QUEEN OF JASTAIN

A Reign of Light novel

Kary Rader

Praise for Kary Rader

and the REIGN OF LIGHT series

Winner of the 2013 Coffee Time Romance Reviewer's Choice Award

Winner of the 2014 RomCom Reader's Choice Award

"I loved the characters and world that Rader created…Rader brings a new dynamic into the fantasy genre."
—MR Wilson, Amazon review

"I found myself lost in the land of Jastain! I would highly recommend QUEEN OF JASTAIN by Kary Rader!"
—Zcrazyangel, Goodreads review

"…a wonderful fantasy adventure with a good versus evil background and a will they, won't they love story."
—Melanie of The Review Corner

STRANGER IN A STRANGE LAND

The horsemen closed in fast, a blur of leather and chain mail charging behind the lone man in some kind of Renaissance chase. Abby's chest tightened. She looked from the man to the riders flying across the valley. They headed directly for him—and her. The lead horseman drew his sword and pointed the rest forward. *That is not a welcoming gesture.* Her gaze flitted back to the man in front of her car. His chest heaved from running, and his blue eyes beckoned her to trust him. There was no time to think this through. God only knew there was plenty to keep her mind occupied.

He could be an escaped criminal for all she knew, but something in his eyes called to her. His voice played again inside her head. "Please, fair one. My name is Avant and I am in need of your help."

"Shit!" She threw the Xterra into reverse and wheeled around to the guy. Leaning over the passenger seat, she opened the door for him.

QUEEN OF JASTAIN

A Reign of Light novel

Kary Rader

www.BOROUGHSPUBLISHINGGROUP.com

Map of Jastain by Allyn Bowker, Dark Leagues Fantasy Mapping

ISBN 978-1-942886-06-8

To my Lord and Savior Jesus Christ,

the one who gave me the gift and the desire to use it

ACKNOWLEDGMENTS

When I started on my writing journey two years ago, I had no idea the number of people it takes to create a novel and make it read-worthy. I also never realized how many people would willingly help me with my dreams.

I want to thank my wonderful family, who suffered from neglect while I was held captive by the characters in my head. Especially, my husband, Bret, who not only allowed me the time I needed but also the encouragement. We made it through, honey, and I pray your sacrifice will reap rewards.

I want to thank my cousins Kendra Highly and Debbie Anderson, who were my first cheerleaders.

Finally, I want to thank Alison Croggon for asking a question that needed an answer. It was that question which set me on this path and I'm forever grateful.

CONTENTS

QUEEN OF JASTAIN

A Seed has been planted
But what will it grow
Darkness recanted
Be there any that know

How can it be thus, when Dark rules as night
Faith free the will to fight the good fight

Closed are the minds
The heart's way is barred
Where love lies and hides
To betray advanced guard

Lay down thy quest to fight and defend
Look for forgiveness to come from within

Wind's breath cannot blow 'til it's released
Nor the sword be wielded 'til it's unsheathed

And the Crown in array of Light cannot see
'Til fruit in its season illuminate the tree

Annum 1567 — Prophesy of the High Priest
Festival Keihev Neous (Festival of New Song)

"But the fruit of the Spirit is love, joy, peace, longsuffering, kindness, goodness, faithfulness, meekness, self-control; against such there is no law."

Galatians 5:22–23

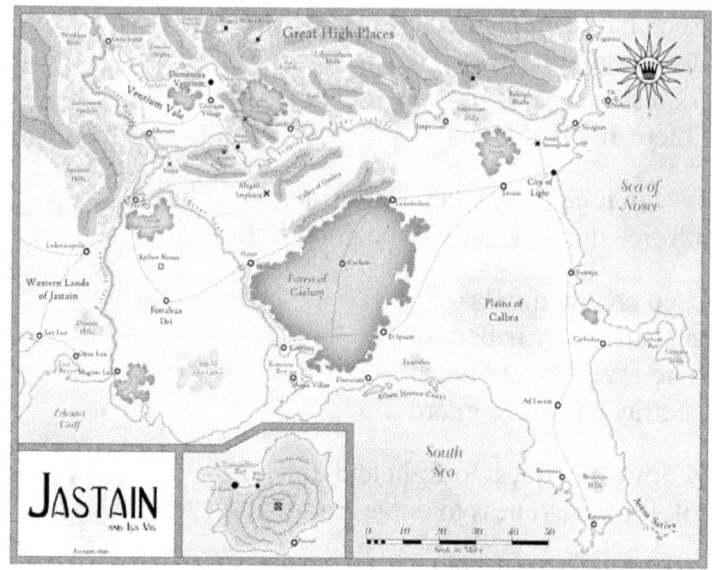

Chapter One

Abby Randall shook her head to clear her mind before opening the front door of her best friend Lyndsea's house. The muffled sounds of music and lively conversation vibrated the door as she held the knob. This was no time for second guesses.

As she opened the door, a blast of cold air hit her face, contrasting with the humid Dallas evening. It was time to make her fashionably late entrance, say good-bye to her recently ex-boyfriend, and get the hell outta Dodge. She squared her shoulders and curved her lips into a smile she didn't feel. She could do this. Just get through the evening and she would be done with it—done with Chad. Her heart sank at the thought.

As she stepped into the living room of the single-story, brick home, a hush settled over the crowd. She craned her neck to see as guests packed in front of her. A dozen or so people blocked the way, but she could hear the lilt of Lyndsea's hesitant voice. Abby rolled her eyes. Lyndsea never had been good at public speaking. That was Abby's job.

"Thank you all for coming. This party was supposed to be a send-off for Chad, but I am excited to say it has become something else."

Something else? A murmur rippled through the group. Abby's heart began to pound.

Lyndsea had agreed to throw the party months ago. When Abby had asked her to cancel it, her best friend had refused, saying too many people were already coming.

The muscles in Abby's stomach clenched. Never a good sign. Her breakup with Chad, just over a month ago, had been hard and hurtful. His leaving would be a fresh start for both of them. *Keep telling yourself that, Abs.*

"This celebration is also *our* engagement party." Lyndsea's voice turned into a squee. "Chad and I are getting *married*, and I'll be moving with him. I've decided to finish college in Boston so I can be with the man I love."

The crowd burst into applause and cheers of well wishes. Abby's vision blurred, and she swayed into the woman next to her, whose face blanched when she saw Abby.

"You didn't know?" Claire whispered as she grabbed Abby's elbow to keep her from falling.

Abby shook her head and tried to swallow, but her muscles froze. Her body refused entrance to much-needed oxygen. Her vision tunneled through the crowd and settled on the couple. Chad and Lyndsea smiled and greeted the onslaught of congratulations. Lyndsea held out her hand. The two and a half carat, vintage diamond ring that had been Chad's birth mother's sparkled on her bony finger—the ring Abby had hoped would one day rest on her own finger.

Her breath returned, and she sucked in a painful gasp, afraid she might pass out or get sick. The throng parted, robbing her of any anonymity she might've had.

The couple's eyes rounded at the site of her. Chad dropped his gaze and swore quietly.

The smile fell from Lyndsea's face. "I-I didn't think you were coming tonight, Abs. I-I'm so sorry."

Abs? The little bitch dared to call me by my nickname? "Sorry to disappoint you, *Lynds*. I apologize. I didn't bring a gift for the happy couple."

Chad looked up at her. "Abby, *please*—"

Abby held up her hand, and her eyes prickled and stung. "There's nothing to say."

Her pulse throbbed in her temples, and she bolted for the door. Her Italian-leather heels clip-clopped down the sidewalk, echoing behind her like a rapidly approaching army. Tonight she wouldn't be overtaken. Not in front of them.

The need to escape gripped her throat like the hands of an assailant. She reached out to the first option she could find: her Nissan Xterra. Beads of sweat rolled down her temples. For now, the SUV would have to do, but it couldn't take her far enough to forget this. Maybe her old standby, vodka, could.

She jumped in the car and screeched out into the street, not looking to see if anyone had followed her from the house. She doubted they would. They'd seemed pretty shocked to see her.

Speeding onto the freeway, she ground her foot into the accelerator. She shook so hard her hands could barely grip the steering wheel. Chad and Lyndsea were...*in love...getting married…moving to Boston.* How could this have happened in barely a month's time?

Did she still love Chad? She'd asked herself that question a lot the past few weeks. Of course she loved him. He was her first love— the only guy she'd ever been with. Her throat constricted, but the tears wouldn't come. She hadn't cried when her dad died, so she sure as hell wouldn't cry over Chad.

Thoughts of her dad pierced her mind like shards of shrapnel in the emotional bomb her life had become. In typical Jonathan Randall form, he'd left her everything: the house, the car, all the patents and book royalties. They were all hers, including the contents of the hidden safe in the study. She widened her eyes to stay the tears that pooled there. Her dad's study, the one place she was never allowed as a child, was now the one place in the world she never wanted to go again.

He was dead. Chad was leaving. And she was alone.

But what Lyndsea had done hurt her more than anything. How could the girl, who was like a sister, do this to her? Lyndsea and her parents were the closest thing to a real family in Abby's life. Her eyes burned, and her breath hissed out in jagged wisps. With her father always gone, Abby had spent most holidays with them. Those days were over now. How could she ever go there again?

Lyndsea hadn't breathed a word of this in the last five weeks. Not a word!

Abby wove the car in and out of the evening traffic like a demon on a mission. The recklessness of her driving mimicked the out-of-control feeling careening through her mind. Her dry eyes masked the sob in her throat. She was about to start hyperventilating if she didn't calm—

A bright light gathered around her, and an electrical sensation coursed suddenly from the back of her jaw through her eyes. *What the hell?*

A bolt flashed, and she was blinded and feeling like her head had been struck with electrical current. She shuddered at the sharp pain.

The Xterra bounced wildly, as if epic potholes littered the road. She still couldn't see from the flash. Not even caring, she slammed to a stop and collapsed on her steering wheel. Let the freeway traffic hit her. Let the fucking car roll over for all she cared.

Heaving dry sobs, she screamed at the loss of her first love, her best friend, and her dad. They were all gone, dead as far as she was concerned. And there was no one else to lose.

Tears finally filled her eyes. She lifted her head to let out a cry, but it hung in her throat. Her jaw fell open. Daylight streamed in the windows. Abby and her Xterra sat in a meadow surrounded by mountains as tall as skyscrapers. *Holy shit!*

A man sprinted toward her with six men on horseback chasing him.

As he neared the vehicle, he held up his hands in a plea for help. She blinked and tried to get her bearings. He stopped directly in front of the SUV. The man shot a look behind him and then turned to her, clearly pleading. His sapphire gaze penetrated her mind, and a voice—*his voice*—echoed inside her head. *"Please help me!"*

The horsemen closed in fast, a blur of leather and chain mail charging behind the lone man in some kind of Renaissance chase. Abby's chest tightened. She looked from the man to the riders flying across the valley. They headed directly for him—and her. The lead horseman drew his sword and pointed the rest forward. *That is not a welcoming gesture.* Her gaze flitted back to the man in front of her car. His chest heaved from running, and his blue eyes beckoned her to trust him. There was no time to think this through. God only knew there was plenty to keep her mind occupied.

He could be an escaped criminal for all she knew, but something in his eyes called to her. His voice played again inside her head. *"Please, fair one. My name is Avant and I am in need of your help."*

"Shit!" She threw the Xterra into reverse and wheeled around to the guy. Leaning over the passenger seat, she opened the door for him.

Chapter Two

Abby eyed the stranger while leaning as far away in her seat as she could. He hesitated, scanning the threshold of the car door suspiciously before squaring his shoulders and climbing in. It seemed he had as many reservations as she did, which was somehow comforting.

Tall and with dark wavy hair, the man looked like he hadn't shaved in a week. He removed his sword belt as he positioned himself in the seat.

Abby shot a glance at the approaching horsemen barreling down on them. Then she looked to the man in leather and linen who, despite his haggard appearance, had the face and body of a god. *No time for ogling the hot guy, Abs. Murderous horsemen on your tail!* "Where to, mister?"

His brow furrowed, and he pointed his finger toward a range of smaller mountains.

The horsemen pulled alongside the SUV as he slammed the door shut. She locked it automatically. Their angry shouts in an unfamiliar language rang above the car engine. A shiver slithered down her spine. Even if these guys weren't after her before, she was now clearly aiding and abetting Renaissance Man.

The lead horseman pulled his sword and banged on the window. Hot Guy gave her a now's-a-good-time-to-go look that arched his eyebrows almost off his head.

"Buckle your seatbelt." Abby hit the accelerator. The tires of the Xterra spun in the damp grass and then, catching hold, propelled them through the meadow.

Sir Hots-A-Lot lurched and grabbed hold of the handle above his head. He craned his neck to see behind them. She glanced in her rearview mirror. The horsemen were frozen, clearly stunned, as they watched the car pull away. With a battle cry she could hear above the Xterra's bouncing shocks, the men galloped after them. Abby squealed and pressed on the accelerator. Who were these guys? And why were they chasing this man?

For what seemed like miles, the horsemen continued their pursuit. In reality—as if there still were such a thing— it was only a few moments.

Abby glanced over. A relieved sigh escaped the man, and a faint smile grazed his lips. Her already erratic pulse shot through the moonroof. If attractiveness equated to trustworthiness—and in her book it did a little—then he was a freaking Boy Scout. But for all she knew, she had just picked up the medieval Ted Bundy. Her gut wrenched at the thought. Why she'd watched that damned documentary was still a mystery. Some things were better left unknown.

The horsemen were small in the background as the Xterra gained a hefty lead. Brutal terrain threatened to jar her fillings loose, but she didn't let up on the gas. The guy held on to the handle with white knuckles and continued to strain his neck around to see. Maybe if she kept him hanging on for dear life, he couldn't rape and torture her.

The sturdy little SUV sped for the mountains, and the pursuers fell farther and farther behind until eventually they were gone. Abby continued to jostle the car across the meadow. When the horses were long out of sight, she let off the gas, and the whirlwind of her immediate surroundings finally caught up to her. She felt like Dorothy in the twister as everything outside her body and inside her mind spun out of control.

"Whew! I think we lost them." Shooting a glance at Mr. Medieval Times, Abby gulped at the startling sight.

He was staring at her with those piercing blue eyes. And what the hell did he have on? Simple linen pants and a cotton tunic-looking thingy stretched over his tall frame and broad muscles. The loose sleeves and V-neck of his shirt were tied with laces, the fabric in shades of brown. She looked back out the windshield, trying not to stare at him. Her nose crinkled as the strong scent of male filled the car. He could use a shower.

Her mind fumbled to come up with a logical explanation for what was happening.

Was she stranded in some strange Renaissance reenactment? Maybe they were filming a new movie. She peeked over again. Her gaze slid the length of him, all six foot plus. He could be an actor. But where were the cameras?

She could be dead. She clenched her jaw. "Or about to be."

He tilted his head and narrowed his sparkling eyes at the sound of her voice. A wavy wisp fell across his forehead. An unintentional sigh hummed from her. Maybe she was dreaming. Had she died on the highway?

Had she traveled to another time or world? With that thought, Abby closed her eyes and said a quick prayer, unable to think of any other alternatives. With just those options, her circumstances were pretty jacked, and the ones that made the most sense were the craziest. *Holy shit!* Where was she, and whom was she with? Bands of panic tightened around her chest. If he was going to harm her, he would have to do it right then. She couldn't handle any more suspense in her life.

She slammed the car to a stop, and Hots-A-Lot tried not to meet the windshield with his face. She turned to the guy.

Questions swirled in her head and wouldn't stop long enough for her mind to capture one and send it out of her mouth. She stared at him, hoping to God he didn't attack. *Abby, start with the basics: who, what, and where.*

"Who are you?" She spoke the words slowly, like that would help him understand a language he might not speak.

The stranger frowned at her and then strained to look behind them again. When some time had passed and still no riders appeared, he turned back to her and lifted his finger toward the mountains.

No English. Great. She shook her head. "No. Not until I get some answers."

His eyes clouded, and his eyebrows drew together. He stabbed his finger, this time more forcefully, in the direction of the foothills.

Abby winced at his insistence but lifted her chin. "Are you trying to silently boss me? This is *my* car, dude."

He sighed and rubbed his forehead. Her father used to give her this gesture. Relaxing a little, she continued to stare at him. If he was frustrated with her, he probably wasn't out to kill her. Yet.

The stranger hissed a word she didn't understand, but guessing by his tone, it wasn't very nice. He leveled a penetrating glare at her. A tingle of electricity pulsed through her, and his voice again reverberated in her mind. *"Fair one, I understand you are concerned and confused. I assure you I will explain. However, we must reach the Tres Frater mountain range."* He again pointed to the mountains. *"We must go."*

He'd called her *fair one* again. The thought made her feel warm and fuzzy, but the fact that he hadn't used his mouth to do it unnerved the crap out of her. Her capacity for suspending logic only stretched so far, and she was at the end of her mental rope. On a positive note, at least she wasn't dwelling on Chad and Lyndsea.

"Look, Mr. ...*Whoever*, I don't speak telepathy, and I need some answers."

He cursed under his breath and fisted his hands, possibly to keep them from ringing her neck. After regaining control, he looked back into her eyes. *"I am Avant and I mean you no harm. You are in the land of Jastain, in the time of the Second Age of Darkness."* His gaze raked over her body accusingly, lingering on her bare legs. *"Clearly, you are from an Other Place and know not the happenings in this land. The king is an evil man who brooks no trespassers and certainly not ones with horseless carriages. Fair one, we are still very much in danger. There are more soldiers on the way. Please. When we reach safety, I can explain."*

His voice rattled her mind, but his gaze absolutely unhinged her. She tugged at the hem of her little black dress. He'd called himself Avant. Sexy name for a sexy guy. Abby sucked in a deep breath and nodded. "OK, Avant, we can go, but it won't do any good to escape the bad guys and go smashing through the windshield. You need to put your seatbelt on."

His face lit in a brilliant smile, and her heart jumped in her chest as if it were leaping toward him. His eyes glittered, and his straight white teeth sparkled like a freaking Colgate commercial. *Ting.* He'd obviously recognized the use of his name but clearly hadn't understood the rest.

She held out her own seatbelt and spoke slowly, enunciating each syllable, as if that would help him understand, "Seat. Belt."

He shook his head and glanced back again.

With a sigh, she unbuckled her belt and reached across him to pull his out. Her arm grazed the solid wall of muscle at his chest, and she squeaked. Her face heated. She caught a chuckle from him as she sat back in the driver's seat. *Driver's seat? Yeah, right.* From the looks of this guy, he wasn't going to let anyone, especially not a woman, in the driver's seat if he could help it.

Avant's quiet confidence charged the air with so much testosterone she needed to roll down the window. Sure, he was cordial enough, but his broad shoulders and straight back exuded a masculine pride she recognized but had only seen in one other place: the football field. Damn jocks. They thought they owned the world.

He clicked on his seatbelt and urged her forward with that unrelenting finger—and those eyes. Following his direction, she put the car in drive and headed for the mountains.

What the hell was a Second Age of Darkness? And *Jastain*? It sounded like the name of one of those girls from the trailer park. Jesus Christ, where was she?

They rode for a time in silence. Abby took in the world around her. Even though she could identify everything, it was like nothing she'd ever seen before, except maybe in a James Cameron movie. To the right, snow covered the soaring peaks. She'd seen the Rockies on several spring break ski trips, but these mountains dwarfed them. Behind her in the distance loomed a forest with trees as tall as the sequoias in California. To her left, a mammoth river flowed from north to south, according to the Xterra's compass, as far in either direction as she could see. It was so wide she might have thought it a lake if it weren't for the obvious current. If everything was bigger in Texas, then Texas had apparently never been here. And even if there were sprawling mountains and towering forests in Texas, she wouldn't be able to see them. It was the middle of the effin' *night* there!

Abby drove slowly through the tall grass and blankets of gold and lavender flowering plants. The sun seeped through heavy cloud cover that choked the sky to the east. She sucked in the fresh air to calm her racing heart. Wherever she was, there was nothing man-made she could see.

Avant reached out his hand. She jumped. He touched the light-gray leather interior of the seat and console. Sliding his curious gaze over the steering wheel and gearshift, he pressed a button on the dash. A cold blast blew into his surprised face.

He didn't know what a car was? He'd called it a *horseless carriage*. Strings of tension bound her hands to the steering wheel. Guess that meant they wouldn't be stopping for a burger. This really *was* the freaking land of Oz. *Tonight the part of Dorothy will be played by Abigail Randall.* She couldn't muster a glance to the sky for fear of spying flying monkeys.

Avant caught her gaze, and the tingle of his words echoed again in her mind. *"What do you call this?"*

"It's a Nissan Xterra. Xterra."

His lips curled into an odd shape as he tried to repeat the word. "Esterra."

His rich baritone sent a shiver down her spine. Although his voice was the same when he spoke in her head, hearing the sound with her ears gave it sexy substance.

She smiled. "Close enough."

When he spoke into her mind—and she still wasn't ready to completely embrace that yet—it was as if the idea took shape; the idea could be communicated in a single thought, whereas it took time to speak individual words.

Hots-A-Lot touched her arm. She jumped again and turned toward him. Her mind prickled with his thought.

"We'll travel the River Sast to the lower range of the mountains. We must hide the carriage there." He pointed in a new direction toward the fork of the river. *"I do not believe the soldiers will find us or the carriage now, but we need to find shelter before nightfall and in the event the scouts return."*

She nodded. His take-charge attitude wrapped around her like her favorite cashmere throw. At least he had a plan, but it didn't negate the tension that thrummed through her at his intense gaze.

As if he'd heard her thought, he arched a single eyebrow and his full lips curved into a cocky half-smile. *"I don't care to tussle with anyone else today."*

It wasn't clear if he was referring to the soldiers or to her. Maybe both. But if he continued to give her that sexy stare, she wouldn't care what he meant. She glanced to the path in front of her and had to swerve to miss a large boulder. *Damn it.* As if she didn't have enough to keep her mind incapacitated, Avant was muddling her brain with thoughts of what a tussle with him might entail.

With furrowed brow, he watched intently out the window. Abby stole a glance at the weapon lying against his leg.

Sheathed in bold filigree, the hilt was the only visible part. Leather wrapped the grip of the silver sword, and two cabochon jewels decorated the sides of the T-shaped guard. The same color blue as his eyes, the large sapphires were of the finest quality and at least three carats each. It was an impressive sight and not something she ever wanted to be on the wrong end of. Although beautifully made, she assumed it wasn't just for show.

Taking a deep breath, she stretched stiffly behind the wheel. What time was it? Her internal clock was all cattywampus. She looked at the digital display on her dash: 12:45 a.m. Not able to see the sun, she couldn't estimate the time in this place. She rotated her shoulders and cracked her neck from side to side. Her weary muscles reminded her of the tense time spent at the hospital the night her dad died and the hollow days that followed.

Too upset, she'd barely helped with the funeral, which her dad had planned to the last detail. It was just one more way he'd removed himself from her. His attorney handled the transfer of property and funds into her trust. Susan, their housekeeper, managed the estate.

Six weeks had passed since the funeral and, except for the breakup with Chad, everything had remained the same. But now, her life was...different. She cut her gaze over to the man next to her. So freaking different, would it ever be the same again? Thoughts of the big empty house flashed through her mind. As lonely as it seemed, at least it was familiar, and it was home.

As the river forked and changed direction, so did they. She scanned the horizon for anything that would give her a clue as to where she was. The horsemen seemed long gone, but a bad feeling swept over her and chills rose on her skin. He'd said there were more soldiers. Why was he being chased?

She stole another glance at him. A straight nose and strong jaw gave him a picturesque profile. His dark hair fell over tan skin, framing blue eyes the color of the clearest ocean at its deepest point. Avant was stunning, possibly the best-looking guy she'd ever seen, even without a shower. Definitely top three. But could she trust him? He didn't appear to want to hurt her. He'd had opportunity, and probably desire, considering his frustration from earlier. If anything, he seemed to be trying to put her at ease, when he should be just as shocked at her appearance as she was. It was almost as if he had been expecting her.

But it didn't matter. She'd made her decision when she opened the door for him, and right now, he was her only option.

They continued in silence. Instead of biting her nails, she plugged in her MP3 player to break the tension. Avant watched with eyes narrowed. When the music started, his face brightened into a sudden smile, and he nodded. Her heart thumped with the beat of the song. She would give anything to know what he was thinking.

Abby swayed to the tune. Hots-A-Lot tapped his foot to the beat of "Pocketful of Sunshine." Something about the camaraderie filled her with hope and warmed her heart. For the first time in days, weeks maybe, she smiled, and it felt real.

As the river narrowed, he pointed out a place between a tall boulder and the mountainside where the car could fit. He looked into her eyes. *"Gather what things you need. I have shelter not far from here."*

Abby shivered as the electric sensation pulsed through her again. Her aching muscles protested against the thought of trekking through the mountains. Hopefully *not far* really was not far.

She dumped the beaded clutch out on the seat he'd just vacated, taking inventory. Out fell the little black box she'd stuffed in earlier. Her eyes filled with tears as her gaze lingered on it.

All the things that meant anything to her were gone, and the emptiness swirled in her heart like a bottomless cavern. She'd wished for escape, and now the unfamiliar surrounded her. Now wasn't the time to dwell on all she'd lost. What she wouldn't give for some vodka. She dashed away the tears and stuffed the small box back into the bag.

Surveying the contents of her car, she discovered an almost-full bottle of Evian and a can of Red Bull.

In the spilled contents of her purse, she found her ID, check card, and her favorite lip gloss—nothing that could help her in this place. She lifted her gaze to Avant as he buckled his sword belt. Her tongue trailed over her lips. Dollars to doughnuts there was a six-pack under that tunic. *For real, Abs? Don't you have more important things to worry about right now?*

Glancing over the backseat, she spied the first aid kit that equipped every Xterra. Considering her imminent trek through the wilderness, that pack might come in handy.

She shoved her phone and purse into the kit. "Lead the way, Hots-A-Lot."

He quirked his eyebrow and knelt in front of her. Lifting his gaze to hers, he frowned. *"Hand me your…shoes."*

She slipped the strappy sandals off and stepped back. He unsheathed his sword. *Whack.* He sliced off both heels with one blow.

A soft sob escaped her for the brutal death of her favorite sandals.

He stood and handed her the eight-hundred-dollar shoes sans heels. She gestured for him to go. Something sparked deep in his eyes. They stared at each other for a long moment before he turned and took off into the trees. She gulped, slipped the semi-flats on her feet, threw the bag over her shoulder, and clipped after him in her new Dolcini strappy sandals. Even without the heels, her feet already throbbed.

One to lead

One to rule

Attempt them both, become the fool

Ancient Jastainian Nursery Rhyme

Chapter Three

Avant kindled a fire, which heated the landing of the large inlet. The damp, stone cavern sat high on a cliff and jutted at least fifteen feet into the side of the mountain.

Having sheltered in this cave many times, he doubted any but he knew of its existence. Here they would be safe from the king's men roaming the lower range. He scanned the valley as he continued to coax the coals, shooting sparks into the air.

"Umbra?" He let out a sardonic laugh. The Valley of Shadows—an unlikely place to plant The Seed of Light—was a wide expanse in the king's domain and already shrouded in Darkness. His gut wrenched at the thought of the spreading evil.

The sun sank low in the sky, bringing the frigid night air. He shot a glance at the young woman's bare legs folded beneath her and quickly looked away. She would surely be cold, although his body heat rose at the sight.

The short black shift barely covered her, and her shoes were the most impractical waste of finely crafted leather he'd ever laid eyes on. Had he any alternative to provide her, he would have. She shivered as the taut buds of her breasts became visible against her dress. He hissed out a breath, and his mouth went dry.

Remembering who he was, he averted his gaze again and swallowed hard. The lump stuck in his throat. Her beauty mesmerized and stirred a desire in him that he dared not pursue. How long it had been since he'd seen so much of a woman. That, certainly, was the reason for his undisciplined response. Still, he expected better of himself.

From where had the young woman come? Who was she? The horseless carriage and other mechanical devices spoke of an advanced society. With thoughts of her world, his mind spun faster than the wheels of her Esterra. Machines that made music and controlled the temperature. Fireless light that seemed to shine without the use of oil, wax, or wick. These signs, coupled with the fact she had appeared from nowhere at the precise moment of his need, were evidence enough she was *The One*. A deeply seeded knowing in his spirit, his Gift, confirmed the belief.

In his dream seven nights before, his father had come to him with a prophecy.

The Stone of Light will be carried in the ear of the Chosen One, transported in a carriage pulled by two hundred and fifty horses.

"Two hundred and fifty horses?" His voice echoed through the cave. She lifted her face to stare at him. Was it possible her carriage was the answer to the impossible riddle? The firelight danced in her eyes. Could she carry The Stone?

The Stone of Light had been missing for more than fifty years, along with all the crown jewels. Though he knew where two were, the remaining seven, including the revered center stone, were lost. The thought of any carriage pulled by more than a dozen horses had seemed preposterous. It must be true. Though how it was possible was beyond his ken.

And what of her world? He'd always believed in other realms and places, but to find they existed in truth was a marvel—and a concern.

Flames flickered and surged with warmth. He glanced at her huddled near the fire. Her shoulders hunched and her eyes drooped, but she continued to shiver.

He strode to his leather pack, pulled out a blanket, and handed it her.

"My lady, you look chilled in the evening air, and this cave will be colder still when the sun gives its final regards. Please take this."

She provided a tight-lipped smiled and nodded. Her eyes darted from him, as if embarrassed, and she quickly snuggled under the soft wool. A wave of tenderness swept over him at her childlike response. He stroked his thumb across his bottom lip.

He'd led her down the stream for three miles, and they'd spent the better part of the afternoon climbing to the cave. She'd struggled and stumbled along the path, hindered by her lack of conditioning and strange clothing. Her black shift adorned with precious stones and the unfathomable height of the spindle heels he'd severed must indicate her rank and importance. Clearly, she wasn't accustomed to walking, as evidenced by her difficulty in breathing during their journey.

Though his eyes appreciated her soft curves, her life of luxury and ease had come to an end. He would make certain he prepared her for the difficulties that lay ahead. That was why she'd come to him.

Never had Avant doubted the wisdom of the Light, but it was far from his vision to see how this young woman would restore the kingdom. To think *this girl*, however lovely, could accomplish such a task seemed pure folly. Nevertheless, the Light had spoken, and as ever, he would see it done.

Avant picked up the metal pot containing the stew he'd made early that morning.

"My lady, would you care for some squirrel stew?"

She politely declined, but her nose faintly crinkled and her upper lip twitched. He chuckled. She would eat when hunger gripped her.

The sunset lit the sky with rich colors of orange and pink. He turned to her. His chest tightened, and his hand burned to touch her golden hair. He clenched his fists at his sides and paced to the mouth of the cave.

By the Light, she is beautiful. Neither the Light nor his Gift had prepared him for this young woman. She was certainly no great mage or disciplined warrior. Nay, she was delicate and privileged, he suspected, based on her appearance and on their limited acquaintance. A dubious laugh escaped his lips as he watched the quiet girl. With her training at hand, he had his work cut out for him. Though it was his own misconceptions that had led him to believe the Chosen One must be a man, she nonetheless seemed an odd choice for the task.

Earlier that day, when the scouting guards spotted him, he'd thought to hide in his cave, but the second band of soldiers had cut off his path. His only recourse was through the valley in the open. It was then the carriage appeared from nothing. He'd immediately known it was his salvation.

Thank the Light, none of the soldiers had recognized him. Not only had he escaped capture, but his true identity remained hidden.

Avant smiled as he remembered the struggle that played across her fair face and her ultimate decision to help him. If nothing else, that proved her bravery and willingness to take risks. She had spirit, to be sure. Those were things with which he could work and a basis on which to begin her training. He frowned. The rest, however, was weather from a different day.

Could she be trusted? A shiver danced down his spine. His deepest secrets would be revealed to her. Avant rubbed down the hair on his arms. He doubted anything could make the necessary intimacy any more palatable to him than squirrel stew was to her.

His gaze flickered over her as she rummaged through her bag of belongings. Being so near a woman taxed his reserve. He'd spent two decades circumventing any intimacy with women. Only taking pleasure in the innocent teasing of the married women in the village, he had avoided young women as if they were the king's sentries. His isolation had worked, until now. He shot her an accusing glance. Now, her soft, full curves were being thrust upon him. He winced at his poor word choice, and the images they evoked.

The vestige of Light she bore precluded her from him, from any man. To restore Light to the kingdom was her purpose, and no man would deter her from the task. Least of all him. Besides, he must gather his own life from ruins and regain his bride lost long ago, if Sentieve would have him. He straightened his shoulders and stepped toward the woman. Both had their respective purpose and fulfill it they must.

The young lady's lessons began now. They had to communicate with one another, or their task would be impossible. Certain of her Gifting, he folded his legs and sat directly in front of her. Avant relaxed his features to hide the intensity that some mistook for severity. In recent years he'd learned to temper his responses…somewhat.

Staring into her face, he spoke using his Implanting, *"Fair one, I believe you can communicate with me as I communicate with you."*

Her eyes widened, and she shook her head in denial of her Gift.

Avant nodded. *"Yes. You can. Look at me and clear your mind."*

The young beauty sucked in a lengthy breath. She looked at him, half-squinting and with every muscle in her face clenched.

"Try to focus your mind, my lady, as if speaking to yourself. Look deep into my eyes. Imagine you stand in a stream knee-deep. Balance your energy and resist the current."

Again her face clenched, and her body shook from the effort she exerted, but nothing happened. She wished to communicate, but her doubt hindered the accomplishment. Dropping her gaze, she shook her head and muttered something in her native tongue. She gave up far too quickly.

Touching his steepled fingers to his lips, Avant studied her response. Failure could not be tolerated. They were people of the Light, called by the Light. And by the Light, they would prevail.

He lifted her chin. His hand tingled when it met her smooth skin, and his countenance softened at the fear reflected in her face. Merciful Light, her eyes danced with pools of blue and green, reminding him of a place he loved.

"Fair one, the difference between success and failure is the direction of your will. It is always too soon to admit defeat." With the force of a storm-swollen river, he thrust his determination into her mind, obliterating the doubt that swirled across her face. *"If you can understand me, you can communicate with me. I am certain of it."*

Avant had learned a long time ago how to use his Gift to superimpose his will onto others. Only the stoutest of hearts could withstand him. Though he rarely used the dangerous Gift, now seemed an appropriate time.

He focused his energy. The power of his Implanting surged into her, filling her with a sense of confidence. She nodded and gazed deeply into his eyes, as if she tried to see behind them. Reaching for his energy source where it touched her mind, she resisted the flow of ideas and emotions there, and the lightning shock of her Gift reverberated through him.

Her forehead creased as if she was thinking. *"My name is Abigail."*

A satisfied smile grazed his lips, and he inclined his head in greeting. *"I am pleased to meet you, Abigail."*

Avant watched Abigail's eyes round as she gasped. She clapped her hands and wiggled on her seat. He laughed and raised his eyebrows. If he hadn't known her exuberance was in response to her accomplishment, he might have thought she needed to relieve herself.

A brilliant smile lit her face. Her eyes sparkled with joy at the small victory and warmed him from a chill the fire could not. He smiled in return and, for the first time in a long while, it reached his heart.

"I am Avant, Lord Ventium of the Freelands of Jastain. Welcome, Abigail. How did you come to be in this land?"

She squinted her eyes and schooled her face in concentration of her energy. *"I don't know. I was driving my car, there was a flash of light, and suddenly I was here. It's a mystery to me."*

He tapped his lip with his index finger. Had she accessed her Gift of Implanting without realizing? Certainly her shift indicated she had come from other lands. To think she accessed so powerful a Gift without knowing was alarming. The power of her Gift must be something indeed and a manifestation of which he, or anyone, had limited knowledge.

"I'm from Dallas, Texas, in the United States of America."

His mind spun with imagination. Thoughts of this place of horseless carriages and other untold wonders filled him with anticipation. Though now was not the time, he intended to find out more about her world.

"I went to a party last night for my ex-boyfriend. I found out he and my best friend were getting married, barely a month after we broke up." Her face pinched, and she scowled past him into the twilight. Remembering herself, she caught his gaze again. *"I was so upset that I drove my car off the road. But when I looked up, I was in that valley."* Abigail pointed over the mountains toward Umbra.

"This boyfriend, he was your lover? He and your closest friend betrayed you?"

She squirmed where she sat, indicating she was uncomfortable with the question. Her cheeks flushed with color, and she barely maintained his gaze. Her modesty was endearing and encouraging. He was, after all, a stranger, and most women didn't relish the idea of confiding their intimate lives with strange men.

"Lover? I guess he was, but that makes it sound glamorous. And, yes, my best friend betrayed me."

The pain from such a betrayal would be great. He, above all people, knew that. *"I can understand the hurt that comes from such a disloyalty."* Avant drifted in thought, remembering how the king had betrayed him and taken his wife. *"We have a saying in this land: 'The Light protect me from my friends. From my enemies, I can protect myself.'"*

She rolled her eyes. *Oh, good. A philosopher.*

Avant furrowed his brow. He'd heard her thought, but it didn't seem she had intended to communicate it to him. Though her inflection held sarcasm, it masked a deeper hurt. The muscles in his arms flexed, and an inexplicable desire to hold her flooded his limbs. My Light, what was wrong with him? He clenched his jaw and pressed his arms uncomfortably against his body.

Her eyes sparkled with newly found confidence. *"My dad died of a heart attack six weeks ago."* Her face fell.

"My condolences."

She lifted her gaze. *"It's okay. He was a really important scientist. Except sometimes I think he wanted to be a priest. He made sure I was taken care of. I'm just sorry I didn't know him better."*

"So you grew up with only your mother?"

"No. Mom died when I was too young to remember. Although they tell me I'm a lot like her."

"Then she must have been a beautiful woman."

Her face filled with mischief, and his heart flopped like a fish on a rock. *"She was drop-dead gorgeous. The desire of every man and envy of every woman."*

He couldn't help himself. He laughed out loud. *"Indeed?"* Her impish ways were not to be ignored. *"And a bit of a trickster, no doubt?"*

"No doubt." Her mind flitted to the next thing so quickly he had to blink. *"So anyway, when Chad and I broke up, I guess he decided my best friend was what he really wanted. It was a pretty quick turnaround. No sense letting the grass grow under him."* She narrowed her eyes. *"I just didn't know my best friend was the new yard he would be parking in."*

He chuckled at the colorful analogy though deep-seeded hurt saturated her words.

"Then a blinding flash of light and poof, I'm here in Jastain saving you from rabid horsemen, right?"

He pressed his lips together into a tight smile and furrowed his brow. *"It would seem so. And rabid is not far from the truth. A Darkness has crept into our land, corrupting all that is good."*

She'd been dealt several harsh circumstances in the past weeks. Her optimism and humor kept the evident emptiness at bay. Again, a compassion for the girl, one he could not explain, washed over him. Perhaps the shocking similarities to his own circumstances caused a kinship with this young beauty. Or perhaps it was something else entirely, but on that thought he refused to dwell.

Based on her description, he believed she had used her Implanting. Unfortunately, without guidance from the Light, he would be unable to instruct her in that aspect of her Gift. Placement Implanting was a rare manifestation and had not shown itself in his lifetime. Even in the Annals of the Great Hall, Placement Implanting was a rare Gift and only bestowed in times of great Darkness. In all his studies, he'd found only two documented occurrences during the first age of Darkness, which was defeated by the great Prince Rheaboam.

"Thank you for sharing your story, Abigail." The tears that pooled in her eyes pierced his heart and halted him from asking more questions. *"However you came to be in this land, it seems perhaps you will not be able to return so easily."*

She barely held back the flood of sorrow at his words. His fingers fisted as he stayed his hand from caressing her face. His heart pounded. It was not his place to comfort her. It was his place to train her and help her fulfill her destiny. This alone was his purpose.

Squaring his shoulders, Avant caught her gaze and held it. *"Seven nights ago, I had a dream that I should seek The One who will defeat the Darkness in this land. Abigail, I believe you are the Chosen One spoken of in my dream and that it is your destiny to restore the Crown of Light and find the missing prophecy. This is, I believe, the reason you have come to our land."*

Her brow arched, and she blinked several times. *"You had a dream about me?"*

He nodded. *"You were the reason for my trip to the Valley of Umbra. I sought One in a carriage pulled by two hundred and fifty horses, which I believe is your Esterra."*

Her face blanched. She shook her head. *"Just because I have a car doesn't mean I'm The One. Lots of people have cars."*

"Not in Jastain. And how do you explain your presence here? Only One of the Light could have come to this land from yours." She may not yet be ready to receive the call of the Light, but it beckoned nonetheless.

She tugged the wool blanket firmly around her and crossed her arms over her chest. *"I don't know how I got here, but I sure as hell don't think it's because I am this 'One' person."*

"And yet you most certainly manifest the Gift of Implanting or we could not be speaking. In fact, I believe it is your Implanting that brought you here."

"Implanting, what's that?"

"The Implanting is what we call our Gift, which can manifest in an infinite possibility of ways. We can Implant our thoughts to one another as we are now. I can Implant direction into objects, causing them to move without touching them. Some are even able to Implant themselves from one place to another without the use of time or space. I believe it is how you came to be here, albeit unknowingly, and if you learn to command the power that is within you, you will find your way home."

Abigail's head jerked up. She stared at him for a long moment then asked, *"You can help me go home?"*

"That is my intention." He suppressed a smile. He would prevail upon her desire for home. Aside from that, the Light must reveal to her the way.

She stared out the mouth of the cave and then looked back into his eyes. *"Can everybody here Implant?"*

He shook his head. *"Only those who are chosen can Implant. It is considered a great honor. And so it is. But I also know it to be a great burden."*

Framed with her beautiful blonde curls, Abigail's face lit with interest as he recounted how Darkness invaded Jastain.

"After the destruction of the First Age of Darkness, laws and decrees were established. A theocracy was implemented that recognized a high priest and a king as joint rulers of the land. This balance of power allowed the Light to rule in Jastain for centuries. But Darkness crept in. Fifty years ago, the previous king murdered his own brother and, upon his own death, set an imposter on the throne. Today, the imposter seeks to unite the splintered kingdom under his evil rule. Until the Light is restored, Jastain and its people will continue to degrade."

Avant studied Abigail as she listened. Her thoughts indicated gratitude. They also indicated her belief that he was touched in the mind. She seemed unaware of having communicated certain ideas, and he was unnerved by such an open window to her inner self. Her heart wasn't open to believe her purpose yet. However, unless his own Gift was wrong, and it was *never* wrong, she was The One. The days of Darkness were numbered.

"Tomorrow we will leave for my home, which is in a valley northwest of the mountains and across the River Itehris. I have a fief there, and you may stay until we decide what next to do."

Abigail wondered if his fief included a wife. His chin tilted to his chest. She was unaware of the communication so he dared not answer her.

How was it he could hear her private musings without her knowledge? From the tenor of her thought, romantic ideas of him clouded her mind. She found him attractive. Warmth poured over him from his head to ignite a flame in his lower regions. He threw his head back and let out a long sigh. She wasn't the only one with a clouded mind, and he must take care on this treacherous precipice. A fall would not only harm them both, but could destroy their chance of restoring the Crown of Light. It was a possibility he could not stomach.

Chapter Four

Sun warmed Abby's face. The cave filled with the sounds of Avant milling quietly, but she couldn't pry open her eyes. After barely two hours sleep, her body ached as if the horsemen in her dreams had trampled her for real.

Even with Hots-A-Lot's blanket, she still froze her ass off. Her back and hips throbbed from lying all night on the rock, and she had to pee. If her legs hadn't been so sore from the climb the day before, she would have shifted closer to the fire. But as it was, she couldn't move more than her eyelids, which finally fluttered opened.

Avant's long legs were bent in a squat as he stoked the fire. His ever-straight spine and the strength of his upper body were evident even under the tunic, and his muscular rear end sat enticingly at eye level. Gasping breaths sounded in her ears, and she realized she was panting.

He looked like he was in his late twenties, but based on all he'd told her the night before, he was likely twice that. Or he was a loon, and she hadn't ruled out that possibility. Though noble and kind, he was also a little stiff and standoffish. Maybe she could help him loosen up. Without her permission, her mind hailed an erotic bus and sped down a road of desire straight to her core. Her cheeks burned. Thank God he couldn't read her mind.

Jeez. She took in a slow breath. He was attractive, but she was stranded alone in some strange world. *A little restraint might be in order here, Abs.* Abby's carnal cravings fought her common sense for dominance, but this was not the time or place for a showdown. She needed to get home.

He'd spent hours explaining how the Darkness had far reaching consequences on the land and its inhabitants. The people of Jastain had lived under the Light for many centuries. Health and long life— according to Avant, two hundred years had been the average life span—blessed them and peace reigned. But a seed of Darkness was planted in the previous king.

As the Darkness grew, sickness and famine replaced goodness and purity. The pride and love with which Avant described his land reminded her of all the reasons she wished for home. She needed to get back to her own time and place to pack and prepare for college.

School would be starting in a couple of weeks. Her heart sank. She would need to find a new roommate.

Avant stood, muscles rippling and flexing under his tight leggings. Her mouth went dry, and she licked her lips. Maybe she could take him with her. Tamping down the unwanted desire, she hoped that she and her guide could be friends. Friend or not, she couldn't stay in this place with the evil king and the trespass police.

According to Avant, the men on horseback were the king's soldiers, and they didn't tolerate visitors. His concern was that they would scour the land for her car. He'd apparently been looking for her (or someone he thought was her) when they'd discovered him. As the leader of the resistance in the north, he would've been killed had they captured him. Raking her gaze down the back of his body, her heart thumped against her ribs. *What a waste that would've been.*

She flexed her arms and pushed up from the rock. A groan of pain that originated from every major muscle group exploded from her mouth.

Avant turned to greet her. *"Ah, I apologize, fair lady, for the inferior quality of the accommodations, but alas, we have at least one more night of the same."* He tipped his head and smiled.

My God, he was gorgeous, but way too…Shakespearian.

He shot her a strange look. *"I know of another shelter we may use tonight, but we must leave shortly to arrive there by nightfall. We have a two-day trip from here to reach my home."*

She focused her mind. Could she still communicate with him? *"Are there roads? Can we take my car?"*

"I am afraid the roads are not open to us and we dare not take your car." He pointed to the ledge. *"If you need to relieve yourself, there is a place down on the next landing to the left."*

Lovely. She couldn't wait to pee outdoors. *"Thank you."*

She half-climbed, half-slid down to the next level and fell on her ass. She found a grassy area with a tree and a small stream of water running off a nearby rock.

God, I must look like a street urchin. And it didn't help that sexy Sir Hots-A-Lot up there thought she was *The Chosen One.* It sounded like some new computer role-play game. Good Lord! There was no way she could be the person he was looking for. Abby giggled, but a chill ran down her arms. What could she possibly do to defeat the Darkness? Shop it to death? *I do wield a mean credit card.*

Even if Hots-A-Lot was delusional, maybe he could teach her to get back home with this Implanting thingy. If that's really how she had gotten here. It was all so convoluted. She looked up to heavens. "C'mon, Lord. Can you throw me bone here? Is anything for sure?"

A shaft of light shone through the trees and reflected off the trickling water.

She rolled her eyes. "That's all ya got?" She shrugged and took a long drink.

Her stomach growled. Before she single-handedly defeated the evil king, she needed food. Just not squirrel stew. She'd hardly eaten anything in the last day and a half. At this rate, she'd be a skinny stick in no time. Smiling at the thought, she gave a booty-wiggle and winced from the pain in her sore muscles. There wasn't a lot to smile about in her current circumstances, but losing weight was something to be grateful for in any world.

When she got back to the cave, she found Avant packed and ready to go. He offered her breakfast, which was the remainder of the soup. Still not hungry enough to eat small rodents, she politely declined.

He went to the "facilities" while she waited. Abby contemplated drinking the Red Bull, but decided to wait until tomorrow. She might need the energy more after a second day of hiking. Also, maybe something better than squirrel would happen along. "Please, Lord."

When he climbed back to the cave, Avant's hair was wet. He'd slicked it back from his face and tied it into a little ponytail with a leather string. The sexy shadow of a light beard softened his angular jaw, and the thick waves of his hair shone with chestnut highlights in the morning sun. It was a good look for him, but then again, what wasn't? Abby ran her fingers through her own tangled tresses and pulled her hair back. What she wouldn't give for a hairclip.

"Would you like a thong for your hair?"

She giggled at the word *thong,* certain that what she pictured was not what he referenced. *"Do you have an extra one? I'd like to get it out of my face, and I don't have anything."* Actually she had her own thong, but she sure as hell wasn't putting it in her hair.

He immediately unlaced the tie at the neck of his shirt and handed it to her.

She gasped and put a hand to her face to hide the heat in her cheeks as his shirt fell open below his breastbone. *"You don't have to do that."*

Her blood coursed wildly at the sight of the smooth muscles of his chest. A soft sprinkling of dark hair beckoned her fingers. She swallowed hard.

"It's all right. Please use it. It will be a hard day's journey with hair in your face." His words rang in her mind so sincerely she forgot her embarrassment, but her eyes kept flitting to his heavenly chest.

"Thank you, Avant, and not only for the lace but for everything you're doing to help me."

Holding her gaze, he nodded once, and her heart fluttered. Was it getting warm in the cave? She wiped the beads of sweat from her forehead.

"It is time to be off if we are to make it to the next shelter before nightfall." He picked up his pack and walked to the mouth of the cave. She grabbed her bag and followed.

Climbing down proved to be more difficult than going up. The muscles required to lower herself from one level to the next worked her thighs and butt like no gym equipment she'd ever experienced. It was like doing hours of squats. She trudged down the mountain with the previous day's tumult weighting her down like the freshman ten. Avant helped her along on the steeper steps, but, for the most part, she made them on her own, clippity-clopping in those damned Docinis all the way down.

When he reached the bottom, Avant disappeared around an outcropping. Abby took the last little step to the base and hurried after him. As she turned the corner, Avant grabbed her arm and spun her around. Driving her back against the rock, he pressed the length of his rigid body against her. His face, barely three inches from hers, clenched in thin lines of stress. Her heart raced with fear.

She was pretty sure it was fear.

Chapter Five

The jagged rock pressed into Abby's back. Avant's taut body molded to hers did nothing to regulate her labored breathing.

Stifling her scream, he cupped his hand over her mouth. *"Please, my lady, there is danger."*

The canter of horses and the voices of men echoed against the mountain. How many she couldn't tell, but it was more than a couple. Although he held her gaze, Avant appeared to be listening to determine their number and direction. Several minutes after the men passed, his body relaxed against her. As if realizing his hand still cupped her mouth, he released his hold but not his gaze and remained inches from her face. Her heart continued to race, but not from fear. At least, not *just* from fear.

The pure blue of his eyes pierced through her, and desire rolled off him in heavy waves. For a long moment, they stared at one another. The harsh lines of his face softened. His eyes clouded as his gaze traced the lines of her lips. Avant's chest rose and fell rapidly, and he seemed as if he might—

He pushed away from the rock and took her hand to help her out of the little cleft in the mountainside. Realizing she'd forgotten to breathe, she closed her eyes and exhaled in a rush. She wouldn't think about what almost happened.

Once a safe distance from the travelers and after her breath returned, Abby stopped him. *"Were those the same men from yesterday?"*

His brow furrowed in a scowl, and his gaze was remote. *"No. They were soldiers sent by the king to spy on the stronghold of the Freelands. Aesdil fears an attack from my men."* His tone again turned cordial, and his face became unreadable. *"I apologize if I frightened you, Abigail."*

Heat spread from her chest to her forehead. He'd done a little bit more than scare her. A vision of his full, dramatically lined lips brushing hers formed in her mind, and she swallowed hard. *"That's okay."*

His eyes widened, and he diverted his gaze to take a swig from his water pouch before looking at her again.

"You don't think there are any more of them, do you?" Avant seemed like he could take care of himself, but she was glad those men hadn't found them. How could he have battled alone against a bunch of trained soldiers?

"It is likely, and we will exercise caution as we go."

"So where are we headed?"

"We have a half-day's walk to the eastern fork of the Great River, called Itehris. There's a place where the northern part of the river narrows and can be crossed on foot. In the Ventium Vale is where we will shelter."

No trace of the earlier distress or the desire showed on his face, and unlike with other guys, she couldn't get a read on him. *"And then tomorrow, we'll reach your estate?"*

"Tomorrow we will journey near the village and then another hour to my fief."

As if to purposely distance himself, Avant quickened his stride, and she had to follow at a half-jog. Taking almost three steps to his one, she struggled to keep up in her little sandals.

He didn't do chitchat very well. The strong, silent, and very Hots-A-Lot type. Of course, he could only speak into her mind when looking directly at her, and that made it hard to talk and walk at the same time. Abby snickered to herself. Plenty of people back home didn't think she could talk and walk at the same time either. The guys at Alpha Tao Omega reveled in presenting her with a new blonde joke every time they saw her.

She breathed out a heavy sigh. Grasping hold of the idea she'd magically transported herself to this place—to this guy—was like trying to catch dollar bills in the wind. One thing was certain, the next time she teleported somewhere, she would bring her effin' Nike cross trainers. The little toe on her right foot was a solid blister and pain stabbed through the balls of her feet. *Damn you, Diego Dolcini, Italian shoemaking asshole.*

She stumbled along a faint trail, following behind Avant. Trees sprawled over the mountainside with low-lying bushes at the base of the rocky terrain. Chipmunks scampered across the way as they walked. She eyed Avant's back, hoping he wasn't thinking about lunch when he saw the little animals.

Avant pointed out some large animal tracks. *"Be alert, Abigail. There are roaring lions about, seeking those whom they may devour."* He flashed a devilish grin, and her heart skipped a beat.

Skirting the eastern side of the range, they moved toward the smaller mountains directly ahead of them.

"Once there, we will stop for a brief rest before reaching the river. I have something I wish to show you." Avant gestured to two closely positioned mountains.

When they reached the pass, Abby looked out over the vista. A beautiful valley, green and lush, descended before them. The mountains, low enough for the sun to infuse the plants with life but protection enough from the other elements, created a garden effect. Cypress and willow trees flourished along the flow of water, and the mossy rocks gave the appearance of small rolling hills. She filled her lungs with a deep breath. Green grass scented the late summer breeze.

Avant sat next to the brook on the soft moss, and Abby plopped next to him, rubbing her aching feet. Fish darted back and forth in the bubbling flow of the stream. She pulled out her Evian and gulped down the whole thing. After refilling the bottle, she drank another.

Avant's gaze honed in on her as he popped the top off his leather pouch and took a mouthful. He looked away when she met his eyes over her upturned Evian bottle. She could feel his stare when he thought she wasn't looking. What did he think of her? He believed she was *The One*, whatever the hell that was. But what did he think of *her*? He'd been about to kiss her earlier. She stole another glance at him. Maybe their romantic moment was wishful thinking.

He unwrapped a small brown paper package to reveal a square cake. Holding it up, he offered her some. She nodded, finally hungry enough to try his food. He brushed her palm as he laid it in her hand. Heat bloomed in her cheeks at his touch.

Giving the biscuit a sniff first, she took a bite. The dense cake smelled like butter and flour and tasted like a cookie, with just a hint of sweetness. She ate the whole thing in three more bites. Her stomach growled for more, but he popped the last bite into his mouth. *Drats.*

They sipped their water and refilled their containers.

"Did you enjoy the panas? It is my favorite. The baker's wife makes it just for me."

Looking at those blue eyes and that smile, Abby just bet she did. *"It was delicious. Thank you."*

He schooled his face. *"Abigail, the Implanting manifests in many ways. No one is sure how or why, but as the Light needs, it empowers the Chosen Ones with Giftings to help accomplish its purpose. I believe you have several manifestations of the Implanting. It is my desire to teach you what I know."*

Avant closed his eyes in concentration and lifted his hand toward the brook. A stone the size of a baseball floated out of the bubbling stream and into his upturned palm. She gasped and blinked.

Holy crap. The Implanting was amazing. Telekinesis and telepathy. She'd always believed in the dormant power of the mind, but never thought she would see or experience it. These people had somehow tapped into their dormant mental abilities.

Avant clasped the rock and held it out to her. *"Take it from me."* She reached out to grab it, but he withdrew his hand. *"With your Gift. Take it from me."*

She concentrated on the rock and in her mind spoke to it. *Come to me, rock.*

Avant watched intently and nodded. *"It is similar to mindspeak but the substance of your thoughts must infuse the rock. All thought has substance, Abigail. No word or deed has ever been that wasn't first a thought. It is the elemental beginning of all things."*

She rolled her eyes at the philosophy crap. Jesus, he was just like her dad.

A cocky half-grin played across his face. Great. What was he thinking?

"Try again. Use your thoughts to meld with the rock and deposit your will into it."

Abby focused her energy on the stone. It fluttered briefly above Avant's hand. She lost her concentration. The rock fell back into his palm.

"Excellent. This manifestation will, at first, drain your energy source. Just as with our bodies, the more it is used, the stronger and more focused it becomes. Try again. This time reach down into the source of your energy."

That was easy for him to say. She narrowed her eyes and gritted her teeth. A power source inside her awakened, a force that flowed from all living things into her and out again. She routed the source and forced her will into the rock. It lurched from Avant's hand and rose above his head. Power surged through her and a feeling a freedom overtook her. Trying to control the movement, she couldn't secure a good grasp on the stone with her mind.

Abby looked into his eyes. He spoke to her again. *"Call it to your hand."*

The blue eyes penetrated to her core and his energy joined with hers. A shock of intimacy reverberated. She lost concentration. The rock fell and bonked him on the head.

"Arrghh." He quickly regained his composure but continued to rub the knot as he stared at her with a puzzled look.

Abby bit her lip and ducked her head. *"Sorry."*

A hint of a smile played across his lips. *"There is no need to apologize. It is my own fault for using a rock. You displayed remarkable control, and your ability to so readily access your Gift is encouraging."*

Pride swelled in her chest. She wasn't sure why, but it was important she hadn't disappointed him or knocked him unconscious.

"I need to go behind that rock for a moment." He raised his eyebrows and pointed behind him. *"There is another small area up ahead. I will meet you there in a moment."*

About twenty yards away, a tall, narrow rock had fallen from higher up, creating a walled-in area. A little shiver of disgust zipped up her spine. Would she ever become proficient in the skill of outdoor toiletry? God, she hoped not.

When finished, she washed her hands in the stream. As she rounded the outlet, she startled, expecting Avant. But instead, she met the gaze of the strangest creature she'd ever seen. Panic raced through her. Her first instinct was to run, but the odd creature did something shocking.

It spoke.

"Hello, Abby."

Darkness in working will always be found
But only by choosing can it be bound

Some fruit as it grows is not always to eat
And denies life to the ones who find it not sweet

Heaven is the moment of purpose to send
On a quest for the answers the help of a friend

By heights and by depths and narrow the way
Gives dawn in the waiting a much needed day

Annum 1560 — Prophesy of the High Priest
Festival Sukkot (Festival of Harvest)

Chapter Six

The creature whispered Abby's name in the loveliest, most-melodic voice. A strange peace settled over her, and her feet froze in place. The serpent-like man was five feet tall and upright on two legs. An air of elegance, refinement even, emanated from the beautiful beast like nothing she'd ever seen or known. Its smooth skin shimmered in bold colors of rosy gold, silvery turquoise, and copper orange, sparkling and giving the appearance of fine clothing.

"Do you trust your companion, Abby?"

A magical warmth wrapped around her mind, and the pleasantly timbered voice rang in her ears. She was about to answer when an intense shock shook her.

"Abigail, do not speak with that creature! Look at me!" The sound of Avant's frantic voice blasted in her mind.

She spun around to find him sprinting toward her.

He was as white as the snowcapped peaks behind him. *"What did you say to it?"*

"Nothing, yet." She was about to ask why, but the urgency of his tone and concern on his face interrupted her.

"Do not answer it! Abigail, focus your mind, gather your energy, and say out loud, 'Begone!'"

The intensity of his statement provided a strong energy pulse. She winced and crinkled her brow. Why would such a lovely creature raise this kind of response?

Yanking her behind him, Avant confronted the creature and said venomously, "Ex tenibris denique Lux stondium tomanco vos, Seppitent! Veritum Lux nos liberabit."

The beautiful creature smiled and cooed, "Certa vos veritus Lux, Avant?" Then it laughed a charming laugh that tinkled in her ears like wind chimes.

She giggled. *"Make it laugh again."*

"Abigail." Avant turned to her and demanded, *"Focus your mind, and say out loud, 'Begone!' Do it now."*

The smile slid from her face. Startled by the command in his tone, she blinked and then focused her mind. Looking directly at the creature, she yelled, "Begone!"

The beautiful thing vanished.

Stunned, she turned back to Avant. He breathed heavily, but the harshness of his face softened in relief. She could hear his thoughts though he stared up at the sky.

"I should not have left her. My Light, what was I thinking?" He turned to her, his face lined with concern. *"Are you all right?"*

The whole exchange had taken less than a couple of minutes, but time had crawled in slow motion. Her mind clouded in a haze as if filled with cotton, and she shook her head to clear it. *"I'm fine. How did it just vanish? What was that thing?"*

"It was Seppitent, the most dangerous creature in our lands. Its voice is a slow poison to the mind that will eventually drive you mad and destroy you from within. Tell me exactly: What did it say to you?"

She cowered at the tenor of his question. *"It greeted me by name in my own language and then asked me if I trusted you."* As she spoke the words, she realized how odd that really sounded.

He narrowed his eyes and scrutinized her face. *"Are you certain you did not answer?"*

"No, I didn't, but I was about to when you screamed my name."

The storm in his eyes cleared, and the look on his face told her that he believed her. He put his hand on his forehead and let out a long sigh. This was the most emotion he'd shown since they met, more even than he'd shown when being chased by the king's men.

"How did it know my name?"

He continued to rub his brow with his forefinger and thumb. *"I do not know, Abigail, but it is good that I got to you before you responded."*

"I realize it was a strange creature, but it didn't seem dangerous. Don't you think it's odd that it could speak my language?"

He responded with a condescending air of authority. *"Yes. Abigail, it is a mystery it knew your name and could talk with you. However, what you think about the creature is irrelevant. It is a monster, and you must never speak to it or listen to what it has to say."*

A revelation of how little she knew about this land and the things that lived here swept over her. But mostly, she realized how little she knew about the man in front of her. What had Avant said to make the creature laugh? *"What did you say to it?"*

His face became unreadable. *"I told it to begone, just as you did."*

She frowned and pursed her lips. Sure he had. *"And what did he say back?"*

"Abigail, we need to go now."

He was just going to walk away and ignore her question like she hadn't said a word? Oh, hell no. Who was he to command *her* to do anything? She'd trusted Avant, but should she? For all she knew, he could be taking her to some hellhole slave camp to do God knows what.

Avant bent over to pick up the pack he dropped. She scowled at him. Blue eyes and a nice ass were only going to get him so far.

He spun around and pinned her with a glare. *"Are you aware that when you think a direct thought about me, I can hear it?"*

"No." Shit!

"We need to move on or we will not make our destination by nightfall. Don't forget your pack." He pivoted and stalked away.

She grabbed her bag, following at a distance. Damn, she couldn't even think he was a horse's ass without him knowing it. *Ugh!*

They continued their trek in silence. Abby attempted to keep her mind focused on other things.

What the hell was a Seppitent? It spoke English and knew her name, and its singsong voice still rang in her ears and clouded her mind. Avant had said more to that creature than he was willing to tell her. Why had it asked if she trusted him? *Should* she trust him was the question. She certainly didn't know anything about him. Their last exchange was evidence enough of that. Abby bared her teeth and hissed at his back.

Just how much of her thoughts had he been able to hear or see? Her face flushed with heat, and she wanted to crawl under the mountain and hide. Oh God, she thought he'd wanted to kiss her— and he knew it. Had he even seen the vision she'd had of him? She was thinking about him again. *Damn it.* Up ahead, he gave no indication he heard her, although she knew he had.

Avant maintained the pace as they crossed the valley to the stony banks of the river. It narrowed and flowed steadily over a rocky bed about two feet deep and fifty yards wide.

Crossing it shouldn't be too much trouble, except she hated the thought of her feet slipping in soggy sandals for the rest of the day. She'd have to cross barefooted and take it slow.

Apparently still miffed about earlier, Avant plunged in ahead of her and started across without looking back. She sat down and took her shoes off, sticking them in her little bag. Stepping into the current, she sucked in a breath. The rocks weren't as jagged as she anticipated, but the icy water numbed her feet. Precariously planted, some of the stones wobbled as she stepped on them.

Moving along, carefully maintaining her balance, she could see Avant was almost halfway across. She went slowly. He could just wait.

Probably hearing her thought, he turned around. Seeing she was some way back and apparently not traveling at his preferred speed, he started back toward her. She kept her deliberate pace as he quickly closed the distance between them. He didn't say a word but grabbed her waist and scooped her up out of the water. Throwing her over his shoulder, he started across again.

She gasped. Her head dangled down his back and her rear end was at his ear. Not the ideal position. *"What are you doing?"*

"Attempting to make it to shelter before nightfall. I could put you down and leave you, if you prefer."

"You're a real piece of work, aren't you?" she said out loud.

"You still have to think it before you say it."

She sighed and rolled her eyes. This whole telepathy thing was not turning out so great, what with him being able to hear her every thought.

"I cannot hear everything, only the things that are directly related to me, and that is only because you have not learned to guard your heart. I'll teach you so no one may take advantage of your ability. Make no mistake, Abigail, what you have is a Gift of great value, and if used wisely, it can be a blessing to many."

That explained why she hadn't heard any of his thoughts, but why hadn't he told her before now he could hear her?

"I wanted to make certain I could trust you, and I didn't want to frighten you. There are things I have yet to reveal, but rest assured, very soon you will know all there is to know. For now it is sufficient for you to know it was not by chance I found you. There is a purpose

to your being here. We have a saying: 'There is only chance in the fulfillment of destiny.'"

"Yeah, I know. The Chosen One, right? Well, we have a saying where I come from too—and you're full of it."

From deep in his chest, a laugh rumbled and burst from his lips, shaking his body as he walked. The happy sound quenched a need in her like Gatorade after a workout, and she grinned.

After stepping up on the opposite bank, he set her to the ground. She hadn't even realized how quickly he'd been moving.

His eyes gazed into hers, but his face remained unreadable. She stared back and tried not to think about how beautifully blue they were. *"Abigail, the Light has brought you here, and I must help you prepare for your purpose."*

Could it be true that she'd been zapped here for a predetermined purpose in some grand plan? Or was she just the lottery winner of some colossal cosmic blunder? She'd never considered there might be a plan for her life other than graduating college and getting a job. The concept was as foreign as the world in which she now found herself. Fear shivered through her. Nothing would ever be the same again.

Avant waited for her to put her shoes back on. He didn't appear winded from carrying her all the way across the river. Her heart fluttered at the thought of how easily he'd picked her up. He started walking again when she stood.

Lifting his eyes to the sky, he furrowed his brow and watched the clouds as they rolled in. *"It is another three hours to the camp, and it looks as if a storm is coming from the east."*

Rain. Yet another thing for which she could be thankful.

Based on the sun's position, it seemed to be mid-afternoon, but soon the storm clouds would overtake them. Hopefully they could make it to shelter before that happened. Apparently Avant hoped the same, because he hit the trail with a heavy pace.

After more trekking in the valley, she struggled up an embankment where he stood waiting. The mountain pass spanned between two ranges. Filled with many trees, some of them so tall the tops were invisible, the valley received the flow of a rivulet that ran as far to the east as she could see.

"Our shelter is a natural cave around the other side of this mountain and on this side of the river. We can make camp, and I'll catch something for us to eat."

Hopefully not something small and furry.

"Probably fish."

"Fish is good." In some respects, she liked that she could now communicate without looking him in the eye. In others, not so much.

Nestled into the mountainside, the deep inlet was elevated on a landing just above the stream. Neither of them could stand to full height in it, but the cave was tall enough to sit and long enough to sleep. Cool and damp, it smelled earthy, reminding her of raw mushrooms. The sound of the rushing water and gusty breeze echoed against the rock. She placed her bag down on the hard stone floor. A booming clap of thunder made her jump.

The rain was almost here.

Avant dropped his pack and left the cave to presumably gather firewood. She followed him up a steep path to a landing with trees above. They quickly gathered enough wood and hauled it to the camp.

He kindled a fire. *"Abigail, you may want to relieve yourself before the rain sets in."*

Oh, he was right about that. Peeing outside during a downpour was not something she cared to experience.

She headed up the path to the trees where they'd gathered the wood. Large drops began to fall and made soft noises as they hit the ground littered with pine needles. She squatted beside a tree. The snap of a twig startled her, and a man emerged a short distance away. The breath froze in her lungs. Dirty and gruff with a beard and animal fur around his neck, he stood maybe six feet tall but had a round belly and wild eyes. As soon as she noticed him, he started toward her. Her heart skipped a beat, and she didn't need time to determine he meant to harm her. Jumping up in mid-stream, she ran for the trail to the cave, pulling up her panties as she went.

Chapter Seven

Avant stoked the fire and then rubbed the back of his neck. Trepidation placed a weight in his mind. Why should he be so concerned? He had little to hide. Still, to think that someone would know every part of him sent a shiver down his spine. There were few who'd ever understood him and fewer still who knew him. In a few days, this young woman would hold every personal and intimate detail. His stomach knotted. It seemed many of his body parts knotted at the thought of her and proved their treachery by drawing near at every chance. He jabbed hard at the fire, sending embers flying into the air. For the Light's sake, he'd almost kissed the woman.

He bit his lip, remembering her soft flesh molded against his and her sweet smell entrancing him. It had taken substantial strength of will to pull away.

What was this hold she had over him? He could not remember a time when his body fought him so discordantly. He sighed out a heavy breath and smiled at the remembrance of her face when he told her he heard her thoughts.

My Light, Seppitent had nearly planted his seed and all could have been lost. Until they reached the northern valley, they would not be safe from the evil that crept over the land. He must take care in the wild.

Turning from the fire, he grabbed a line and hook. He'd promised the lady fish for dinner, so he better be about it before the rain—

"Avant!" Out loud and in his mind, Abigail's scream pierced through the silence of his thoughts.

Dropping the fishing line, he bolted up the trail in four strides.

A man hooked one filthy arm around her neck while the other arm forced his vile body against her from behind. Avant's blood boiled, and his pulse pounded in his head.

The rain poured in a torrent.

Avant unsheathed his sword and grasped it with both hands in front of his body. "Halt or I will kill you!"

The man's head jerked up. Using the sudden distraction, Abigail stomped on the reprobate's foot, shoved her elbow into his ribs, and wrenched away. She scampered toward Avant, and he moved to position himself between her and the man who stood six paces from him.

Avant glowered at the beast, who blanched and said, "Commander Avant?"

The derelict's face became visible and recognition coursed through Avant's mind. His body stiffened. "Yes, I live. Does that surprise you, Retalis? Considering our last encounter, I see how it might."

The memory of an arrow lodged in his chest and a large gaping wound in his gut flooded his mind. The sound of his men retreating and leaving him in the enemy camp was the harshest sound he'd ever heard. His chest tightened.

"Commander, I had nothing to do with it."

"Indeed? And what are you doing attacking innocents? Your alliance with the Darkness has deteriorated your heart. From the looks of you, you have wandered these woods alone many days. Were you so base as to be expelled from even the king's guard?"

"You know nothing of me or what I've suffered. I'll kill you."

He chuckled. "Kill me, the man who trained you and saved your life? You've already failed once in that endeavor. I know full well you have neither the courage nor the skill to kill me. What's more, you know it too."

"Perhaps not, Commander, but what I do know is the king would be interested to hear of your survival. I am certain the queen will wish to hear of it also."

At these last words, Avant squared his shoulders and stood tall, pointing his sword at the man's chest. "If you value your life, you will leave these woods. Tomorrow my forces in the Freelands will canvas this forest with orders to kill any renegade soldier or spy."

"*You* are Lord Ventium?" The man's face lost all color.

Avant gained purchase in the degenerate's mind with his Gift. He did not speak nor did he release the man from his gaze. He forced his will into the tormented mind.

Retalis raised his hands to his skull and screamed. "Stop. Stop with your witchery!" With his palms lifted in surrender, he backed into the trees and disappeared.

Avant felt as if someone sat on his chest. He sucked in a labored breath and lowered his sword. Immediately turning his attention to

Abigail, he looked into her frightened face. Compassion poured over him like the rain, and his hand reached out to her. *"Are you all right, Abigail?"*

She stared back, her eyes glazed. Her thoughts swirled in a frenzy of emotion and poured from her like an overflowing washtub. *"My father is dead. My best friend and my boyfriend have betrayed me. I've been ripped, suddenly and without explanation, from my home and sent to a place I have never heard of, with no idea how to get back. I haven't slept or really eaten in three days, have been charmed by a witch-creature, almost raped by your hobo mountain friend while peeing outside with no toilet paper, and everything I think and feel is open to public display. I'm soaking wet and now so are my shoes, and I stink! No, I would not say that I am in any way all right!"* She began to sob and shake, tremors racking her body.

He put his arm around her and led her back to the cave, where the fire blazed. She was shivering so hard she seemed unable to stop her teeth from chattering. She couldn't cease crying. Avant took an extra tunic and wool cloak from his pack and handed them to her. He turned his back and sat near the fire while she changed.

After removing his own rain-soaked shirt, he laid it out to dry.

Still trembling, Abigail laid out her wet clothes and sat down next to him. He put his arm around her and pulled her close. She leaned her head on his chest and a sweet warmth, like honey over hot bread, slowly covered him at her nearness.

"Abigail, you have lost much, but you also have much for which to be thankful. You now have me, and I am a steadfast and faithful friend. Even if you do not know it yet, you are strong and powerful, with a Gift that can effect immense change in whatever world you find yourself."

She never acknowledged his words, but her shudders subsided and her teeth stopped chattering. Her body melted in his arms, and the strawberry scent of her hair filled his senses. Soft tears tickled as they fell onto his bare skin and slid down. She nestled into him and laid her hand on his chest. With that one small gesture, Avant, for the first time in many years, felt as if he were home. She fell asleep in his arms and left him to ponder just who comforted whom.

He tightened his grip and rested his chin on the top of her head as the exchange with Retalis replayed in his mind. The man had not been in the service of Aesdil for quite some time by the debauched look of him, and certainly his actions told of the corruption inside. Seppitent's work, no doubt.

But the thing that played over in Avant's mind was the mention of the queen. Would Sentieve even want him back after all these years? His anger at the king surged, and his muscles tensed. Abigail stirred. He forced his body to relax. Nuzzling his nose deep in her hair, he breathed in her soothing scent and she stilled.

The king would pay for his evil deeds, and Avant would reunite with the woman who'd been his wife.

Annova's prophecy came to him: *You must trust your own Gift, Avant. It will lead you in the right path, although I see the path is not what you now think it to be.* The path would not be what he thought? When he had prepared to receive the Chosen One, he certainly had not expected the young lady in his arms, but the Word of Light had to mean more than that. He stared out of the mouth of the cave, seeking an answer, but there was only rain.

Doubting Retalis's threat to inform the king of him, Avant became more concerned with the men who had crossed their path in the valley. The king had gotten bolder, seeking information from spies. Avant snorted. Aesdil, though not a fighter, was a strategist. He, of course, would know the growing numbers of Lord Ventium's troops, but Retalis confirmed that the king did not know Lord Ventium's identity. It was only a matter of time, however. This made the training of the Chosen One a priority of the utmost urgency.

The volatile timeframe loomed before him. He would have to Implant his thoughts into her as soon as possible. Closing his eyes, he shook his head, sickened by the thought. Could he trust her? Glancing down at the slight body of the sleeping girl, his heart leapt within him. An even more frightening question came to him. Could he trust himself?

For many are called, but few chosen.

Matthew 22:14

Chapter Eight

Abigail yelled, but her voice was swallowed in the darkness. She reached out to feel her surroundings, but emptiness greeted her fingertips in the blackness.

A white light shone from behind her. She spun to find the source, but the beam followed the movement of her head. Everywhere she looked, the light was already there, turning with her.

Her eyes adjusted. With the beam in front of her, the smaller independent shadows that made up the nothingness ran to get out of its way. The fear that gripped her ebbed. Though it was the smallest glint of illumination, the darkness could not extinguish the bright shaft of hope.

Two other lights, deep blue in color, appeared. Added to the power of her light, they revealed more of the room. The shadows moved restlessly inside the darkness to keep from being touched by the glowing beacons.

Four more lights appeared, two in green and two in red, almost fully illuminating the room. The shadows retreated to the far walls. Dark wood panels and furniture of fine quality imbued the space with an air of familiarity, but she still couldn't tell exactly where she was.

Finally, two purple lights blazed, and all the shadows evaporated. In full illumination, four people stood with their bright lights shining, though their faces were hidden.

A familiar voice spoke, but it wasn't from any of the light-bearers. "Chosen One, seek the Way in the land of your father's father, and there will you learn how to return My Light to the kingdom."

*****

Abby woke early. The storm had passed, but dawn hadn't broken. Her head rested against her bag near the fire. She pushed up from the stone floor and scanned the cave. A strange dream still played in her mind. Warmth from the coals blanketed her, though the fire had all but gone out. Avant slept nearby.

His protection and kindness of the previous evening came rushing back. How long had he held her after she'd fallen asleep? This man couldn't be real. She must be in a fairytale. He really was a valiant knight. She studied the face of her savior and resisted the urge to push a wisp of hair from his peaceful face. Avant was so different from the guys she knew.

The guys back home were always looking for something more or better. They had no chivalry, no honor. Abby had loved Chad because he seemed removed from them. She'd trusted him. A sob stuck in her throat, and she stifled it. The thought of Chad made her head hurt.

She stood and stretched her arms over her head. Her body, though sore, surged with renewed strength from sleep. Avant's soft cotton shirt and wool cloak hung on her like an oversized hospital gown. The ecru tunic glistened in the glow of the coals. Intricate dark chocolate and gold embroidery decorated the edges of the V-neck, and the loose-cuff sleeves were too long for her arms. Lifting the sleeve to her nose, she breathed in the scent of fresh cedar and pine with a hint of musk. Out of nowhere, a vision of Avant tenderly kissing her flooded her mind.

Caught breathless, she gasped. The warmth and softness of her own lips kissed him, and her hair fell soft and silky in his hand. Slow and sensuous, the kiss deepened and went on and on. Finally pulling away, he looked into her blue-green eyes, and a plunging current of passion swept over her.

A heavy sigh from Avant slammed her back to reality, and the vision vanished. She bit down hard on her knuckle. *Please don't wake up. Please don't wake up.*

How had her mind jumped so quickly into that kiss? There was something odd about that vision, but whatever it was flitted out of her reach. Why had she seen her own face and not his? Where did that passion come from? She'd never felt that deeply about anyone or anything. She'd never had a reason to because nothing had ever been that important to her. He was attractive, yes, but jeez. *Show a little self-control, Abs, for God's sake.*

She needed to splash some cold water over her heated body and change out of his clothes. After gathering her things, she tiptoed from the cave. The stream was nestled less than twenty-five feet away from the cave, but uneasiness kept her from venturing farther than a whisper.

After washing in the freezing water, she dressed in her own clothes and crept back into the inlet just as the sun cleared the horizon.

Abby laid Avant's shirt and cloak folded neatly next to him. The vision of the kiss flooded back to her, making her stomach flutter and her heart race. She needed a plan before he woke up or he would see that kiss in vibrant HD. She might as well fling herself from the nearest cliff if that happened. Maybe she could sing a song to clear her mind if the thought assailed her again. That could work, right?

She pulled out the Red Bull and popped the top. Avant opened his eyes.

"Sorry." She smiled and took a gulp.

A flicker of something crossed his face, but it was gone so fast she couldn't identify it.

"Good day, fair lady. I see you have awakened the sun for us."

"I guess I did. Late night?" She swigged the energy drink.

He shook his head. *"You seem in better spirits. There is nothing like the dawn after a storm to provide us with hope and fill us again with faith. Weeping may endure for a night but joy comes in the morning."*

Uh-huh. God, he sounded just like her dad, which was a creepy idea after she'd just imagined— *Ninety-nine bottles of beer on the wall, ninety-nine bottles of beer, if one of those bottles should happen to fall, ninety-eight bottles of beer on the wall...*

Avant gave her a suspicious look and the last portion of the panas before going to wash in the stream. She sang the whole song—twice.

In the excitement of the evening, they hadn't eaten, so he also fished for trout. He cooked his catch, and they shared it for breakfast. Fish for breakfast was not her first choice, but it actually wasn't bad. The white flaky meat melted like heaven in her mouth, and her body immediately absorbed the protein. A new energy filled her, although that could've been the Red Bull.

Packing up the camp, they headed toward his home.

"We'll bypass the village and journey to my fief by way of a footpath a short distance to the east. I would rather not explain your

presence quite yet. Your visit will be rumor enough in time, and the villagers are somewhat prone to gossip."

"Do you rule the people of the village also?" She could understand how her presence might cause talk if he was their leader. Especially if he wasn't married, or even more if he was. Her heart sank and then her cheeks heated with the revelation that *again* he'd heard every word.

His face lit in a cocky smirk.

Damn. Damn. Damn.

"It is a modest village where everyone is known, and in your current attire, you could not possibly go unnoticed." He raised his brow as his gaze slid the length of her. *"I'll have Petra get some proper clothing for you tomorrow, as well as anything else of which you have need. And, in answer to your unspoken question, I have no wife on my fief."*

Abby's heart lurched into her throat, and she couldn't meet his even gaze. Not only did he know she lusted after him, he thought she was dressed like a tart. This was starting out to be another banner day.

Trying to refocus her mind, she concentrated on his last words. *"Who is Petra?"*

"Petra is the bailiff of my lands. He has lived with me for almost eight years. Though not by blood, he is my son."

Abby breathed a sigh. *"Your son? How old is he?"*

"He is nearly twenty summers old."

He had a son her age. As if the awkwardness couldn't get any thicker. He chuckled.

Indignation burned in her throat. *"I'm not sure what you're laughing at."* She wasn't the only one with a secret attraction.

With that thought, he masked his face in impassivity. And she was the one who smiled in smug satisfaction.

Picking up the pace and walking ahead of her, Avant left the sparkling stream in favor of a trail between two closely formed hills of the eastern mountains. The late summer foliage remained green, but the chill in the wind told of cooler weather to come.

They spent several hours ascending the wooded path through uneven terrain. The moisture in the air increased, and the sound of rushing water grew louder the farther they walked.

Abby's feet felt like they would fall off. The eight-hundred-dollar shoes had succeeded in producing huge blisters on at least two toes of each foot and had rubbed off all the flesh on the back of her heel. Fairly certain her Achilles tendons were now exposed to the elements, she never wanted to see a pair of designer sandals again as long as she lived.

The night's rest in the cave had given her some relief from the fatigue that drained her. Still, the travel and stress left her feeling like she was carrying the mountain instead of climbing it.

She'd come to accept that she didn't know where or when she was. The realization she was trapped indefinitely in this world had finally sunk in. Maybe it was her breakdown last night, but her mind embraced the possibility she would have to stay here.

A brilliant smile lit Avant's face as he turned to her. *"We'll stop here for a short rest, because I could scarcely pass my favorite place in the world without a moment to enjoy it."*

Feeling downcast but warmed by his smile, Abby trailed after him through a narrow clearing between two trees to a small, grassy area on a cliff.

Stepping out, she gasped. "Oh my God!"

She stood on a ledge halfway down from a taller cliff to her left. Pouring over the rock forty feet high, a waterfall spilled into a teal-green pool below. All around the falls were the tallest of the snowcapped heights encircling them like a crown. The sun-kissed mist created multidimensional rainbows that glistened and arched down, brightening and fading as the clouds glided overhead.

Each of her senses overflowed with the experience. The light shone and water roared with effortless strength. The ripe scent of pine permeated the air and a caress of moisture touched her skin. It was by far the most stunning and intimate setting she'd ever seen, and she doubted anything she would ever experience again in heaven or earth would be so lovely.

They sat down on the grass in silence, drinking in the beauty of the falls.

"Abigail, you have been dealt a difficult circumstance. I cannot tell you the future will be easier, but what I can tell you is eventually this new life will seem familiar, and you will be able to find peace and joy within it."

He'd apparently caught the tenor of her thoughts from earlier and was trying to lift her spirits. The words rang through her mind, genuine and heartfelt. She wasn't sure how she knew, but he spoke from his own experience.

"I will give you the language and culture of Jastain through my Implanting, which should help you adjust to life here."

"I can learn by Implanting?" Her dad had been wrong—she could learn by osmosis? Cool.

"It is possible to Implant my learning into your mind so that you will know our world, language and way of life, but it is a process of which I am unsure. I cannot tell what other…information the seed may carry." His eyes darted from her. He shifted his weight uncomfortably.

What did he mean? Maybe she didn't want to know.

He got a far-away look in his eyes, and it was a moment before he continued. *"Abigail, you may dwell in my home and work on my fief, but when your destiny calls, you must offer the sacrifice asked of you."*

Looking out over the falls, they were silent for a long while. *Sacrifice?* Her dad had once said something about sacrifice but at the moment she couldn't think of it. A shudder ran down her spine. The word *sacrifice* did not conjure warm, fuzzy feelings. She hoped he didn't expect her to throw her non-virginal body into a volcano or some crap like that.

"I cannot say what the Light will require other than your unconditional obedience. That is also my requirement in exchange for training you in your Gift and providing for your needs. While I have no specific knowledge of the Implanting you employed to bring yourself here, I have sufficient knowledge to hone your Gift and in all else I trust the Light. I can help you Abigail. Do we have an accord?"

She glared at him. He was blackmailing her. She stiffened her spine. *"And what if I don't agree?"*

His face clouded with deep-seeded pain. *"Then hope is gone, my lady."*

Dread filled her, but Abby couldn't stand to see the hurt in his eyes for a moment longer. If he was crazy, then it wouldn't matter. Destiny would never call anyway. And if he was right, well, she'd cross that proverbial bridge later.

The despair in his eyes caused tears to well in hers. A pain pierced her heart and even telepathically she couldn't speak the words fast enough. *"Okay. I'll do it. I promise."*

He shut his eyes and spoke a quiet word she was certain was a prayer of thanksgiving.

After a while, he stood. *"Now it is time for us to be on our way. We should reach the fief in an hour."* He grabbed his pack and began to walk.

Taking a cleansing breath and one last gaze at the falls, she grabbed her pack and then followed after him. She would definitely be coming back here.

Chapter Nine

Avant allowed Abigail to lead their descent into the valley. He listened to her thoughts as she replayed the conversation again in her mind. Catching glimpses as they related to him, he hoped to gain insight. The Light had not yet revealed to her its purpose, and she had strong doubts. In truth, he had his own doubts. He hesitated, measuring her as she walked ahead. His purpose was clear: to prepare her, whether she believed or not. The Light would provide the rest in due time.

"Avant, what is the Crown of Light?" She stopped to look at him. Her teal eyes glittered in the light of noonday.

"The Crown of Light, set on the head of the king, will yield fruit in the hearts of the people and cause peace to reign in the land."

She turned and began walking again. *"What kind of fruit grows in the heart? Is this philosophical symbolism again?"*

"The fruit of the Light is all righteousness and everything which is good and true. Each jewel set in the Crown represents a trait of the Light, but now, without the Crown, the Dark holds sway over the land. Those gifts are lost or forgotten."

"What happened?"

"Forty years ago, the last high priest prophesied the new king. But unlike years past, the king's son was not the chosen successor. This enraged the ruling king, who would not countenance his son to be snubbed. In an act of defiance against the Light and treachery toward his own brother, the king killed the high priest and attempted to kill his own scribe, the only other witness to the prophecy." Avant closed his eyes and mourned the death of his father at the hands of his uncle. When he opened them, Abigail stared at him with such compassion and intensity his heart burned within him and his arms ached to hold her again. Their attraction grew, and he knew they tread upon dangerous ground.

He staunched his desire and continued with his tale. *"Being forewarned, the scribe escaped with the Crown and the final prophecy. Since that time, there has been no Light, no high priest, and no peace. Though the current king did not choose his own path, his reign is an abomination and governed by Darkness. And he has since fallen to the Dark. The land is splintered, and the kingdom, broken."*

Abigail's face glowed with understanding, but her tone was filled with doubt. *"Avant, I'm sorry about your kingdom, but you're wrong about me. I can't be the one you're looking for. I can't help you find your crown."* Her brow furrowed, perplexed. *"I plan parties and go shopping. I don't help restore kingdoms of Light."*

"I did not say it was my crown, although I believe it is. And whether you know it or not, you are the one to restore the Light, just as I am the one to rule. Neither of us asked for these appointments, and yet they fall to us just the same."

She stared at him for a long moment, but her thoughts were closed.

He spoke the truth. Avant's dreams told him he would one day be king. On many occasions, visions of himself in the castle, leading the people of Jastain in a new reign of Light had come to him. The deep-seated knowing of his Gift, as well as the foretelling of others, confirmed this belief, but without the final prophecy there was no way to prove what he knew. No way to overthrow the reign of Darkness. Finding the prophecy was as important as finding the Crown, and to do that, he needed the Chosen One. He needed Abigail.

He stooped to pick a wildflower and handed it to her. *"It is a Queen's Cup lily."*

Looking up at him through long lashes, she smiled and a faint blush colored her cheeks. A feeling of contentment ran through him like a river flowing across the desert.

Taking the white flower, she held it to her nose and then drew the delicate petals across her cheek. His breath quickened as he found himself wishing it were his lips feathering her skin instead.

He shook the thought from his mind. *"We will speak of Jastainian politics later, but now we are home. At last."*

*****

Abby let her gaze travel across sprawling fields of grain and pastures where herds of cattle and sheep grazed. Off in the distance, a large slate-stone manor came into view like a picturesque scene from some new Disney movie. She half expected Julie Andrews to break into song. The charcoal color of the large estate house popped against the late summer greenery and crystal blue sky. *Sweeping* was the word that came to her mind.

A warm smile lit Avant's face, and his eyes sparkled. *"Welcome to my fief, Domentus Ventium."*

As they approached the manor, several workers waved to Avant. Still feeling vulnerable after the previous night's close call, she peered down to the ground, embarrassed by her appearance.

Avant picked up the pace and she hustled to keep up.

This whole place was his? Massive and beautiful, the bright fields spanned as far in the distance as she could see. She swept her gaze over him. He must be the catch of the county.

"You were not clear on the size of your farm. It is a bit bigger than I expected." She smirked accusingly.

"My apologies. I do hope you will find it comfortable and welcoming." He dipped his head with cordial formality.

"I'm sure I will." She held the graceful flower to her nose again. Its soft floral scent filled her, and her heart melted like ice cream in the Texas sun.

They walked the long drive to the mammoth house and entered through a side door. A huge fireplace with built-in structures that held various copper pots and pans dominated the cozy kitchen. A small pig cooked on a spit over the fire, and the smell of slow roasting meat made Abby's mouth water. A busy little cook prepared some kind of dough on a long wooden table.

When she saw Avant, the squat woman's hands paused. "Dominus Avant, ha vetrie il siat."

He answered back, allowing Abby into the conversation by speaking into her mind. *"Yes, thank you, Helean. It has been a long journey, and we are both in need of a hot meal and a bath as soon as possible."* He gestured toward her. *"This is Abigail, a guest who will be staying with us for a while. Please let Master Petra know we have returned."*

The sturdy woman eyed Abby up and down, her shock evident. She looked back to Avant, curtsied, and then hastily departed.

Abby crinkled her forehead. She realized Avant wasn't just any Joe Shmoe. But a curtsy? Really? To top it off, Avant's eyes twinkled with amusement.

Leading her upstairs, he showed her the restroom, which was basically a hole covered by a wooden seat. The gaping darkness of the drop resembled the pit of despair, and the smell confirmed the belief. He left her there, saying he wanted to check on something he'd requested. She shook her head in distaste, and it crossed her mind that she might prefer the outdoors.

After using the facilities, she returned downstairs. Wandering to the front of the manor, Abby inspected each room as she passed. The main entrance to the house encompassed a large room with several doors leading to smaller adjacent rooms. Fine-quality furnishings made of rich woods and jacquard fabric decorated the beautiful slate-stone house. She ran her fingers across the satiny purple fabric of a settee.

One door led to a cozy parlor where she picked up a handwritten, leather-bound book and thumbed through the pages. The colorful drawings adorned in gold ink seemed to lose none of their detail due to size.

The clap of leather on the stone floor sounded behind her. Avant had returned to get her. She turned to greet him but gasped. Her heart caught in her throat. It wasn't Avant, but a chillingly familiar face.

"Chad?" She blinked her eyes and shook her head.

The man's hair was longer and his shoulders broader, but the eyes were the same. He seemed just as stunned by her, and they stood there, gawking at each other.

He raised a tentative hand in greeting. "Geta, san ty Petra."

This was Petra? "I'm sorry. I don't speak Jastainian." She couldn't tear her eyes from his face.

He flushed crimson, but his gaze stayed fixed on her. The awkward silence engulfed them but neither could shake it.

Avant strode into the room and abruptly came to a halt. She never broke her gaze from Chad's mirror image.

"Petra, this is Abigail, our guest." Avant's voice rang in the room and her mind.

Though they both heard, neither she nor Petra acknowledged him. Avant cleared his throat. Abby finally closed her eyes and turned her head, which seemed to release Petra from the spell. He greeted Avant but kept glancing over at her. Her hands trembled, and she tried to steady her breath.

"Abigail, this is Petra. He is the bailiff of my lands. He can get you anything of which you have need, if I am...not...around." Avant regarded her through narrowed eyes that held an emotion she couldn't quite describe, but it wasn't happy. *"Is something wrong?"*

The sharp edge of his tone startled her, and she shook her head. *"No, nothing."* How could she tell him his bailiff looked exactly like the guy she was zapped away from, the same jerk who'd broken her heart?

Abby, deep in thought, barely heard as Avant thanked Petra.

How could two people in different worlds look so much alike?

Petra's voice jerked her out of her thoughts. He asked Avant a question. Avant laughed uncomfortably and said, *"No."* The young man made a slight bow and left the room. Her gaze followed him until he was out of sight.

Avant stared at her for a long moment, running his index finger over his lips, his face unreadable. *"It seems my young landmaster is somewhat besotted with you. He is not one to be led by his emotions, and yet you obviously affected him."* He straightened his stance with feet apart and hands clasped behind his back. *"What did you say to him?"*

Abby threw up her palms and rolled her eyes. *"I didn't say anything. I don't speak Jastainian, and I can't imagine what there is to be besotted about. I'm sure I look and smell like hell."*

As if he realized the accusatory tone of his question, he quickly said, *"Of course, you didn't. I was surprised by his reaction to you."* His features smoothed and he spoke softly, reverently, *"You do, however, underestimate yourself, Abigail. Even likened to hell you are quite beautiful."*

Her cheeks flamed, and she averted her gaze. *"Thanks."*

Avant had her emotions in a tailspin. His hot and cold reactions confounded her.

"Come. Your bathwater will be getting cold."

*****

She soaked for a long while and scrubbed her filthy flesh with the washcloth and the little carved soap. The water soothed her sore muscles, especially her feet. A firm belief settled in her bones—

strappy sandals were of the devil. She sighed and sunk deeper into the tub.

Petra had apparently rounded up a linen sheath and wool socks for her to wear until they could cover her with "proper attire." She shot a dubious look at the plain dress.

Who was this Petra? How could two people look so much alike and not be related? He'd reacted strongly to her too. There had to be a connection with his reaction and his resemblance to Chad. But what?

The Chosen One. Abby scrubbed her face. What was Avant smoking? Find the missing prophecy and restore the mysterious Crown of Light? Ha! Good luck with that. She couldn't find the match to at least ten pairs of earrings and even more socks. How was she going to find his crown?

In all other ways, Avant seemed sane and balanced, if not a little formal. It didn't make sense that he put so much faith in this Light stuff. How did he know with such conviction? What caused him to believe? It was obvious that paranormal activity was a way of life in Jastain. She'd seen things she never thought possible. But how did that automatically translate to her being The One?

After her bath, Helean, the house manager and cook, ushered her to a table where the men waited. Her gaze immediately locked with the eyes of her enigmatic host, who stood as she approached.

Avant was clean and freshly shaven. His dark hair waved around his handsome face and made his eyes look an even deeper shade of blue. Dressed in fine brown pants and a midnight-blue linen tunic with rich silk embroidery, he looked every bit the part of Lord Ventium. She frowned, disconcerted with the change. Was this the same man who tapped his foot to music and sheltered overnight in caves eating wild rodents? He looked more like the pushy commander who pissed her off.

Clearly, Avant had said something to Chad…uh, Petra, because he scarcely glanced at her and quickly averted his eyes when she did happen to catch him looking.

She took a seat at the large table, and the men sat. Helean served delicious food on simple metal plates. A fork-spoon hybrid utensil and a very sharp knife lay in front of her. She picked it up and studied the spork. KFC was the only place she'd ever seen one.

"Abigail, was your bath satisfactory? And the clothing?" Avant spoke in her mind and out loud to include Petra.

She smiled and nodded. *"The bath was great and the clothes are...uh...nice."*

Avant laughed out loud.

Taking a bite of the delicately roasted pork with turnips and carrots, she closed her eyes and moaned in delight. Avant watched her with amused interest and seemed pleased she enjoyed the food at his table. She devoured the mouth-watering bread slathered with honey butter. But the best part of the meal was the mead, an alcoholic drink made with honey and clove spices. She drained three full glasses before she realized it.

Her eyes conspicuously roamed around the room, not landing on either man. Because of the difficulty in communicating with anyone other than Avant, the silence lengthened uncomfortably between them. Abby was anxious to engage Petra in conversation, but it seemed he was unable to communicate using his Implanting.

After the meal, Avant led her back to the small living room. He walked to the window and stared out into the evening.

"I am certain the events of today were a little overwhelming, but sometimes the Light will speak to us in the simplest matters. For me, revelation comes in the form of dreams."

The blood drained from her face as her dream from the night before played in her mind. *"How do you know your dreams are inspired?"*

"They have never failed me. I have learned by difficult paths not to ignore them. My dreams have been the one true constant in my life. The one thing on which I could always depend."

She walked and stood behind him. *"Last night I dreamed I was in darkness, alone and afraid. But a small light shined, and I wasn't afraid anymore. Then more lights came and the darkness dwindled until four others joined me, shining different-colored lights."*

Avant turned from the window to face her. His eyes sparked with interest.

"Finally, a voice spoke, but it wasn't the people with me, it was someone else. Someone familiar, but I can't place who, and it said, 'Seek the way in the land of your father's father, and there will you learn to return Light to the kingdom.' Do you know what that means?"

Excitement danced over his features. *"How many lights including the first shone in the room?"*

"Nine. Everyone but me had two colored lights, but my light was just white." She stared at him and pictured the final scene of the dream. *"Like this. Does it mean anything to you?"*

His brow relaxed and he looked past her, tapping his finger on his chin. *"This dream is our starting point to find the jewels. There are nine jewels in the crown. Two stones are amethysts, then two rubies, two emeralds, two sapphires, and the Stone of Light the center."*

Her heartbeat raced. *"The colors of the lights in my dream correspond to the colors of the stones."*

He paced in front of her. *"Indeed they do. When Jo-naphen, the scribe, took the Crown, he removed the stones and hid them for safekeeping with several devout followers of the Light. I have two of them in my own keeping."*

The sapphires on his sword? She still had doubts about her role, but Avant seemed so sure of her involvement, and it did seem possible this dream correlated to the Crown. *"Where are the other stones?"*

"That is something I hoped you would know. Do you recognize the place of your dream? The picture you presented appeared hazy."

She shook her head. *"It's like a song I know all the words to but can't remember how it starts. If someone could give me the first line, I could sing the whole thing. But, as it stands, I can't remember."*

"When the time is right, you will."

He guided her upstairs into a nice-size room. A cozy fire flickered from the fireplace. The warmth removed the chill as night crept in. Sweeping windows opened to the east, and a stunning view of the mountains spanned the horizon. The late evening sun danced off the snowy peaks Avant had called the Great High Places. A simple four-poster bed made of dark wood took up most of the space. She smoothed her palm over crisp ivory linens and a fluffy down comforter that appeared to be brand new. A delicate table sat by the bed next to a straight-backed chair with a crimson velvet cushion. Someone had placed her first aid bag on top of the spindle-legged, two-drawer dresser. Simple but clean, the room was a welcome change from the cave floor.

"Fair lady, do these accommodations meet with your approval?" Avant cocked his head and eyed her.

Abby smiled. *"Yes, these are the finest accommodations I have seen in your great land."*

His eyes narrowed, though a smile played at the corners of his mouth. *"Hmm. I am not certain that is a compliment."*

Her heart fluttered at his tease. A wisp of his wavy hair fell across his forehead, and his strong lips met in a perfect line over his slightly cleft chin. It should be against the law for a man to be so sexy. She stepped closer and took a deep breath, breathing in his clean, woodsy scent. Feeling the mild effects of the wine from dinner, she twirled her hair with a finger, remembering how it felt to be wrapped in his arms with her head against his chest. *"I slept very soundly in the accommodations provided last night."*

He cleared his throat. *"Yes, well, get a good night's rest, and we will start working on our plans in the morning."*

"Thank you. In the morning, then." She frowned and dropped her gaze as he strolled out the door.

A candle burned on the table and a long-sleeved nightshirt waited for her on the bed. Abby pulled on the soft shirt and sank into the feather mattress. Wrapping her body around the long cylinder pillow like a lover, she fell fast asleep

INTIMACY, n. A relation into which fools are providentially drawn for their mutual destruction

Ambrose Bierce

Chapter Ten

A banging on her door echoed through the room and woke Abby from sleep. She sat up and stretched, trying to clear the cobwebs.

"Yes." Her sleep-weary voice broke.

The sun spilled light into the space. Avant strode into the middle of the room, carrying an armful of clothing and a leather pack of goods. His face was drawn in tight lines, and the rigidity of his stance screamed *foul mood. "It is time to get dressed. We have a lot to do today."*

Helean bustled in behind him, setting a bowl and pitcher of water on Abby's dresser. The woman shot a furtive glance at Avant and left. Abby couldn't blame her. She wanted to climb back under the covers and hide. Yawning, she tried to focus her eyes to meet his gaze. *"What's up, Lord of the Ringlets?"*

He frowned at her humor. *"We have much to do in a short time, and today I will attempt the Implanting."* He unceremoniously dumped the items on the end of her bed. *"You have half an hour to get ready."* Then he pivoted and marched out of the room.

Abby sighed and rolled her eyes at Sir Grumpy. Welcome to the Freelands.

She climbed out of bed and washed her face with the tepid water before putting on the new clothes, which fit as if they'd been tailored for her. The forest green skirt flowed almost to the floor. Complimented with an ecru muslin top underneath, the dark brown corset laced in the front and emphasized the soft curves of her body. The colors accentuated her blonde hair, and the corset was comfortable enough, better than the Victoria Secret bra she'd worn for three straight days.

After propping the small hand-held mirror up on the dresser, she brushed her hair behind her ears, tying it back in a half-ponytail. Her dad had always loved it when she wore her hair like that. A wave of grief swept over her.

God, she missed him. She could use a few of his bright inventions in this place. *Hell, heated water would be an improvement.*

Stepping lightly into the soft leather ballerina slippers, she could've been a character in a fairytale.

She descended the stairs and found Avant in the kitchen waiting with breakfast. He turned to speak but stopped short. His appreciative gaze slid like silk across her skin and made her breath quicken. Still feeling put out with him, she just stared.

His self-satisfied smile churned her stomach. *"So the clothes fit?"*

"Apparently." She broke his smug gaze and marched to the table.

"Sit. Let's eat." He pulled out a straight-backed chair at the small table, where a bowl of oatmeal and a piece of fruit waited. They ate in silence.

What was up with him? Just because she was at his mercy with nowhere else to go, didn't give him the right to be rude. And she wasn't a little doll that he could dress up and sit on a shelf either. Though, she had to admit he'd done a good job getting her sizes right, and the colors weren't completely unfortunate either. He glanced over, his eyes sparkling. She stared back brazenly. Let him hear.

When they finished, Avant stood. *"I think we will be more comfortable in the parlor for what we have to do."*

He waited for her at the door, allowing her to walk to the small library where they'd spoken last night.

Large square windows faced the southern fields. The beveled panes filtered the light and sent rainbows across the floor in the morning sun. An intricately carved mahogany mantel adorned the white and gray marble fireplace. Above it hung the most beautiful oil canvas in the house. An ornately gilded frame encased the substantial painting, which depicted the very falls she and Avant had visited the day before. They sat on the sofa. Large brocade pillows lined the back of the crimson couch. Abby placed one in her lap as she shrank back into the corner, trying not to bite her fingernails.

Avant took a deep breath and forced it out. *"Abigail, I must explain something before we do this. There are things in my past few people are aware of, and if those…things ever became known, it could be a danger to us."* The worry in his eyes and the stress lines on his face softened her heart.

"You can trust me." Even though she was still irritated with him, she smiled and squeezed his hand. He'd done a lot for her. How could she refuse him and those blue eyes anything?

He smiled wanly. *"Thank you. It is a hard thing to discuss my past, and I am sorry if I have been unkind this morning. This next step is urgent and must be done or all our hope to defeat the Dark will be lost."*

What could be so bad and why the hurry? The king's men didn't seem like nice guys, but based on the military barracks they'd passed, Avant's forces could defend the Freelands.

"Aesdil's father, Sudael, was my uncle. He took care of me and my mother after my father died. It wasn't until years later that I learned the truth—that he had killed my father, his own brother. When Aesdil was crowned king after Sudael's death, rumors abounded and the kingdom was divided. Whispers of betrayal splintered the peace between the lands of the south and east. Wars broke out." Avant stood and paced in front of her as he relived the story.

He wandered to the window and fingered the fringed drapes, absorbed in the telling. *"Having never needed a peacekeeping force, the City of Light was threatened by the attacks. Fortunately, the attackers were less knowledgeable than I was about warfare. I was the only one in the kingdom with any training, and much of that I'd learned on my own in the Hall of Records. My tutor, Galwyn, taught some military strategy, but combat skills were unknown to us at that time. Aesdil was my closest friend, my cousin. He appointed me commander of his newly formed army. Sometime after my appointment, the king conspired with a few of my men to have me killed during an uprising in the southern plains. Once the enemy attacked, the forward-most troops pulled back and left me for dead. It wasn't until after miraculously surviving the incident that I discovered his treachery. That was twenty years ago."*

Twenty years ago? How old was Avant?

"Forty-eight," he answered her.

She gaped at him. God, he barely looked late twenties, but she'd already guessed he was older than he appeared.

"Without the proper king, our condition will continue to deteriorate, and the hearts of men have become so base that they kill each other rather than wait for the elements of nature to destroy them. The Crown of Light must be restored and Aesdil defeated."

She came to the question his story begged. *"If the king was like a brother and you were the only one who could fight, what made him want to kill you? Why would he do that?"*

His eyes filled with the pain of heartbreak. *"Because he coveted my wife."*

A lump formed in her throat. *"Your what?"*

"My wife, Sentieve." Avant said the words with such reverence there was little doubt as to his feelings.

He was married to a woman he clearly still loved. *Well, that sucks.*

"After I was left for dead, the king took my widow, Sentieve, as his own wife." A flash of anger crossed his face. *"Aesdil thought he could command the army I'd trained, and, without me to challenge him, he thought he could stand. But his plan failed. I am still here to oppose him, and I intend to claim my kingdom and reclaim my wife."*

Her heart plummeted. She knew a guy like Avant was probably taken, but she'd hoped. Maybe. Leave it to her to end up in the middle of some other chick's fairytale.

"I am certain Sentieve was manipulated. I knew Aesdil held feelings for her, but never believed he would harm me. She loved me. I am certain he played on her fear and grief. She was expecting a child at the time of my death. He deceived her into a marriage he founded on murder."

His fisted hands shook with bridled anger. Waves of loathing rolled off him, causing the hair on her arms to rise.

Something about that story with his wife didn't add up, but Abby let it go for the moment.

"So, you have a child?" Who was twenty years old.

"The child died less than a year after it was born." He fired a gaze at her. The rage reflected in his eyes caused a shiver to run down her back. What he must have gone through. Abby couldn't imagine…yes, she could. Lyndsea and Chad had screwed her over to be with each other. The wound stung, and Avant's hurt had to be even worse. Twenty years? *"Couldn't you get her back before now?"*

"I've been seeking nothing else, trying to find a way. But the Light has required my silence and inaction. As of yet, the king is unaware I am still alive."

Her heart broke for him. She couldn't fathom the faith it must have taken for him to sit idly by for twenty years. Again, the story didn't quite add up. Avant didn't strike her as the wait-and-see type. What was he not telling her? She eyed him speculatively.

She'd never endured anything near what this guy had. An overwhelming tenderness swept over her. *"You've been waiting all these years for the Chosen One to come help get her back?"*

He stiffened his spine and sat next to her on the sofa. *"Yes. And now that you've come, I can finally avenge myself."*

This was heavy stuff. The pain he'd suffered: the loss of his life, his love, and his baby, without anyone to comfort him, must have been awful. She would've turned into a raving-mad monster from the heartbreak. She took his hand and squeezed tightly. *"Avant, I don't think I'm the One you're looking for, but I'll help you in any way I can. What do I need to do?"*

Hope leapt in his eyes, quenching the rage or, at least, burying it. *"We must find the Crown, reset the jewels, and restore it to the proper ruler. It is my hope we can infiltrate the castle and help Sentieve get out. Then we will march against Aesdil and his armies. With my Implanting and yours, he cannot stand against us and the Crown."* Avant lifted his chin. *"Now you know the whole story. Aesdil's armies are great, but he still thinks he fights against an untrained enemy. If he was to find out I'm still alive, that I am Lord Ventium, an attack would be imminent. Secrecy gives us an advantage we require."* He resolutely placed his hands on his knees. *"Are you ready to receive my Implanting?"*

She smiled half-heartedly. *"I guess so. Do you have any idea what I can expect from this Implanting?"*

"Yes, I have an idea." He didn't meet her gaze, and a slight flush swept over his face.

He was blushing? What the crap was that about? Dread tightened around her throat. *"Are you going to tell me?"* Maybe she didn't want to know.

He'd just revealed the most intimate secret he had, but *that* hadn't embarrassed him. Her stomach clenched. Never a good sign.

"You will most likely receive all of my feelings, my thoughts and my memories." He gazed into her face, blue eyes searching for the answer to a question he hadn't asked.

Heat flushed her cheeks and her stomach flip-flopped. *Oh hell.*

"I do not relish the idea of baring my soul, but it is a necessary step in gaining the upper hand against my enemy. I imagine, for you, it will be like living inside me and through me—and there are things there I wouldn't wish on anyone, especially you." He blew out a long, whistling breath.

"W-what do you mean...your feelings...and thoughts?" Awkwardness flooded her brain, and her thoughts stumbled. The urge to run like hell tingled in her legs.

She needed a drink. Glancing around the room for a means of escape, she searched for anything that could help.

All the things she'd done in the privacy of her life ran through her mind. A chill swept over her and she shivered. No way would she ever reveal those to anybody for any reason.

She would have memories of his sexual fantasies? And what he did with them? Eww. Every hateful thought would be revealed. Ouch. Every time he picked his nose. Eww again.

"My God!" The words came out in a gasp, and the corset cinched her lungs closed.

"There is no way to separate my experiences from my thoughts and feelings of those experiences. You will have them written upon your memory like the words of a book. I am fairly certain you will have firsthand knowledge of my mind and heart. It is an unfortunate result of the process and one I deeply regret, but it is not to be helped."

Was he trying to convince her or himself? *"Avant, I don't want to. Please. Let's not do this. I can learn the language—we can find another way."*

"No! This is how it must be. Do not tempt me. It is the only way. Time is of great importance. The Light has spoken; now we must act." He seemed on the brink of violence, and she didn't dare push him further. Standing, he paced to the window.

Shit. Her stomach churned. She would never hurt him, or use the information against him. But it's not like she wanted to know all of his business, either.

He took a deep breath and then turned to face her. *"I think you can expect more of the same energy you experience when we communicate. Let's try."*

She couldn't look at him.

He lifted her chin and stared into her eyes.

With his straight back and set jaw, he looked so stoic. She couldn't imagine wanting something so much that she'd be willing to do this to get it.

"Please, Abigail."

Abby winced but nodded. *"I need a drink first."*

He walked to a large leather box and opened it. Inside the folding liquor cabinet sat a crystal bottle filled with amber liquid. So that's where he kept the good stuff. He poured her a small glass and handed it to her. Downing the drink in one gulp, she coughed and choked as the liquid fire blazed a trail to her belly. His furrowed brow and intense gaze, evidence of his disapproval, kept her from asking for another glass. That, and her vocal chords were singed from the alcohol content equivalent to moonshine. She handed the glass back.

After closing the box, Avant turned and stared at her. He hadn't wanted to give her the drink, but he needed her, or at least he thought he did. The liquor had been a bribe.

She was being a baby. He was the one at risk. If he wasn't scared, why should she be? How bad could it be? She steadied her legs and stood. *"I'm ready."*

She gathered her strength, and the light amassed. The room around her, the world, dimmed—except his gaze. His sapphire eyes glowed with an infinite spectrum of emotions. A light burst from deep within him. They were the same—their hearts mirrors of one another. Both raised without parents, betrayed by family, and forced to begin a new life after tragedy. But Avant held a strength she didn't and a wisdom that came from years of struggle. Rage darkened his heart.

Brave in battle, his skills vanquished even the strongest of foes, but his fear lay in revealing his true self. Even in his dealings with those closest, he withheld so much.

His life exploded in living color, all of him laid bare in an instant, leaving nothing hidden. Unable to breath, Abby's heart ached at the sensations. Tears streamed down her face. He felt so deeply, fought so tenaciously, and was utterly alone.

The intensity of him broke her wide open, shattering her heart to make room for him. A rush of life she'd never lived swept through her: the joy, the regret, the torment, and the love. She knew him as surely as she knew herself. And with that knowing came something frightening: Her heart tangled and merged with his, in that moment forever changed.

With the exhaustive knowledge of his essence, a love for him she was unable to restrain flooded her. He was part of her heart. The bond they shared could never be undone. Upon knowing and receiving him—in an act of communion she could only equate with the most intimate lovemaking—her heart was lost.

She clasped her head in her hands. Concern for his vulnerability had driven her—never had she suspected her own heart was at risk. She lay spiritually naked, exposed and open, as if her heart were spread like a lover to receive him. A painful cry escaped her lips as she fell forward into unconsciousness.

Chapter Eleven

Avant blinked and staggered. When he regained his sight, Abigail lay on the floor unconscious. He rushed and lifted her to the sofa, certain he'd heard her scream.

Propping her head up with a pillow and brushing the curls from her face, he was unable to tear his gaze away from the creamy texture of her skin and how it glowed in the morning sunlight. She should not have had to endure this, but it was the only way. He closed his eyes and pressed his fist into his forehead.

He smoothed back her hair and stared, and then tried to bring her to by tapping her cheek. She didn't stir.

Long dark lashes rested on her rosy cheeks, and her pink lips fell slightly apart. Would she forgive him for putting her through this? At least she would understand his motivations. If she despised him when she awakened, she certainly could exact her revenge. She would know his every secret fear and weakness.

Reaching out, he ran his thumb over her cheek and across her lips. The silky feel of her skin ignited him with a passion he'd never experienced. As if drawn by some unseen force, he leaned closer until his lips hovered above hers.

She exhaled and he snapped back, losing his balance and falling on his behind. *By the Light!* What was he doing? He jumped up and retreated several steps.

All these long years, he had disciplined his body and mind into submission, awaiting the return of Sentieve. Now, at the moment of possibility, he let his guard down? Even if he hadn't shared a bed with her in twenty years, she was still his wife and deserved his loyalty.

He walked to the door, turning in the threshold. Abigail would know of his desire when she woke, and *that* he could not face. He needed time. The one thing he didn't have. With one more sweeping glance at her, he turned and left.

Stopping by the kitchen on his way to the stables, he asked Helan to make certain his guest was taken care of.

Outside, the bright sun of late summer hit his eyes and he squinted. A beautiful day. Somehow he felt lighter, as if sharing his life relieved him of the lonely burden. It was foolishness to think so, for they were still his experiences regardless of who knew of them. He marched to the stables. "Good morning, Landmaster."

"I thought you were working with Abigail today?" Petra glanced up from the horse he groomed.

"We've completed our work, and now I must go to the vineyards for the harvest. I'll be staying with Hossa and Annova until after the festival."

"Why? What of Abigail while you're gone?"

"What of her?" He shifted his weight and stared, attempting to hide the awkwardness charging the air. "She needs to help prepare for the festival like everyone else. Have her gather the eggs in the henhouse."

Petra tilted his head to the side and narrowed his eyes. "I thought she was a guest."

"Never mind. Just see to it."

Petra's face lit with obvious joy, and he licked his lips. "I intend to see to it. Rest assured, I'll make the most of my time with the lovely Abigail. May I bring her to the festival?"

A jealous fire raged through Avant's veins. He fisted his hands, suppressing the urge to jerk the man up by the scruff of his neck and slam him against the stall. Instead, he chose his words carefully. "Abigail is not here for your pleasure. She has been gathered here by the Light for a purpose that has *nothing* to do with you. I want no distractions for her. Keep your attraction to yourself! Am. I. Understood?"

Petra's eyes rounded, and he reared back. "I-I understand." His eyes studied Avant's features. "Are you sure this is only about Abigail's purpose?"

Avant squared his shoulders and placed his fists on his hips. "What do you mean?"

"I mean, you seem pretty emotionally charged for someone who is just interested in her *purpose*. Are you certain there's no other reason you'd like me to stay away from her?"

"What other reason could there be?" He shifted uncomfortably under Petra's gaze.

Petra shook his head. "You tell me."

"I have no idea what you're talking about." Avant stared at him for a moment and then turned to saddle his horse for the ride to the vineyards. From the corner of his eye, he saw Petra shrug his shoulders and return to brushing the horse.

Avant's breath came out in a whoosh. He hadn't meant for the command to sound so harsh, but the anger incited by Petra's attraction had been completely involuntary. Of course it was because of her purpose. Abigail was the only way to get revenge on the king and get Sentieve back, and he had waited too long for retribution. There could be no other reason.

He traveled south through the village, stopping at the bakery for some of his favorite panas. He breathed in deeply. The smell of the bread and the friendly villagers gave him a feeling of community. This time of year was his favorite, and the bustle of the workers preparing for the Harvest Festival in three days reminded him of the bounty his people enjoyed.

He ate his panas as he strolled to the dressmaker. Greeting the passersby with a cordial nod, Avant strode into the shop. "Good morning, Gessup."

With the tinkling of the door chime still ringing in the quiet storefront, Avant perused the various dresses in different stages of completion. A little man with a round face and white hair shuffled out of a back room with a cloth measuring tape draped around his shoulders and a lavender dress across his arms. He smiled pleasantly. "Lord Ventium, what brings you to my shop this fine harvest morning?"

Avant smiled. "Gessup, I am in need of a dress." At the wide-eyed look from the dressmaker, he laughed out loud. "For a guest of mine. And I have specific requirements. Do you have anything in a teal green?"

"My lord, I have but one dress in that color." The elderly man shuffled to the back room and returned with a beautiful silken taffeta gown. He held it out to Avant for inspection.

Taking the dress and holding it up, Avant noted how the blue-green color saturated the shining fabric. The style would be most agreeable for Abigail's curves. He shook his head. "This dress is too big for the lady in question. Do you not have a smaller one?"

"Not in that color, my lord."

"It must be this color, Gessup." He rubbed his chin with a forefinger. "What do you need to alter this dress to the appropriate measurements and have it ready for the festival?"

"Well, my lord, with all of my current orders, I'm so busy and haven't the time for additional alterations."

"I did not ask you if you could do it. I asked what you needed to make certain it gets done. What do you need to ensure this dress is ready in two days' time?" Avant smiled because his words carried the message with enough force.

The little man pursed his lips and sighed. "Well, my lord, I'll need the services of Bardon's wife. She helps me sometimes when I have more than I can do, but she is expected to help bring in the harvest. Her family relies on the wages from the work."

Avant weighed the cost. He would lose a good harvest worker and would still need to pay her wages, in addition to paying Gessup for the actual dress and alterations. No matter. Abigail must have that dress. Pulling out his moneybag, he turned to the man. "I'll send Bardon's wife this morning. Here is payment for her wages and the dress."

Avant rode to the house in the vineyards at the end of the valley. The straight rows of heavy-laden vines were ripe for harvest with rich grapes that produced the best wine in all of Jastain. The soft breeze wisped his hair and filled his nose with the sweet scent of ripe grapes. He reached from his horse and pulled a cluster from a vine adjacent to the trail. The juicy, acidic tang assured him the vintage was destined to be a good one.

Walking up to the gray stone house and into the front door, he called out. "Greetings. Is anyone here?"

Annova came from the kitchen, wiping her floured hands on a cloth. "Avant, my sweet, how wonderful to see you." She kissed him lightly on the lips, her auburn hair brushing his cheek.

Annova had found Avant injured and left for dead. She and her husband Hossa, fleeing from the king themselves, took him from the southern plains and escaped to the Freelands. The three of them then established the community of Domentus Ventium for refugees fleeing the treacherous lands ruled by Aesdil.

As prophet of the Light, Annova was Avant's spiritual advisor. She was also like a mother to him.

"Are we prepared for the harvest?" He grinned at her.

"Of course, my lord." She eyed him suspiciously. "You've found the Chosen One, then?"

"I have indeed found the Chosen One." He could no longer hold in his excitement.

"And I take it you are pleased with this discovery? But there is something else in your eyes. What is it, Avant?"

Why need there be something else? Was not finding The One enough? "I found the young woman three days ago in the Valley of Umbra just as my Gift told me. I have already Implanted into her, and she is at the manor even as we speak."

"Young woman? Truly?" Annova studied his face, and a knowing smile crept over her lips. "Is that why your countenance is lighter than I have seen it in years?"

"Yes, of course. Abigail is The One to restore my life. Why should I not feel lighter?" He sighed. Why must everyone assume he desired her youth and beauty? Could he not just be glad for the Light's provision?

Annova's eyes narrowed, and she stared at him for a moment longer. A glow emanated from her, and Prophecy overtook her. "Do not lose faith in your Gift, Avant. It will lead you in the right path. And though I see, indeed, this young woman will help restore your life, it will not be what you now assume. Dark times are ahead and a need for great faith in the things we hold dear, for things we love are not always as they first appear. And when the night is dawn and morrow is yet breaking, it is the path of love we esteem worth taking."

They stood silently for a time. Avant closed his eyes. His experience with Annova's Gift gave him assurance that she spoke the truth. "This is the second time you have spoken those words to me, Annova. Where do I assume this path to lead?"

In his heart, he knew her words were key to the Chosen One's purpose. Avant's dreams indicated he would one day be king over the new kingdom, but exactly what part Abigail would play after the restoration was unclear.

"Avant, I cannot tell you what the words mean. Only that they are the truth, and when the time is ripe, you will comprehend."

Chapter Twelve

Abby woke. Her eyes fluttered open to reveal a quiet room bathed in sunshine. As she tried to lift her head, saliva filled her mouth. A cold sweat misted her face and nausea tainted her stomach.

How long had she been unconscious? What had happened to make her pass out? Avant had attempted to Implant his knowledge, but after that, her mind went blank.

A sound echoed from the hall. A plump little figure entered the room and shuffled toward her. Helean.

"Are you feeling better? You've been out for some time. I was getting worried about you. Lord Ventium said you'd fainted. No doubt from your long travels the last few days," she chatted absently. "My dear, do you think you can sit?"

"Where's Avant?" Abby sat up. Her head reeled from the movement, and her stomach churned. *Oh, God.* She felt worse than the time she challenged a group of frat boys to a game of Mexican Minesweeper, a drinking game played with tequila shots. Only this time she was fairly certain she hadn't won anything.

"Lord Ventium is gone. He went to the vineyards to prepare for the harvest. He won't be back until after the festival."

It suddenly occurred to her that not only had she understood Helean completely, she'd spoken in Jastainian. She could speak Jastainian?

Helean's words finally registered in her mind. The festival was in three days and she wouldn't see Avant until then. She leaned over and threw up.

*****

Abby lay alone on the sofa for most of the day, watching the sunlight glide slowly across the floor. She hadn't even been in this world a week, and already it felt like a lifetime. Maybe Avant's Implanting caused the effect. Everything was all at once foreign and strangely familiar.

Avant had left her there, passed out on the sofa, after she was doing everything in her power to help him. What was up with that?

An awful aching gripped her heart in a steely bear trap. Home seemed impossibly far.

The events from earlier in the morning were hazy at best. She could barely remember having breakfast and then talking with Avant. So much seemed like a dream where her memories lurked on the edge of consciousness. Memories she wasn't sure she wanted to surface.

As the sun set, she gathered herself and trudged up to her room for the evening. She slept in fits all through the night. Frenzied dreams of fighting and death, an evil king, and a beautiful woman with brown hair and doe eyes infiltrated her mind.

Early the next morning, Helean woke her for breakfast and work. "Come, my dear, you can't sleep the day away again. It's time to rise up and meet your new life."

Abby moaned and covered her head. *Is everyone an effin' Socrates around here?*

"The landmaster has requested your presence at breakfast. He has a task for you this morning." Helean bustled in with the washbasin and a pitcher of water.

At the mention of Petra, Abby sat up in bed. "Helean, what do you know about Master Petra?"

The brown-haired woman turned to survey her. "Oh, as much as any, I suppose. Lord Ventium made him bailiff a few years ago. Master Petra is charmed, they say. The fief has more than doubled in yield under his leadership. He has a way with the animals, and he's a good boy. I expect he'll find a wife very soon. He has his pick of any maid in the village." Helean sighed. "But he is too much like Lord Ventium—waiting for something."

Helean would be a valuable resource in the house, and Abby loved harmless gossip. "Thank you. I'll be down in a minute."

She dragged herself out of bed in the early morning for the second day in a freakin' row. Didn't these people need sleep? At least she didn't feel dizzy anymore. She washed and dressed herself in the clothes from the previous day and pulled her hair back in a loose ponytail.

Padding downstairs, she went to meet with Petra, who waited at the kitchen table for her.

"Good morning." Petra stood awkwardly as she walked in. "I'm glad you're feeling better. We've a few things to do before the festival tomorrow."

God, he looked like Chad. She smiled in greeting, and his cheeks flushed. "What would you like me to do?"

"Avant wants you to help prepare for the festival while he's away, and tomorrow you can ride with me to the celebration." He raised his eyebrows and grinned playfully, showing beautiful white teeth and a hint of a dimple in his cheek.

"The party's going to be in the main square tomorrow night?" Abby sat in front of a small bowl of oatmeal and an apple.

He nodded. "There's much to be done before then. Please eat, and then I'll show you your task. We'll have you at the grinding stone today. Avant specifically requested you tend the chickens."

She felt all the blood drain from her face. "Chickens...oh, I don't know. I'm not good with live animals." Or dead ones for that matter. She never cared for animals, and didn't have any pets back home.

"You'll do fine, my lady." His eyes twinkled with encouragement.

He was adorable and exuded much more personality than Chad. The familiarity of his face gave her a measure of comfort—even if it did remind her of the rat bastard who had screwed her over. It was still something from home.

She finished eating, and Petra led her to the chicken coop. He explained all she had to do, handed her a small basket, and left her to the task.

After almost an hour and several attempts to enter the disgusting lair of the demon fowl, she'd gathered one egg. One. She scowled as she handed it to Helean, who seemed wise enough not to ask.

This was ridiculous. She hadn't come to this place to be Avant's servant girl. He could kiss her ass, because she wasn't doing any more of his menial labor. Wasn't she the revered Chosen One? Never having actually worked a day in her life, she never thought her first occupation would involve a chicken coop. *Damn it.*

Abby rolled her eyes and stormed up to her room. She threw herself across the bed and sulked. Her mind buzzed. He expected her to be his *servant*. Well, screw him. She wasn't taking another step inside that coop.

A groan escaped her lips. The idea that she might disappoint him made her heart sink. His blue eyes pierced her thoughts. He might as well get used to the fact she wasn't who he believed she was. *Never would be.*

Abby stood and paced to the window. Outside, laborers hustled around with plenty of work to be accomplished in a short time. The windmill stood empty. That was where she was supposed to be. At least, that was where Petra told her to go. Nowhere in this whole place was where she was *supposed* to be. She was *supposed* to be at Macy's buying new school clothes. Still, she had promised to help. Blowing out a long sigh, she headed downstairs to do what she could.

Making the best of the situation became easier now that she could speak the language, and so far, everyone was friendly. Although unasked questions remained in their glances, their smiles seemed sincere and welcoming. She worked hard all day until Petra came and got her for dinner. She trudged after him to the house, ate, and then went back to work until well after midnight. After finishing, she lugged her weary ass to bed and slept like a stone all night long.

The next morning before the sun rose, Helean scurried around her room. "Get up, my dear. The day will start without you. You must get up, up, up."

Abby curled her lips into a snarl. She liked Helean, but if something other than her pillow had been within reach, she would've thrown it at the perky little wench. Her arms were made of lead, and her neck rebelled against the task of holding her head up. "Can't I sleep for a couple more hours? I worked until after midnight."

"My dear, everyone worked until after midnight, and we're up already. This is what you do during the harvest. There is much still to be done before tonight, and I promise to let you have a bath and dress this afternoon. Come, come."

Shit.

Practically everyone in the fief and the village had spent the last two days in the vineyards picking grapes for the new wine. That night they would celebrate the harvest.

Based on the limited memories that had appeared in her mind, the party would be filled with eating, drinking, and dancing. Hopefully she wouldn't fall asleep.

Abby wasn't exactly clear on all the traditions, but since Avant's Implanting, his memories were beginning to fill in the holes. It was a strange phenomenon.

When she met new people, their name would come to her mind along with all of Avant's thoughts and feelings about them. His memories told her he loved Petra and thought highly of his landmaster's Gift and work ethic but found him to be a bit of a clutter bug. Helean he respected and admired for her organizational skills, but he knew she was prone to gossip. He'd caught one of the field hands in the barn with a milkmaid and planned on insisting they marry.

Avant knew the people who worked for him, and he used this knowledge to draw the most and best from them. His strategy was ingenious, but the most striking thing was his motives. He genuinely cared for his people and wanted them to be the best for themselves. She could've never imagined all that went on in his head. As of yet, no memories or thoughts of her had surfaced. Not that she really wanted them to.

Blowing out a haggard breath, she dragged her reluctant butt out of bed and plodded downstairs. At least someone else had gathered the eggs.

She helped in the kitchens most of the morning and cleaned up after the cooks who came in from the village.

After taking a quick break, Abby headed back to the kitchen, but she stopped short outside the threshold, hearing the women chattering inside.

"…I don't know where she came from, but the dress she had on was not decent. She was wearing strange underpants and no corset," Helean was whispering.

"No! Well, is she the lord's mistress?" asked a plain-faced woman from the village Abby had met earlier.

"It seems likely, but I can't tell. He may have brought her here for the landmaster. They seem to be about the same age. And the young master is quite taken with her," Helean said in a matter-of-fact tone.

"Surely Lord Ventium wouldn't have brought her here to marry. Although he is still a bachelor and needs to be settled, if you ask me. He as good as gave his blessing for my Saundra to wed Master Petra. I can't imagine he would have brought the girl here for someone other than himself," said a little round woman whom Abby knew to be the baker's wife.

Abby cleared her throat and walked into the room. The ladies looked up and smiled. Yep. It was the same everywhere. Old crows were gonna gossip.

Helean clapped her floured hands together, causing dust to billow. "My dear, are you ready for your bath? We must prepare you, and I have already drawn your water on strict instructions."

Were they Petra's instructions or Avant's? Either way, she could use a bath.

"Thanks. I'm ready."

"Now, dear, your clothes for the festival are already upstairs. You can wear the robe from the bath to your room and leave your work clothes for the laundry."

"There are special clothes for the festival?"

"Yes, dear. For you, there are."

"I didn't realize…" Great. One more thing for them to gossip about. *The lord's mistress.* Hardly. Then a memory of Avant's wife surfaced in her mind. They apparently had no idea about Sentieve. What kind of a name was that anyway? *Sentieve.* Abby curled her lip and wrinkled her nose.

"That's all right. Run along. Busy. Busy. It would not do for you to not be up to specifications."

Abby rolled her eyes. She went into the little adjacent room, undressed, and soaked in the steamy tub. The warm water soothed her, and her eyes drooped. She scrubbed her dirty face with a cloth. The sound echoed in the quiet room.

Why had Avant left her without so much as a good-bye? The murmur of voices outside amplified her loneliness.

And what of his wife? She hadn't remembered Sentieve until now. An unfounded hatred for the woman filled her. He'd waited twenty years for that woman. She shook her head. As far as she was concerned, the mousy, doe-eyed twit could wait another twenty before she found out he was alive. The harshness of her thoughts shocked her. Why did she even care? Had something happened during the Implanting? Is that why Avant left?

Struggling with her thoughts and her work-weary limbs, she finished her bath and headed to her room.

A shimmering teal-green dress lay across her bed, greeting her as she came through the door. Next to it lay a choker in rose gold, intricately designed in a leaf pattern and set with sparkling green stones.

She ran to the bed and picked up the long silk gown, twirling in a circle. It was hard to believe that a man could've picked these things. In her experience, guys didn't know clothes. But these were perfectly matched to her size, shape, and coloring. Whoever had chosen them for her had a keen eye.

She missed Avant. Now that he had Implanted into her and she was a full-fledged member of his world, would he treat her differently? She would know in a few hours.

Her heart fluttered at the thought she would see him soon. She rushed to get ready.

Using her new comb, Abby French-braided her hair and tied it back. Even without a full-length mirror, she felt sure the dress flattered her. If she'd handpicked the gown herself, she couldn't have done a better job. The necklace added a perfect touch, but she needed color on her lips. She pulled out her bag and unzipped it. Finding the beaded clutch, she searched for her favorite lip-gloss. Out fell the little black box.

Abby picked it up and opened it, smiling sadly.

Jonathan Randall had been a dentist by trade, but, in his heart, he was a philosopher. In demand all over the world for training sessions and speaking engagements, her dad was the most brilliant man she knew, except for Chad.

He'd called a few weeks before her birthday, as he always did, to ask what she wanted for her present. She never got what she really wanted—just to see him—but she always got whatever she requested.

His schedule wouldn't permit him to come home, but he said that to turn twenty years old was a *milestone birthday, and she would soon embark on a new season of her life, learning things about herself she couldn't have imagined.* Could he have known what would happen to her? He always said shit like that, though.

She'd told him she wanted diamond stud earrings.

"Diamonds? When you accept diamonds, Abigail, there's always a commitment of sacrifice. But if there's love, then the sacrifice is worth taking."

He'd made it sound like a life or death choice. With her dad, nothing was ever straightforward or easy.

A week and a half later he'd died of a heart attack on his way home. It would have been the first time he'd been home to see her in over a year. The earrings were given to her, along with all of his personal effects, when she claimed his body at the hospital two days before her twentieth birthday. She remembered thinking he'd made it home for the occasion after all.

Looking down at the icy sparkle of the three-carat stones, she drew in a heavy breath. Most people would never wear even one diamond the size and quality of her pair. But she saw them as she saw her father, with admiration and longing, and she would trade them in a heartbeat for someone who loved her and a place where she belonged. Tears dripped onto the velvet. Maybe that was what he meant by sacrifice. She had all these beautiful things in her life, but without the love he'd spoken of, they weren't worth anything.

She wiped away a tear as she pulled the diamonds from their nest. Her dad had wanted her to have these, and she would wear them for the first time to the Harvest Festival. Now that was what she called destiny.

Chapter Thirteen

Abby giggled with giddiness. She skipped downstairs to wait for
Petra in the empty kitchen. After all the recent hustle and bustle, her
footsteps echoed eerily in the quiet. She and Petra must be the only
two left in the house to leave for the party. A driver waited outside to
take them in a horse-drawn carriage to the village square. Having
missed Avant more than she could understand, Abby poured herself
a glass of mead to calm her nerves. What would she do when she
saw him?

The back door opened. Dressed in a tunic of fine crimson and
gold brocade, Petra stood in the threshold, and his chocolate-brown
eyes sparkled in the lamplight. The look fit his title of landmaster.
Abby smiled and his jaw dropped open. Lighthearted ease sprang up
in her heart and her confidence soared with his appreciative gaze.

He studied her like a fine painting. "Abigail, you look beautiful
tonight."

His attention filled her like an empty pitcher. "Thanks, Petra.
Please call me Abby. You clean up nicely yourself."

"And scarcely anyone will notice me as long as you are nearby.
Nonetheless, I hope that will be my misfortune." His eyes twinkled
with a mischief that charmed her.

Petra might look like Chad, but he was so different.

"Somehow I think there will be plenty to notice you tonight,
Landmaster, and I will be the most envied lady at the party."

His cheeks reddened, but he continued to stare at Abby as he
stalked toward her. Her heart beat rapidly. With a cocked eyebrow,
he bent, took her hand, and kissed it. She held her breath. He cut his
gaze up to her and grinned impishly.

She exhaled and laughed.

"Do you like your dress?"

"Yes, as a matter of fact, I do. Did you pick it out?"

He took a glass, poured a drink for himself, and then refilled
hers. "No. It arrived from the village this morning. I assume Avant
had someone get it for you."

The corners of her mouth fell, and her heart sank a little. To be
disappointed that Avant hadn't picked it out himself was just plain
silly. She couldn't expect him to be perfect in every way. Besides, he

still wanted his stupid wife. Abby smirked. *Maybe not for long if I have anything to say about it.* She downed her drink.

"Are you ready?"

His question drew her from negative thoughts. She nodded excitedly, pleased for the distraction. "Let's go."

The carriage jostled over the road to town. She and Petra talked and laughed like old friends and warmth surrounded her while he was near.

He reached out and touched her arm, which tingled from the gesture. "The baker's bull only wanted to mate with the innkeeper's cow. The poor animal stood at the edge of the property and bayed like a lovesick troubadour. Avant sent me to talk with the animal. It seems the baker's cows didn't smell appealing. The baker had much wild garlic growing in the pasture. So I spoke with the baker, and we moved the cows to a pasture with clover. The baker now has two calves and plenty of fresh milk. And the bull, well, he gets his fill of love."

She laughed so hard she fell against him. He caught her and pushed her up straight. She wiped the water from the corners of her eyes. "Ugh. Cow sex. Gross."

Petra told her more funny stories about the fief and Abby told him about her experience with the chickens.

She gave him a carefree smile. He gave his undivided attention, and it was the shortest trip of her life over the bumpy road to the village. As they approached, the sounds of music, laughter, and a gathering crowd drifted in the night air.

The driver took them directly into the square and opened the door of the carriage. Abby stepped out, like a princess, into a picturesque little village. A quaint stream churned through a watermill and flowed under a cobblestone bridge. At the end of the main square, rich colored papers and fabrics decorated the festival gathering. A Thomas Kinkade painting had come to life with lights and colors in the brightest hues. The smell of freshly baked pastries and roasted meats permeated the air, and lyrical music lilted over the friendly din of conversing voices.

Petra took her hand and led her through the crowd. They could hardly go a few feet without someone stopping them to talk to him and eye her keenly. Petra kept hold of Abby's hand and always politely introduced her.

Abby spotted Helean across the square and waved to her. Helean waved back and then bent to whisper in another woman's ear. Several of the farmhands and their wives ate and drank at a far side table. Scanning the crowd to see if she knew anyone else, she waved to the baker and his wife. A pretty young girl dressed in lavender, who was probably their daughter, gave her an evil glare. *Yikes.* The young lady shot a gaze at the handsome landmaster, who appeared oblivious to the attention. Two more girls smiled at Petra and scowled at her. Just like she thought—the claws were coming out of all the village maids. She giggled.

Diligently she searched the crowd for the one person she wanted to see, but he wasn't there. Her heart sank a little, and she clasped Petra's arm and pulled him closer.

Petra leaned over, his breath tickling her ear. "Abby, I need to introduce Lord Ventium and the winemakers to start the celebration. Can you wait here?"

She nodded, understanding now why she couldn't find Avant. Her heart started to pound and sweat covered her palms.

Petra stepped up onto the dais, and the crowd stilled to a hush.

"Men and women of the Freelands of Jastain, welcome to the Harvest of Wine Festival." The villagers applauded and cheered, and the musicians played loudly before quieting to a hush. "Let us begin the festivities by introducing the fine ruler of these lands, our Lord Ventium." The crowd again gave a chorus of claps and yells.

Dressed in black pants and a charcoal tunic with bright blue and silver appliqués, Avant glided across the stage. Her heart caught in her throat. He looked magnificent in a waist-length royal-blue velvet cape. Embellished with silver embroidery and fastened across the top of his chest with a decorative chain, it flowed like a billowing current behind him as he walked.

He spoke a word of welcome, but Abby didn't hear it. Her heart beat like a frantic humming bird caught in a thorn bush, and she forgot how to breathe. All of the memories—*his memories*—flooded back to her. His thoughts now shared space in her mind. His emotions, his heart, were a part of her.

She remembered something else—she loved him. A loud gasp escaped her and she stumbled.

He caught her gaze.

For a brief moment, she viewed herself though his eyes, as if she still looked through the window of his soul, and a surge of passion ripped through her.

The solid gate of his mind slammed shut, though he seamlessly continued to speak. Abby staggered and grabbed the arm of a man next to her. The glacier of Avant's empty stare bit into her, and she couldn't seem to draw in enough air.

Avant introduced the winemakers, Hossa and his wife, Annova. The woman's auburn hair blazed over her emerald green dress. Catching Abby's gaze, she smiled knowingly. *Great.* What had Avant told her? Avant was the one who had revealed all his secrets, and yet Abby was the one who was vulnerable and insecure. What a pisser.

The crowd applauded again, and as the music started, everyone began to sing. Though she knew the words, she didn't sing along. Avant turned his gaze, but she couldn't. Trapped by her heart, she loved a man who was still in love with his wife.

She tried to regulate her breathing, and her heart finally settled into a steady rhythm.

Someone touched her arm, and she jumped. "Abby, are you all right? You look pale." Petra furrowed his brow.

"What? Oh, yes, I'm fine, but I need a drink. You were great up there, a natural speaker." Could everyone tell how flustered she was?

He stopped a server and took two cups of wine. She snatched one from his hand and downed it like a shot, then grabbed the other. Not seeming to mind, he got two more, and she guzzled those too.

Petra stared wide-eyed at her alcoholic intake. "I suppose you were thirsty."

After she finished the last of another drink and soaked in Petra's attention, her confidence returned. She smiled and laughed at his good-natured gossip about the villagers.

Petra leaned over and asked, "Would you care to dance?"

"I don't know." She loved to dance but shot a gaze up at the dais. Avant stood with his back to her.

"It's easy. I'll teach you."

His wheedling tone and warm hand on her shoulder convinced her. "Okay. Let's dance."

Petra led her to the dance floor and spun her around. Abby allowed his closeness to lighten her mood. During a slow and elegant tune, Petra waltzed her around, floating as if their feet hovered above the ground. A faster tune played and they skipped across the floor, exchanging partners back and forth. The unfriendly glances of several young maidens scathed her, and their unhappiness rippled in waves toward her. She bit her lip and smiled at Petra's obliviousness.

The girls were right to be jealous. Petra was a dream. He told the funniest stories and seemed completely at ease. The way he looked at her infused confidence into her frail feminine psyche. *I am the luckiest girl in all of Jastain tonight.* Then why didn't she feel like it? Her gaze flitted back to the dais. Avant was seated and speaking quietly to the group at his table.

After several dances, Petra led her off the floor. He parked her at a long table under the stars and left to get more drinks. She fanned her sweaty face with a napkin and twisted to see the festivities behind her. All around, the villagers danced, chatted, and enjoyed the party in lively fellowship. They celebrated, genuinely happy with the bounty of harvest they'd been given. Quite a few watched her, too. Her head spun. *What did they think of her? Could she ever be one of them?*

Avant remained seated on the dais with the winemakers and never offered a hint of acknowledgement. *How could she be in love with him?* She needed another drink.

A reassuring hand clasped her shoulder, and as if on cue, Petra handed her a full glass. He smiled, his face half in shadow. She shook Mr. Couldn't-Care-Less from her mind and chugged down the delicious, spiced wine. Petra chatted and they drank. Then he grabbed her hand and pulled her up to dance.

Gliding her around the floor, he said, "It's almost time for the Lord's Harvest Dance. Don't be surprised if he asks you."

"Don't be surprised if *who* asks me *what?*"

"Avant. He's allowed to choose a dance partner from among all the ladies. The one chosen wears a crown of grape leaves for the remainder of the evening and is greeted by all the guests."

Abby's heart began the hummingbird shuffle again. "Oh, I don't want to do that."

"You'll be fine. Besides, it's a requirement. Avant specifically requested your participation in this event."

She wasn't ready to face *him* yet, but Petra's warm eyes reassured her. She cupped his cheek. He flushed red and desire sparkled in his soft brown eyes. Abby smiled. With Petra by her side, she could handle anything, except maybe if Avant chose someone else.

The music stopped and the platform cleared. All the women, young and old, gathered around the perimeter. Petra pulled her toward the edge of the dance floor, between two old ladies. Shoulders squared, Avant strode out confidently. Abby's heart beat so wildly the old folks next to her could probably hear it. Laying a hand over her breast to staunch the rapid flutter, she tried to wedge herself behind the two women. What would she do if he picked her? What would she do if he didn't?

A shameless flirt, he scanned the floor and made eye contact with each lady, causing some to blush. Quickly glancing past Abby, he didn't acknowledge her, but continued his visual trek around the floor. He'd told her he didn't want to draw attention to her, and she could understand why she might not be his first choice. But the thought of his rejection caused tears to well.

He stepped to the center of the floor facing the far end. Gazing at his profile, she could tell from the set of his jaw he'd decided. Her heart sank as he took two strides forward. *Another time, maybe.* Then he pivoted and walked directly to her. Her heart lurched in her chest as if it were leaping to reach him. He caught her gaze and bowed low. His velvet cape swept the ground. A sigh escaped her, and excitement danced down her spine. Taking her hand, he led her onto the floor.

"Do you know this dance?" He smiled to the crowd as he spoke into her mind. The villagers applauded loudly, and the music began.

"I think so, but I hope I don't try to lead you." She grinned and bit her lip.

"I hadn't thought of that." He cocked his eyebrow, and swept an arm around her waist. *"Not to worry, I'm a strong partner."*

Her body hummed at his touch, and everything but him slipped away. She closed her eyes as he whisked her around the floor. Instinctively, she knew the steps, but he danced surprisingly well. She could easily have followed him without knowing the moves. Having done her share of two-stepping back home, she recognized the ability of someone who could lead a woman around the dance floor. A vision of Avant in blue jeans and cowboy boots assaulted her, and she laughed out loud. That was something she'd pay top dollar to see.

She breathed in. He smelled so good, cedar and pine, woodsy with a hint of musk, like his shirt in the cave.

He asked aloud, "How do you like our festivities?"

The sound of his strong tenor voice filled her ears like the music, and had she not been dancing, she would have wanted to. "It's a great party. I couldn't have done better myself and, you know, I am a party expert."

"You look stunning tonight. Do you like the dress?" He turned his gaze to her, and she knew he was reading her response.

"I love it. Please thank whoever picked it out."

He tilted his head, a bright smile lighting his face. "I picked this dress to match your eyes."

He was flirting. Her heart fluttered and a flush of heat covered her. So he *had* picked it out himself. "It's lovely, and the necklace is beautiful." Dropping her eyes from his intense gaze, she fingered his velvet cape. "So, is that a theme of the party? To wear the same color as your eyes?"

He laughed. "No. I merely thought you would like it, and it's the color of the pool at the falls."

Her breath hitched as she remembered the falls. She hadn't really thought about the color—but apparently he had.

It had only been three days, but she wanted to see it again. "Avant, I would love to go back to the falls." At the sound of his name on her lips, a heady wave washed over her.

"We will." His eyes lit with an idea. "Tomorrow, maybe."

She beamed. "You know what? This is our first real conversation."

He grinned. "I am enjoying the sound of your voice."

He was flirting again. His strong arms around her waist and his smooth gait ushered her to paradise. Maybe the musicians could keep on playing? The song could go on, and she could dance with him all night. *Wake up, sleeping beauty. Not your fairytale, remember?* "So what happens after this dance?"

He narrowed his eyes and a devilish smile stole over his face. "I'm going to kiss you."

Chapter Fourteen

"Kiss me?" Abby knew from his memories it was a perfunctory kiss of tradition, but she suspected Avant just wanted to see her flustered, which admittedly she was. The thought of touching him, lips to lips, for any reason caused her stomach to turn flip-flops.

His smug smile irked her. Armed with the boldness of several glasses of wine, maybe she could turn the tables on him for a change. Shifting her gaze sidelong at him, she allowed herself a tight-lipped smile and searched his face for any hint of revelation.

When the song ended, everyone cheered and clapped. Abby pushed her intentions to the back of her mind and hoped to God Avant didn't read her thoughts. Her heart hammered with anticipation. She was going to get him good.

A tall man in military regalia handed Avant a wreath of grape leaves, which he in turn placed on her head. Then he gracefully bent and pecked her on the lips. But as he pulled away, Abby wrapped her arms around his neck and drew him into a *real* kiss.

Her lips embraced his with exuberance. Her senses heightened in awareness, reaching for a full experience of him. His touch. His smell. His taste. He expelled a sigh into her mouth and seemed too stunned to do anything but kiss her back.

Surprisingly soft and warm, his mouth responded to the light rhythmic pace she set. His lips parted, and the moist expanse engulfed her to breathlessness. His arms encircled her waist and drew her closer. Her breasts brushed against him. Intensity radiated between them. Their bodies buzzed with awareness like a live wire split in two and held in close proximity. A feeling of being all at once too close and not nearly close enough warred within her. Their breaths became labored as he deepened the kiss. For a precious stolen moment, she lingered in her fantasy and pretended he belonged to her. But all too soon reality set in. The murmur of the crowd broke the spell and reminded her of where she was.

Reluctantly, Abby slid her arms from around his neck and placed her palms flat against his chest. His heart thundered beneath her fingers. She pulled from him. A groan escaped his lips. She got the feeling that, had she not pulled away from him, he wouldn't have stopped. Looking into his surprised blue eyes, she bit her lower lip and smiled sheepishly.

The crowd roared with laughter and applause.

The raw desire in his gaze gave way to fury as he yanked her hand and pulled her to the receiving line in front of the dais. Not sure if he was angry that she'd started the kiss or ended it, she couldn't help but giggle. He'd blushed! She did a mental fist pump.

"What was that?" he stormed into her mind.

"You said a kiss. I just thought we should give the crowd their money's worth" She shrugged her shoulders and almost laughed. She could read him like a book. The Implanting had given her insight into even the slightest nuances of his body language. The slight twitch of his lip and the barely perceptible lifting of his chin told her he was unnerved. He despised not being in control. *"How was I supposed to know you'd accept the invitation and stay a while?"*

His eyes narrowed. *"I believe there are a great many things you know about me. Too many."*

Shit. He was reading her thoughts again. Oh well. What was that saying regarding turnabout and fair play? She couldn't read his thoughts like he could hear hers, but thanks to the Implanting, she understood enough. She shot him a glance. He growled under his breath. He was pissed. She also knew what they said about paybacks being hell, and if his glare was any indication, she was in for it.

Avant smiled for the crowd, but his blue eyes kept darting scowls to her between introductions. *He needs to get over himself.* His eyes flickered with an emotion that made her pulse race and heated her in private places.

As the villagers filed through the receiving line, he introduced each one. Many spoke of how lovely she looked and how funny they thought the kiss was. After a while, even Avant loosened up and laughed too—until Petra came through. He would hardly look at her, but he glared at Avant, who hung his head in guilt. Abby's stomach dropped. She hadn't meant to hurt Petra's feelings. Surely he knew it was a joke. He'd been so good to her. She would make it up to him.

The intense redhead and her husband were the last to greet them.

Taking Abby's hand, the woman penetrated her with a knowing stare. "My lady, I am Annova, and I am graced by your presence at our harvest gathering."

"Thank you. I'm Abigail." Abby couldn't make eye contact. The woman made her feel like she wasn't wearing skin.

"My dear, guard the precious Light that's in your heart. Its yield in due season will be far greater than mere fruit."

Abby's smile wavered. What the crap did that mean?

The exchange was not lost on Avant, and he nodded knowingly to Annova. What had he told this woman about her? That she was this Chosen One? Not that she didn't trust Avant, but she was as likely the savior of Jastain as Lady Gaga.

Once she and Avant finished with the greetings, he swept an arm around her back and turned her to face him. "Thank you for the dance." His eyes sparkled with mischief and her heart thumped again. "I must formally end the festivities but I'll be back at the house later. We can discuss our plans for tomorrow." He brushed a hair from her face and trailed his hand down her cheek.

Abby's mind spun, whether from his touch or the wine she couldn't be sure.

He bent and brushed her cheek with his lips before he whispered, "Later?"

She stepped away and tried to remain upright. "Okay. See you then."

He cocked his head and gazed at her with a tenderness she hadn't ever seen from him before. Her chest welled with so much love that it almost knocked her over.

She floated in a dreamy haze as she left to find her date.

Searching for Petra, she finally found him sitting with shoulders slumped, staring down at his clasped hands. She brought him two drinks as a peace offering. "My handsome landmaster, which of these drinks is yours?"

"Well, if they're anything like the others from this evening, neither." He lifted his gaze to meet hers without moving his head, his long lashes unable to mask his hurt pride.

She smiled. "Wrong. They're both yours, and so am I for the last dance." She pumped her eyebrows. He begrudgingly smiled, took the first drink, and downed it in a single gulp. Then he drank the other. Having consumed quite a few herself, a reckless feeling invaded her veins. Fortunately, she had a high tolerance for alcohol, but her propensity for trouble while intoxicated was well documented on various social networking sites. Thank God Jastain didn't have the Internet.

Shrugging off the thought, she grabbed two more drinks on the way to the dance floor and handed one to her handsome date. They slammed them down and went to dance the last dance. Petra, as good a dancer as Avant, slid her gracefully around and around, laughing and talking.

"So have you enjoyed our festivities, milady?" His words slurred slightly with too much wine, but he'd apparently forgiven her for the earlier indiscretion and was now focused completely on her.

She smiled and pulled him along in the dance. "Can we do it again tomorrow?"

"Only if you take care of the chickens." He bust out in a big, belly laugh.

She shoved him playfully. "Not a chance, stable boy."

When the dance was over, they staggered to the carriage. Abby breathed in the fresh scent of harvested grapes and peered up at the star-cluttered sky. She smiled, then swayed, and almost fell over. Petra caught her and helped her into the carriage before stumbling in after her.

She yawned and scratched her head as she nestled against the carriage window. Wasn't she supposed to do something when she got back to the house? "Hey, Landmaster, I had a great time tonight. How 'bout you?"

Petra's head lolled with the lurch of the coach. "Yes, milady. I had the time of my life dancing with you this evening."

Abby broke into song. She pointed to him as she sang "Time of My Life" in English. Petra chuckled.

The tune "Kiss Me," a song from her favorite movie, popped into her mind. She didn't sound too bad, except to those few people who might still be sober. "...so kiss me."

As she sang the last note, he pulled her to his lips. So accustomed to his feel, she didn't flinch but simply wrapped her arms around his neck and kissed him back. She parted her lips, and his tongue gently teased between them, stroking hers with great tenderness. The warmth of his mouth comforted, and pleasure swept from the point of contact over her. Soft and slow, he lingered, savoring her as if it were their very first kiss.

She drove her fingers through his silky hair and deepened the kiss. His arms banded around her, cinching her to him. She could feel the strong rhythm of his heart. His familiar lips and the feel of his long hair…long hair? *Chad doesn't have long hair.* Her eyes flew open. "Oh my God! Petra, I'm so sorry." She put her hand to her mouth and blinked, trying to focus through the haze of lust and drunkenness.

"I beg your pardon, but I kissed you, Abby." The wine gave him a cocky confidence and his topaz eyes sparkled.

Definitely not Chad. "Yes, but I kissed you back thinking you were someone else."

He frowned and dropped his head.

"Oh, honey, no…I didn't mistake you for Avant, if that's what you think. It's that you look so much like my boyfriend back home. In fact, you two could be twins."

"Oh, *that* makes me feel so much better." He rolled his eyes. "You have a *boyfriend*?" He wrinkled his forehead.

"Well, I guess technically, he's my ex-boyfriend. He was my"— she used her fingers to form little quotey things—"*lover*. At least, that's what Avant called him."

"A lover?"

She tried not to wince at his disapproving tone.

"And Avant knows this?"

He still looked a little confused or maybe he was just drunk. "You mean does Avant know that my boyfriend—ex-boyfriend— looks like you? No, he doesn't know that."

He slapped his leg. "I knew it! I told Avant you felt something when you first saw me, but he denied it. You know, he actually told me to stay away from you." Petra swayed in his seat and pointed his index finger at her. "I've never seen Avant so agitated. I think he was jealous because you had a strong reaction to me."

Avant was jealous? Chad…umm…*Petra* must've been mistaken. Abby's head whirled like the carriage wheels, and she still felt Chad's kiss on her lips. "You look so much like him, but your personality is completely different. He's shy, and you're…not."

Abby heaved her shoulders and adopted her most motherly tone. "I'm sorry I kissed you, but we've had a little too much to drink, and it absolutely can't happen again, okay?"

Petra locked in her gaze. She swallowed hard. His eyes filled with passion. "All right *for now*, but I reserve the right to renegotiate later."

"Fair enough." She held out her hand for him to shake. Instead, he pulled it to his lips and kissed her palm. His sweet warmth washed over her. Why couldn't she be with this guy again?

The carriage pulled into the manor drive. Petra jumped out and then helped her down. "You were by far the loveliest woman at the festival, and as I predicted, no one even noticed me."

Abby rolled her eyes and staggered at the dizziness it caused. Was he seriously that dense? "Right. No one except that gaggle of girls who followed behind you all night, hoping I would fall off the planet and you would ask one of them to dance." Abby leaned over and kissed his cheek.

She said good night and stumbled upstairs to her room. Thank goodness a candle was lit for her. She didn't want to burn the house down trying to light one. Her hands fumbled to unlace the dress, and it fell to the floor. She pulled on her nightgown, undid the French braid, and picked up a brush. It was so relaxing to brush her hair, even though it would give her the frizzies in the morning.

Another song popped into her head as she remembered her dance with Avant—and his kiss. She grabbed her pillow and twirled around the room, singing "I Could Have Danced All Night."

There was a knock on her door.

She giggled and jumped on her bed. "Yes."

Avant slowly opened the door and looked inside. "I thought we were going to meet about tomorrow's itinerary." Was that a pouty look on his face? *Hmm.*

"You're right! I knew I was forgetting something. Well, c'mon in and take a load off."

He stepped in and stopped awkwardly at the end of her bed as his gaze raked her body. Noticing the dress, he frowned, picked it up, and laid it carefully across her dresser. He turned and sat in the chair next to her bed.

She snickered. Which looked more stiff, him or the chair? She slapped the bed. "I can't talk to you way over there. Come sit by me."

He eyed her cautiously but moved to the bed. "You've had quite a bit of drink this evening, I would say."

"I wasn't the only one, was I?" She giggled as she thought of Petra and how intoxicated he was.

Avant's face clouded and he looked away. He acted so strange sometimes.

"Ya know, I'm still kinda mad at you for leaving me passed out on the couch two days ago." She poked him hard in the arm with her finger. "That wasn't a very Prince Charming thing to do, now was it?"

Avant grinned at her endearment. "No. You're right. I must apologize, but I had many things to which I had to attend, and I knew you would be well looked after."

"By whom? The chickens?"

At this, Avant laughed out loud, and her heart floated in the happy sound. A desire to make him laugh like that every day filled her. He angled his body so he could look into her face, desire filling his. Her cheeks flushed and her eyes wouldn't focus. She fanned herself and brushed her hair back behind her ears to cool herself down.

Avant stared at her with an intensity that made her heart beat in double time. Reaching his hand to the side of her face—*what is he doing?*—he turned her cheek to the side and touched her ear. Shivers slid down her neck.

Seeing her reaction or more likely hearing it, he said, "Forgive me, Abigail. It is that…you have stones of Light in your ears." He studied her earrings.

That figured.

"Stones of Light are precious in Jastain. There are few who ever see one. It is said in the Ancient Ways, stones of Light can move life and hold sway over even death itself, and you hold them in your ears." Avant said these last words with reverence, and Abby vaguely understood the noble regard in which he held the diamonds.

"They were a gift from my father." Remembering her dad was a real buzz killer. She stared down at her comforter.

"That was a kingly gift, indeed. Even the royals of this land have not seen stones of Light for many years. I myself have seen only one other." Avant gazed at her with an amazement she didn't quite understand. She waited for him to say something, but his sapphire eyes became distant, and he didn't continue.

She knew the other diamond was the ring worn by his wife. But she was too drunk to bring the memory forward. Or maybe she was blocking it on purpose. The only ring she could picture was the one that sat on the bony finger of her ex-best friend.

She'd conveniently forgotten about the wife when she kissed him. God, had she been reduced to the *other woman*? Shaking the thought from her mind before he heard, she tried to break the silence. "So, tomorrow are we going to the falls?"

"Yes. We will pack a lunch and travel there. Can you ride a horse?"

"Uh no, unless I can from your memories." She still wasn't sure what his memories would allow her to do. She was certainly able to recall the dance steps tonight and the words to the songs, but what other things translated she wasn't sure.

"Well, tomorrow you will try. Get some rest." Avant pulled back her covers, and she snuggled under them.

*****

Avant sat on Abigail's bed studying her beautiful features. She had fallen asleep as soon as her head hit the pillow.

The Implanting had worked. She was as fluent in the language as anyone in Jastain.

My Light, she looked lovely in that dress. He traced the outline of her mouth with his gaze. The memory of her kiss flooded his mind. Her tender lips and floral scent made his throat go dry. The only thing he could wonder when she pulled away from him was why had she stopped. He could have kissed her all night and begged for more. Avant covered his lips with a finger, as if that would stop the flow of desire overtaking his will.

He could no longer conceal his emotions from her. She read him too well. He was not certain if that disturbed him or not. And, she had hidden her thoughts from him. That kiss had to have been premeditated. All of these things forebode trouble. Yet he could not bring his heart to heed the warning.

Tomorrow he would begin the first lesson in the exercise of her Gift, and the falls was the perfect setting for such a lesson. Perhaps he would even show her his secret discovery. He smiled and exhaled deeply.

He brushed a stray curl behind her ear and studied the stone in her earring. *Could one of these be* the *Stone of Light?* His dream had foretold the Chosen One would have the Light in her ears, and his own Gift confirmed the truth. *It must be.* But she was unaware, and he could not tell which was the true Stone. The Light would reveal it to them in time.

He ran his thumb over her lips as his mind replayed the kiss for the hundredth time. His body bucked with desire. After so many years of lying dormant, his passion threatened to overrule his will. He had isolated himself from temptation and foolishly believed in his ability to control his will. With her damnable kiss, this beauty fractured his reserve and threatened to take his control.

Rising from her bed, he strode to his own room. With the discovery of what was surely the Stone of Light, he came one step closer to his destiny and his wife, but the thought of Sentieve brought him neither pleasure nor pain.

Chapter Fifteen

"Ugh." Abby woke the next morning with a monster hangover and clouded memories of the night. The sun streamed in through the windows, and the song of morning larks filled the quiet room. Helean must've brought her the basin with water and her daily clothes but hadn't awakened her. She wet her frizzy hair and pulled it back in a loose ponytail.

As she dressed, the dance with Avant and their kiss played in her mind. Her pulse quickened at the memory of him so close. What had she been thinking? The look in his surprised eyes tickled her, but the taste of his lips kissing her back for that brief moment was like oxygen, causing her to expand with life.

Avant. She sighed. What was their trip to the falls about? Had he missed her as much as she'd missed him? Other than the dance and the kiss, he'd practically ignored her. The kiss, however ill conceived, had been real.

What was his plan? Maybe today was a date. She frowned. That seemed unlikely. With the Implanting, she knew of Avant's attraction for her, but she also understood his sense of duty. He'd never succumb to his desire, probably wouldn't even admit it. His will was too set and too strong. Even if he loved her as she loved him, he was as immovable as one of those mountains in the distance. A tight smile stared back at her from the mirror. But his resistance wouldn't keep her from trying. She looked forward to seeing him today.

God, she hated that her heart wasn't her own, but she couldn't regret the love for him that coursed through her. She just hoped he would give her a chance.

Feeling queasy with the shakes, she hurried downstairs to get some water and a bite of food. Helean had already prepared a lunch and had her breakfast waiting on the table. Abby drew a cup of water from the bucket and gulped it down.

"Well, my dear, you caused quite a stir in the village last night. Everyone is talking about how delightful and charming you are."

She smiled guiltily and chugged another cup of water. "Oh, I hope I wasn't too forward."

"I must say, you were a little bold for our humble gathering, but it was entertaining to watch. Lord Ventium is such a flirt with the ladies. They often talk of how he shamelessly makes them blush. It was exciting to see the shoe on the other foot."

They both giggled.

"Well, someone needed to take him down a notch. With those eyes and that smile, it's hard to imagine he doesn't make most women blush."

"'Tis too true, and he knows it well, my dear," Helean said with a wink. "Although, I have never seen him settle his sights on any lady in my many years here. This, of course, has given rise to vicious rumors and has made your arrival of even greater significance."

"You mean, since you've been here, he's never had a girlfriend...*lover*?" She winced at the word.

"Never. As you already guessed, he could have had any number. It's strange to me that a man as kind as he is would not have the love of a woman in his home."

Abby hadn't realized it until that moment. No illicit relations of any kind tainted his memories, only love for his wife. In fact, his thoughts were as chaste as a choirboy's. Surely he wasn't gay. No, she knew he desired women, but he never allowed himself the freedom to fraternize or fantasize. My God! He must have an ironclad will or a severely disabled libido.

Avant strode into the kitchen and ensnared Abby with a smoldering gaze. An unexpected and unnerving vision shot through her, taking route between her legs and up her spine. Lodging itself in the back of her brain, it forced her to stifle a gasp. No. Definitely no disability there. She shivered.

"Greetings, my lady. I trust the conversation has been *stimulating* this morning."

Crap! He'd heard her thoughts again. Abby swallowed hard. "Good morning, my lord. Helean and I were just talking about the festival and what a wonderful time we both had."

Avant turned his attention to the little woman, who wouldn't meet his gaze. "Helean, what are the villagers saying about our Abigail this morning? I imagine she made quite an impression."

"Yes, my lord. She endeared herself to them well. We are all happy with this match, if I may be so bold." The woman blushed and went about her work.

"What?" Abby choked and water came out her nose.

"Yes, I was certain that would be the talk this morning. Thank you, Helean." He looked at Abby with a mocking smile.

"Aren't you going to clear up this misunderstanding?"

"Why should I? They will think what they want no matter what I say, and you did not help your cause with last night's bit of trickery."

"Yes, b-but Helean, she thinks…" Abby stared at him.

"Yes, she does." Out loud, he said, "Are you ready?"

Avant picked up the basket, headed to the door, and then turned in the threshold. "Helean, please check on Master Petra. He looked an interesting shade of green when I saw him earlier."

Oh God. Petra. She'd forgotten all about their—

"Come along, Lady Abigail."

Abby followed Avant out the door to the road, where two horses waited. Naturally, Avant's horse was a big silver stallion. After all, what would a noble knight be without a white charger? The other horse nudged Abby playfully in the neck. The dark russet mare with jet-black tail and mane had a sweetness that Abby immediately gravitated toward.

"This is Imperial. She is as gentle as she is sure, and I trust her with you as you learn. My mount is Spiritus, and he will lead the way for us today."

Avant easily lifted her onto the back of Imperial. She lightly held the reigns as he mounted his horse.

"They're beautiful. I just hope I don't fall off."

He started down the trail at a leisurely pace. She followed. The Implanting, apparently, worked with riding, too.

She broke the silence. "So now the entire village thinks we're a couple?"

"You mean, they think we're lovers."

Her cheeks heated, and she scowled. "Yes, that's what I mean, but how does that help your cause?"

"Why does it bother you?" He gave her a cocky half-smile. What was with him? He was in rare form this morning.

"Because it isn't true." She rolled her eyes, but she was curious about something. "Helean said you never had a woman in the house. Is that true? I mean, I don't have any memories of other women from you." Her cheeks heated. "Other than your wife."

Abby hadn't dwelt on *those* particular memories. Thinking of them seemed like too much of an intrusion of his privacy. It didn't do her any favors either. Thoughts of him making love with his wife occasionally, like twenty or thirty times a day, tried to invade her mind. Just the visual memories of his naked body overheated her. Luckily, there weren't too many of those. It never occurred to her before how little one actually looks at one's own naked body. However, it surprised her there had never been another woman. Ever. Not even in the twenty years since his presumed death.

Avant was quiet for a while. "No. There has never been anyone else. I will be able to tell her that I was never unfaithful to her."

"But isn't she remarried?"

"She does not know I'm alive." His anger flared and, even from two lengths back, she could see his jaw tighten and clench.

Abby halted her horse and spoke softly into his mind. *"I know. Your faithfulness is a testament. Any woman could only hope to be loved so much."* The words broke her heart to say. As long as he held out for his wife, Abby could never win his heart. Somehow she had to make him see he belonged with her and not a woman who'd forgotten him two decades ago. She was here now and she loved him. That had to count for something.

"I am sorry, Abigail. I have never spoken with anyone of these things, though I have thought them every day."

She rode even with him, tilted her head to the side, and smiled. "Maybe me knowing all your secrets will be more of a blessing to you than a curse."

His face relaxed, and he smiled at her. "Maybe it will."

The horses trotted down the trail, and Abby made small talk to ease the tension. She told him the story about the chickens, making him laugh so hard he almost fell off the stallion. They discussed their dance—but not the kiss—the significance of the crown of grape leaves, and how drunk she and Petra were.

When she mentioned Petra, Avant's jaw tightened and his voice hardened. "Petra did not attempt any unsolicited affection from you, did he? He is young and much infatuated."

Her stomach churned at the memory of their kiss in the carriage. She steadied her voice and tried to sound casual. "Why would you ask that?"

Avant spun the horse around to face her. His voice lowered an octave. "That is not an answer, Abigail. Is there something you wish to tell me?" His face became unreadable.

Damn. She was busted. How did he know? He could see right through her diversion tactics just like her dad, the only one she could never fool.

She sighed. "Not really, but I'm not going to lie either. He kissed me and I kissed him back."

An unmistakable jealousy flared in his eyes.

Her heart pounded. She panicked and blurted out, "Please let me explain—it was a case of mistaken identity."

"And how is that possible?" The coolness in his voice chilled her.

You better tell him the truth, Abs. "Petra looks exactly like Chad, my ex-boyfriend." Abby projected an image of Chad into Avant's mind. "I was drunk and got mixed-up. It's so embarrassing. I know Petra feels strongly about me, and I like him but—" She wanted to say, *but I am so in love with you, I can't see straight,* but she stopped herself before that embarrassing tidbit fell out of her big mouth.

Avant remained quiet for a moment, contemplating something. "Well, it is no concern of mine, other than I specifically told him not to engage you. For your part, that certainly explains your first meeting."

He wheeled Spiritus around and started down the trail again. Abby cringed. The formality of his tone told her he'd shut down his emotions. He thought less of her now. Why would he tell Petra to stay away? That seemed like a strange thing to tell someone. It wasn't like there was anything going on between her and him, right?

They rode in silence.

Finally Avant broke the stalemate. "This Chad, he was your only lover?"

Abby smiled at the way he always said "this Chad," as if it left a bad taste in his mouth to say the name. "That's kind of a personal question to ask a lady, isn't it?"

He smirked. "I'll count that as a 'no.'"

Abby rolled her eyes. He had her in a catch-22. If she didn't speak up, she would seem like a slut. If she did, he won the answer to his nosy question. "Yes, he was the only one, and how did we get on the subject of my love life all of a sudden?"

Avant cocked his brow and smiled roguishly. "I didn't want to dominate all the interesting conversation."

They reached the falls a half-hour later. This time, he guided her down a lower path that led to the side of the pool. He spread an old blanket on a patch of soft grass under a tree, and they sat and ate their lunch. The place was every bit as magical as it had been the first time, and the steady flow of the waterfall filled her with strength and life.

"I'm pleased you love the falls." He studied her.

"I've never seen anything so beautiful."

His face cleared of emotion, and he turned businesslike. "Abigail, I want to teach you how to put a wall up in your mind. It is the first step in learning how to control your power."

"Okay, tell me what to do."

"I think you have some idea since you hid your devious little plan from me last evening." He pointedly inclined his head and raised a brow.

Biting her fingernail, she shrugged her shoulders and smiled sheepishly. "I wondered about that. You really were shocked, weren't you?"

"You have no idea." He shook his head.

Her mind was off in a sprint, reliving the moment of that kiss. Warm lips pressed against hers made her mouth tingle again. At the time, he'd seemed as affected by it as she'd been, but now she couldn't tell.

His voice interrupted her. "The concept is the same. If you think something, it must be buried deep inside your mind. Practice compartmentalizing your thoughts and then you can begin to differentiate between the different aspects of your Gift." He reclined back against a tree trunk. "Think something about me but try keeping it from me."

A fleeting image came to mind, and she stuffed it deep in the recesses. "Okay. I've got it. Can you see it?"

"No. It is hidden from me. What it is?"

"It's your sword. The sapphires on the hilt are the color of your eyes."

"Good. Now try to imagine it in action."

He glossed over the flirtation and forced her to focus. The picture of Avant running to save her in the rain and pulling the weapon from its sheath filled the back of her mind. "Did you see that?"

"Only fleetingly. Show me the full memory now."

She drew the memory to the forefront—the awful man, Avant's rage, and the sword held threateningly in front of him. Her own fear rushed back. "I didn't realize at the time that man was one of the king's guard, but I realized he knew you."

His eyes clouded.

They sat silently for a long while. Pain reflected in his face, and all she wanted was to ease his hurt. "I know what you need. This is something friends do for each other where I come from."

She knelt behind him and placed her hands on broad shoulders that rippled at her touch. The wall of muscles crunched as she applied pressure. He groaned, but she wasn't sure if it was in pleasure or pain. Maybe both. Jesus, he was tense. "Are you smuggling rocks under here?"

He laughed and his shoulders released some of his tension.

Kneading his tight flesh, she worked the stressed tissue. Eventually, his muscles relaxed and gave way. His grunts and groans gave way to yawns. He lay on his stomach and fell asleep.

Leaving him to snooze, she waded into the shallow waters of the pool, allowing the chill to soothe her feet. Dancing the night before had made them sore and they hadn't fully recovered from her mountain trek in sandals. This place was a balm washing over her.

Out of nowhere a vision infiltrated her mind—of him leaning in and tenderly kissing her. The same slow sensuous kiss as before. Her soft lips kissed him back and her silky hair slid through his hand. When he pulled away, her teal-green eyes shone with love and her own voice spoke: "I love you." He kissed her again with so much passion that the thought made her lightheaded.

The vision left as quickly as it came, and she sucked in a breath. She splashed her face. The more she thought about that vision, the stranger it seemed. *Oh my God.* It hadn't been her vision—it was his. His mind unguarded in sleep had allowed her access. She darted her gaze to him. How often did he dream of kissing her?

Chapter Sixteen

Still feeling the remnants of a hangover, Abby lay down next to Avant on the blanket and took a nap. Well, she tried. Lying next to his big, warm body put all kinds of ideas in her head, but eventually the soothing crash of the falls and the mild breeze lulled her to sleep. When she awoke, he was sitting next to her, watching intently.

"There is something I want to show you." His mouth was set in a half-smile. The excitement in his eyes warmed her. He was itching to reveal whatever it was.

She stretched and stared at him, still amazed that the Implanting gave her so much insight into him. "What is it?"

"A secret cave, but you'll have to trust me to get to it." His eyes danced, and he flashed a boyish smile.

There was no way she could resist him. "Where is this cave?" She narrowed her gaze in suspicion, remembering how far he'd pushed her the day they'd met. "You aren't going to make me hike a mile up a cliff, are you?"

He chuckled and gestured toward the falls. "It's behind the falls at the backside of the pool. I've already got dinner set up over there with a campfire. Come. It'll be an experience."

He didn't need the wheedling tone. He could have convinced her with just a smile. Whatever his reasoning for showing her the discovery, it was clearly important to him. She searched her mind and found vague memories from him of a cave behind the falls.

She raised a skeptical eyebrow. "How do you expect me to get over there without getting soaking wet?"

"You'll have to take your clothes off." He grinned devilishly.

Her heart skipped a beat, but she put on her best poker face. "You do this to all the girls, don't you? Pretend to be honorable, and then you get them out here alone so you can take their clothes off."

"You're the first. I've wanted to share this place with someone, but...never have." Avant searched her face. "Do you trust me?"

It was that question again. The one the Seppitent asked, and the answer was the same. "Yes. I trust you. Remind me what I have to do."

"Remove your outer clothing."

She frowned.

He laughed. "I'll place them in the saddlebags, where you can retrieve them later. Swim to the rock behind the falls. Beneath it, on the right side, is a short tunnel."

Was it such a good idea to take her clothes off? She would be in her undergarments. God only knew, her hot-pink bikini was significantly more revealing than Jastainian underwear, and she'd never thought twice about going out in public wearing it.

Without further debate, she shucked off her clothes while Avant turned his back, and then waded out in the freezing water. "Brrr. Crap, it's cold." She darted a glare back at him. Had he planned this from the beginning of the day or was it spontaneous? She had to admit the mystery was enticing.

When she got past the fall of water, she could see the opening down by her knees, and the memory of it came to her.

She heard his strong, reassuring voice in her head. *Trust me. It is a short distance, and it opens into a lovely cave.*

"Here goes." She took a deep breath and dove underwater into a tunnel about three feet long.

Bursting out of the icy pool, she sucked in a breath as soon as her head cleared the surface. She wiped her eyes and panned her gaze around the large cavern sparkling with golden walls. Abby shivered as she climbed out, gaping in wonder.

On the banks, a palette of soft moss beckoned to be lounged upon, with dinner set for two. A flickering fire sat to the side, and the smoke filtered up through a hole in the top of the mountain like a chimney.

The cave was an amazing discovery, with veins of gold that glistened deep into the rock. Warm firelight danced with sparkling colors in every direction, and the rhythmic sound of the water set off a calming echo. Lilies and fresh earth perfumed the moist air, and toward the back near the glittering wall, a natural hot spring bubbled like a top-of-the-line Jacuzzi.

Scanning the scene in awe, she marveled, the seduction of the setting crashing into her core like the relentless falls. Her breath quickened, and her body thrummed with yearning. *Avant has to be the most romantic man in the universe.* And as far as she was concerned, if he wanted to make good on the village gossip, he was welcome.

He rose out of the water bare-chested. Her tongue stuck dry to the roof of her mouth. His muscles glistened in the firelight. Several deep scars smattered his chest and a fine line of dark hair trailed under the waist of his pants. Her breath adhered to her lungs like school glue on construction paper. Taking in air proved impractical. Her knees gave way, and she sat on a rock to keep from stumbling. Desire fought brutally with her mind as she pushed down erotic images warring with her good sense. Thank God she was learning how to hide those thoughts from him. Otherwise, her sex fantasies would've been plastered in his head too. Not that the thought was unappealing, but it was a little embarrassing.

He stepped onto the bank and pulled her to her feet. His face shone with excitement and delight laced his voice. "Abigail, I cannot tell you how much this means to me. I've always wanted to share this place with someone." He pointed over her head. "Is this not an incredible structure of nature?" He stepped to the far wall and pulled her along. "Look over here. It is a natural hot spring! I suspect it to have healing properties. Would you like to get in?"

The secret places of his heart were known to her, but to have him openly share this touched her deeply. Before she knew what had happened, her heart hinged opened like a golden locket. An unstoppable desire flowed from the depths of her. She wanted him. *Right here. Right now.*

Without a word, she took his hand and led him to the spring.

He climbed down into the bubbling water and lifted her in. Submerged to mid-chest, he sat on a rock that formed a natural bench. The heated bubbles tingled against her skin and stimulated the craving that coursed through strategic locations in her body. Liquid need pooled between her legs.

She stared into his unguarded eyes, and without hesitation, climbed astride him, resting her knees on the rock at either side of his thighs. Tilting his head up, she lightly kissed his lips, running her fingers through his wet hair. *You feel like heaven.* She drew in the sweet flesh of his bottom lip. He softly growled. Waves of want washed over her.

Trailing his hands up her sides, under her arms, and around her back, he caused her body to throb. *Oh God.* She placed her lips flush with his and opened her mouth. His tongue needed no further invitation but slid inside, discovering the backside of her lips and the straight edge of her teeth. The ache between her legs became more intense. Moving their mouths in rhythm to the softly drumming current, they explored, teased, and tasted in a sensual experience that Abby drank in like spiced wine.

He grasped her hips and pulled them down, settling his erection at the juncture in between. Moaning into his mouth, she encouraged him on, grinding against him. Her heart sought that union with his, and her body searched for intimate release. His arousal pulsed. He wanted her just as much. She smiled against his lips. Her aching desire would be realized.

But in a sudden jolt, Avant released her hips, pressed his hands to her arms, and yanked himself away from her. He rose so fast, had he not held her shoulders, she would've been upended in the water.

They stood with chests heaving, only the strength of his arms holding them apart. Abby fought frantically against his grip, trying to reach him before he shut her out. Struggling to be back in his embrace, she seized his gaze and silently pleaded in a communication of her heart that was deeper than telepathy. She opened herself, became vulnerable.

His eyes shuttered. He pushed her away and turned his back.

It was over.

The door of his heart was closed, and it wouldn't open again. His will was settled, and she knew he would never change his mind.

A heavy sigh blew from her lips and her chest ached from his rejection. She had to get away, escape, *now*. A light amassed around her, and her jaw tingled.

"Abigail!"

Shaking from her trance, she stared at his face, which was white with concern. Sympathy filled his eyes.

The light faded around her. Tears welled, but she held them back with surprising resolve. She could stand anything but his sympathy. *That* she couldn't tolerate.

She jumped out of the spring and dove into the icy water, swam through the tunnel, and climbed out the other side. Shivers wracked her body as she dressed. She mounted Imperial and took off for the manor as fast as she could without falling.

*****

Avant gasped for breath as he watched Abigail go, unable to stop her for fear his resolve would fail.

For the Light's sake, what had he been thinking? He hadn't been thinking. Not with his mind. His recklessness had hurt her and put the entire quest at risk. "Damnable Darkness!"

The pain in her eyes ripped at his heart like the teeth of mountain lion. She'd almost accessed her Gift to leave. He slammed his fist into the rock. Two knuckles crunched and blood ran down the wall. He welcomed the pain, earning every moment of it.

Where had he gone wrong? Not having realized her intent until the soft flesh of her lips brushed his, it had been too late. Her kiss had rendered his will powerless. He flexed his bleeding hand and wiped the sweat from his brow. Overconfident in his self-control, he never could have imagined such a test.

He glanced around the large inlet. Having found this cave during a dark and lonely time of his life, he had wanted to share it with her. He would never be able to return without thinking of her. A sickening feeling churned his gut.

What a knave! How could he have allowed this? He bent in front of the meal he'd so painstakingly set and laughed mirthlessly. His carelessness had placed Abigail in harm's way. To seduce her had not been his intention. Far from it. He had merely hoped to communicate with her in companionship.

Picking up a piece of crusted bread, he twirled it between his fingers and let it fall back on the untouched food. She'd never gotten around to asking him how he'd gotten the supplies into the cave.

He'd thought Abigail could be a companion, a friend, but their fierce mutual attraction precluded that from happening. He was a fool for thinking otherwise.

His conduct was intolerable and unforgivable. The memory of her openness and abandon assailed him. After the Harvest Festival, he'd known she cared for him, but now, he'd seen the love she held for him and silently cursed himself.

"Argh!" He hurled a plate of food at the wall. It splattered with a loud clang.

He wanted her. More than he'd ever desired any woman, including his wife. Had it not been for the thought of the restored kingdom, he would have taken her without a second thought. He shivered at how easy it would have been. *Still would be.* Even now his mind betrayed his will with a vision of her in his arms, and his body still throbbed with the need to feel her soft flesh beneath him.

A sense of duty, the Light itself—whatever had brought the Crown of Light to his mind, he would never know, but had it not come, he would have given in to his lust. He had *already* given in. Desire wielded his flesh like a sword, and he had fully intended to take her.

Disgusted with himself, he stomped out the fire and slammed the supplies into his bag.

His purpose was clear. His wife awaited him. This could not, would not, happen again. Regardless of his desire, he would not put Abigail's heart at risk. *Ever.* His focus would be her training, and he would make certain to guard himself from even the appearance of impropriety. *That is how it must be.*

*****

Still shaking, Abby dropped from the saddle and led the horse to the stables. She fought back tears, not wanting Petra to see her cry as she approached. "Will you please help me with this animal? She needs tending. I have some idea what to do but have never actually done it." Her voice cracked, and she swallowed the lump in her throat.

Hurt filled Petra's eyes, but he took the horse and motioned for her to follow. "Come on. I'll show you."

Was he hurt because of her trip to the falls with Avant?

Glancing back as he led the mare into the stall, he scrutinized her wet clothes. "Abby, is everything all right?"

"Why do you ask?" She shifted her weight from foot to foot.

He unsaddled Imperial without ever glancing at his hands. "Because you left with Avant and now you're alone and soaking wet."

She shrugged and tried to smile with half-hearted effort. "Right. We had a…misunderstanding. I left him on the trail from the falls, but no need to worry, I am sure he'll be here shortly."

Petra nodded and dropped the subject. Relief flooded her chest. He couldn't know how much she appreciated his understanding.

He showed her how to remove the saddle and how the animal should be tended. His practicality put her at ease and the sharp pain in her chest abated.

Abby's stomach growled. "Are you hungry? I'm starving."

"I'm a little hungry. I haven't eaten much today due to the festivities of last night." He grimaced.

She smiled at his mention of the evening. "Come on. Let's go get something to eat."

They walked up to the house and into the kitchen. The sun sank below the horizon. Helean finished preparing dinner while they watched. The sturdy little woman stared at Abby with a tilted head. Abby shrugged her shoulders. She and Petra washed and ate a small meal. They talked about the previous evening and exchanged gossip. Neither mentioned their kiss or Avant.

"So what do y'all do around here for fun on non-festival days?"

Petra pushed his seat back from the table and dropped his napkin in his plate. "Not too much. There's always something that needs to be done and no time for fun."

"This is a tragedy we'll definitely have to remedy." She stood and took his hand.

They made their way to the parlor. Abby tried to think of something they could do. All the games she knew were either drinking games or had to be played with some form of technology. She did know a few of jokes, especially blonde jokes. So putting on her best comedy routine and drinking a full glass of "the good stuff" in the parlor, she entertained Petra.

He grabbed his sides, and his rich laughter washed over the room. The tension in her eased. He told her a few jokes, and the smile on her face became more than a façade. Petra emanated genuine warmth, and she gravitated to him. Just like last night, Petra made her feel safe and cared for. He was unassuming and lighthearted. His gentle comfort filled empty places within her.

He sat on the sofa, and she on the floor between his legs, while he massaged her shoulders. Her eyes rolled back in her head and she moaned. Hands strong from labor carefully kneaded crunchy muscles with perfect pressure. God, she was tense. Avant had apparently rubbed off on her. She snorted. No, he hadn't, and that was the whole problem.

She took a deep breath and focused on the man with her. "How did you come here, Petra?"

His hand squeezed the back of her neck. "Avant found me in the forest after my parents were killed."

Goosebumps rose on her arm. "I had no idea. What happened?" She could never have guessed the tragedy of his past by his demeanor. The epitome of grace under pressure, he gave no indication that his life had ever been anything but sunshine and wildflowers.

"My parents had been in hiding for several years, but the king's lands had become so vicious we sought asylum in the Freelands. I led the horse carrying our family possessions behind my parents. Several men came from behind the rocks and ambushed us. My father was killed immediately." He paused and a tremble ran through his hands. "My mother was…killed too. I tried to help her, but I was knocked unconscious. When I came to, they were gone and so was the horse. I buried my parents as best I could. I was twelve years old. I'd been wandering in the forest for several days when Avant found me starving and half-crazed. A wooden box was all that remained of our possessions. It had fallen off the horse and I clung to it with all my strength." He stopped rubbing and his hands began to shake, sending tremors through her body.

Abby got to her knees and turned around to hug him. To think that someone could do that was unbearable. "Oh, honey, I am so sorry. Nobody should have to endure such horror." His eyes held a distant rage that frightened her with its absolute contrast to his normal disposition. She put her arms around him and stroked his hair.

The shaking subsided. He exhaled. "I've never told anyone that story. Not even Avant."

Abby pulled away to look him in the face and touch his cheek. She didn't know what to say but his face relaxed and the sweet sparkle in his eyes returned.

He asked, "So, what happened with Avant?"

She shook her head. "I don't know. I feel like I've lost part of my heart, and I don't know how to get it back. He certainly doesn't want it."

Petra gazed at her and nodded. "Avant has a way of drawing you to him with his charisma, and it can feel overwhelming. But he has a hard time reciprocating with his emotions. His presence requires so much from those who love him, and he is mostly unaware of the effect he has over people. He's an intense man, but a great one."

"I know what you mean." She stared up at the picture of the falls over the mantle and then dropped her gaze. "I think you are in need of an Abby Randall special back massage. Sit here, fine sir."

He laughed as they traded seats. Abby rubbed his back and neck as she explained the finer points of her world, like shopping, studying, and Mexican Minesweeper.

"Oh, please don't talk to me about drinking. If I never take another swallow, it will be too soon."

They laughed at their previous evening's escapades. But in mid-chuckle, Petra froze and then jumped to his feet.

"W-What—" Abby's gaze fell on the dark shadow in the doorframe.

Petra stepped toward the door. She grabbed his arm. "Petra, you don't have to leave."

The look that stormed in Avant's eyes told a different story. How long he'd been standing there was unclear, but she suspected it had been a while.

Petra turned to her. "I'll meet you for lunch tomorrow."

Abby nodded and let him go. She glared up at Avant. "What the hell is your problem?"

"Abigail, I need to speak with you." His face was a mask of formality.

"Why? The situation is pretty clear." The emotion in her words made her voice rise. She gazed up at him, hoping for a miracle, but his eyes were remote, closed off.

She knew he cared for her and battled a fierce attraction. She'd wanted to give him time to come to terms with how he felt. That is, until he opened his heart to show her that damned cave. The cave he'd never shown anyone. Mistaking his gesture, she'd assumed he'd recognized and accepted the feelings he had for her. She'd assumed wrong. Or maybe she hadn't.

She glared at him. "You can pretend that you don't feel something for me."

He didn't speak but stared at the rug.

"You can say that you made a mistake—because that's what you were going to say, wasn't it?"

"Abigail, it was a mistake."

"I thought so." She smirked. "And you can deny that I stir something in you that you've never felt, but save that bullshit for yourself. Because I know the truth."

He lifted his chin. His eyes flickered with all the emotion she'd felt in his kiss, but the door slammed shut again. "I never meant to hurt you."

"Don't," she spoke in his mind. *"Just don't."* She squared her shoulders and stomped to her room. All of the pain rushing down on her again, she threw herself on the bed and cried herself to sleep.

Chapter Seventeen

Abby rode Imperial to the falls. The autumn trees poked spindly fingers into the crisp blue sky. The mare's hooves crunched through the dry leaves scattered across the trail, where the wind had gathered them in piles. She pulled her new wool cape tightly around her shoulders to ward off a chill. This was most likely one of her last trips to the falls until after spring. Petra had said that once winter set in, it would be too cold to travel there.

In the three months that followed her arrival on the fief, Abby had settled into a routine. Each day Helean woke her before sunrise. She rose and ate and then helped around the house until midday, when she met with Avant for several hours. In the open field behind the stables, he trained her to use her Gift, driving her like a demonic taskmaster hell-bent on conquering the world.

He taught her mind exercises that strengthened and increased her control. She worked hard every day. He didn't tolerate slackers. Her Implanting improved quickly. In a short time, she'd gained skill and could exercise basic control over it. She moved small objects with her mind and spoke thoughts into the minds of animals. She and Avant could still communicate, though they rarely did.

He also required her to do physical labor on the fief, in the mill, and with the animals.

"Abigail, the state of your body is merely a reflection of your inward self." He straightened his spine and lifted his chin, which he always did in *instructor mode*.

Abby rolled her eyes. "Fine, Tony Robbins. Just show me what you want me to do."

In the weeks since her training commenced, Avant had pushed her well past what she considered her physical limitations and brought her to tears many times. Forcing her to run exercises regardless of the weather or how she felt, he barked out commands and expected perfect compliance. *Is he putting me through military drills or is he just pissed because he hasn't gotten laid in two decades?* She made sure he heard that thought.

They never spoke of that day at the falls or what had happened. Avant remained reserved and formal, rarely speaking of anything personal. Abby hid her emotions deep in her heart and tried not to think about them.

Holding Imperial to the trail, she winced as her mind reflected on her training session that afternoon. During an exceptionally difficult exercise, her concentration had slipped and a fifty-pound bag of feed fell on her, crushing her chest. Avant rushed over and threw the bag aside. Lifting her to a seated position, he knelt facing her. "Abigail! Are you all right?" He tenderly brushed the hair from her face, looking with concern into her eyes.

Caught off guard by the touch of his hand and his kindness, Abby's heart softened and all of her feelings flooded back. She nodded, unable to break his gaze, and then lifted her hand to his cheek.

Seeing the emotion in her face, he looked away. "I am sorry. It was too much weight for you to bear." His mind closed, and his voice filled with the sympathetic tone he had adopted for times when he couldn't handle his own emotions.

Rage and rejection thundered in her. She'd stood and stormed to the stables, wincing at the pain in her chest, physical and emotional.

Saddling up Imperial, she pulled the cinch tight. *Why won't he accept his own feelings?* She mounted the faithful horse and took off down the trail to get some breathing room.

Sympathy. He'd looked at her as if she had some schoolgirl crush on the hot professor. "Humph!" She wasn't alone in her attraction, but she'd play hell ever getting him to admit it. She shook her head and spurred Imperial forward. For him to show sympathy insulted her intelligence and the memory of what they'd shared. Whether he wanted to admit it or not, he felt something and one day would have to face it.

At the falls, she dismounted and walked to the landing where Avant had brought her that first time. She sat on the grass. The higher trail seemed preferable today. Typically, she went to the pool's edge, but she wanted the panorama to ease her tension. The falls changed in beauty with the seasons, and each, though unique, thrilled her senses.

She wished Petra could have come with her. Just as if her wish had been his command, his strong hand was on her shoulder.

"I saw you race off and figured you might want some company." His easy smile warmed her against the chilly autumn day as he folded next to her.

"I might."

"So, you want to tell me what happened?"

Petra had become a helpful distraction. But more than that, he'd become one of the best friends she'd ever had. He'd taught her about farming, animals, and the ins and outs of daily life on the fief. Funny and unassuming, he strengthened her confidence and gave her a peace she found nowhere else. They usually ate lunch together, and Abby spent evenings with him in the stables. She could talk to him about anything. Though their friendship was important to her, she always knew he wanted more. She looked into his rich brown eyes, blond wisps of hair blowing across them. Maybe it was time to give him more. She reached up and pushed the unruly strands back and tucked them behind his ear. "You need a haircut."

His smile fell and desire flared in his eyes at her touch. She dropped her hand with a shock. Her heart pounded, and she gulped. He schooled his need and took her hand, his warm fingers clasping hers. "Tell me what happened."

"Avant happened." She pulled her hand from his grasp but scooted closer to him, leaning back against the tree, their shoulders touching. "I've tried every seductive trick I know, and he refuses to notice me." She plucked a blade of dried grass from the ground. "He leaves in the morning before I'm dressed and is only available for our afternoon training sessions, which he runs like a freaking boot camp, all military discipline. He takes dinner in his room or at the military compound. When was the last time he ate at the house with us? Even though I know he—" She stilled and looked over at Petra, who was staring at her.

"Maybe you should forget those people who aren't around and look at those who are."

His words rang in her heart and his gaze never left hers. The crashing sound of the falls filled the silence.

Petra cared for her, maybe more than anyone ever had. He'd listened to her, comforted her, and cheered her on. And he was right. He was here and Avant wasn't.

*****

Lying on her bed, Abby stared at the wood-slated ceiling, not really able to sleep. Too cold to go outside, she lounged on her bed until it was time for her afternoon drills with the taskmaster.

Though she bitched about the training, her slim body rippled with defined muscles from the daily exercise. The purity of the food and drink gave her loads of energy, and the fresh air filled her with endorphins. Still, would she ever get back to Dallas? Did she even want to?

The months had passed. At night, Abby dreamed of Avant, and sometimes her dad, but she always woke before the dreams finished. Even now tears threatened.

Winter brought the snow and bitter cold. She spent her days in the parlor reading or playing checkers with Petra. He'd made the board out of a small end table and the checkered pieces from a branch they'd cut at the mill. She'd soaked half of the pieces in wine so they were a different color. Occasionally Avant joined them, and tension filled the air. But mostly she and Petra sat alone.

She sighed and sat, propping herself up with her bolster. No sleep for her. Pulling her black bag out from under her bed, she dumped the contents, combing through each piece like a graphic novel of what used to be her life. How was her Xterra doing? Probably covered in snow. She eyed her phone. Just to see if it would work, she turned it on and, to her surprise, it lit up. As she scanned the screen, the date caught her attention, December twenty-first. Four days until Christmas!

As a child, her Christmases had been lonely. Her dad rarely came home for the holiday. Generally pawned off on the housekeeper, Abby could count on one hand how many times her dad had spent Christmas with her, but he always sent presents.

In recent years, she'd spent Christmas at Lyndsea's house. She attended candlelight services with them on Christmas Eve and spent the night to wake with them on Christmas morning.

Last year, she and Chad spent Christmas with Lyndsea. Chad was adopted by an older couple, and his mother was overbearing and obnoxious. His dad died when he was in high school, and his mom couldn't stand Abby. The feeling was mutual.

A melancholy smile tinged her lips. She'd always wanted a big family for birthdays and Christmases. Maybe someday. Her heart ached with the vision that flashed in her mind. She might as well put that one away in the when-hell-freezes file.

She loved the planning, the excitement, and the anticipation of the season. Her mind spun with a new idea like an SUV on black ice. Quickly she stuffed all of her things back into the bag and put it away. She flew downstairs to find Helean.

A tizzy of excitement filled the next two days. Avant and Petra watched her run around, looking on in what appeared to be wonder and concern. She directed Petra to chop down a fir tree on the edge of the forest, and then made him drag it back to the house.

Without them knowing, she rode to the village and bought gifts with a trade of the crystal beads on her little black dress.

On Christmas Eve it snowed. A real white Christmas. She hadn't seen many of those in Dallas. Having finished up the last of the treats for the next day, Helean prepared a goose with vegetables and made Christmas pudding. The little lady caught the guys poking their heads in the kitchen and shooed them away. Despite themselves, the men seemed to be getting a curious to see what all the fuss was about.

Abby gathered them in the parlor, where they talked, laughed, and drank spiced cider well into the night. Avant sat silently and watched her. His eyes sparkled with an openness he hadn't shown in months.

The next morning she banged on their doors. "Get up. Santa has come and left you something."

Making them come down to the parlor in their nightclothes, she brought blankets to keep them warm while they opened their gifts. She heated the spiced cider and set out the panas, which she'd decorated with colored icing Helean had helped her make.

She handed everyone their stocking filled with fruit, nuts, and a little wooden toy, and then passed out their gifts. Bouncing in her seat, she rubbed her hands together to watch them open the presents.

Petra untied the bow and tore into the wooden container like a kid. She'd found him a wooden chess set in the village. The pieces were intricately carved and the board finely made of several inlaid types of wood.

He reached over and pulled her close, squeezing her so tight she couldn't breathe. "Thank you, Abby. I love it."

She'd played chess as a child and understood the general rules. Apparently, Avant had played quite a bit when he was a boy and promised to teach Petra. They vowed a chess match for later that day with a little side wager having to do with trudging into the snow to gather eggs from the coop.

Helean opened her gift, a knitted shawl in bright jewel tones. Abby was fond of the woman, and loved to listen to her lighthearted gossip. In the evenings when Helean took the leftover table food out to the animals, she covered herself in an old shawl with holes in it.

Tears came to Helean's eyes as she wrapped it around her sturdy little shoulders. "My dear, this is the most beautiful thing I've ever received." She hugged Abby and kissed her on the cheek.

Abby's heart beat wildly, and her breath quickened when she handed the little black box to Avant. He fingered the velvet, turning it over in his hand, and offered up an inquisitive look. Opening the box, he stared at the single earring inside. The others gasped.

Silent for a long moment, he finally said, "Abigail, this is not a gift to be given lightly."

"No, it isn't. Someone told me once that it was a kingly gift. The lord of these lands is certainly worthy of such a gift, and I couldn't think of anything better to express my gratitude. Besides, I still have one. See?" She pulled back her hair to reveal the one in her own ear.

His face was unreadable, but he accepted the gift with grace.

Petra smiled impishly. "And did our Lady Abigail think that she could escape without a gift of her own?"

"What did you do, Petra?" She looked at the others, and they grinned too. Avant strode to the next room. He brought in a large box and a tall stand covered in brown paper with the most pathetic bow she had ever seen.

"Petra, I told you to have Helean make the bow." Avant squinted as if it hurt his eyes and then laughed as Abby squealed.

"You are the sweetest, most wonderful people in Jastain. I can't believe you surprised me."

Petra pulled her to the gifts.

She tore off the lopsided bow. "This is a beautiful bow." Putting it around her neck, she kissed his cheek and then ripped the paper to reveal a full-length mirror. How did they know?

Inside the large box lay a crimson dress with gold embroidery and a necklace of rubies to match. Knowing who had picked that out, she glanced at Avant.

He smiled and gave her a cordial nod.

She hugged all of them.

It was the greatest Christmas. Ever. They ate their meal and a snowball fight commenced in the front yard afterward.

The day would have been perfect if she hadn't lost the blasted chess match and had to go gather eggs. Trudging through the snow and chicken poop, she vowed to one day return the favor to Avant. Calling him out on a wager would be her life's ambition. But she doubted she could ever beat him at chess. Poker, maybe.

Chapter Eighteen

Abby moped around the drafty house, stuck inside unless she wanted to freeze her ass off with Petra out in the stables. After Christmas, the cold, dreary days lingered like an uninvited party guest. She flopped down on the sofa in the parlor and thumbed through a leather-bound book she'd read four times at least.

Now fairly skilled in the art of her Gift, she could easily move large, heavy items at will. Earlier that morning, she'd practiced by gathering eggs from the chicken coop without having to enter it. When she got really bored, she rearranged the furniture, which always sent Helean into a dither. She giggled as she moved several armoires to different rooms. Moving large items took concentration. Her body seized and muscles spasmed as if she'd physically moved the impossibly heavy items. Not that she needed the extra workout, because Avant had no mercy.

Forcing her outside regardless of the weather, he pushed her to the ends of her endurance. When she collapsed with exhaustion, he yelled and required her to continue. Some days she would've strangled him with her bare hands if she could've lifted them. He couldn't read her thoughts at all anymore, and she regularly said things to him in English that would have gotten her ejected from a baseball game.

Why did she have to do this stupid training? Yes, she'd learned a lot, but under such duress, anyone would've. If she was the Chosen One, why didn't she have any clue what to do to help *restore Light to the kingdom*? Avant grasped at straws, trying to make her into his hope for the future. Why couldn't they just live in peace here at the fief?

Since the holidays, Avant had actually warmed a bit and smiled on occasion, when he wasn't barking orders. He'd eventually realize she was a hopeless cause in the savior-of-the-world sense. Maybe then he'd finally accept his feelings. *Nah. Probably not even then.*

The months passed, and she marveled at her genuinely happy life. The best part of her days were the evenings spent in the parlor. Since Christmas, Avant, and sometimes Helean, joined her and Petra to talk about the day, play a game of checkers or chess. Abby's skills at chess had advanced almost as much as her Implanting, but she still couldn't beat Avant. It didn't keep her from trying.

She stared at the board and glanced up at him without moving her head. He tapped his finger on his lips. Shit. That meant his next move was *check*. She stared harder at the pieces.

A sound of approaching horses filled the manor. Never in the whole time Abby had been on the fief had there been a visitor. They all rose and went to the window. Avant opened the door.

"Greetings, lord of the fief. It is the humble winemaker and his wife." A tall man stepped from his carriage.

"Hossa, my friend, come in from the cold." Avant went outside to greet them. Annova stepped to the ground, and the winemaker escorted her to the door.

Avant took her hand and led her in the door, leaning to kiss her sweetly on the lips. "Annova, love, how are you?"

Abby wanted to yank the redheaded woman bald. Why does she get the soft smile and a kiss?

"Avant, we've missed you these months. You haven't been to see us." She stared at Abby. "I met you briefly at the Harvest Festival. I'm Annova." Of course Abby remembered her. A stunning woman with her cream-colored skin and auburn hair, Annova emanated a sacred air of grace that commanded reverence.

Abby couldn't hold the woman's intense gaze.

"Abigail is the newest member of our family," Avant said as he wrapped a protective arm around her shoulder.

Abby smiled and reveled in his touch. Since that night in the cave, he'd gone out of his way to make certain they never touched. When she'd hugged him at Christmas, she might as well have been hugging a tree for as stiff as he was. She winced at the memory and pushed the thought from her mind.

Moved that he introduced her as family, she cocked her head at him before taking Annova's hand. "It's nice to meet you again. I know how important you are to Avant."

Annova looked meaningfully into her eyes and smiled. "Thank you, Abigail. You too are important to Avant."

Heat rose from her chest to her forehead.

According to Petra, Hossa and Annova had worked for the former king in the palace. When the new king, Aesdil, was crowned, Annova had a prophetic vision that told her to find the rightful ruler of Jastain. She and Hossa fled southwest in the middle of the night. On the south side of the Forest of Caelum, they'd found Avant lying in a pool of his own blood, left for dead. Taking him with them, they'd crossed the River Sast and headed north to the Freelands.

"Hossa, Annova, how are you?" Petra rushed to greet them.

Avant led them to the cozy parlor and strode toward the kitchen. "I will let Helean know we'd like some wine and cheese."

"Hossa, take a look at my chess set, and tell me of this season's vintage." Petra directed the hulking man to the little table.

Annova took Abby around the shoulders and led her to the sofa, speaking softly, "I've come to speak with you, my lady. You've found your time in our land happy?" The mystical sparkle in her eyes told Abby she knew everything and then some.

"Yes."

"Your time is almost ripe. Your destiny knocks at the door. Are you prepared to go?"

"Go where?" Abby wrinkled her forehead.

"Away. You cannot stay here, my dear. This is not your home."

Abby's heart sank. This felt like home. It felt more like home than anyplace she'd ever known. "I don't think I have the strength to leave."

Annova took her hand and gave it a motherly pat. "You will when the time comes. I've seen your heart, young one. Your sacrifice will not be in vain, but how it will turn, who can tell. You'll find a familiar voice and a way to the end."

"What does that mean? It doesn't make sense to me." Why did these people always have to speak in effin' hieroglyphs?

Annova laughed as though she'd heard Abby's thought. She probably had. "It will. A word of advice—keep your heart guarded. In the end, you may be rewarded with its chief desire. You understand *that*, do you not?" She said this with a knowing smile.

"I think so." Abby's heart leapt for joy.

"He loves you, my dear, but you must first know your own heart, and you'll be surprised when you find it. He still has to work out his own heart. There's a long journey ahead. Prepare yourself."

Abby shivered and rubbed the crimson velvet on her arms. How could this woman know so much about her? Was it possible Avant could really love her? But what about his wife?

Avant strode in with a tray of cheese and bread, and a bottle of wine. They ate and talked but Annova said no more to her.

Hossa played a game of chess with Avant and beat him soundly. Abby was impressed, and Avant spent the rest of the evening brooding. He didn't lose often enough to do it well.

*****

The lights came, one by one illuminating the room. A familiar voice spoke: "Seek the Light in the house of your father's father. Up in the High Places, you must seek the Way of the old prophet."

She shot up in bed, the dream still fresh. The High Places? To seek some old guy, but who? *The house of her father's father* didn't make any sense.

Was Annova right? Was her life on the fief over? A sick feeling wrenched her gut and tears pooled in her eyes.

Avant's words came flooding back to her. *Abigail, you may dwell in my home and work on my fief, but when your destiny calls, you must offer the sacrifice asked of you.*

In this place she'd known the happiest time of her life. She had found people whom she loved and who loved her. She belonged with them. Now she had to leave? How was that fair? Not that she didn't want to help these people—she did. To leave them would break her heart.

But she'd sworn to Avant that she would go when the day came, not actually believing the day *would* come. Would she have to go by herself? Was she not meant to belong anywhere? Was she not meant to be loved? Some people were just meant to go it alone.

She paced in the dark. No one knew about the dream. She could just not tell. Maybe it wasn't a message at all. Her heart betrayed her. She knew it was a message as sure as she'd known anything. As her Implanting increased, her ability to discern did too. It wasn't the wine or the visit with Annova. This was her wake-up call. She needed to tell Avant. *Now.*

Abby lit a candle. She'd never been to Avant's room, at least not when he was actually in there. Helping Helean do the laundry, she changed his bed linens all the time but never dared go when he was there.

Padding lightly down the chilly hallway, she scooted her bare feet and tried to keep to the narrow rugs. She took a deep breath and hesitated at his door. Her heart pounded in her chest. Maybe this wasn't such a good idea. She stared at the door across the hall. Petra, at least, would comfort her. No. Petra couldn't help her with this. As much as she hated to admit it, she needed Avant.

Knocking lightly, she tried to rouse him out of sleep. She opened the door and whispered, "Avant."

He stirred as she made her way to him.

His hulking four-poster bed with thick midnight-blue draperies and linens dominated the room. A fireplace taller than her heated a comfortable sitting area with bookshelves. The glowing embers cast long shadows across the dark floor. In the corner near the eastern windows, he kept a writing desk and armchair where he corresponded and managed the paperwork of his holdings. Sometimes during days when she felt lost, she would secretly go and sit at the desk. Smelling the leather, ink, and paper reminded her of her dad.

"Abigail, what's wrong?" Avant asked in a hoarse whisper, his voice laced with concern.

"Nothing's wrong. I just need to talk to you."

He propped himself up with an elbow and slid over so she could sit on the side of the bed. "What is it?"

"I had the dream about the lights again." Her voice broke. Shit. She was trying to hold it together.

He laid his hand over hers. Warmth and confidence radiated from it. She could do this. "And I know it's time for me to leave."

"Leave? To go where?" The words seemed to catch in his throat.

"To the High Places to find some old prophet who can tell me what to do. Do you know who that might be?" She teetered again on the verge of waterworks. A wave of emotion built inside her. Swallowing hard, she wrapped her arms around her chest to keep from shivering.

His eyes glistened in the candlelight. "There is a man, a prophet, who lives in the High Places. It does not surprise me he would be the first step on the journey."

"Can you tell me how to get there?" She closed her eyes, dreading to hear the direction of her exile, and a single tear slid down her cheek.

"I've been there before. We can go in a few days."

We. Relief at his words swept over her. The words rushed out. "Thank you, Avant. I-I didn't know where or how or anything and...I was so afraid I'd have to go alone." Tears coursed down her cheeks, and she was unable to stop to flow.

He placed his hands around her waist and pulled her into bed next to him. He whispered against her ear, "Abigail, you're not alone as long as there's breath in my body."

She melted back against him and closed her eyes. His arms wrapped tightly around her. The fear ebbed, and with her heart reassured, she slept.

Waking, she lay against Avant, the cedar scent of him filling her nose. His strong arms encircled her, and she felt safe. Too safe, too comfortable. And all too vulnerable. Fear struck her heart.

The candle had burned down, but the faint glow from the fireplace threw soft shadows around the room. She hadn't meant to spend the night. Moving gently, she tried to slip from his arms without waking him, but he tightened his grip and pulled her closer.

"Stay for a little bit longer." His words in her mind seeped into her and she couldn't move.

He held her with a strength that promised protection from any danger and comfort through any sorrow. The last thing she wanted to do was leave. Her heart drummed blissfully, but her head warned of the trauma to follow such a careless act. She should go. Now. He reached up and stroked her hair. Trails of desire followed the path of his fingers.

Since the incident in the cave, he'd been closed and formal. Even at Christmas, he barely touched her when she hugged him, making it easier for her to keep a distance, but now all those emotions flooded back. Like a night of too much drinking, it felt so good, but she would pay the price in the morning.

"I need to go," she whispered.

He held on and dropped his face into her hair, breathing in deeply. Sensing his struggle, she lay perfectly still, afraid to stay but despising to go. The silence pressed in.

Finally relenting, he released her.

Quickly sliding out, she hurried from his bed. She lay in her dark, cold room, imagining the warmth of his arms securely around her.

She tried not to love him, tried to deny her heart, but she always ended back at the same place.

Why had she gone there? Couldn't it have waited until morning? It seemed like such an obvious mistake now, but she'd been so scared. She buried her head into her pillow, preparing for the onslaught of pain, which obligingly came.

The next morning Abby lay awake when Helean came bustling in. After dressing quickly, she padded downstairs.

Avant waited at the kitchen table for her. Her heart caught in her throat. He didn't normally eat breakfast with her. Looking up, he smiled casually as if nothing had happened. *Damn him! How does he do that?* She had to work on just keeping herself upright. He gave her his typical look of sympathy, and she nearly slapped it off his face. Shooting him a glare, she sat and started eating.

"We need to decide when to leave. It will be a hard journey, but spring is coming early, and I sense the weather will be in our favor."

"How long will we be gone?" she asked, not meeting his gaze.

"I expect it will take at least ten days. We can be ready in two days' time. I plan on taking the bridge in the north valley to a trail through the lower range of the Labyrinthum Hills and then up to the Massilia Pass." He drummed his long fingers on the table and looked around in contemplation. "You'll need warmer clothes, and we will need traveling packs with provisions. We can take the horses as far as the mountain trail and leave them in the valley hills to graze while we travel the mountains on foot. I've journeyed there and know of several shelters along the way."

Avant had apparently not slept either but had spent the remainder of the night mapping out the trip. With that thought, he captured her gaze. Her heart leapt. For a brief moment his eyes were unguarded and filled with—

He quickly looked away.

The next two days were spent in a flurry of preparations. Petra wouldn't speak to or even look at her, and Helean took every opportunity to tell her every horror story of the mountain trails. *I am so looking forward to this trip.*

Avant went to the village for traveling clothes and bulky fur coats. He purchased her boy's clothing, because he said it didn't make sense for her to wear a skirt. *Sure. Now I get to wear pants.* Helean packed dried fruits and meat, crackers, and some cheeses.

Avant put in some spiced wine and their favorite panas from the bakery.

Packing the leather travel bag, Abby included a change of clothes, extra stockings, her first aid kit, and a warm blanket.

She tried to talk with Petra, but he was too hurt to have a conversation. Not angry out of jealousy, he was worried for them. He'd lost so much in his life, and she and Avant were all the family he had. She understood. They were the only family she had, too.

On the eve before they left, Petra sat next to her in the parlor. He took her hand in his. "I wish I could go with you. My heart feels like it's ripping from me. I know Avant will keep you safe but—"

She wrapped her arms around him. "I know. I wish I didn't have to go." A heavy sigh blew from her lips.

Somehow she knew if she didn't go, her destiny would find her anyway. She preferred to meet it on her own terms rather than be hunted down and dragged away. It wasn't just Avant that she loved. She loved it all: the manor, Petra, Helean, the village, even the disgusting chickens. She loved her life. But more than that, Abby loved who she was—who she'd become—and the thought of giving it up was like losing her world all over again.

Chapter Nineteen

Big flakes floated to the ground, draping everything in a priestly mantle of white. Abby held out her hand to catch one that melted against her skin. Catching snow was as elusive as finding a home. A chill hovered in the air, but the wind wasn't bitter. Avant loaded the horses, insisting they get an early start.

Petra hugged her tightly. "Abby, take care not to fall off the mountain." His hand pressed her head to his chest. "And come back so I can even the score of our chess matches."

She hugged him around the waist and kissed his cheek. "Good-bye, honey. Take care of yourself. I'll be back as soon as I can." A knot caught in her throat, and she didn't know if she could go.

"I am not certain when we shall return but certainly not before a month's time. You have all you need for the fief. I know it will be in the best hands." Avant placed his hand on Petra's shoulder.

"A month? You'll be fortunate if you come back and I haven't taken over as lord." Petra smiled and hugged Avant briskly.

Petra stood silently in the door of the stables as they mounted the horses and rode away.

Heavy wool clothes and fur coats insulated them from the elements. She wasn't sure what kind of fur it was, but her body warmed as if she snuggled near the fireplace in the parlor.

They followed the road through the northern part of the valley and across the Itehris River at the northern bridge. The winter wonderland was a spectacle to see. Cardinals sat on leafless branches and snow carpeted the meadows, leaving only a path for the stream.

She'd never traveled this way. All the settlement and activity seemed to be south. There were a few farms scattered about but after that, only rolling hills Avant called the Fiat Foothills.

Avant pointed at the trail ahead. "There's a small village on the edge of the settlements that we can reach by nightfall. Tonight we'll stay at the local inn."

By Abby's internal calendar, it was early March, but spring hadn't come to the Freelands. Avant thought the weather would be mild, but apparently his idea of mild was different from hers. She let her gaze linger on him as she did sometimes when he couldn't see her. Being around him every day had given her even more insight.

Though she knew him intimately, his persistence and work ethic astonished her. His straight back and squared shoulders said he was ready for the journey, but there was an urgency in his manner that compelled him forward.

It chaffed her a little that he didn't seem the mildest bit concerned about the sacrifice she was making. Who knew what this journey would bring? He wished nothing more than to plunge headlong into the task, regardless of what it cost.

Three nights ago when she dreamed of the lights, she knew her life would change. On this path, the fear of the unfamiliar engulfed her. Something in her heart shifted, as if a rope of destiny pulled her toward whatever loomed at the end of the road. Her life depended on the success of this trip, and what she found would change her forever.

"Avant, after Aesdil tried to kill you and you knew your life was lost, how did you find the will to make a new life?"

"Hossa and Annova. They took me in and healed my wounds. Annova spoke to my heart when Darkness threatened to overtake me. Had it not been for her, I would have abandoned all that was good."

"Is that why you're helping me, because you understand how it feels to lose your life?"

"I'm helping you because I know you are the Chosen, The Seed of Light."

"You didn't have to help me, Avant. You could've dumped me on any doorstep in the village, but you brought me to your home." Her heart twisted in a knot and pain shot through her chest. She'd deceived herself into believing Avant was helping her because he cared about her, not because she was the Chosen.

"I'd waited more than twenty years for justice and restoration. I knew you were The One who could finally help me. You needed to be trained. I was the only one who could do that."

An avalanche of grief fell, and she couldn't breathe. She'd refused to consider he was only helping her to get what he wanted most: his wife. She'd been such a fool. He'd told her of his intent on the day of the Implanting, but she hadn't listened. Devoted to his wife, he bridled to be reunited with her. Abby's love for him had blinded her. He felt something for her. She was sure, but it wasn't enough. Only enough to retreat from his feelings so as not to hurt her. Only enough to give her sympathy. Not enough to give his heart. The story of her life.

In the daily routine of the fief, she'd thought he'd eventually realize his feelings for her, but now she recognized the error in her logic. He had held her at bay so he could reunite with his wife, not because he couldn't accept his feelings.

She stifled a sob, staring blankly at the reigns in her hands. "I hope I don't let you down."

"We'll succeed in this, Abigail, or we'll die trying."

A pain ripped through her heart. He was willing to die to get Sentieve back, and apparently, he was willing for her to die, too. Alone as she'd ever been, she'd been lying to herself with ideas of family and love. Annova was right. The fief wasn't her home. Nowhere was.

In the dark cave-in of her heart, she struggled to hold back the depression and hopelessness.

They rode the rest of the day in silence and came to the inn before dusk. She said an early good night to Avant, telling him she was tired from riding all day and wanted to get some sleep, which was true enough.

Riding out before dawn, they traveled the mountain pass toward the lower ranges. They journeyed the next two days through the hills, edging closer to the heights of the great mountains. The snow had stopped, but the wind picked up. The ride became miserable.

The desire to quit and run back to the fief consumed her. But even if Avant would've let her go, it would never be the same again. He seemed so driven, as if he could see his long-awaited desire and rushed toward it. How could she blame him? He'd waited so long and suffered so much. Her heavy heart burdened Imperial, and the mare lagged under the weight.

On the fourth day, they stopped for the evening in a shelter of thick trees with an overhang of rock. Avant coaxed a fire. She unpacked the supplies and unsaddled the horses. Using her Gift, she spoke to Imperial, telling the mare not to run off but to graze in the field until their return. The farmer of the land agreed to watch over the horses and shelter them until their return.

She and Avant had barely spoken. Both were absorbed in their thoughts. Abby, burdened by the fear of the unknown, nursed her wounded heart. They ate a quiet dinner.

Avant studied her, his eyes full of concern. "Abigail, you've been much in thought the last few days. Rarely have I seen you so quiet, and you've gotten so skilled with your Gift, I scarcely know what you're thinking anymore. Is anything wrong?"

Not meeting his gaze, she shook her head. "I'm worried about finding this man. Who is he, anyway?"

The weight of his stare fell on her. "His name is Naphen. Do you not have memories of him from me?"

"I think I do." She searched and found a hazy recollection of a man in the mountains.

"He was the high priest before my father. He is a great man who sees clearly the workings of the Light. I came to him many years ago after my life was stolen. He helped me. He told me how my father was murdered, and he gave me these." Avant unsheathed his sword and handed the hilt to her. She fingered the beautiful cabochon stones. "They'd been entrusted to him by his son, Jo-Naphen. They are the sapphires from the Crown of Light. He held them for me."

"Because you're the rightful king of Jastain?" A vision dawned in her mind. For a brief moment, she saw Avant not as he was, but as he would be. Regardless of what he believed, this journey wasn't about Sentieve; it was about him becoming who he was born to be.

And as quickly as it came, the vision vanished.

"My Gift has told me that I am to be king. There are many who believe that I am, but no one knows for certain. Jo-Naphen took the final prophecy, which named the new king. Without that prophecy, we may never know who the rightful ruler of Jastain is."

Clarity of vision came to her and understanding flooded her mind. Her throat tightened. Chills spread across her body as tiny hairs stood on end. Her voice broke as she spoke. "Jo-Naphen was the scribe who took the Crown from the king, and Naphen is his father?"

"Yes." He narrowed his eyes.

She gasped for a breath and remained quiet a long time. Softly, she said, "My father's name was Jonathan. Did you know that? In my dream, the voice said I needed to seek the way in the house of my father's father."

Avant looked blankly at her, as if he didn't understand what she meant.

"You don't think I could be related to this man, do you?"

Avant's voice was quiet and filled with wonder. "Abigail, the voice of the Light is truth. Yes, I believe you could be."

Could her dad really be the scribe who escaped with the Crown and prophecy? Was it possible that this land was her rightful heritage? Her destination suddenly seemed more urgent.

*****

Avant lay awake, staring through the trees at the frosty night sky. The clouds had cleared, and the stars shown like beacons to far-off places with horseless carriages. Although he loved sleeping outdoors, the conversation with Abigail had unsettled him. Truth be told, her demeanor unsettled him. Something was wrong. Her heart grieved in loss. Initially, he assumed it was leaving the fief, but now it seemed like more. The sly twinkle in her eye was replaced with a burden she seemed too weary to carry alone, but as of yet, she had refused to share.

Reaching to his ear, he twisted the stud that pierced his lobe. How the Stone of Light could come to such a young woman had puzzled him. He smiled ruefully. Could she be the granddaughter of Naphen? It certainly explained many things about her circumstances—and her personality. Remembering her disdain for the philosophical, he laughed out loud and quickly glanced over to make certain he hadn't woken her. Yes. It made sense.

He'd come to care for this young woman, and prayed the Light would watch over her during what was certain to be a long and arduous journey. She'd trained as well as any soldier in his company, and although he never told her, he was proud of her. Her Gift and conditioning was without equal of any woman he'd known. Aye, and most men, too. Though she fought him stubbornly, she was as prepared as she could be, and he took solace in that.

At the end of this journey waited the Crown of Light. The task of restoring the kingdom fell to him and Abigail, but ruling would be his alone, and much needed to be done. Sentieve would have to decide if she wished to remain queen. He blew out a heavy breath and the mist of it lingered in the air above him.

His wife had not dominated his thoughts. It had been months since he dreamt of her, although his dreams were far from empty. He gazed at the beauty sleeping near him. Her golden hair spilled across the fur of her covers. He fisted his hands in his own fur, and a pain stabbed his heart.

Near enough to touch, but too far to hold.

*****

Her dad sat in the darkened study. The light on his desk illuminated the room in a golden glow. A young Abby entered, though she wasn't supposed to disturb him. Frightened he would scold her, she ducked her head. But when he saw her, his face lit with joy, and he held his arms open wide. She ran to him, and he picked her up, setting her in his lap.

"My angel, I've missed you. Have I told you how proud of you I am? I know this has been hard, but you're Chosen. Everything you need you will find here, Abigail, but you must guard your heart. I love you." His voice remained strong, but the vision faded.

"I love you, too. I love you, Daddy." The sound of her own voice woke her. Crying quietly in her blanket, she wished she could talk to Petra. He always knew what to say.

After the dream, she couldn't go back to sleep. Her mind flashed with too many thoughts. Rising before dawn, she quietly started packing and then stopped to gaze at Avant's peaceful face. Her heart beat unevenly with an ache. She walked to the stream, deciding to wake him after she returned.

Leaning over to splash her face with water, she startled at the sight of the familiar sparkling skin.

"Hello, Abby," the lovely voice chimed. "It has been a while since last we met."

She looked up into the face of the strange creature—she hadn't remembered how charming it was until now. "How do you know my name, Seppitent?"

"I know a great many things about you, Abby." It smiled. "We're alike, you and I. We can survive in different worlds and find the treasures in each."

She said nothing but looked at him with distrust.

He gazed back with hypnotic eyes and pleasantly sang, "You can talk to me, Abby. I'm a friend. It pains me how your companion uses you, stringing you along to get what he wants. The queen's true love treats you so cruelly."

A thorn pierced her heart, and the creature gave a sad sympathetic sound like a lover's lament. His voice lilted, "You don't have to complete this task, Abby. It will only mean ruin for you. Turn back, and everything will be as it was."

That was a lie! Nothing was the same, and it would never be again. She knew that as surely as she knew her own heart. A light amassed around her, illuminating his deception. She immediately saw the creature for what he truly was: a hideous thing, full of loathing, despicable and vile.

It was about to say something when the light grew in Abby's heart. She found the strength to lift a large rock with her mind and hurl it toward him. The stone struck the creature in the head and shattered to dust. Through the noise, she couldn't hear his poisoned words.

In her mind and with her voice, as loud as she could thunder, she yelled, *"You're a liar, Seppitent, and you must begone!"*

He laughed hideously, the sound scrapping her soul. He vanished.

She'd been an idiot to speak to him! He almost had her bound in his spell. The tentacles of melody he'd wrapped in her mind still had her dazed. After splashing water on her face, she turned to find Avant behind her, his sword drawn.

"Abigail, are you all right? I heard you scream. What happened?" He looked at her as if afraid of what she might say.

"It was Seppitent." She couldn't meet his gaze.

"You know his words are lies. He twists and manipulates the truth to cause pain and sow distrust. Do not believe him." He pleaded with her. "Please look at me."

She looked into his eyes with a coldness she'd never communicated before. "Some of what he said was a lie."

He reached toward her. She flinched.

"Please do not let this creature divide us. You are too important to me."

"Yes, ironically, I know I am, Avant. Don't worry. This won't hinder our task." She brushed past him. "But now we need to go." The thorn in her heart throbbed like someone pounded it with a hammer.

Chapter Twenty

Abby stared up at the sky. A cold, empty feeling stole through her bones like a thief. The sun shone through the high wispy clouds but gave no warmth, and bitter wind bit into her face.

They packed up the camp in silence and ate a meager breakfast, setting out on the climb through the lowest mountains. Leaving some of the supplies at the campsite for the return trip, they took with them only the minimum required. Pressing against the piercing gusts and steep incline, Abby couldn't shake the feeling that Darkness loomed.

Her mind still reeled from the incident with Seppitent—and Avant. He wouldn't look her in the face and hadn't said a word since that morning. The hurt in his eyes caused her pain. But the question kept swirling in her thoughts like the strong winter gales: Had she not been the Chosen One, would Avant have helped her?

What difference did it make? She pulled the fur tight around her body, trying to staunch the chill. Finding her purpose was the most important thing. She journeyed to her destiny, her family, and anything else could only be on the periphery. Pushing Avant from her mind, she focused on other things.

What would Naphen be like? Would he know who she was? She replayed the dream with her dad. A longing to know him pulsed inside. Had he really fled Jastain? Her dad, the prophet. It certainly answered some questions. But why hadn't he told her?

Steep and unrelenting, the path mired their progress, but her body responded valiantly to the challenge. Avant had made good on his promise to prepare her. Physically she was ready for the grueling road. Emotionally—well, that was a different story.

They made good time to a sheltering cave in the cleft of the mountain. Avant gathered wood and started a fire. She unpacked and made up their beds for the night. The cold sliced through to the bone, the temperature dropping further as the sun sank. Avant sneezed and shivered. Abby fixed an offering of dried beef and the last of the panas.

After they ate, Avant finally broke the silence. "Abigail, please talk to me. This is not merely about Seppitent. You've been distant since we left the fief. What have I done to offend you?" Bloodshot eyes encased in dark circles implored her to open up to him, but her heart was too hurt to budge.

"You haven't done anything to offend me. I'm fine. Really. I've just realized the true nature of our friendship, and the importance of our task. We need to find my family and get you back yours." She stared into the flickering fire as it danced in the draft of the inlet.

The weight of his gaze rested on her, but she didn't meet it.

"Abigail, you are my family, as I hope I'm part of yours."

"Your wife might have something to say about that. I know I would if I were her." She looked him in the face.

His blue gaze penetrated like ice daggers. His voice rasped hoarsely and hinted at his frustration. "My wife will love anyone I love and welcome them."

She narrowed her eyes and shook her head. For such a wise man, he had no clue about women. "Really? You don't think she'll mind our Harvest Festival dances or midnight conversations in the dark? What about picnic dinners in secret caves?" She glared at him. "She must be very understanding."

Avant rubbed his brow. "Regardless of what you think, you're family to me, and I expect you to be in my life. I understand, in the beginning, your feelings were a little confused, but I thought we were past that."

He did not just say that! How could he be so dense? The anger flew from her like a vicious wasp with intent to harm. "You're right, Avant. I was a little *confused,* but I've been thinking, I should take a lover. It shouldn't be difficult to find one."

His voice lowered an octave, and his eyes flashed with that familiar flame of jealousy. "That is not how things are done here, Abigail!"

Knowing she'd hit her target, she pressed on. "Why not? I have no commitments. I'm very fond of Petra, and you know how he feels about me. Just think, if things work out, you could walk me down the aisle at our wedding, and could even be like a grandfather to our children. What a perfect family we could be, now that I'm not *confused* anymore."

She knew her sarcasm struck a low blow, and he couldn't have looked more shocked if she'd slapped him across the face. Had he never considered the situation? Maybe he hadn't wanted to, but those blue eyes reflected a revelation that appeared as unwelcome as Seppitent. He spoke no more but continued to sneeze and shiver.

The cold night formed a barrier between them, and the wind beat at her body. She huddled, stiff and miserable, under her fur but still felt like she slept in only her shirtsleeves. Avant coughed and shuffled under his covers.

An hour before sunrise she got up and started packing. Avant shivered and rose. He looked worse than he had the night before.

She stopped and studied him. "Are you going to be all right today?"

"I will be fine. Are you ready?" His voice croaked and his cough rumbled deep in his chest.

They ate a small breakfast. She pulled a leather pouch from her bag and handed it to him. "You might feel better if you drank some spiced wine."

He looked at her. Snatching the pouch, he gulped the contents.

They climbed switchbacks across the face of the mountain for most of the day. Avant followed behind. This, more than anything else, told her how sick he was. He hated following anyone, and his pride wouldn't let him get too far behind, though he struggled for breath in the high altitude.

By late afternoon, though still cold, they'd gotten a reprieve from the piercing wind. Abby stopped to take a break, and Avant sat on a rock next to her. His chest rattled as he gasped.

"You can't continue like this. Is there a shelter nearby where we can stop for the day?"

He put his head in his hands. Then lifting his gaze, he scanned the area. "I believe there is a cave on the next switchback right above us, but the trail leads away from here before climbing back."

She threw her head back and studied the cliff. A flat rock about twenty-five feet directly overhead created the next level of switchbacks. They might be able to scale the side of the mountain to reach it directly instead of following the trail all the way around. "Do you think you could climb this cliff to the next landing?"

Looking up, he calculated for a minute. "I think so, as long as the wind doesn't start blowing again."

They found a place where the mountain jutted out, giving them more protection and a grip of the rocks as they climbed. Avant climbed up first, and she followed. Straining her newly conditioned muscles, the cliff proved a challenge. If either of them slipped, they risked falling several stories down the mountain. Taking a deliberate path, they carefully placed feet and hands as they scaled the rock wall.

They climbed for thirty minutes, making it more than halfway to the top. It would have taken another three hours to walk the trail around. Avant set a slower pace than he would normally, but he made sure his feet were securely planted before pulling up each step. Abby followed about eight feet below him. Her arms burned and sweat rolled into her eyes even in the cold.

After a little more than an hour, he finally reached the top and pulled himself up. She continued, but as she reached for the ledge her fingers lost their grip. Her foot slipped. She closed her eyes. A fall was imminent.

A strong hand clasped her forearm and pulled her up.

She fell against the sturdy wall of his chest. He wrapped her in his arms. His body burned with fever, and he shook. The thorn in her heart throbbed, and though he'd saved her, she couldn't bring herself to reach out to him. She pulled away without a word and left him there.

Avant made a fire while Abby unpacked the supplies. Hopelessness overwhelmed her. The thorn in her heart bit her in two like the piercing mountain blasts.

Avant continued to cough and wheeze, but rose the next morning to continue their journey. They filled their water bottles in the mountain stream. She gave him Tylenol from the first aid kit to help keep his fever down, but feared he might be getting pneumonia. He wouldn't look her in the eyes at all anymore. Their silence widened the gulf and made their harsh journey more miserable.

On the seventh day of climbing, they came to a small footpath off the trail. They walked the little path for an hour. A heavy wooden door emerged right from the side of the mountain. Avant banged on the door, but no one answered. He tried the knob. The door swung open. Darkness engulfed everything inside.

He turned to face her. "You wait here. I will go in and make sure it's safe."

She shook her head, her mouth making a tight, straight line. "I'm going with you."

He closed his eyes and took a leveling breath. His chest rattled. He gave her a frustrated nod.

Avant stepped in first, keeping her directly behind him. As their sight adjusted to the dark room, they saw bright orange coals burning in the stone fireplace, revealing a small sofa and side table.

Avant called out, "Naphen, it is Avant. Is anyone here?" A rustling noise from another room broke through the silence.

He turned to look directly into her eyes. With a voice the brooked no opposition, he spoke into her mind. *"You stay here. I will call to you if it is safe."*

Abby shrank at his fierce gaze and nodded. With his hands clasped on the hilt of his sword, he stole into the shadows.

She stood in the faint embers' glow and strained her senses. Her heart pounded in her chest. Whispers and quiet murmurs floated through the air.

After a while Avant returned, his face pale and his eyes filled with a stew of emotions too tangled to name. His hands shook. He closed his eyes as he spoke. "Abigail, Naphen is ill. His time of passing is near. He has been waiting to see you. Do you want me to go in with you?"

"I'll go alone."

He clearly wanted to come with her, but he nodded and stepped aside.

The room was hewn into the rock. Naphen lay on a straw bed, covered in a patchwork quilt. The frail man looked at least a hundred years old, and his wispy white hair was in disarray. His blue-green eyes sparkled, lucid and bright, but the skin on his weak body grayed with fatigue. He raised a wrinkled knobby hand, motioning her to his bedside.

Warmth covered her as he took her hand, although his fingers felt cool. Tenderness for this little man filled her heart.

He spoke in a gravely whisper. "Child, you come to seek the wisdom of an old man, and I have only my love to give. I've wished to see you many times, and now my desire is fulfilled." His eyes twinkled with love that filled her from crown to feet. Her grandfather.

"I didn't know you existed. I'm sorry for missing time with you, but I'm here now." Her voice cracked and tears pooled. All she'd ever wanted was a family and to feel she belonged. She leaned over and hugged his frail body and kissed the top of his head. Her tears fell on his cheek.

Using the last of his life to speak, he labored for each breath. "Child, I am your past. Release the hardness in your heart, and you will find your way. I'm sorry for what you've lost, but it is the journey that allows the Light within you to shine. It was always there." His eyes closed. There was nothing she could do but hold his hand.

He breathed one final breath, smiled, and was gone. She sat there clasping the bony fingers, holding on to the only piece of her history she knew. Mourning the loss of a man she hadn't known, she imagined her dad as a boy in this land. She imagined them together. They'd been great prophets of the Light. They'd been her family. And like everything else, they were gone.

Abby let go and went to find Avant. He knelt at the fireplace, preparing a hot meal over the flame. He rose, faced her.

"He's gone." She looked past him into the fire.

Avant walked over and reached out to embrace her. At his touch, a cold wind blew away the warmth of the old man, and she flinched. He dropped his arm.

Though she felt the plea in his gaze, she couldn't meet it. "We should bury him."

"Aye, he has it all prepared. He told me where." He continued to study her as if he thought she might crumble.

Her face void of emotion, she looked at him, feeling nothing but emptiness. She didn't have anything inside to reach out to him, and even if she did, she didn't want to.

They ate porridge before taking the frail body for burial. He'd dug his own grave down the trail in a small wooded area. Dug his own grave. Abby couldn't fathom the years he'd spent alone on this mountain.

With Naphen wrapped in the quilt, Avant carried him to the grave and gently laid him down. He sang a lament as he shoveled the dirt over Naphen, prophet of the Light, her grandfather. His strong baritone penetrated like a sword, and she bled her grief into the ground.

They lingered a few more days.

Naphen had lived simply in his mountain dwelling, having few possessions. She took a small stack of writings from a wooden box and a pewter candle stand from his bedside.

On the evening of the third day after his death, Avant spoke. "We must leave tomorrow to return to the fief."

She wanted to stay longer, to hold on to the small glimpse of her past, but there was no reason. She'd lost the only connection as soon as she'd found him. This place held nothing more for her.

The thought of returning to Petra filled the ache inside. She'd missed him so much. His calm practicality and the way he made her laugh was the healing she needed. She still hadn't spoken to Avant about what Naphen said. She hadn't really spoken to Avant about anything. Every time she started to, a sharp icy pain would pierce her heart.

Warm light illuminated her father's study. She read a parchment, and the rays glowed from the paper, revealing the room. The familiar voice—the one she couldn't place— said, "It is time to return. Seek the Light in the house of your father and there you will find your Way."

Abby shot up from the sofa and went to the writings in her pack. She'd already read each page several times but hadn't seen anything that might help her. She lit a candle and read through each one again.

Chapter Twenty-One

Abby slung her pack over her shoulder and gazed around the hewn hole in the rock.

Avant held the door open and allowed her to walk through.

"We'll travel a different path on the return trip. It's higher up the mountain in the Inubibus Range but eliminates two days of switchbacks. The weather was harsh on the journey here, but now I believe it will hold for us."

Their stay in the mountain home had helped him, but a faint rattle still sounded in his chest.

Silence continued to grow between them, and other than to communicate something of necessity, they never spoke. Avant gave her glances that invited her to open up in dialogue, but she wasn't ready. He'd been respectful of her solitude and given her space to grieve, taking extended walks or gathering wood and water. He prepared all the meals and cleaned up afterward. His domesticity made her almost smile, but she couldn't bring herself to look him in the eyes. It hurt too much.

On the second day of travel, they stopped at a cave off the peak of one of the mountains. It appeared more of a fissure in the rock caused by some cataclysm rather than a formation. The terrain had been easier to climb, but the wind blew fiercely across the trail. At times, Abby feared they might be blown off.

Avant went to gather wood while she unpacked. It was the routine they'd adopted, each of them understanding their place and counting on the other to fulfill their task. She pulled her blanket and fur from her pack.

The ferocious roar of a mountain lion slashed through the silence. Avant cried out in pain. Abby's heart skipped a beat. The sound of a struggle ensued.

She dropped the bag and bolted to him. Fear banded around her chest. Panic struck her like lightning, and all the hair on her body stood at attention. The first thing that came to her mind was *what if...*

She yelled and reached for his mind. *"Avant?"*

No answer.

As she reached the scene, she saw the animal pinning Avant, crushing him into the ground. Her mind buzzed. *Think, Abs.*

She focused her energy. *"Stop, animal! In the name of the Light, stop!"*

The lion lifted its head from Avant's shoulder, its mouth covered in his blood. A shriek tore from her lips. For a moment, it seemed as if the animal would attack her. Then it bounded up the rocks and disappeared.

She ran to Avant, who lay unconscious on the ground. The faint movement of his chest proved he lived, but blood seeped from a deep gash high on his right bicep and from a bite on his lower left abdomen. His clothes hung in tatters around his bloody body. *Calm yourself and think.*

She bolted back to the cave and grabbed her first aid kit. Sprinting back to his side, she dumped the contents and found a roll of heavy gauze. A piece of ripped clothing served as a tourniquet. She wrapped his arm tightly. The wound on his stomach didn't appear as serious once it had been cleaned, and she realized most if it was just the scar from an old injury. After dressing the wound, she tapped his face to wake him, but he didn't respond.

The sun sank. Soon it would be dark. She needed to get him in the cave, but she couldn't lift him by herself. Pacing the ground, she tried to think of a way to maneuver him, but he was too heavy. *Too heavy?*

She'd moved pieces of furniture three times his weight. Hope sprang in her heart. She *could* move him.

Concentrating her energy, Abby saw the light reflecting from her, dancing around him. He levitated off the ground and into the cave. She lowered him gently to the floor. Pinching her eyes closed, she staved off a torrent of tears and heaved a sigh.

Inside, she set up camp. A feral stench and carcasses of dead animals littered the back of the deep fissure, obviously the home of the mountain lion, which explained why it had attacked so viciously. It was gone now, and she didn't have time to worry if it was coming back.

She laid out the blankets and furs, gathered wood, and unpacked the supplies. How was she going to start a fire? Avant always did that, and she'd never paid much attention. She removed his torn clothes, cleaned his wounds, and moved him to the pallet before she set her attention on the fire.

For kindling, she placed small, dry leaves and brush around and on top of the larger limbs in the fire pit. Taking the flint from his pocket, she struck it with a pair of scissors from the first-aid kit. Sparks flew and a small amount of the kindling caught fire. She nursed the little flame for a long while before it began to burn the wood. Then she piled on more wood until heat filled the space.

Avant shivered from fever and shock. She sat next to him and tried to give him some water. Most of it ran out. Freshly clotted blood caked the deep scratches down his torso, and bruises colored the length of his body.

The vulnerability of his condition and the innocence of his face as he slept caused Abby's heart to expel the painful thorn left by Seppitent. The depth of her love for him swept over her, love she hadn't allowed herself to feel in months. In her pain, she'd been callous and hurtful, withholding kindness. What if he didn't wake up?

She whispered his name. *Avant.* "Avant, I need you. I can't do this without you, and I don't want to."

Brushing the hair from his face, she caught the glint of something at his ear. She pushed the brown waves away to reveal the diamond. He'd pierced his ear? She twisted the stud. He'd worn it for a while. Drawing in a ragged breath, she stroked his hair. What would she do without him?

A prayer spilled from her lips. "Lord, you brought me here to help Avant regain his kingdom. I'm smart enough to know I can't do this by myself. But you can. Hands of grace cover me to do what you've spoken."

She slid next to Avant and wrapped her arms around him to keep him from shaking. He relaxed at her touch, and his tremors subsided into shivers.

About midnight, Avant finally stirred. Weakened and in pain, he couldn't speak or even keep his eyes open. Awake just long enough for Abby to get three pills and a cup of water down his throat, he passed out again. Once the Tylenol took hold, he stopped shivering and slept until just before dawn.

"What happened?" His voice was barely audible.

"You were attacked by a mountain lion. You're pretty roughed up, tough guy. You've been unconscious for most of the night."

Avant looked at her through a haze and winced when he tried to move. She gave him two more Tylenol, and after a few minutes, he slept until midmorning.

He appeared coherent but in more pain. His arm still bled so she redressed it. She'd held vigil at his side except to tend to the fire.

He swallowed the water she fed him. "How did I get in the cave?"

"I Implanted you here."

He closed his eyes and smiled weakly.

"Seems like your fever is broken, but you're weak. Get some rest. We're not going anywhere today." She brushed the hair from his face and stroked his cheek.

"You spoke to the lion—you stopped its attack." He tried to move so he could see her but couldn't manage.

He fell asleep, and Abby went to gather more wood for the fire.

They needed water. She'd used a good portion to clean Avant's wounds, and there was little left for them to drink. She hadn't stopped in the last few hours to think about much except taking care of him. For the first time since the attack, she realized how much she'd changed.

She took a cooking pot outside and filled it with fresh snow. Placing the pot next to the fire, she went to gather wood.

Walking a distance from the cave, she gathered small limbs.

A clearing emerged ahead. Light hit the space in a strange way that seemed unnatural, as if rising from the ground. The wind blew hair in her eyes, but the brightness drew her. She stepped from among the trees into the light. A gasp escaped her. The unhindered view caught her breath and her eyes widened, taking in the sight. She stood on a precipice that hung out from the mountain. A panoramic vista of the rich and fertile world of Jastain lay before her.

The biggest peaks rose like giant knees beside her to the northeast and spread to the lap of the valley all the way to the sea. The trail that would take her home wound through the rock like a giant thread. Down below, to the east, sat the kingdom of Aesdil. A dark haze hovered over the city. Fresh green draped the rest of the land but neglected the castle. Her heart grieved to see the beauty of her world covered by Darkness. She hissed out a breath and desire revealed itself—to stop the Darkness from overtaking her simple, unspoiled world.

She swept her gaze over the Valley of Umbra, where she'd first come to Jastain. A smile touched her face as the memory of that day replayed.

From up on the heights, everything below seemed small and quiet. Nothing down there could stop her from accomplishing her task and fulfilling her destiny. No power that roamed the land could hinder the Light from returning. For a brief moment, a bright ray broke through the haze, and the castle walls glistened in its path.

The power and grace of the mountains filled her lungs, and she gazed to the heavens, marveling at the nearness of His majesty. The revelation of a prepared plan lay before her.

Destiny provided the truest thing in her life. The thing that made her who she was—The One, the Chosen, the Seed of Light—and she *would* restore Light to the kingdom she loved. She drank in the vista as if the sight filled her with necessary fuel to accomplish her task and complete her journey.

It was after midday when she finally returned to check on Avant.

He sat ashen and concerned on the edge of his pallet. "Where were you? You've been gone for hours."

She dumped the wood and rushed to check him. "I'm sorry. I went to gather wood and get water. I didn't mean to scare you." She studied his face and inspected his dressings. "Lay down. I'll warm some water, and we can both bathe. Then we'll eat."

His shook his head, and his eyes filled with wonder. He repeated her words, "'I plan parties and go shopping. I don't restore kingdoms of Light.' *Indeed?* I suspect now, my lady, you can do whatever you will."

For the first time in a long time, she gazed without pain into those blue eyes. "Well, if that's true, it's because of you." Then she smiled seductively. "Now, take off all your clothes."

His jaw fell and his face paled.

She giggled impishly. "So I can wash them."

He chuckled and winced.

Abby washed first and then helped Avant. She rinsed out his hair, matted with sweat, and gently cleansed his bruised body covered with dried blood.

She bit her lip and sighed. Under other circumstances, sponge-bathing Avant might have been a pleasurable experience. However, his broken body and stubborn pride made it worse than trying to help Lyndsea bathe her cat that time in high school. Abby giggled under her breath, remembering how they'd both ended up in the tub as Skittles hid behind the toilet. Maybe that had been worse. Avant growled when she hit a tender spot on his chest. Maybe not.

When she finished, she kissed his forehead. "Well, at least the beast didn't scratch your face, pretty boy."

He rolled his eyes, not amused.

After redressing his wounds, she secured clean bandages. The pain and stiffness limited his movements, so she dressed him in clean clothes and fed him. He made known his displeasure with her coddling by continuously telling her how she could do things better.

"Guess what, Commander? Next time somebody gets shred to ribbons, you can do it your way, okay?"

She washed their clothes in hot water and laid them by the fire to dry.

It took six more days before Avant was able to travel a little way, but each day he grew stronger. After his brush with the mountain lion and her mountaintop experience, her heart had healed and hope sprang up. She still loved Avant; she would never stop loving him. But her purpose was clear. Whatever he decided would have no bearing on what happened now. She didn't think any more about the future. She had enough to do in the present.

A week after Avant's attack, they packed up and traveled the path. He could move without too much pain in his side, but his arm remained immobile in a sling.

"We have at least five days before reaching home."

He seemed different, too, but Abby couldn't put her finger on what exactly made her think that. He certainly hadn't lost any of his pride. Though he knew full well she could set up camp, he insisted on gathering wood and starting the fire himself—with one good arm. She rolled her eyes as she watched him struggle with a pile of kindling.

The mountain lion had broadsided him and knocked him cold before he could even use his Implanting on the beast. She knew he viewed the attack as a failure on his part, but she was finally glad to see he wasn't actually Superman.

The travel wore heavily on him, and she made sure he ate everything she gave him. He slept deeply during the night and strengthened daily. Several times she caught him staring, but he looked away when discovered. What he was thinking?

Since the attack, they'd slept side by side, sharing their blankets and furs. It allowed for more comfort and warmth because they could pad the rock surface with his blankets and cover themselves with hers. The close proximity didn't bother her, and her lack of concern seemed to ease any apprehension Avant might have had.

They didn't always find a cave. Sometimes it was just an overhang to keep the elements out, but whenever a need arose, something emerged to meet it. They were guided by destiny, and Abby marveled at how everything fit perfectly into place. She was finally where she belonged and it wasn't a place—it was a purpose.

On the fifth day of travel, they reached the valley, finding the supplies they'd left and the horses nearby. The late afternoon sun beamed into the cave in blinding hues of orange as they set up camp for the night.

After they ate, Avant appeared to be deep in thought.

She watched. "What are you thinking about?"

"I'm concerned. I felt certain this trip would provide the next step in our journey. While I believe it was important, it has not yielded the answers I'd hoped. Frankly, I'm at a loss as to what to do next and I sense time is short."

She hadn't spoken to him about her experience on the mountain or the dream she had in Naphen's home. "I think I know where our next step has to be, but I'm not sure how to get there. The last night we were in Naphen's house, I had a dream of my father's study. And I realized that's where I need to go."

His brow furrowed, and his voice lowered an octave. "Why did you not tell me of this before? You're not going back there without me, Abigail."

She rolled her eyes. "Fine time to go all protective, Commander. It doesn't matter anyway. I don't know how to get back, so nobody's going anywhere until we can figure that out."

They both sat silently in thought.

Avant's face lit. "You told me the night you came here, you'd discovered this Chad and your friend had betrayed you?"

Abby wasn't sure where he was going with this, but she nodded. "Yes."

His face clouded in myriad emotions. He dropped his gaze and sighed heavily. "Did you know you almost left by Implanting in the cave at the falls? It took all my power to hold you and bring you out of your energy."

He showed Abby his memory of that evening. She'd glowed like a lantern. His energy had held her back as he called her name.

Since that evening, Abby had not spoken to Avant about the incident. Neither had she afforded herself permission to think about it. "I didn't realize that had happened. I just knew I had to get out of there." She looked up into the sky, trying to stave off her own memories.

Bringing her out of her thoughts, Avant spoke softly, "It seems emotional trauma opens that aspect of your ability. If you could recreate the energy of the emotions, then you could Implant."

"No way!" She frowned and furrowed her brow as she shot him a glare. "Why don't you relive the moment when you found out your wife married the man who tried to kill you?"

He held up his palms in peace. "Abigail, that isn't what I meant. I'm talking about the energy of your emotions. If you can recreate that energy, then the Placement Implanting will open to you."

Her shoulders relaxed. She considered it for a moment. With the other aspects of her Gift, she was able to concentrate her energy to Implant, but apparently teleportation had an emotional connection. "Do you have any idea how I can Implant without reliving the worst moments of my life?"

Sighing, he shook his head. "Not at this time, but allow me to think on it."

"Avant, can I ask you a question?"

He pulled a piece of grass from a tuft growing in the cave and nodded.

"How long have you been wearing the diamond earring?"

A brilliant smile lit his face brighter than she'd seen in months. "Since the day you gave it to me."

Her heart melted into her chest and she dropped her gaze to pick at a loose thread in the hem of her shirt. "Really? Who pierced your ear?"

"I did it."

She winced, imaging the pain. "Oh my God, how could you do that to yourself?"

"It was a small price to pay for the privilege of wearing it."

The words warmed her more deeply than the campfire. "I'm so glad you liked it. I wasn't sure, but I knew how you regarded it."

He gazed into the fire and then turned the full force of those blue eyes on her. "You gave me the best you had, and nothing you could have given me would have touched me more."

His words held strong emotion, and something she hadn't seen in a long time flicked over his face. Her heart sped up a few beats. What he'd said reminded her of something her dad might've said, and the thought of Jonathan Randall opened the floodgates of her mind in revelation. *Holy shit!*

Avant reached for her hand, their fingers barely touching. "Abigail, I—"

"Avant! My dad gave me these earrings. Do you think one of them is the missing Stone of Light?" She stared at the diamond in his ear and pulled her hand from his to touch the one in her own ear.

His eyes immediately shuttered to hide some emotion, and he studied her face. "Yes. I am certain one of them is the Stone of Light, but which one I cannot tell."

Chapter Twenty-Two

Evidence of spring teemed all around as they rode the northern valley. The freshly tilled fields offered proof that Petra had been busy planting crops and managing the lands. The early wildflowers bloomed in bright hues and colored the meadows like large pieces of confetti. The new growth of grass permeated the air in the sunshine as the horses trotted the dale.

As Avant predicted, they'd been gone thirty days, and early April fell upon them like the newly found peace that had descended on her.

Petra apparently heard their horses because he dashed out of the stables to greet them. At the sight of his face, Abby jumped from Imperial and rushed to him.

He picked her up and spun her around. "I'm glad you didn't get blown off the mountain." Squeezing her tightly, he rocked from side to side.

The scent of leather and hay and warm male tickled her nose. She exhaled into his chest like a heavy weight had been removed. "I'm so glad to see you. It was a hard trip." Pulling back to gaze into his face, she touched his cheek and smiled. "Avant was almost killed." She turned her head back to gesture at Avant over her shoulder, but flinched at the raging Titan in his eyes. Without a word, he dismounted Spiritus and stormed up to the house, leaving her and Petra in wide-eyed bewilderment to tend the horses.

"What was that about?" Petra narrowed his eyes as he watched Avant stomp into the house.

Abby bit her lip. "Oh, don't worry about him. He probably had something he needed to do." Her eyes lingered on the doorframe as he disappeared. Then she shook her head and focused on Petra. "So, anyway, he was attacked by a mountain lion, and I thought he was going to die."

They tended the horses, and she told Petra about meeting her grandfather, his death, Seppitent, and her horrible fight with Avant, leaving out one little part. She also told him about her mountain vista experience, something she hadn't told Avant.

After they'd cared for the horses, Petra had a few things to finish up, and she needed a bath. He promised to meet her for dinner at sunset.

"Abby, I missed you." Petra took her hands in his.

Staring into his brown eyes warmed her in a way that made her feel like she could never be cold again. "I missed you, too. I thought of you every day."

He smiled and pulled her close. She closed her eyes and allowed her heart to drink in his affection. Kissing the top of her head, he sent her off to the house.

She made her way into the kitchen, where Helean busied herself preparing dinner. When the little woman looked up, she squealed and dropped what she was doing to hug Abby. "My dear, the house has seemed so lonely. I haven't gotten a decent night's rest since you left."

"We're home safe now, and glad to be here, so you can sleep well tonight." Abby patted the sturdy little shoulders.

"I've got your bath water heating. It will be ready in a bit, my dear."

"Thanks, Helean. I've missed you." Abby kissed her on the cheek and hurried to soak in a hot tub.

She'd missed everything about home, but especially Petra.

What had gotten into Avant? Pursing her lips, she suspected she knew, but to dwell on it would open a whole can of emotions she wasn't prepared to consume.

After her bath, she sauntered to her room and combed out her wet hair. She put on clean clothes and padded downstairs to see if Helean needed help.

Hearing Avant and Petra talking in the parlor, she smiled and redirected. When she got to the door, Petra's voice stopped her short before she could enter.

"You are not in love with Abby; therefore you are not entitled to jealous rages!"

"What gives you the right to say such things to me?" Avant spoke in a low growl that meant he bordered on rage.

A lump formed in her throat, one she couldn't gulp down.

"My right is that I'm in love with Abby, and if it weren't for your mixed signals, she would love me, too. Let her go, Avant. You will only hurt her. Is that what you want?"

The breath left her lungs and chills crawled up and down her arms. *Oh my God.*

In theory, Abby knew Petra was in love with her. It was hard not to know, but to hear him say it out loud felt like warm liquid pouring over her. Was he right? Would she love him if not for Avant? He was her best friend, but *love him*?

Avant bit back, "How could you possibly know what my feelings are?"

"Are you really prepared to give up the hope that Sentieve will again be your wife? If you are, then you have my blessing to pursue Abby." Petra said the words with such contempt, Abby wasn't sure Avant wouldn't hit him.

"I do not need your *blessing*, Petra."

"Go ahead. Try to give her what she deserves."

"What do you mean *try* to give her what she deserves?" Avant's indignation flared, but he hadn't answered Petra's question about Sentieve.

She winced at the obvious sidestep.

"I don't think you can make her happy. I know her better than you. She talks to me, and I can assure you that you don't make her happy. You make her miserable."

"You have no idea what I *know* or what I *feel*, and you are now overstepping the bonds of our relationship, young landmaster."

To hear him speak to Petra like that wrenched her heart.

"Then let me leave you with this: If Abby is your heart's desire, you should let her know before you find she's in love with someone else." Petra stormed from the room and found her in the hall.

Her eyes widened. He paused to meet her gaze, and her cheeks flushed with heat. He gave her a soft laugh that held no humor and left her gaping after him.

Abby flitted in a fluster to the kitchen. Why hadn't she just gone here in the first place? She and Helean set the table and called the men in to eat.

Abby sat between them. They brooded and scowled at each other as they filled their plates. Whenever she tried to speak to Petra, Avant interrupted with questions about the planting of the fields.

After the third time, she threw her spork into her food and glared at Avant. "May I speak?"

He held up his hands as if he had no idea what she was talking about. "Of course, Abigail."

Petra sat silently and stared into his plate. It reminded her of that awkward first meal in the house. Determined not to let their issues ruin her first night back, she told Petra more about the mountain lion attack, about making fire, and about lifting Avant. Finally she asked him, "Are you available for lunch tomorrow? I was hoping we could go to the falls."

Petra met her gaze and smiled with such warmth her heart fluttered.

She could have sworn she heard a low growl come from Avant, but then he spoke quickly. "I'm sorry, Abigail. Petra is needed in the southern field tomorrow and won't be available for lunch."

She turned to look at him. His face was unreadable, except the slight twitch of his upper lip that indicated agitation. She glanced back at Petra, who had finished his last bite and stood.

"I'm sorry, Abby. It seems I'm occupied tomorrow." His gaze landed on Avant and smoldered with contempt. The tension was tougher than the venison steak, and she doubted even a finely forged blade could break it.

"I will, however, be available for dinner tomorrow evening, and I intend to spend it with you." He cupped her cheek and left.

Petra's face fell as he walked from the room. Avant's goading had upset him. She pushed her chair from the table to go after him, but Avant caught her arm. "Abigail, I was hoping you would allow me to peruse the prophecies from Naphen this evening." She stared down at his grip on her wrist and he released her. "I must meet with my captains in the morning but will be available to take you to the falls for lunch tomorrow." His eyes glittered, and his face lit in a brilliant smile.

She blew out a heavy breath at his obvious diversion, but how was any woman supposed to combat that smile? She returned his smile and nodded, and then headed off to get the papers.

The next morning Abby's head throbbed in pain. All night she had dreamed of dark shadows grabbing at her.

She washed and padded downstairs before sunrise. Finding Helean in the kitchen, she scoped out the tension. "Good morning. Are the boys already gone?"

"Master Petra is in the south field and Lord Ventium has gone to the village. He said he would be back by midday to take lunch with you."

"Thanks, Helean." She sighed and went to work on the breakfast dishes as the songbirds chirped outside the kitchen window.

Thoughts of the previous evening filled her mind, but she wasn't able to sort the swirling contents. Petra was her best friend, her confidant. He knew her better than anyone in the world, but she couldn't be in love with him. She loved someone else, didn't she?

I'm in love with Abby. His words played over and over in her mind. Who doesn't want to be loved? Her heart pounded, and she tossed the cleaning rag on the table and hurried to the stables. She needed to see Petra before having lunch with Avant.

After saddling Imperial, she galloped toward the southern field.

Supervising a crew of farmhands atop his blue-black stallion, Dalitus, Petra waved and rode to meet her. "Is everything okay? What are you doing here?"

He dismounted the horse and hurried to her side.

Bewilderment set her mind in motion. Why *had* she come? "I-I don't know. I wanted to make sure you were okay." She stared down at the reins in her hands. "I was worried."

"Were you?" Petra asked, genuinely touched. He helped her dismount. Pulling her down by the waist, he set her on her feet.

She gazed up into his rich brown eyes, which were more familiar than anything in Jastain. As if seeing them for the first time, she allowed their warmth to flow through her. Her heart thumped a strong beat and a flush of heat rose in her cheeks.

At first Petra's eyes narrowed, but then they widened as realization came over his face. "Who am I?"

She creased her brow. "What?"

"What's my name?" He gazed intently.

Confused, Abby looked sideways at him. "Petra."

His mouth descended on hers as he took her in his arms, hesitating for just a moment. When she didn't pull away, he made full contact, his lips brushing hers like a gentle wind against the new growth of barley. The mint and lemongrass scent of his skin infused her, and his soothing arms conveyed security but not confinement. Her mind scattered like apple blossoms in the breeze. Was this why she'd come?

He pulled from her lips to gaze into her face. Her chest rose and fell heavily as she tried to focus.

Petra smiled and whispered, "I'm invoking my right to renegotiate. Have we an accord?"

She didn't know what to say. Petra was like home, easy and comfortable. Looking into his face, she knew she loved him. How could she help but love him when he loved her so freely? She laid her palm on his cheek.

He leaned in again. His tongue gently parted her lips, beckoning her to take part in his pleasure. Her stomach fluttered like small moths in the grass. She opened her mouth, her heart, basking in the warm sunshine of his love, as new and bright as the spring. Lacing her arms around his neck, she moved her hand into the satin hair at the back of his head and pulled him closer, her kiss matching his, stroke for tender stroke.

The sweetness of their kiss smoldered and became more urgent. Petra's arms drew her flush against his strong body, and his hands roamed her back. Passion stirred in her core. She sighed. He deepened the kiss, and the evidence of his arousal pressed into her.

A vision of Avant penetrated her mind, and her heart responded with a sharp spasm. She pulled from the kiss. Her heart fractured; his broke.

"Petra, I'm sorry. I can't." She leaned her forehead against his chest. *Damn it.*

"Abby, every time I kiss you, you end up apologizing to me." He smiled sadly. "I understand you're conflicted. It's all right."

A sick feeling knotted in her stomach. "I don't know what to say."

He whispered into her hair, "Say that you love me."

She lifted her gaze. "I do love you, Petra, more than I knew or thought was possible."

He closed his eyes and listened, like it was his favorite sound in the world.

"But—"

He put his finger to her lips and shook his head. "There's no need to explain, and I can't bear to hear the words." His hands warmly cupped her face. "I love you, Abby. I can make you happy. I'll never be the one to break your heart. And I'll be here waiting, until you decide."

She closed her eyes and held back the tears. Gladly, she would give him anything she had. But her whole heart wasn't hers to give, and he deserved nothing less. She hugged him with all her might and kissed him gently. He helped her back on Imperial, and she rode to the falls.

What a mess. She did *not* want to see Avant right now. Could she even look him in the eyes? Crap. Avant felt something for her, but he still loved his wife. She didn't owe him *anything*, but her heart disagreed.

When she got to the falls, Avant waited for her. She took a deep breath before she dismounted and walked to him. He turned when he heard her approach.

"Ahh!" She gasped.

It wasn't Avant. This man had the same dark hair, but his cold gray eyes betrayed the resemblance. Aesdil. Her pulse shot up like an arrow, and her body trembled.

The harsh lines of his face made him appear older than Avant. Not quite as tall, the king possessed the same air of formality. The sharp edge of his voice cut into her with mock civility. "You must be the fair lady in my lands about whom I have heard so much."

"These are not *your* lands." Abby glared at him, trying to keep from shaking. Nothing good could come from this meeting.

He laughed and took a step toward her. "I see you've been speaking with my dear cousin, whom, until recently, I had assumed dead. How is Avant?"

Abby ignored his taunt and glanced behind her. She might make it to Imperial. He didn't have a horse nearby that she could see.

"You've caused quite a stir in my kingdom. It seems you've been traveling to the Great Heights. What could a gentle lady such as you need in the Great Heights?" He took another step.

How much did he know? Was Avant in danger? She had to get back to warn him.

Abby took off in a sprint but an unseen force restrained her. Struggling against the invisible bonds, she heard Aesdil call out. Five soldiers rushed from behind the trees to grab her. Thinking quickly, Abby amassed all of her energy and started slinging stones in their direction. Hitting three of the five soldiers, she knocked them back before they caught her. She pushed her will against Aesdil's Implanting. His grip loosened. As she reached Imperial, two of the soldiers caught her from behind. Abby told the mare to find Avant as fast as possible.

Abby screamed Avant's name in her mind, hoping he was close enough to hear her.

Then everything went dark.

*****

Avant finished the meeting with his captains. The news hadn't been good. Aesdil's spies had returned to the forest in the southern vale. Avant's troops had caught two of them and chased three others across the Itehris. Using creative interrogation techniques, the spies confirmed the king planned to attack the Freelands. According to the men, Aesdil had information that Lord Ventium had traveled the Great Heights and had not yet returned.

Avant raked his fingers through his hair as he paced the room. What else did Aesdil know? Was he aware of Abigail? If he was, their time ran short. The prophecies weren't widely known, but the king was aware of them. If Aesdil suspected Abigail was the Chosen, he would use all his means to lay claim to her. They must find the Crown and the jewels.

He sank in a chair and rubbed his tired brow. Tossing and turning, he'd spent the night thinking of Abigail. So used to having her next to him, he couldn't sleep without her, and though he lay in his own bed, he'd found no rest there.

A heavy sigh blew from his lips. His fractious exchange with Petra had given him much to consider. Petra was right. He had no justification for his jealousy, but he could not control it. For years, he placed his body and emotions under submission. He'd lived in complete self-control, but at the thought of this young woman, he unraveled.

Sitting in the empty room, he rested his head in his hands. His feelings for Abigail had changed, or perhaps they would no longer be denied. *She* had changed, grown. Her destiny had called, and she had responded. Avant lifted his head and smiled, remembering how she had cared for him on the mountain.

But what of Sentieve? His duty was to his wife, to the kingdom, but like it or not, she now shared his affections with another. What that meant, only the Light could know. The task was at hand, and the fate of Jastain took precedence over matters of his heart.

He left the command post and strode to Spiritus. His heart leapt with joy at the thought of meeting Abigail for lunch. Lying awake the night before, he'd thought of a way to help her tap into her Placement Implanting, but she would resist. He rolled his eyes. The stubborn woman always resisted. A smile spread over his face.

He rode hard from the village, anxious to see her. In the distance, a horse bolted toward him. Imperial. He sped toward her, but a sick dread hit his gut as her empty saddle came into view.

The horse galloped straight for Spiritus and stopped when she reached them. Avant spoke to her mind, *"Where is Abigail?"* Imperial neighed and twisted her head toward the falls.

Without a second glance, he took off in that direction with Imperial following behind. He flew to the water's edge and jumped off his stallion. "Abigail!"

Tracks lay in the mud at the pool's edge and a struggle had taken place by the trees.

The sick feeling spread from the pit of his gut over his whole body. He mounted Spiritus and rode for the south field.

When he pulled up hard in front of Petra, the boy looked white as the snowcapped peaks. Did he already know something was wrong?

"Have you seen Abigail? I found Imperial wandering alone near the falls. I believe she has been taken."

"What?" He dropped the plow from his hand. "Abby was headed to the falls when I saw her this morning."

"Could she not have gone back to the house or to the village?" Hope tried to spring in his heart, but his Gift told him it was in vain.

"She wouldn't have had time and Imperial wouldn't have left her. Something's happened."

Petra was right. Imperial's loyalty was the only reason Avant had allowed Abigail such freedom in traveling the valley.

"That is the same forest where my parents were killed." Petra's voice wavered with rage.

Avant dismounted Spiritus and collapsed to the ground. His elbows rested on bent knees. If anyone harmed her, he would rip them to pieces.

Two of Avant's captains galloped up on their mounts. "Commander, our spies on the eastern road have spotted the king and his men. My lord, they had Lady Abigail with them."

Avant shot from the ground and reached for his horse. "As the Light is my witness, I will kill him!"

Petra tackled him and held him back.

"Release me! I'll stomp that damnable snake into the ground once and for all."

When that defining moment presents itself—for it always presents—what choice does one have but to become the sum of her experience and act in accordance with all that she is?

Raieda Randall, on sacrifice

Chapter Twenty-Three

When Abby woke, her cheek lay on cold stone and her body ached. A trickle of water echoed off the surrounding rock. She lifted her head and tried to focus. A torch flickered against the slate wall across from her barred cell. Her head throbbed and she rubbed the knot where the soldiers had clocked her. The mingled smells of raw dirt and urine permeated the dank air.

How long had she been unconscious? What day was it? Her head dropped back to the floor, and she passed out again. Dreams of Petra and Avant swirled in her mind. She imagined their happy faces in the parlor, laughing, joking, and spending time together. Her love for them washed over her, and happiness wrapped around her in a shield of protection. She was home.

Rousing to a sound of clanking metal and heavy footsteps, she lifted her foggy head. How long she'd slept she couldn't tell. The footfalls halted in front of her.

"I must apologize for the inferior quality of the accommodations, my lady." The king's sneer made her queasy. "But this will be your home until you tell me where to find my Crown."

She scrambled to her feet and retreated to the wall in the rear of the cell. So, he knew she was here to find the jewels. What else did he know? "I don't know what you're talking about."

"Abigail, I think you do know, and you will tell me or there will be consequences." He flashed a sickening smile that chilled her bone deep.

"I don't know anything."

"On the contrary, Chosen One. You know much. Please don't make me harm you."

This is bad. She'd seen enough horror shows to know she couldn't withstand much torture before she would spill her guts. But he didn't know that, did he? "I won't tell you anything, you rat bastard!" Maybe he wouldn't see that she was trembling like a California quake.

The king studied her and then taunted, "Not to worry. I am sure Avant will save you."

"Don't you even speak his name, you sick monster!" Abby seethed.

"Ah, I see the noble Lord Ventium has won the heart of the lady. He is so very charismatic." His venomous words spewed like acid, and his gazed raked her body. "But knowing Avant and his sense of honor, I can imagine he has not taken his place in your bed. A mistake I would never make, my lady."

Her empty stomach heaved and tears streamed down her face. Would he try to rape her?

Even in his fine robes and with a false crown on his head, his authority could not withstand Avant. No wonder he feared Avant. Abby stared at the man with disgust. She'd fight him with everything she had, but she wasn't sure that would be enough.

"Unless you reveal to me what I want to know, I will finish what I started long ago, my lady. In the meantime, I want information on this mysterious horseless carriage." Aesdil turned toward the hall. The heavy oak door creaked open and light spilled down the corridor. The sound of marching feet echoed around her. Her body wouldn't stop shaking.

Two soldiers appeared. One carried a short whip with small tails.

Her knees gave way, and she crumbled to the floor, sucking in ragged breaths. Her fear embodied the two soldiers as they unlocked the cell door and stalked toward her, their long shadows reaching her before they did.

Tears coursed down her face. She couldn't swallow the bile in her throat. "Lord, please help me."

Light gathered all around her. Her hands glowed from within. She held them up, turning them from side to side. A tangible force encompassed her. It coursed through her like electric current looking for a grounding wire. The soldiers froze. She illuminated the dungeon like it was high noon, and her Gift appeared as a force field advancing toward the intruders, pushing back against the shadows.

Aesdil cursed and then yelled to his men, "Retreat at once."

They rushed from the cell, slammed the door, and hurried down the hall.

Aesdil's body illuminated with a glowing mist rather than light, and he spoke into her mind. *"Your Gift is impressive, Abigail. Though it may have given you reprieve this day, it cannot save you."*

He pushed against her Implanting. Her light faded. He pivoted and stalked out.

She curled up in a ball on the floor until the tremors subsided. Never had fear gripped her so completely. Trying to regain control of her frantic heart, she played through memories of Avant. She thought of his smile, his broad shoulders, his implacable will, and those blue eyes. Her body stilled and her breathing calmed. Her thoughts turned to her current predicament.

Aesdil planned to use her as bait to lure Avant to his death. That wasn't going to happen.

She had to get out. Avant would be frantic by now, looking for her. Petra would be worried sick. *Petra.* The memory of his kiss washed over her, soothing her mind and confusing it at the same time. She had to get back. To both of them.

Sometime later, though how long she couldn't tell, a soldier brought a meager meal and water. She stared at the gray gruel. Deciding to brave the food and water, she ate and soon was overcome by sleep. *Note to self: definitely drugged.*

The sound of footsteps woke her. Raising her head, she eyed another meal and water. How long she had been unconscious was unclear, but days had passed since her abduction, she was sure.

She dumped the meal and drank the water, which didn't seem to be altered. Then she passed the long, dark hours singing songs, playing word games in her mind, and trying to think of a way to escape.

Escape was necessary but was it possible? How could she use her Gift? If she could only access her Placement Implanting, she'd be out of this hellhole in a flash, literally. She tried to focus her energy and pull the torch from the wall, but the braided metal fastened into the stone. No concentration of her Implanting could remove it. Nothing else she had would knock a man unconscious. The cell itself lay bare except the tray with a small wooden bowl and cup. She went to the bars and tried the door and then looked down the hallway as far as she could see. Nothing. She was stuck.

Where was a gun when you effin' needed one? If she ever got back to Dallas, she was bringing a gun, and maybe a couple of grenades too. Then she would see how tough that scumbag was. If he hurt Avant, she would blow him and his thugs to kingdom come.

A plan dawned and she smiled as she worked out the details.

The next day when the soldier came to bring her food, Abby gathered her energy and pulled with as much force as she could amass, slamming him into the iron bars. Knocked out, he fell to the ground. She pulled him next to the cell and searched his body. No keys! No weapon. Nothing but the tray. *Shit.* She rattled the bars with her hands.

Eventually, the soldier regained consciousness. He rubbed the front of his head and scowled at her. Grabbing the empty tray, he left without saying a word.

More days passed. Abby didn't know how many. A soldier brought her food once a day, or at least she thought it was once a day. It was hard to tell. She ate every third tray and slept for at least a day afterward from the drug. Her stomach bloated in starvation. She'd never experienced hunger before. It sucked. Her stomach growled and cramped, and food dominated her thoughts. The only thing that took her mind off her dire need for food was thinking about Avant. She imagined his broad shoulders and firm grip. A genuine smile flexed her face when she remembered how that one wisp of hair never stayed put but fell in a perfect wave across his forehead. Her heart ached with need for him like her stomach ached for food. Against her better judgment, she allowed her mind to wander into forbidden places.

Imagining him in the cave behind the falls, his body glistening and filled with desire, she entertained luscious dreams of endless passion where he sated her every need to be loved and cherished. At times, he was a gentle lover, calming her fears and bringing her sweet release. Others, he was a fierce warrior who took her shamelessly in feral need. However he took her, his strong arms always wrapped her in safety and heat.

Her need to stay lucid became a daily struggle. Floating in and out of consciousness, she counted what she thought was nine days since she'd seen the king and estimated she'd been in the dungeon two days before that. She hadn't eaten the drug-laden food in a couple of days and wasn't going to be able to make it much longer without nourishment. What she wouldn't give for a Big Mac and some fries.

Sprawled on the cold stone, her heart gave way to an overwhelming sense of loss and hopelessness. The threat of death became substance. She reached down in the recesses of everything she'd ever known to find something she could cling to, but it eluded her, just outside her grasp.

In a last-ditch effort to regain her faith, a prayer sprang to mind and her parched lips spoke the words, "Lord, thank you for my life and all of the love you've given me. I know you haven't brought me this far for me to die in these dungeons. Please help me out of here."

There had to be a way out. Avant would be trying to rescue her. Her heart caught in her throat, and she gasped. If anything happened to him—

The door creaked open, and light footfalls pattered down the corridor. Abby's head jerked up, and she stood in the middle of her cell, anticipating the approaching figure.

Her heart pounded in her head. A woman glided to the iron bars of the cell wearing a long, hooded cloak. A whoosh of air caused the torch to flicker, and her shadow danced long on the rock wall of Abby's cell. Pushing back her hood, the woman revealed brown hair pulled back from the lovely lines of her neck and the silky skin of an oval face.

Abby gasped at the sight of the warm doe eyes she knew intimately, though they'd never met. Tall with an air of elegance, Sentieve, with her regal beauty, was everything a queen should be, and everything Abby wasn't. With just a glance, it was easy to see why Avant had fallen in love with the woman.

"My lady, have you been harmed?"

The queen's satin speech rang oddly in Abby's ears after not hearing a pleasant voice for so long, or any voice for that matter, for almost two weeks.

Abby shook her head but continued to study the graceful woman. "No, Your Highness. I'm just hungry. What are you doing here?"

Sentieve was older and more careworn than in Avant's memories, but her countenance appeared genuine. Reaching into the deep pockets of the gray cloak, she pulled out a small loaf of bread, a piece of cheese, and an apple. She offered the food between the bars. "My lady, I need to speak with you. My sources tell me that you may be the Chosen One. Is this true?"

Abby quickly took the food, not even caring if it was poisoned. "Yes, it's true." How often had she thought of Sentieve? Never had she imagined the queen would be helping her.

"Your name is Abigail?"

Abby nodded as she took a frantic bite of bread and barely chewed it before she swallowed.

Sentieve waited for her to eat a few more bites of bread and cheese before speaking. "You look so much like your mother."

"You knew my mother? How?"

Raieda Randall had died in a car accident before Abby was two years old. She had only vague memories and a few old pictures of the woman.

"Raieda was my mother's best friend, and she helped me."

Abby gulped in air and bent over, trying to catch her breath.

Sentieve stared past Abby as if a long-stored memory returned to her mind unwillingly. She breathed in sharply. "My sources tell me that someone has been helping you, Abigail. Someone by the name of Lord Ventium. Do you know Lord Ventium?"

In all the moments of Abby's life, in every experience she'd ever had, these words brought more fear than any others ever had. Her body shook and her voice trembled. "Yes, Your Highness, I know him." The utter truth of her words—truth the queen would never suspect—struck her as painfully ironic.

Speaking slowly, deliberately, the queen said, "I believe I also may know Lord Ventium."

Steeling herself, Abby took a deep breath. "Yes, Your Highness, you know him."

Sentieve closed her eyes and grabbed hold of the bars, relying on them to keep her upright. "I had thought him lost and have only recently... Is he well? Are you and he—" She opened her eyes and tried to ask, but it seemed as if she couldn't bring herself to the words.

The defining moment of Abby's life stared at her with familiar brown eyes. Finally, she understood the true meaning of sacrifice. "Avant is well. We're friends. He's been seeking a way to reconcile with you for more than twenty years." A pain pierced her heart like a sword. "He still loves you."

Sentieve turned her back. Her body shook beneath the cloak, and her chin lowered to her chest in quiet sobs.

After a long moment, she turned to stare into Abby's face. "Thank you, Abigail. I must go now. I will return tomorrow. Eat no food brought by the sentries and hide any remains of what I have given you." She quickly turned and padded away.

Abby heard the clank of the door and exhaled a sharp cry. She fell to her knees. Sobs came easily but in her dehydrated state, the tears wouldn't flow. Even knowing all along this was her destination, she couldn't bring herself to believe it. She had a bad habit of not accepting the reality of a situation. Escape was what her life was all about, even before her birth, but there would be no escaping this.

The pain reverberated inside her like the echo of footsteps that stole her heart's desire. Avant would take up his life with the woman who obviously still loved him. He was lost to her. Gone, and she would never recover from it. *"Lord, the price is too high. I can't pay it."*

A single tear ran down her cheek as the only lament her body could afford.

Laying in a fetal position on the stone floor, she eventually fell asleep.

Shaken out of a dream by the sound of footsteps, Abby stood at the approach of her daily meal. She'd awakened in the night and eaten all the food Sentieve had given her, hiding the apple core away in her corset to eat later.

The soldier, as always, didn't speak but placed the new tray on the floor and removed the old. Abby met his cold gaze with defiance before he stalked away.

After he left, she ran to the water and drank it in one gulp, the cool liquid soothing her parched throat.

The ripping pain from yesterday's encounter was replaced with a dull ache that made her head throb.

Sentieve was still in love with Avant and he loved her. What else was there to do? If Avant were in her shoes, what would he do? He would stand behind that ironclad will and endure. That's what she would do, too. She had to find a way to get out and to bring the queen with her.

Sentieve had said she would return. Abby just had to wait until she did, and then they would figure out a way to escape.

Hours passed. The door creaked open, and the patter of light feet echoed softly. Abby stood and went to the front of her cell.

Sentieve glided across the floor, her long cape billowing, giving her the appearance of floating.

Her eyes were grave and her face gray with exhaustion. "We must be quick." Sentieve took out a key and unlocked the cell door. "Please come with me."

Abby hurried out of the cell and down the hall. The queen opened a huge wooden door, which swung out to a winding stone staircase. The women stole up two flights and out a side exit of the castle.

The queen led Abby into a small room. Abby spoke before she turned to face Sentieve. "Your Highness, you must come with me. Avant will protect you. It has been our plan to rescue you."

Sentieve shook her head and whispered, "I cannot go."

"Your Highness, how can you stay? Avant is alive and wants you with him, and the king is dangerous. You must come."

"I cannot go with you, Abigail." Sentieve breathed in and looked up at the ceiling as if it could give her support.

What was holding her back? Abby couldn't imagine not wanting to run all the way to Avant after hearing he was alive and still loved her. What was the crazy woman waiting for?

"After Avant's death, I married the king and had a child. He was beautiful, strong, and Gifted, and having heard rumors by that time of the king's treachery, I feared for his safety. Abigail, I did not know of the plan to harm Avant. I loved—*love* him." She stopped and placed her long, elegant fingers across her mouth as if she'd said something she herself didn't realize. She inhaled. "I had to get my son out from under the king's clutches."

Abby gasped in horror. "Oh my God. Aesdil killed him?"

"He didn't die." Sentieve evened her gaze.

"Your son is alive?"

"With the help of your mother, I created the illusion of his death and sent him away with Raieda. I sent with him two of the Crown jewels that had been entrusted to me by my father. Raieda took him to a place where Aesdil could never find him."

"Avant's son is with my mother?" Abby sat absently in a wooden chair with a narrow back that spanned a foot over her head.

Sentieve looked at her with a sadness Abby couldn't understand. "I don't know if he is Avant's son, but the last time I saw him he was with your mother. That was nearly twenty years ago."

Abby shook her head, trying to understand. "Not Avant's son? But Avant said you were expecting a child before his accident."

"That is true." Sentieve dropped her gaze in shame.

Abby looked at her with a revelation of disgust. "You were unfaithful to him while you were married? Do you know he's been faithful to you for twenty years? He won't allow himself to love or be loved by anyone because of *you*."

Deep lines of pain etched the woman's face, and her voice was filled with inconceivable sadness. "I can imagine what you think of me, but believe me, I have paid for my indiscretion. I am telling you this because if you find my son, you will find the emeralds you seek."

Abby's head was so full of new information she wondered if it leaked out her ears. Two things stuck out in her mind: Avant may have a son and that son had two of the jewels.

"What is your son's name, and how can I find him?"

"Chatham would be twenty-two years old. Your father will know where to find him."

"My father is—"

A noise shuffled in the corridor. They stood in silence, not daring to move.

The queen whispered, "Abigail, it's time for you to go. There's a horse waiting outside with provisions. If you follow the river to the Northern Passage, you can cross on horseback. Do not take the roads or bridges. They will be watched."

"Thank you, Your Highness." Abby paused, hesitant. Resolve filling her, she continued, "Please come with me."

Abby could no more describe the look of sorrow on Sentieve's face any more than she would ever be able to forget it. The queen was a woman bound to a hell of her own making.

"You may tell Avant of my betrayal. He is released from his vow. When you find my son, tell him I love him." Sentieve opened the door to the outside world and fresh air swept across Abby's face with the sweet smell of freedom.

The haze veiled the stars in the night sky, with only the brightest shining through. It reminded her of the sky back in Dallas. A dark horse tethered to a nearby tree stamped his hoof on the ground impatiently.

"Skirt the perimeter wall of the castle for a half-mile to the west. There you will come to a guard gate that will be unlocked and unattended. Ride north for five miles to the River Itehris, and follow the river to the Northern Crossing."

Abby remembered the place where she and Avant had crossed on foot months ago.

Sentieve inclined her head in a queenly gesture of dismissal and closed the door of the castle.

Abby mounted the horse and took off for the perimeter wall. She tentatively rode through the eastern gate. As the queen had said, it was open and unguarded. She rode hard through the night until well after dawn, wanting to make sure she was far away when they found her missing.

Mid-morning, Abby stopped and searched through the packs on the horse's saddle. Finding bread and dried meat, she ate half the loaf. She drank from the river and let the horse rest for a short while before riding out again.

Riding hard until nightfall, she could see the mountains where she and Avant had camped the first night she met him. The sturdy horse attacked the trail with a steady pace. Weariness and fatigue sank deep in her bones, but she pressed on with an endurance she didn't know she had. Cell phones and satellites could never have taught her, and in that other life, she could've never become who she was, who she was destined to be.

The knowledge of Sentieve's betrayal should have been welcome, but it wasn't. It reminded her of the time she ate a spoonful of cocoa powder thinking it would be like chocolate candy. The dry bitterness was all she could taste. The pain it would cause Avant was unfathomable.

After hiding the horse, she made camp in a small grove of trees and then slept for a few hours. She left the next morning before dawn and, a little after midday, reached the northern point of the river, where she crossed on horseback. She could make it to the small cave by nightfall and camp there before heading to Domentus Ventium.

The trip with Avant and those first days played in her mind. That seemed so long ago. This was her world now. She smiled, remembering how Avant had scooped her out of the water and carried her across the river. He'd been so arrogant. Abby's heart ached to see his tall frame and gaze into his blue eyes. If it hadn't been for him, she would have died, then and now. But for him, she would still be a helpless party girl looking for escape. He'd made certain she was prepared to survive, and she loved him for it.

Sentieve said Abby looked like Raieda. Her father had told her that too. Why hadn't Avant told her that he knew her mother? Was it possible she was still alive?

Abby neared the campsite around dusk. Two horses stood near the stream, and the glow of a campfire lit the cave. Her heart thumped in her chest. Could the king's men already be looking for her? She turned the horse around, preparing to leave quietly. Instead, she found herself at the point of a silver blade, two sapphire eyes staring up at her.

Chapter Twenty-Four

Avant's eyes widened, and he dropped his sword. He lifted Abigail from the horse and held her in his arms. "Is it really you or am I dreaming again?" He pulled away and stared into her gaunt face. Barely a wisp, she appeared as frail a newborn foal.

"It's really me." She tucked a lock of hair behind his ear, and her delicate touch sent tingles through his body.

He pulled her close again and kissed her forehead. Feeling as if a great weight had fallen from his shoulders, he sighed into her hair. "Are you all right? You're so thin. Did they hurt you, my angel?"

"You mean, other than holding me hostage, drugging me, and starving me half to death? No, it was a blast." She smiled, but it never reached her eyes. She had clearly faced trauma. The thought pierced him.

Avant's heart leapt within him to hold her in his arms. He'd nearly lost his mind with worry. That treacherous animal had imprisoned her. Seething rage bubbled in his veins. "I did not know if I'd ever see you again. If anything had happened to you, Abigail—" His voice broke and he fought to regain composure.

Despite her mild protests, he carried her to the cave, not even allowing her to take a step. She laid her head against his chest. He bounded up the rocks, holding her emaciated frame with ease. Folding down at the fire, he cradled her in his lap, unwilling to let go. Neither said a word. She melted against him and cried silently.

The feel of her in his arms reminded him of their previous time in the cave, and for the first time in weeks, his unsettled mind gained a foothold on some kind of peace.

Petra entered. When he saw Abigail, his face lit in affection. "Abby. Where did you come from?"

She wrestled out of his grip and jumped into Petra's arms. Bereft by her absence, he glared up at them.

Petra held her close, nuzzling his nose in her hair. Avant softly growled. Looking past her, Petra quickly pulled away and wrinkled his nose. "Abby, you need a bath."

She laughed. "No kidding."

Sitting down between them, she told the story of how Aesdil had captured her.

Avant listened to her recounting, but there was one thing he didn't understand. "Abigail, why were you alone at the falls?"

She darted a glance to Petra, who quickly looked away. Avant shifted his gaze back and forth between them. He tapped his lip with his index finger but said nothing. Those two clearly were hiding something.

A guilty look crossed her face, and his heart plummeted. "I had ridden out to see Petra that morning and thought I would stop by the falls afterward."

"Abby, you said they drugged you," Petra said.

"Yes, they put it in the food. I think they were keeping me drugged to prevent me from using my Implanting."

"That seems likely," Avant said. "How did you escape?"

Her face went ashen at his question, and she hesitated before speaking. "The queen helped me."

Avant stared unbelieving.

"She released me from the dungeons and gave me the horse. I don't know how, but they know I'm the Chosen One and that you, Avant, are alive."

His airway constricted, and he could not breathe. Sentieve knew he was alive?

Abigail's face lined with concern. "I tried to get her to come with me, but she wouldn't."

Why had Sentieve not escaped with Abigail? His mind flailed, and he could not discern his emotions. The walls of the small cave closed in around him. He needed to think. Rising, he left the cave.

*****

Abby's heart left with Avant. She walked to the cave entrance and watched him until he disappeared upstream. All of her emotions flooded back when he'd held her in his arms and only Petra's appearance could have torn her from him.

After a long silence, Petra stood behind her and wrapped his arms around her shoulders. She leaned back into him and sighed.

"I'll get you some water so you can wash, and I brought a change of clothes for you. We'll finish our conversation later."

As usual, Petra's calm practicality eased her heart and served as a balm to her raw emotions. She grabbed his arm before he walked away and leaned her head against his chest. His arms went around her.

"I couldn't have stood it if something had happened to you. I was so worried." They stood in a tight hug for a moment. He finally released her and went to get water from the stream. Heating it over the fire, Petra unpacked his supplies and gave her a cloth and some soap. He had to be the most prepared guy in the world, in any world. She loved him for it.

She touched his face. "I'm sorry you were worried. All I could think about was getting back to you and Avant. There's a lot more to the story, but I don't think I should tell Avant—at least not yet."

"We'll talk in a little while. You get washed up, and we're going to get some food in you." He squeezed her hand. His actions communicated his love and relief at finding her.

For the first time in weeks, she felt like smiling. He left the cave to give her privacy.

She removed her ragged and filthy clothes and then washed with the warm water. Her hair she soaped and rinsed last. She dried with an extra blanket, and changed into the clean clothes. After finishing, she called to Petra, who returned and prepared something to eat.

They sat in front of the fire and watched the flames flicker into the cool evening.

"Where's Avant?"

Petra shrugged as he took a bite of bread. "I'm not sure. He took Spiritus upstream and will probably be gone a while. He was crazed when we got word that the king had captured you. I had to hold him back from storming the castle. We spent a week gathering our troops and formulating a plan to try and get you out. We were headed to your car, thinking that might give us some advantage if we could make it run."

She searched his face. "You didn't tell him about what happened, did you?"

"Are you crazy? He would've killed me, Abby. As you are aware, Avant and I were not exactly on the best of terms. After you were taken, he broke. I would have sworn he was in love with you. Maybe he is." His face creased in pain to speak the words. "But clearly, he still feels something for the queen."

Sentieve. "Oh, Petra. That woman doesn't deserve ten minutes of his suffering, much less twenty years. She admitted to me she was unfaithful to Avant while they were married. She doesn't even know who the father of her son is."

Petra stared at her wide-eyed. "You mean the one that died?"

"The one whose death she faked, and who is still alive." Abby couldn't conceal the contempt in her voice.

"*What?* Avant has a son?"

Abby, still fearing hunger, tore into a small roll and spoke with her mouth full. "Could have. And she sent the emeralds from the Crown with him and my mother."

"Your mother is involved in this? The emeralds? By the Light."

She took a big gulp of spiced wine and swallowed. "Sentieve thinks she might still be alive. Should we tell Avant?"

Petra sighed and rubbed his brow. "We'll have to tell him, Abby. This isn't something we can rightfully keep from him, but we need to wait. Something happened to him when you were captured. I've never seen him so vulnerable. It scared me. He has always been a rock, even when something devastating hurt him. He seemed diminished, like all his strength left when we didn't know what had happened to you."

Petra loved Avant and she trusted his judgment. Tight bands of worry weaved through her chest. Avant *had* seemed different. They finished their meal.

"I have to find a way back to Dallas. That's the next step in finding the answers we seek." She sighed and chewed her fingernail. "I've never used my Gift like that. At least, I've never controlled it."

Petra wrapped an arm around her shoulders and pulled her to him. "I wish I could be of assistance. That's out of my realm of expertise, but I know Avant can help you. He said he'd thought of a way."

She rested in his arms and they talked a little while longer, filling in the gaps of their stories. Avant didn't return. Abby's eyes fluttered in weariness, and as much as she wanted to wait for him, she couldn't stay awake any longer. Petra made a pallet, covered her up, and she fell asleep.

*****

Avant traveled upstream and sat under a tree near the water. Staring into the flowing brook, he tried to sort through his emotions.

Sentieve knew he was alive, as did Aesdil. Leaning his head against the tree, he exhaled and raised his gaze to the stars. All these years he had feared the unknown of this moment, wondering if Sentieve would still love him and want him back. He had locked that fear away, but it had haunted him. Until recently. Never once had he considered whether he would still love her. Yet that was the position in which he found himself.

Picking up a rock, he chunked it into the bubbling current. He had not acted gallantly in his marriage with Sentieve. He'd made many mistakes for which his heart now grieved. Guilt over how he'd denied her his love that last morning stung his mind. He closed his eyes. If he were honest, it had been his guilt these many years, and not his love, that motivated him toward reconciliation. But reconciliation would not right the wrongs of the past, and would be a worse offense toward her.

When his thoughts drifted to the future and he envisioned his reign in the new kingdom, the woman he saw at his side, his queen, was not Sentieve. He had tried to suppress the vision and *that* dream. The one damnable dream that reoccurred almost nightly, and he could no longer fight its meaning. Sentieve was his past. She was lost to him the moment Aesdil plotted against him.

Abigail was his future, but an uncertain future, at best. Their quest, now more urgent than ever, rested in returning to Abigail's world as quickly as possible. He had a plan.

He rose and mounted Spiritus, patting the stallion fondly on the neck. He headed toward his future.

Avant returned to the cave a short while before dawn. He knelt next to the waning fire, gazing at the flaxen locks splayed across Abigail's pallet. Her form, though worn and frail, brought peace to his troubled mind. My Light, he'd missed her, feared for her. He moved closer and stroked her hair. The dawn would break within the hour, and they would get an early start. She stirred and stretched. Her eyes fluttered open and sparkled in the dwindling firelight. Petra slept soundlessly nearby.

"I am sorry." He gazed into her comely face. *"I did not mean to wake you."* They had not spoken with mindspeech for a long while. Too long.

"It's okay. I'm glad you did. I was worried about you. Are you okay?" She furrowed her brow and clasped his forearm. The warmth of her touch melted the chill of the spring morn.

"No, Abigail, I'm not, but I am better now I know you're safe." He continued to stroke her hair, taking small strands and gently wrapping the curls around his finger. *"Abigail, do you have any memories of me telling my wife I love her?"*

Her gaze shot high and to the right in recollection. She shook her head. *"No, I don't have any."*

"Do you not think that strange?"

"A little. Why didn't those memories Implant?"

"Because there are none. I never said the words to her."

"Avant, you can't beat yourself up over that. Some people don't say it. They show it. I think that's what you did. She knows you love her."

He dropped the strand of hair and stared into her eyes. *"But do you not believe hearing it is as important?"*

"Yes, I guess it is."

She hadn't understood, but she would. He would not repeat the mistakes of the past. He shot a glance over at Petra. Now was not the time for that conversation. He spoke softly. "I've been thinking how I might help you use your Implanting, and I have an idea."

She sat up on the pallet. "That's good, because I feel a sense of urgency now we've been discovered. The king will come after me, and he wants you, too, Avant. I don't think it's safe for us to go back to the fief."

"You're right. He is gathering his troops even now and is preparing to attack the Freelands. We cannot return. My troops prepare for him and can hold back an attack, but I regret the losses they will suffer. I am confident that, even with smaller numbers, we can prevail over him in our own land. However, if you and I are not there to capture, he might not risk an attack at all. This morning I will send Petra back to the fief to notify my captains that I have found you and they are not to march on the castle as planned."

"Avant, you don't have to stay with me. Petra could stay. You can go back to lead your men in battle."

He studied her intently, trying to read her motives. Clearly, something had changed between her and Petra. He had taken note of it last evening, but what that change meant he dared not think. A rage already brewed at the merest glint of the thought. He sucked in a breath. "Is that what you want, Abigail, to be with Petra?"

She shook her head. "I don't want to take you from your responsibilities. I've cost you so much already, and I'm not thrilled with the idea of Petra in harm's way."

"Nor am I, but I am confident he'll be safe. I will not permit him to fight. He has to run my lands." In truth, the fief was the safest place for Petra, which was Avant's chief reason for sending him. "Abigail, regardless of whether Petra stays or goes, I will not leave you. You are my priority."

She sighed. "Okay, then. Petra leaves at sunrise, but where will we go?"

"We can return to the cave where we camped our first night together. It will provide the security we require to practice your Implanting."

"How do you think you can help me?"

"I want you to Implant yourself into me as I did with you."

*****

Abby's heart skipped a beat. Oh God. That was not what she expected. Implant into him so that he could know her every thought, memory, and emotion? No effin' way.

The first light of dawn illuminated the small cave, and Petra stirred and sat.

"Did you hear all that?" Abby asked Petra.

"Yes." Hurt laced his voice and he wouldn't meet her gaze.

The sun rose, and they packed up camp.

Petra was taking the horses back to the fief. She and Avant would travel on foot to the other cave. She surveyed the leather pack Petra had filled with provisions. It was the right plan, but she didn't want Petra to go.

When Avant left to wash in the stream, she grabbed Petra and held him close.

Downcast, Petra wrapped his lifeless arms around her. "I understand the wisdom of this plan, and agree it's for the best. Yet I feel I'm losing you. I can't explain it, but I know things will be different when this is over."

Since returning to their company last evening, she'd sensed the same thing and knew Petra was right. "No matter what happens, I love you and I always will. You're my best friend, confidant, and personal cheering section. No one has been better to me than you." Abby wasn't sure why, but she felt compelled—she put her hands on either side of his face. "Whatever is meant to be, will be. But, Petra, you are not second best!"

Tears sparkled in his eyes. She placed a lingering kiss on his cheek and finished packing before Avant returned to the cave.

Avant embraced Petra, and it seemed any breach was healed. They tethered the horses, and Petra left for the fief. She watched him until he was out of sight and then left the cave, following Avant in the opposite direction.

They traveled through the woods and reached the river before noon. Everything stilled in the quiet forest. Not even a bird chirped. A soft rain disturbed the face of the smooth flowing river.

Avant glanced over at her and cocked his eyebrow. "Do you want me to carry you across again?"

She smiled at the playful note in his voice. "I can make it on my own this time." She lifted her foot. "Now that I have proper clothing."

He chuckled.

They plunged into the biting water and started across. Halfway into the river, Abby spied a garrison of six soldiers on the bank in front of them. Avant swept her up out of the water and turned to run back to the opposite side, but six more soldiers lined the bank behind them. He set her on her feet.

"I can take three, maybe four of them, Abigail, but that still leaves two."

Abby barely heard him because she was already Implanting stones from the water and hurling them at the men in both directions. Avant gaped at her before doing the same. They waded quickly in the direction of the cave. Three of the soldiers in front were knocked unconscious by the flying boulders, and the other three ran for cover. The six soldiers on the other bank started across.

Abby made her way as swiftly as she could, but wading in the knee-high water felt like frame by frame on her DVR. She continued a barrage of stones until they reached the bank.

Avant glanced at her and nodded once. *"Look for their horses. If we can take one and run off the rest, we may get a head start on them. I don't believe they can track us to the cave."*

She scanned the perimeter. *"The horses are in the trees."*

"We need to run quickly. Keep your eyes open. I believe there are more men than we have seen."

Two of the soldiers on the ground began to stir, and two more came out of the brush and tall grass. Abby and Avant sprinted toward the horses, but before they could reach the animals, four soldiers surrounded them. Avant unsheathed his sword and speared the soldier in front of them. Blood poured from the wound. The man gurgled and fell with a thud. Abby's heart lurched and her stomach churned like a thirty-year-old washing machine.

"Abigail, run!"

Avant engaged two more soldiers, allowing her to slip through the ranks and head for the tethered animals. Blood pounded in her temples. She moved reflexively in the face of danger. The sound of the remaining soldier's footsteps echoed against the mountain.

Abby reached out for the horses' minds, telling them to be ready to run. She Implanted a large piece of driftwood, hurling it at the man chasing her. He leapt to the side so it wouldn't slam him to the ground, but the limb still knocked him back. The blow gave her enough time to reach the trees.

She loosed the reins on the eight steeds and sent seven of them flying in the direction of the castle. As she mounted one of the stallions, another soldier grabbed her from behind and pulled her foot from the stirrup. She fell to the ground, flat on her back. He stomped her in the stomach.

"Ugh." She whooshed out the breath in her lungs. Pain stabbed at her, but she still tried to get up. He laughed and kicked her in the head. The last thing she saw before she lost consciousness was a silver blade through his chest.

Chapter Twenty-Five

Abby became aware of someone calling her name from far away, or maybe he just whispered. "Abigail. Abigail, please wake."

Opening her eyes, she saw that she lay in the darkened cave. Avant cradled her throbbing head and stroked her face. Not able to take a deep breath, she closed her eyes again and slept.

The next morning she woke, her head resting in Avant's lap. He sat asleep, leaning against the cave wall. Trying to reposition her aching body, Abby shifted. A pain stabbed into her side. Avant opened his eyes.

She smiled up at him and murmured, her voice dry and scratchy, "You carried me and all the provisions up the mountain, Superman?"

Relief flooded his face. He smiled back. "It was still much faster than when you climbed up yourself."

"I thought you intended to kill me that day, but you were too cute not to follow." She tried to stretch and thought better of it as pain prevented a deep breath. "So what's the damage?"

"You were kicked in the head, which I believe broke the man's foot." He flashed her a rascally smile. "And you have at least two bruised ribs."

"Were you hurt?"

"I am all right. I killed five of the eight soldiers, but there were six more across the river. I am certain they'll comb the rocks below for days. I do not believe they'll climb this far, and I sent the horse in another direction." He rubbed his neck and stretched. "Abigail, we cannot linger in this place as I'd hoped. We have access to water, but we'll eventually run low on provisions. We cannot risk going for food." Worry lined his handsome face, but if she knew him, he had a plan. He *always* had a plan.

"What do you suggest?"

"You need to Implant into me as soon as possible. I'm convinced I will be able to help you if you do."

Anxiety cinched a chord around her throat, doubling her heart rate in a half-second. "Avant, I'm not prepared for that yet."

He brushed the hair from her face and stroked her cheek. "I understand you're still too weak today. We can do it tomorrow."

Tomorrow? She rolled her eyes. Whew, what a nurturer. She wasn't going to be ready for at least a decade. Knowing she had no choice but to Implant into him, she considered other drastic alternatives, but in the end, logic forced her to return to the idea.

She sighed. "Okay, tomorrow, but I need to tell you some things before then."

He bared his pearly whites in a knowing smile. "Abigail, are you ashamed of things in your past?"

Oh, he didn't know the half of it. "Yes, I am, but those are the least of my concerns."

They stayed in the cave for the remainder of the day. Her body ceased to throb in several places after she drank something and had a few bites of panas.

He made them a pallet. "It is too dangerous to build a fire that someone might see. We can lay together for warmth." His eyes sparkled, causing a tingling sensation to scamper up her spine. Something about him was still different, and she still couldn't quite put her finger on what it was.

The sky colored with warm hues of the day's end. Avant lay close behind her, propped up on his elbow with his arm resting around her waist. They watched as the sun set beyond the horizon. Stars crowded the sky. Abby had forgotten the panoramic vista from this cave. She sighed and leaned her head back against his chest. He nuzzled into the hair above her ear, drawing closer so the lengths of their bodies touched. Oh my God, he was spooning with her. *Definitely different.* She rested, content in his arms.

Sleeping long from exhaustion, neither woke until mid-morning. They ate a small breakfast of fruit and nuts. Avant carried her down the rocks to the next level so she could relieve herself and wash.

Her ribs protested with any sudden movements but breathing came easier. Maybe they weren't too bruised. After returning to the cave, she took the last of the Tylenol from the first-aid kit. When she came back from Dallas to Jastain, she was bringing a gigantic Costco-sized bottle of Advil with her.

Avant sat cross-legged in front of her, placing his palms on his thighs. "Are you ready?"

Her stress level hit code red, and her heart went into overdrive. "Right now?"

"Yes, because to think too long about doing a thing often becomes its undoing. So let us hasten to do what we must do."

Abby shook her head. His philosophy was about to turn to tragedy. She bit her lip and crinkled her brow. "Avant, I really need to tell you a few things so they don't catch you by surprise."

He patted her knee. "Abigail, you do not have to be ashamed of anything in your past. I will not sit in judgment of you."

"My thoughts aren't only about things I've done, and I'm afraid some of them will hurt you."

Avant stared at her for a while and then looked away. "Has something happened with Petra?"

Crap! She'd been so worried about Sentieve that she'd totally forgotten about that. "Yes, but that's not what I am talking about."

"You two are lovers, then?" he snarled through clenched teeth, his gaze flaming with jealousy.

She rolled her eyes and blurted out in frustration, "No! Is sex all you think love is? I have information about your wife that you need to know."

His face was dumbstruck. "Sentieve? What about her?"

She took a deep breath. "Sentieve told me…she faked the death of her first child and sent him with my mother to keep him safe from the king. She believes he's still alive, but she doesn't know where he is." Abby paused and studied Avant. "Sentieve had the emeralds from the Crown, and she sent them into hiding with him."

His eyes narrowed and his voice raised an octave. "Sentieve sent our son into hiding, and he is still alive?"

"He's alive as far as we know—and she thinks he's your son."

"What do you mean *she thinks he is my son?*"

"She isn't sure he is." Abby hated to hurt him with the horrible words.

"But she was expecting the child before—"

"Yes, she was."

He remained quiet, his gaze fixed on the rock behind her. His chest rose and fell in a rapid but steady rhythm. "Is that all, or is there more?"

"That's all."

He seemed oddly in control, which was somehow more frightening than the rage. "Then you're ready?"

"Avant, don't you want to wait—"

"No."

"Please say something."

He stared deep into her eyes. Hurt reflected there, but oddly relief did, too. "Abigail, I've learned one lesson in the past twenty years: Some things are simply out of my control. If I want to find my son, I need your help."

He'd taken it far better than she'd hoped, but she was afraid of the proverbial other shoe.

After a brief reminder from Avant on how to Implant into him, Abby centered her energy and stared into the sapphire eyes that would soon know everything—in living color. She looked past his eyes, resisting against his thoughts and feelings, and in an instant deposited all that she was within him.

A stream of energy left her body, filling his heart and mind in the world's most intimate download. She caught flashes of the information as it transferred and glimpsed a few things she wished she hadn't seen go by. She was reminded of every stupid thing she'd done, like that pole dancing class. A returning current refilled her like a circuit. Avant infused her with his energy as her life was written on his heart.

He passed out and fell sideways on the cave floor. He came to around midday and sat up from the pallet where she'd laid him.

When she caught his eye, an electric current stabbed through her. The circuit remained open. She quickly closed her mind. He blinked and took a deep breath, as if to stave off a wave of nausea.

She stared at him, waiting for the oh-my-Light gasp. When it didn't come, she tentatively asked, "How are you feeling?"

Avant blinked at her, apparently still trying to process everything. He closed his eyes. "I've felt better, but I'll survive."

Abby remembered the dizziness. "You will—but *will I?* Now you know everything. I have no secrets."

His blue eyes opened, and Abby felt like she'd plunged from the top of a cliff.

"Yes, I know everything," he said with a sad laugh.

"And…"

"And…I'm sorry I hurt you so deeply. I'm sorry I did not understand what happened when I Implanted into you. I'm sorry I pushed you away and could not give you what you sought, but at least you found it with someone else." The hurt in his tone was evident, though his face remained neutral.

"You mean Petra."

"Yes, I am referring to Petra. You're in love with him."

"Am I? I suppose it's hard not to love someone who loves you so completely." She made the statement more of an accusation than a declaration.

"Yes, it is."

Avant still denied her love for him. Why? It seemed ridiculous since they both knew the truth. At least he wasn't giving her the sympathetic-teacher gaze. She really didn't want to have to beat the crap out of him, since she still needed his help to go pee.

He changed the subject. "I think I know how you can get back home."

"Really? How?"

"It's your love. That's what brought you here and almost took you away."

"What do you mean?"

"Abigail, when you give your love, the energy of it flows from you and then returns again in a perpetual loop. That loop replenishes the supply of energy from which your Implanting draws its power. As the love accumulates and flows out, it keeps your Implanting in balance and harmony. Love is the answer."

He sounded like a freakin' hippy. "Huh? I'm not sure I understand."

Avant gazed to the ceiling as if searching for a way to explain. "Snow falls on the mountains. The sun melts the snow, and it runs down to make rivers and provide water to the land below. The sun takes the water up from the valley into the sky, and it falls again on the mountains. If you stop the sun from shining, the circle would be interrupted. This is what happens with your energy when your love is unrequited or rejected. The flow of the loop is halted, and the energy of your Implanting is unchecked and out of balance."

"How can I stop loving?" Abby bit her lip.

"I do not think you have to stop completely. You only need to interrupt the flow momentarily. Long enough to Implant somewhere to get back into balance."

"Oh. Okay. Still not sure I get it, but what do we do next?"

"We test my theory, but not today. You're still not ready to travel, and neither am I. Since we're not sure where we might end up, perhaps it's best to wait a day or two." Then the most devious little twinkle lit his eyes. "In the meantime, my lady, you can explain to me the benefits of Mexican Minesweeper, because, based on your memories, I see none."

She laughed so hard it hurt.

They spent the next two days in the cave. Abby was still sore, but the fog had cleared from her head. It even seemed like she was gaining her strength back, if not any weight. She and Avant had more in common now. They talked each day and late into the night. He hadn't said anything about Sentieve, but he talked a lot about Chatham. He would love the boy whether they were related or not. She hoped he wouldn't be disappointed.

"Abigail, I am fascinated with the inner workings of your thoughts. I never imagined that when I say a thing, it could be analyzed or interpreted in any way other than intended. Yet you can find three different inferences and analyze them in an instant, determining the most logical. Do all women think this way?"

Abby laughed at the perplexed furrow of his brow. "You mean, do we all try to figure out what a man is thinking when he says something? Pretty much."

"The love you experience is a paradox of delicacy and strength. Your heart is fragile toward those you love but fiercely protective of them." He shook his head as if he couldn't fathom the concept. "Having insight into your mind and heart is a privilege, Abigail. Please don't ever Implant into anyone else. We must discourage the use of the Gift in this way. It is too dangerous." His eyes became remote. "Although, to some extent, there seems to be a built-in safeguard."

Abby reared back. "How is it dangerous?"

He gazed at her with a look of incredulity. "Do you mean that you cannot see how to make an advantage against me from my Implanting?"

She shrugged her shoulders. "I guess not. I figured I was the one who got the short end of the stick in that deal."

His face clouded with thick emotion she couldn't read, and when he spoke, his voice was soft and reverent. "That is because your heart is pure."

Since her Implanting, there was something different in the way Avant looked at her that made her think he'd changed again. Could he have had the same experience with her Implanting that she'd had with his? Her heart rumbled at the thought, though she tried to push it down. He held her that night as they watched the sun set and fell asleep.

The next morning she woke to a sweet breeze across her face. As she opened her eyes, Avant's lips descended and brushed against hers in a soft kiss. Abby's heart leapt to life and she breathed in his scent, luxuriating in the feeling, until she realized he wasn't even awake. The following morning, something rock-hard pressed against her abdomen and roused her out of sleep. He wasn't awake for that either. At this rate, she might *get lucky*, and he would just sleep right through it. She rolled her eyes and stuffed down her own desire as she gently pulled away and went to wash in the stream, the cold stream.

On the evening of the sixth day in the cave, Abby dreamed of her dad's study. *She opened the safe and lights shone out from far away.*

She sat up in the pallet. It was time to go.

"Avant." She lightly shook him.

"Is everything all right?"

"I had another dream. It's time to Implant. What do I need to do?"

He sighed and stretched, trying to wake himself up. She loved how she didn't have to explain about her kooky dreams to Avant. He just believed her.

"I think you should concentrate on something or someone you love and then try disconnecting with your feelings. My theory is that you will be sent someplace where your energy can return to balance."

"Do you think I should try right now?"

"You can try. I doubt you'll be able to make it work on your first attempt. Maybe you should try with Petra."

She shot him a sideways glance. "All right."

She missed Petra and had thought of him every day, hoping he was safe. She concentrated on her love for him, the sunshine in his eyes, and the way he made her laugh. She focused on the flow of love, feeling the invisible energy radiating from her heart to his and back again. Time and distance were irrelevant in the exchange. She made a deliberate effort to halt the flow of love. For a brief moment a light flashed, and electricity coursed through her head.

She sat cross-legged on a rug in a dark room. Hearing the light breathing of someone sleeping, she was afraid. Eventually her eyes adjusted and she could make out the room.

As quietly as she could, she got to her feet to see if she could find a door. She took two steps to her right and tripped over something on the floor, making a sound that was sure to wake everyone within a mile.

A candle lit behind her. Petra sat up, looking more than a little startled.

"It's me."

"Abby, what are you doing here? Are you all right?"

She went to his bed and sat on the edge. The bed linen rode low on his hips and his glorious body glowed in the candlelight. She swallowed hard and looked away from his bare chest. "I'm fine. Well, except for a couple of bruised ribs. I Implanted here from the cave. Isn't that unbelievable?"

He nodded at her in wide-eyed amazement. "Is Avant all right?"

"He's fine. We were attacked crossing the river but managed to escape to the cave and have been hiding there since we left you." She told him the story of her Implanting into Avant and how he took the news about Sentieve.

"The king's army is marching on the Freelands, but two neighboring lands to the southwest have sent troops to help. Aesdil is a coward. He'll back down once he gets the report from his men that you and Avant are not here."

They talked for half an hour before Abby remembered Avant alone in the cave. He would be out of his mind with worry. She hugged Petra and thought again of her love for him. She made a deliberate effort to stop the flow and…nothing happened. How was she going to get back to Avant? To get back to Avant, did she need to think of him?

Bringing him to her mind was like eating forbidden fruit. *Avant.* She'd allowed herself limited access to those feelings since the episode at the falls. To open her heart and let the love rush through her like a river, strong and steady, was frightening and heady. She thought of his strong arms, his heartbeat, and his blue eyes, and then focused on stopping the flow. A light grew. A shock reverberated through her head and with it came a flash.

She gazed into the blue eyes that she loved. They weren't happy eyes. She pursed her lips. "Don't look at me like that. You were the one who didn't think I could do it that quickly, and I didn't mean to leave you behind."

He frowned. "Where did you go? And why did it take so long?"

"I ended up in Petra's room. It was so dark, but I could hear him sleeping."

"Was he wearing clothing? I've warned him about that."

She rolled her eyes and continued. "We talked. Apparently, I have to think of the person I want to go to. Are you mad?"

His face softened. "I'm not angry. I was worried. How is Petra?"

Abby told him about the king's army and the southern villages. He was pleased with the news.

They packed up camp and left the supplies in the back of the cave. Still several hours before dawn, they decided to leave. Based on her memories, Avant's best guess was a time difference of twelve hours, which would put them in Dallas at three p.m.

"Isn't it exciting? Did you ever believe anything like this was possible? I can't wait to take a shower and drink a Diet Coke."

"I admit it is more than I thought possible. I am ready to see the world from which you came, and to find my son."

Avant put his arms around her, holding her in tandem. She thought of her dad and how much she hadn't known about him. Now that he was gone, she knew him better than when he was alive. Wishing she could talk to him, she halted the flow of love as it filled her heart.

A light flashed. They stood in her dad's study, Avant's arms firmly around her.

Chapter Twenty-Six

Avant blinked, the light momentarily blinding him. As his vision returned, he gaped at dark wooden shelves filled with leather-bound books. The transition had been instantaneous and seamless.

"Ouch! Avant, please loosen your grip. My ribs are still bruised." Abigail winced.

"I'm sorry."

He released his hold. She rounded the large, oak desk and sat down. There he stood in another world—*Abigail's world*. He turned in a circle, taking in the room: the sights, the sounds, the smell.

Since the day of their first meeting, he'd desired to see it, but after she Implanted into him, Abby's memories locked around him and drew him here to *Dallas*. Hundreds—*thousands* maybe—of books lined the shelves, books printed by machines. He ran his hand over an armchair near the stone fireplace. The leather and textiles of the furniture were all crafted by machines. It was an age of superior technology and discovery, but spiritual infancy and moral decay. He shook his head.

Abigail rummaged through the documents in the desk, upon which sat a light illuminating the contents. She held the…telephone—*yes, that was it*—and she pressed buttons on the handset.

"Susan, this is Abby." She spoke in English. "If you come to the study, I'll tell you. Can you bring some coffee with you—and two cups?"

She glanced over at him and nodded to a chair in front of the desk. "You can sit down." She began sifting through papers and lit up a windowed machine on the desk, a *computer*.

He sat in a leather, winged-back chair and picked up the quill…*pen* from the desk. The writing instrument, made of weighted metal similar to that of his sword, felt sleek as he turned it in his hand.

A few minutes later, a large woman pushing a cart came wheeling into the study. Abigail jumped up and ran to embrace her. According to Abigail's memories, she was the house manager. "Susan. How are you?"

"Abby, girl, where have you been? You've been gone for almost a year, and— Good Lord, child, what are you wearin'?" The woman held Abigail's arms from her body and studied her ragged appearance.

"You wouldn't believe me if I told you, but I'm back now. For a little while, anyway." Abby motioned for him. "This is Avant. He'll be staying with us."

The substantial woman eyed him with suspicion.

She was important to Abigail, and he needed to make a good impression. He bowed, took her hand, and kissed it. He smiled his most charming smile and said, "It is a pleasure to meet you, Susan."

She blushed, and Abigail rolled her eyes. *"Avant."*

Glancing up to his beauty, he grinned and sat back in the chair. They would need Susan's help for many things during this visit. He was already fond of the woman who looked at Abigail with such love.

Susan smiled sweetly. "Avant, honey, can I get you a cup a coffee?"

"Yes, thank you."

Susan poured two cups of coffee. "Your daddy knew this would happen, honey. He left Doug and I specific instructions on what to do if you disappeared. We've kept things pretty much the same and have been tellin' people you were travelin' in Europe."

Hmm. Jo-Naphen had prepared for the contingency that Abigail would Implant to Jastain. That must mean he had also given her direction on how to find and restore the Crown.

"Susan, I need to get into Daddy's safe. There's something in there I need."

"Well, Abby, it's your safe now. You should have the combination in the papers Doug gave you from the will."

Confidence surged in his chest. What they sought would be in the safe. The Light had revealed it to Abigail through her dream. This had to be it.

Susan looked at Avant and asked, "Do you take cream or sugar, honey?"

He smiled. "You decide."

Susan raised her eyebrows. "Oh, I think you'd like a little sugar."

He chuckled as Abigail pursed her lips at the exchange. He sipped the hot beverage, which had a rich roasted flavor with a hint of sweetness.

After their cup of coffee, Abigail asked, "Susan, could you make us some of your pancakes and bacon? We need to bathe and change clothes."

"You know I will, honey." She wheeled the cart back toward the kitchen.

The clothes he'd worn for days clung to his skin. A bath would be a welcome friend. Abigail led him upstairs to what he assumed was the master chamber, her father's. The dark wooden furniture filled the lightly colored room. Though the pieces were substantial, the delicately carved wood gave an air of elegance. A solid color rug, made from a textile he'd never seen, spanned from wall to wall across the floor.

Framed photographs—captured moments in time—sat atop a chest of drawers. He wandered over and studied each photo as Abigail flitted about the room finding him supplies. A beautiful blonde child with bouncing curls in a formal dress next to a Christmas tree. Jo-Naphen with her on his lap.

She darted into an adjacent room lined with clothing and tossed a pair of pants at him. "Can you wear these?"

He tried them on. The waist fit but the legs were too short.

She crinkled her nose and shook her head. "You can wear Daddy's flip-flops and shorts to the mall, and we'll get you some clothes after we eat—and I open the safe."

What might a *flip-flop* be?

He watched her flit and scurry, and he chuckled as she gathered things in her arms. She was his little take-charge captain. To see her in her element both fascinated and frightened him. If he relinquished control of the quest, would he ever regain it? She shooed him out of the way to open one of the drawers. He tightened his lips. *I doubt it.*

What if she loved her world too much to return to Jastain? This had been his primary fear all along. "Abigail, how does it feel to be back?"

She halted her flurry to ponder. "Strange…and familiar." She scanned the room and lit with a smiled. "C'mon. I have a special treat for you."

My Light, she was a vision, even rumpled and weatherworn. He followed her into a large tiled room. She opened an oversized door made from glass and turned a knob on the wall. Water sprouted like a fresh spring. Steam gathered as Abigail handed him a long plush towel, washcloth, soap, and some kind of handheld machine.

He turned the small instrument over in his hand. "What is this?"

She grinned. "I guess I don't have many memories with this, do I? It's an electric razor." She flipped a button on the handle. It buzzed to life. She held it to his face. Moving it in a circular motion, she touched a small area of his jaw. The instrument vibrated against his cheek.

He reached up to feel where she'd stroked. The skin was as smoothly shaven as if he had used the sharpest of blades.

The mirrored room fogged.

"Enjoy. And let me know if you need anything. You may not want to leave after this." She pumped her brows as she left him there. A bolt of desire shot through him.

Watching her leave, he considered asking her to stay. My Light, she precipitated a response in him that made him pulse with heat from his nose to his knees. The now-familiar Implanted memory flooded his mind for the third time that day, and he hissed out a breath to maintain control of his body. If his self-control was in jeopardy before her Implanting, it now crumbled under the weight of her memories.

The hot water methodically pounded his tense shoulders, relieving the tension. Abigail's massages were the only thing that had ever released the tightness in his shoulders. His eyes rolled back into his head as he thought of the pleasure her hands afforded him. Unfortunately, her hands caused other tension within him.

He let the water beat against his back as he shaved and washed. Feeling more relaxed, he dried and dressed. Abigail was correct in thinking he would enjoy the shower. But wearing the new undergarments restricted his freedom. With a frown, he donned the T-shirt and shorts she'd tossed at him.

*****

Abby hurried to her own bathroom and showered until all the hot water was gone. She washed and conditioned her hair, shaved her legs, exfoliated, moisturized, spritzed, and sprayed anything she could find among her many toiletry items.

Her favorite jeans fell off her hips. Pulling on her skinny jeans, she surveyed herself. They fit but were loose. She pumped her fist in the mirror. *Yeah!*

After she dressed, she found the paperwork and the combination to the safe. She went to the study and opened the locked casing. Inside were several files filled with papers and an empty oval box made of inlaid wood.

She flipped through the various legal documents. In the middle of them lay an envelope with her name written on the front. Abby opened the letter.

My Dear Abigail,

If you are reading this, then something has happened, and I wasn't able to make it back to you. I'm sorry I can't be there. I'm sorry that you're alone on this journey. I've regretted every moment away from you, but please know you have been in my thoughts.

The first thing you need to do is find Chad. He loves you and can lead you to me. I will explain everything in detail when you find me.

Be careful. There are those who seek to destroy you, and they are closer than you think. Trust no one in your father's house or employ, and tell no one where you are going or what you plan to do.

I hope to find you soon and find you well.

All of my love,

Raieda

The letter was dated this past December, after her father's death and her disappearance. Her mother was *alive*—and somehow she'd placed the letter in the safe without anyone knowing. Abby put the paper back in the envelope and stuffed it in her pocket.

All the years of missed time with Raieda came rushing in on her. She'd lived without a mother all of her life and rarely thought of having one. Now Abby was to welcome her with open arms? She replaced the contents and closed the safe.

Raieda must've had her reasons. Hope sprang in her heart, but years of solitude held her emotions in check. *They better be good reasons.*

She headed to the kitchen to find Avant.

*****

Avant peered down at the strange, ridiculous shoes. The little fastening between his toes, which provided the only means to secure them to his feet, rubbed annoyingly. He sneered. *Flip-flops.* The name did them justice. What other indignities must he endure? He sighed and clopped downstairs toward the smell of food.

In the kitchen, Susan prepared him a plate of round flatbread called *pancakes*, which she covered in butter and a thick, sweet liquid similar to honey. He moaned at the delightful flavor and ate them in five bites. The kind woman brought him another, larger stack with pieces of fried pork.

Abigail stepped into the kitchen, her face pale with concern. Something was wrong. "What is it? Did you open the safe?"

"Yes, but there was nothing there that can help us. We'll have to look somewhere else. Maybe Daddy had something placed upstairs. We can look when we come back from shopping."

"Avant, we can't trust anyone. I've found something. We'll talk when we get out of here."

He nodded his understanding. What had she found? Whatever it was, it had clearly shaken her.

"Are you ready to go get some new duds?" Her eyes twinkled. "Susan, is Daddy's car in the garage?"

"Yes, ma'am. Hector's been usin' it to run errands, so it should start just fine." Susan pointed to a set of small metal objects hanging from the wall. "Should I make dinner for y'all tonight?"

Abigail stepped over and picked up the dangling metal. "That'd be great. I think Avant needs to experience Tex-Mex." She glanced in his direction and raised her eyebrows. "Can I still use my credit cards?"

Tex-Mex? It sounded a lot like flip-flops.

Susan turned to face them. "You should be able to, but you can use the checks from your trust, honey."

"Oh, right. Thanks."

Finished with breakfast, he followed her into the garage. A large, shining black carriage waited in splendor. It was beyond anything he could have fathomed. His fingertips slid over the supple leather like fresh butter over bread, and it smelled just as mouth-watering. He walked around the vehicle. His heart pounded in his chest.

He lifted his gaze to Abigail. "I want to drive."

Her brow furrowed. She hated relinquishing control as much as he did, but this was a lesson she needed to learn if she was to be his queen. And the truth of the matter was he did want to drive the car.

"I don't know, Avant. Driving a car is not like riding a horse, and Dallas traffic is the worst."

"I am aware of that, Abigail. Are you so loath to allow me into the driver's seat?" Coaxing her in this instance might be the best way.

The familiar struggle played across her face, and he knew from experience the war raged in her mind. "Do you trust me?" He held her gaze, waiting for an outcome.

She sighed and rolled her eyes. "Oh, all right. Here." She tossed him the keys.

He understood how much relinquishing control meant and he was humbled by her gesture. The desire to kiss her overwhelmed him. Barely concealing a smile, he stalked to her and swept an arm around her waist. Her eyes rounded like a doe's in the hunter's sights. Blood pulsed in his head, drowning out all noise. His vision focused on her lush lips, which parted slightly as he lowered his head.

Brushing his lips over hers was the purest heaven. Her sweet flesh yielded to his, and she sighed. His body bridled to claim her. *Slowly, Avant.* Slanting his mouth, he deepened the kiss but never sped the pace. She tasted of sweet maple and pecan. His hand braced her head and fisted in her hair. He kissed her long and deep, drinking in their shared desire like festival wine.

Chapter Twenty-Seven

It is not yet time. With an act that tested the outer boundaries of Avant's will, he pulled from the kiss and smiled. Abigail stood with her lids closed, swaying as if she might lose her balance. Slowly she opened her eyes and stared at him with such love and desire he forgot his purpose.

Finally regaining some of his senses, he sucked in a deep breath and opened the passenger door for her, before rounding the car and slipping behind the steering wheel.

Luminescent numbers and characters glowed across black glass on the dashboard and a black lever sat enticingly between the two front seats.

Still appearing a bit dazed and disoriented, Abigail pulled a letter out, which he took from her trembling hand and read.

By the Light, they could not linger here. He tossed the note on the center console and rubbed his face. Danger lurked in this world. *Who here could know of the existence of Jastain?* He started the car and backed out of the drive.

"Abigail, I am bewildered. We must find what we seek and return to Jastain. This ominous danger is unsettling. How can we defend ourselves from it?"

She shook her head as the car raced smoothly down the road. "I don't know. I didn't find anything else in the safe. This has to be the clue we're looking for."

He stared ahead as he traversed the crowded streets. The power of the car's engine thrummed through his body, energizing every cell. His Gift told him the letter was not the clue they sought, but for now, it was all they had. They must move quickly. In his world, he could protect her, but here, the unknown moved in every shadow.

It was clear they must go to Boston. *Damnable Darkness.* He'd not prepared for a face-to-face meeting with *this Chad.* Avant seethed at the thought of the man. He hadn't anticipated the possibility that the Darkness had allies in her world. His foot ground into the accelerator and the car roared to life with the surge.

Since Abigail had Implanted into him, two things had happened: Avant was now hopelessly in love with the woman. And, unfortunately for him, the memories of her and *this Chad* making love assailed his mind relentlessly.

These memories shook him to his core. The sheer volume of the encounters and the variety in which they occurred drove him to madness. His marriage had been loving, as far as he knew, but his marriage bed was wrought with formality. Perhaps had it been more passionate, Sentieve would not have strayed. Her betrayal pained him, but he felt a measure of responsibility and accepted at least a portion of the blame.

In his world, unspoken rules governed the relations of lovers, to which most adhered. However, the obvious pleasure the unfathomable variations brought to the couple—to her—forced him to reevaluate those restrictive standards.

One particular memory he battled incessantly to keep from his mind. The erotic thought made him rage with jealousy, but it also made him rage with desire—a desire he could no longer deny. It had been too long, and the well of passion he suppressed was too full for these memories. His will was formidable, but it was also fallible. More than once Abigail had taken it to task, and as his love for her grew, desire for her engulfed him.

They had a mission to complete. The future of Jastain must be paramount. His Gift told him the time was near for the battle to begin. His Gift was never wrong. However, regarding his desire for Abigail, his Gift was silent other than the dream.

When he became king, he would marry Abigail, and she would be his queen. Then he vowed to systematically replace every memory he had been viciously forced to endure with a new image. He knew exactly where he would begin.

The beeping sound of technology startled him out of his thoughts. He winced, in pain from his arousal, and took several deep breaths. Abigail had activated her new intelligent phone on the car's technology.

Avant drove into the parking lot of the shopping mall. He knew well where it was and where she liked to park because of her numerous memories.

Volumes of merchandise filled countless storefronts and multitudes of people milled in and out. The moving staircases loped along, transporting people up and down several floors. Even the marketplaces of the Eastern traders could not compare. Scantily clothed women occupied the windows of a pink store, and the smell of ginger and strawberries held him captive at the door. *Victoria's Secret, indeed.* Based on what he saw, it did not appear Victoria was leaving anything a secret.

"C'mon, Commander, you might get into trouble in there." With a mischievous smirk on her face, Abigail pulled him along.

In less than an hour and a half, she'd purchased five new shirts, two pairs of pants, two pairs of shoes, and undergarments called boxers, which were less restrictive and more in line with his normal attire.

He constantly shifted his eyes through the crowd, worried about the danger. Abigail had refused to allow him to bring his sword. Wearing the damnable shorts and without his weapon, he might as well have been completely unclothed. He stared into a storefront and frowned. At least he fit in.

Though he had Abigail's Implanting, he was out of his element and unsure of his defenses in the event of a battle. "Abigail, I understand the letter says it is from your mother, but something is not right. Why would she not attempt to find you before now?"

"I don't know, but I'm sure she had her reasons. Don't you want me to find my mother?"

The hurt in her tone tightened bands around his heart, but he wasn't certain he did want her to find her mother. At least, not until a few other things became clearer.

He drove the carriage back to the house, gripping the steering and allowing the speed of the vehicle to thrum through him like wine. It was exhilarating, intoxicating, and Abigail was right: He could get used to it.

"Tomorrow, we'll Implant to Boston first thing in the morning, after I get some cash. But we'll still have to find a place to spend the night once we get there. Unless you want to stay with Chad."

Ignoring her jibe, Avant said, "I'm not delighted with the idea of this Chad being the only one who can help us. It seems strange that your mother would entrust him with such an important task."

Avant had never met Raieda nor had he realized Sentieve knew her. Abigail's family had long fled Jastain when he married. "Perhaps Raieda was the one with the Gift of Placement Implanting. It is a rare gift, and it does stand to reason that she would use it in the service of the Light."

"And it would make sense that I also have the Gift of Placement Implanting."

He nodded and returned to the other subject that plagued his mind. Avant didn't know how he would control the rage he felt for this young man, unless he could stop the mental barrage. "I do not care for the idea that this Chad is still in love with you, Abigail. Although it makes me wonder if there is any man who can resist your charms."

She shot him a perturbed glance. "Some seem to manage just fine."

When they returned to the house, she took a nap. He found the hot tub and television a welcome retreat. He settled into the warm, bubbling water, which reminded him of the hot spring in the cave. He'd been a fool that day when he'd allowed the intimacy between them and he'd been a fool to push her away after the fact. He'd wished a thousand times over to relive that moment. One day he would, one day soon. His body and heart had known what his mind had yet to comprehend: Abigail was his life, his destiny. He loved her and would stop at nothing to protect her.

That letter. If Raieda had the Gift, why had she not used it to find Abigail? The facts were amiss, but troubling his angel with them now seemed unwise. She was still struggling with the news that her mother might be alive. He would just have to stay on guard until the mystery was revealed.

The letter had said Chad still loved her. Of course, Chad still loved Abigail. She was foolish not to realize that he'd jumped into relations with her friend out of heartbreak. Avant would wager, even now, the man would have her, if Abigail wanted him. If she wanted him. Did she? The thought was too painful. Avant already shared her heart with Petra, which was his own fault, but he would share no more. She belonged to him, and he belonged to her, by more than mere sentiment. It was time he claimed her as his own. He doubted any two people were ever more intimately connected than were he and Abigail.

"You know that thing will turn your brain to mush, right?" Abigail stood over him, apparently looking to see what he was wearing.

He flashed her a sly smile. "I can certainly understand how one could waste away in front of it. I've been watching this CNN, and they're speaking of so many evils I cannot comprehend the scope of it all. Abigail, your world is frightening."

Her gaze roamed his bare chest. "This isn't my world, not anymore. My home is with you. You're my family."

Love and desire for her engulfed him, and he pulled her into the hot tub.

"Avant, now I have to blow dry my hair again!"

Joy welled and laughter rumbled from him. He loved the feel of her, the smell, everything.

Water dripping from her cheeks and soaked to the bone, she stared with that huntress gaze that thrilled and disturbed him. She drew closer and laced her arms around his neck. He looked into her eyes and filled himself with the offering he found there. His breath sped. To claim her in this moment was not his plan. As she leaned in to kiss him, he turned his head, allowing her to kiss his cheek instead. He lifted her arms from around his neck and pulled from her embrace.

Her eyes blazed. "Why are you pulling away? Again?"

He labored to steady his breathing. "Why do you insist on being the aggressor?"

"What?"

He stared into her lovely eyes. "Have any of the relationships you initiated with men borne healthy fruit?" Her memories indicated they had not. Abigail's father, though mostly absent, was the only male in her life who didn't succumb to her dominant personality. This was the reason she equated Avant with him. It was also the reason Avant could not allow her to direct their relationship.

"So you're asking me to relinquish the driver's seat?"

She was as sharp as a forged blade. He held her gaze and nodded once.

"And what if you never start the car?"

"That is the rub with relinquishing control, is it not?" He brushed a drop of water from her cheek.

She dropped her sights and climbed out of the water, dripping with disappointment. He watched her leave, noting the way the wet clothing clung to her, revealing the sensual curves of her body.

Be patient, my angel.

*****

Abby stomped upstairs, stripped the wet clothes from her body, and threw herself across the bed. *What an overbearing, arrogant asshole!* He was such a control freak.

Was he trying to piss her off? But the look on his face hadn't indicated he did it out of spite or control. His heart had shone in his eyes. Still, he rejected her. Again.

What did he mean the *fruit* of her previous relationships? He knew she'd only had one long-term boyfriend. He also knew nothing good came from it. She huffed out a breath.

Chad had always given in. Accepted into the MIT post-grad program, he was a nuclear engineering major on full scholarship. Generally quiet, Chad was the kind of guy who let her lead. The casual ease of their relationship had given her the security she desired and provided Chad with a social outlet.

Now she saw the truth. She'd never respected him. In fact, when he'd confronted her about her late nights and heavy drinking, she'd kicked him out of the house. The moment he'd tried to influence her, she'd shut him out.

Avant was right. *Damn.* She was the control freak. It chapped her that he called bullshit and didn't let her get away with trying to manage him. It also filled her with respect for him, and made her want him even more, as if that were possible.

She smiled at the thought of his face as he sat behind the wheel of the Beemer. The thrill in his eyes tickled her. *And that kiss.* That kiss set her on fire. It was the first time he had ever initiated anything with her. She gulped at the memory as heat pooled low in her belly.

Abby packed their clothes in a suitcase, along with other essentials, and hid the bag under her bed. She straightened her hair and dressed in a sleeveless white blouse with a ruffled V-neck, and a black gauze skirt. God, everything was so different. She was different. Peering in the mirror was like staring at a different person. She didn't look anything like the girl she'd been.

She knocked on Avant's door and walked in. "Hey, pretty boy. Are you ready for dinner?"

"I'm ready." He sauntered out of the bathroom wearing the crisp, white button-down shirt and blue jeans.

Abby's knees turned to mush, and she almost fell to the floor, where she could have picked up her jaw.

It was a silly schoolgirl fantasy, but since the night of the Harvest Festival, she couldn't help but wonder what he would look like in blue jeans. The answer more than justified her desire to see it.

"Oh my God. You are so cool!" Her eyes raked his body, and she wished she could touch him—everywhere. "You look *hot!*"

He laughed. "Your colloquialisms are amusing. It is a strange thing that one could be *hot* and *cool* at the same time."

"But you are!"

They ate tacos and enchiladas for dinner. Abby laughed so hard she snorted iced tea from her nose when Avant took a bite of jalapeño and had to down his drink to quench the three-alarm fire. She couldn't stop staring at him. Here in her world, where he wasn't the feared commander, he lost some of his stuffiness—not all but some. Even if he wasn't exactly relaxed, he didn't stand on formality either. The fact that he was the best damn looking man she'd ever laid eyes on didn't hurt either.

Still wiping the tears from his eyes, he asked, "Was there nothing else in your father's safe, Abigail?"

"Only documents and an empty box."

"I know it is likely fruitless, but I wish to peruse the papers. Perhaps something will reveal itself to me."

"It's worth a try. We don't really have much else to go on."

After dinner, she left Avant in the study with the papers and went to her room.

She turned on her computer and sifted through email. Several friends had graduated. A couple had gotten married. One had gotten arrested. The Aggies had a decent football season but basketball was looking up. *Sweet Sixteen in March Madness. Gig 'em.*

The radio played a familiar tune, and her foot tapped to the rhythm. God, she'd missed music. A new song played, one she'd never heard. The music caught her up, and thoughts of Avant filled her. His smell. His kiss. She danced around the room as her innermost fantasies sprang to life, warming her heart and heating her body. Images of him holding her, making love to her, spending his life with her, filled the space in the beautiful song. Closing her eyes, she swayed with the music, her love and desire thrumming strong inside her.

The song ended. Her eyes opened. Avant stood in the doorframe, watching.

Shit. Those thoughts had been unguarded. A tidal wave of humiliation and embarrassment flushed her from head to toe. What could she do about it now? It wasn't like he didn't already know about her sexual fantasies, but to have him catch her red-handed was beyond mortifying.

She squared her shoulders and met his gaze, prepared for some kind of rebuke. Her heart skipped a beat. She didn't see the usual look of sympathy or restraint he normally possessed—his eyes flamed wild with passion.

A new tune played, familiar, sensual. For a moment, they stood with just the song between them. The desire emanating from him pounded as severely as the beat of the music.

In an instant, he spanned the distance between them in three strides. With one arm around her waist and the other behind her head, he pulled her into a rapturous kiss. His passion, a breathtaking rush, swept over her and continued to spill like a waterfall, thrashing with powerful current.

Slanting his lips against her mouth, he took as he pleased, and she tried to keep up. Hot and forceful, his tongue danced across hers, his velvet strokes sending electric shocks coursing through her core. Dizziness threatened her balance, and breath was in short supply. She could only hold on. His urgency possessed her like a demon spirit, and heat burned between her legs.

After a time—she couldn't say how long—his pace slowed, but his kiss, still deep, became languid and full of promise. Leisurely and fluid, his mouth moved but never relinquished his hold. She molded to his chest and would've given her fortune to stay in this moment for the rest of forever. His hold loosened, and the kiss slowed like a carnival ride coming to a stop.

Finally, he pulled from her lips. If he let go, she'd melt into a pool on the floor.

He released her body and walked to the door.

She sucked in a breath and held out her arms for balance. Her pounding heart sank and her eyes refocused. *Damn.* It was over.

But then he closed the door and turned around.

Capturing her in his sight, he unbuttoned his shirt as he stalked toward her. She let out a gasp and stepped back.

The feral desire in his eyes left little doubt as to his intent. A chill swept over her where flame had burned, and she continued to retreat. Never releasing her from his gaze, he slipped the shirt from his shoulders, discarded it, and reached for her. The back of her knees hit the bed. She swallowed hard.

Pulling her close, Avant whispered into her ear, "Why are you afraid, little rabbit?" He slid his hands under her blouse and pushed it up over her head. Then he brushed his lips down her neck, over her shoulder, and across her chest, which rose and fell with force. Her senses heightened and every touch intensified. She felt his lips and breath like velvet on her skin, but most of all she felt the heat. It radiated in waves. He slipped his fingers under the waistband of her skirt and pulled it past her hips until it fell in a *whoosh* to the floor.

God Almighty. Is this really happening? His warm tongue trailed over her skin, indicating it was. Her eyes fluttered closed. He released the hooks on her bra and slid the straps from her arms. His hands trembled as they cupped her breasts. Pleasure shot through her core as his thumbs stroked her hardened nipples.

Any fear incinerated in the wake of his touch and only desire existed. Her hands slid the length of his chest down to his jeans, the muscles rippling under her fingers. He blew out a hot breath. Their hunger for one another drowned anything else in its way. Abby shimmied from her panties and scooted onto the bed.

The look of want and need in his eyes pulsed heat between her legs.

*****

Avant drank in the vision of her naked body like cool water on parched soil. He removed his jeans and boxers and then slid into bed next to her. Slipping one arm under her and the other on her hip, he pulled Abigail to his mouth, drowning her in kisses. How long he'd waited. His need to have her beneath him, to make love to her, overtook his will, and he relinquished control.

Everything dimmed but her softness. His heart slammed against his ribs. With insistent lips drawing in her sweetness, he took possession of her with a ferocity that shocked him. He wove his hand into the back of her hair and pulled her head back. She sighed and trembled. The fear and vulnerability in her eyes had intoxicated him, and in his drunkenness, released his doubts. He couldn't do anything but give himself over to passion.

Brushing her neck with his lips, he exhaled in her ear. "My angel. My beautiful angel."

A treasure in his arms. Where to go first? His hands, finally free to roam her silky skin, caressed her sides and hips. He slid his palms around her waist and down her backside, where he grabbed and pressed her firmly against his thigh. She shuddered and moaned. If she continued, he'd not be able to withhold his release.

He bent and filled his mouth with her dark pink bud. He teased the tip with his tongue and sucked in the pebbled flesh. She arched into him. Her warm hands explored him, moving across his shoulders and back, intensifying the throbbing need to penetrate her.

Her fingernails raked over his hips, and her fingers kneaded his behind, pressing the length of their bodies together. A growl from deep in his chest rumbled from his lips. He seized her thighs and pushed her legs apart. He trailed his fingers along the length of her satin folds drenched with desire. She whimpered. The sound of her pleasure was his undoing. He could wait no longer.

He rolled on top of her and positioned himself between her legs. Then mercilessly, he thrust into her with a force that caused her to cry out. Had he not been connected to her mind, he would have thought her in pain. The untamed need within him took her unashamedly. He pulled back and drove deeply again and again, capturing her, claiming her with each thrust. Their bodies merged along with minds and hearts. Light gathered and electric current circuited through them. She threw her head back and arched into him, meeting him stroke for stroke. The pleasure that engulfed him built, and he could not contain it. He withheld nothing but pounded with his relentless passion.

Her thighs tensed. She came with a rapturous explosion of sounds and shudders that swept him over the cliff. His long-denied desire roared through his heart as his seed pulsed into her body. Light shattered. Raw energy and emotion, in an ebb and flow loop, gave as aggressively as it received.

Their bodies became a reflection of what their hearts and minds already were. Intertwined. Merged. One.

He collapsed onto her, breathing in the faint strawberry scent of her hair. His heart raced and sweat streamed down the sides of his face. Rolling to his back, he pulled her to him. She wrapped an arm around his waist and a leg over his thigh, nestling her head into his shoulder.

"Holy fuck!" Her words came breathy and labored.

Through his panting, a hearty chuckle escaped his lips. "Yes, wasn't it?"

"If I'd known letting you lead would produce these results, I'd have surrendered months ago."

A feeling of invincibility spread through him at the thought of giving her so much pleasure. After the Crown was restored, he would make Abigail his queen. She was for him. He glanced down at his angel with gold-spun tresses. Her creamy skin against his filled a longing he never believed could be sated, and he drank her in.

Her desire for him was just as great. Warmth spread through him at the thought of how she loved him, and he pulled her in tightly. *Mine.*

Smiling in satisfaction, he was pleased with the memories he had created. He glanced down at her body draped over him, finer than kingly robes. He was by no means finished creating new memories tonight. *Let her dwell on these images tomorrow and feel the aftereffects of my claim on her.* This Chad should take care, or he would find himself at the end of a sword.

The exquisite pleasure of her flesh set his body into motion again. By the Light, he would tell her tomorrow that this passion needed to be shelved until their task was completed, when they could properly marry. Humph. He scowled at her. To think he could abstain now he had tasted her was folly, and she would be no help to his cause. Tomorrow they would cloak their passion and wait for its time, but tonight….

He silently held her and then made love to her again. And again. Exploring her like a new treasure, he unlocked the hidden places of pleasure she'd never articulated. Her secret desires lay bare before him, and he intended to fulfill. Every. One.

Chapter Twenty-Eight

Abby's head lay on Avant's chest, his heartbeat providing comfort and security. Her body felt like butter at room temperature—the slightest movement would cause her to irreparably melt into the mattress. If the house caught fire, she'd just have to go down in flames, because there was no way her jellied limbs could save her.

With his middle finger he traced her arm, shoulder to elbow and back again. "Abigail, have you considered what you'll do after we accomplish our task?"

The sound of his husky baritone poured over her. "Mmm." She sighed. "I haven't really thought much about it."

"I want you to live in the palace with me." His heartbeat quickened under her, and he swallowed. "Have you ever considered being queen?"

Had he just proposed? She lifted her head to see his face. "Queen? What do you mean?"

"Abigail, I expect to be in the castle after this is over, and I expect you to be there with me." He bent his head and kissed her. "My Light, you will make a beautiful queen."

Her heart pounded in her chest and tears stung her eyes. She held him tightly and smiled. "Queen? It just seems so unreal. Wow. Of course I want to be with you."

After all these months, he'd finally allowed himself to open up. He wanted to marry her? To live with her? Holy crap. She was going to be a queen.

"Then we need to regain our kingdom. I searched the files you gave me but found nothing. My Gift tells me this Chad is not the answer we need. Are you certain there was nothing else in the safe? It seems the most logical place."

"There were only the files—and the empty box." A revelation flooded her mind. "Why would my father leave an empty box in the safe?"

Apparently Avant was thinking the same thing. He jumped from the bed and slid on his jeans. She threw on her robe, and they trailed down to the study.

After she opened the safe, Abby carried the box back to her bedroom. She flipped on a lamp and sat cross-legged in the middle of the bed. Pop music played softly as they studied the oval container of inlaid wood. Opening the lid, she let out a frustrated sigh. Still empty.

He reached over. "Let me see it."

She absently handed it to him. Where would her dad have hidden something for her? This had to be it.

"This looks strikingly similar to a box my father made for me." He opened the lid. Feeling the inside edge, he found a button that opened another compartment underneath. "Abigail, look. The rubies!" Avant gasped as he gently removed two papers and handed them to her.

She laid the papers to the side and moved closer to look in the box. The stones sat securely in the bottom of the secret compartment. "We found them." She wrapped her arms around him and captured his mouth, but he captured hers right back. In a delicate tug-of-war, their lips playfully battled for supremacy.

Avant pulled from her kiss. "Where are those papers?"

She caught her breath, handed one to him, and then opened the other.

Abigail,

I trust you have found this letter when the time was ripe. You'll find the Crown and the sapphires in the house of Naphen, your grandfather. I was entrusted with the Stone of Light and have given it to you to keep until the Crown is restored. The mated earring is a diamond for which I paid a high price, but if the stones have found you, all is not lost. The amethysts and the emeralds have been entrusted to Kasten. Raieda had possession of the rubies, but upon her death, I've placed them in this box. She was known by the evil one to be your mother, and could not risk your life by being with you. She loved you, Abigail.

I write in haste and regret I couldn't share more. My angel, we have each made our own sacrifice to the Light, and you not least of all, Chosen One. To reset the Crown will not be an easy task, but I foresee the end and your great accomplishment.

I've always been proud of you, and I've always loved you. — Daddy

She laid the paper at her side. A lump formed in her throat and tears dropped on her leg. *I wish you were here, Daddy.* But he'd confirmed her mother's death. Was it possible Raieda had gone into hiding and was still alive? Or was something else going on?

This letter confirmed everything. Her father had known of her destiny. He'd hidden her away until the right time. All those years of thinking she wasn't good enough, that he didn't love her enough, were a guise to keep her safe so she could return to the place where she belonged. He had known she would marry the king, that one day she would be queen.

Avant still held the other parchment. He appeared to be rereading it.

"Avant, you need to read this letter. It's from my dad. All we need are the amethysts, the emeralds, and the Crown—and, of course, we have to confront the king's army…. Avant? What is it?"

The blood had drained from his face, and he swayed as if he might pass out.

"Honey, are you all right?" She touched his arm. His chilled flesh shook beneath her fingers.

He tossed her the paper and rose from the bed. Pacing to the window, he peered out into the dark. She glanced down and unfolded the parchment. Perfectly formed, scrolling letters decorated the aged paper. Her father's writing.

On the last eve of her twentieth birthday, The Seed of Light will be fully grown and the Crown of Light fully known.

A song for the singing
Life for growth
Love now in bringing
Hearts once were smote
Hope to the wise
The tree now is green
Crown her the Head
Make her the Queen

Blessings and bitterness at dawn will they duel
The Keeper of Stones crowns the new rule
The Chosen One now chooses
The fruit borne is seen
A king rules no more

The Reign belongs to the Queen

Annum 1567 — Song of the High Priest
Festival Keihev Neous (Festival of New Song)

She finished reading the last prophecy of Avant's father, the high priest, as transcribed by Jo-Naphen, her father, over forty years before.

Avant's voice was soft and strained. "Abigail, do you understand what this means?"

The final pieces of her destiny fitted into place with a resounding clank. The spiritual weight of her people rested solely on her shoulders. "Uhh, yeah…I think I do."

*****

The next morning Avant was gone from bed when Abby woke. She stretched under the soft sheets. A flush of heat spread over her as the events of the previous evening replayed in her mind. She could still feel him inside her as she got up and headed to the shower.

Once Avant decided on something, there was no turning back. Exhaling heavily, her body quivered at the thought of his touch. Places she didn't even know she had were tender and sore. She'd never experienced so many climaxes in one night, not even with battery-powered equipment. Turning on the water, she stepped into the steaming flow.

After reading the letter and finding the missing prophecy, they'd not spoken. Avant had climbed back into bed, and she'd curled up next to him.

She knew he'd expected the prophecy to name him the king, but so what? He was still going to be king. *Like she could rule a freaking kingdom by herself.* They would do it together. She smiled. They made a good team. Warmth pooled in her lower regions at the memory of just how good.

After her shower, she went to the kitchen for breakfast, where Avant was eating bacon and eggs prepared by a doting Susan.

A nonchalant smile curved his lips.

Rolling her eyes, she knew the drill by now—pretend nothing happened—so she smiled back. "Did you sleep well?"

"Well enough. And you?" His eyes twinkled but underlying concern dimmed their shine.

"I must've, because I don't remember *anything* after we ate dinner." She sighed in teasing innocence.

Avant narrowed his eyes. "Indeed?"

"Indeed." She bent and hovered over his lips before she kissed him.

He swept an arm around her and pulled her into his lap. His mouth captured hers and drew her into a kiss that tasted like bacon. She wrapped her arms around his neck and pressed into him as if their bodies could blend into a single being.

They stopped by the bank, where she withdrew seven thousand dollars from her trust fund. Avant had insisted on driving but otherwise hadn't said a word. When they got back to the house, Abby told Susan they were leaving. She just couldn't bring herself to think Susan would do anything to hurt her. She hugged the stout woman and promised to check in once in a while.

As they entered her room, she turned to face Avant. "Are you okay? Something seems not quite right."

"We need to go." His eyes wouldn't meet hers.

She raised her eyebrows and wagged her index finger at him. "No way, mister. You're not pulling that caveman bullshit on me this morning. Not after what happened last night. Out with it. I can handle anything you have to say, but I can't handle silence."

He looked at her as if she had grown a third eye. "I'm concerned about our trip—and our meeting."

Abby pursed her lips and nodded. She sauntered toward him and pulled his face to hers. "You have nothing to be concerned about." Kissing him, she ran her fingers down the zipper of his pants.

He groaned, halted her hands, and kissed her back. After a way too short a kiss, Avant pulled away. "Abigail, we need to go."

She growled and frowned. That got her at least a half-smile.

"There will be time for this later." Avant wrapped his arms around her from behind as she held the luggage. She could hardly think of anything other than his hard body against her, and she quivered with the memory of the previous night. When she melted back, he bent and brushed her neck with his lips.

Reluctantly, she thought of Chad. A light flashed, and they stood in a deserted corridor of the MIT Nuclear Science Building. Following a short hallway, they made their way to the reception area. Chad would be in the lab.

Already in a mood, Avant waited by the front door, scaring people as they entered. Abby rolled her eyes. They hadn't even found Chad yet.

She approached the security desk. "Can you let Chad Smyth know there's someone waiting to see him?"

She tapped her foot on the linoleum. A few minutes later, the door to the lab buzzed open and Chad came out. His mouth opened in surprise, and she smiled.

"God, Abby. What are you doing here? Is something wrong? Are you okay?"

"I'm sorry to bother you, but I really need your help. Is there a time and a place we could meet to talk?"

He nodded, his gaze never leaving her. "I can be done with this lab in forty-five minutes. Where would you like to meet?"

"I don't know. Someplace...private?" She searched his face for any inkling that he already knew the reason for her visit.

"I live about two miles from here. Would you like to meet there?"

Abby furrowed her brow and shook her head. "I don't really want to see Lyndsea."

"What? Lyndsea...no...Abby, we haven't been together in over six months."

"Oh, I didn't know. Well, okay, your place. What's the address?"

He gave her the address, which she entered into her phone.

"We need to check into our hotel. I'll meet you there in a couple of hours. Do you mind if I bring a friend?" Abby asked, not daring a glance back.

"I don't mind." He opened his arms wide and hugged her. "I've missed you, Abby."

She smiled and watched him go back through the lab door. The shock of seeing him struck her harder than she'd thought it would. He'd changed. His hair was shorter and his glasses different. He looked older, and there was something else different about him too, but Abby couldn't put her finger on it.

She turned to find Avant glaring at her.

Clearly, Chad wasn't the only one who would be dealing with a nuclear reaction in the next forty-five minutes.

Chapter Twenty-Nine

Abby debated whether to take Avant with her to meet Chad. The commander needed to calm down, but would probably be worse if she left him. If he'd even agree to that.

They found a hotel less than five blocks away and checked into the room. Then they took the hotel shuttle to Chad's place.

The high-rise apartment complex sat right off the edge of campus. Chad most likely walked to the lab or rode his bike if the weather permitted.

"I am astounded at his resemblance to Petra, which will make it more difficult to run him through with the blade of my sword."

Abby squinted up at him. "Ha. Ha. Very funny. You have to control your temper. We need Chad's help. If I can forgive him, then you should be able to."

"Abigail, this man betrayed you with your best friend. I will attempt to be civil, but that is the best I can offer."

She sighed. At least he was speaking to her again. She knocked on the door.

Chad opened it quickly, his eyes widening. "Uhh. Hi, Abby."

He seemed taken aback by Avant, who stood almost a head taller.

"Hey, Chad. This is Avant." Abby elbowed Avant hard in the ribs, and he smiled—sort of.

They entered the simple apartment, which had a scenic view of the city. She and Avant sat on the sofa while Chad sat in his favorite armchair across from them. She gazed around the room. "I can't believe you kept that chair."

"Yeah, I got rid of most things but couldn't part with the old chair. I still have my same bed, too."

The sound of every knuckle in Avant's hands cracking punctuated the awkward silence, but she didn't dare glance over at him.

"Abby, I know why you're here. Your mother found me a few months ago and said you'd come looking for me."

She explained to Chad the things that had happened in the past year, as best she could. She told him about her Gift and her purpose. Chad, as she suspected, took it all in stride, never indicating even a hint of disbelief. He listened, but she knew the wheels of his analytical mind were spinning in multiple directions.

When she finished, he simply asked, "Can you show me what you can do?"

She nodded and then focused her mind, opening his refrigerator door and making a Diet Coke fly to her. As it floated by, she grabbed it and popped the top.

"That's impressive. Avant, can you do this as well?" Chad focused his gaze on Avant.

"Yes." She answered for him, looking out of the corner of her eye.

Avant's jaw clenched, and he drummed his fingers on the arm of the sofa. *"This Chad is still in love with you, Abigail."*

"You're wrong, Avant."

Then Chad spoke into her mind, *"No, he isn't. I am still in love with you, Abby."*

Oh my God. Her mind swirled. She wasn't sure what stunned her more: the fact that he still loved her or that he'd heard the unspoken conversation and responded in kind.

Rising to his feet, Avant demanded, "Did he just say he was in love with you, Abigail?" Avant stormed toward the man. "He used the Implanting, Abigail!"

Abby stared wide-eyed at Chad, who shrank like cotton in a dryer. She stood and placed herself between the men. *"Avant, you need to calm down or leave. Which do you prefer?"*

"To leave—with you now!"

Bringing him had been a mistake. "Chad, I'm sorry, but Avant needs to go...do something." She turned to glare at him. "I'll meet you in the lobby after I'm through."

Chad watched with eyes the size of saucers but never said a word.

She walked Avant to the door and pushed him out. *"Please, I won't be long."* She shut the door and turned. "I'm sorry, Chad. He's a little overprotective."

"Is he your...boyfriend?"

Boyfriend? Lover? What the hell was Avant? Abby had to laugh but it held only irony. "No...yes...I don't know. It gets a little confusing sometimes, or so he tells me."

Chad stood and took her hands. "Abby, why did you break up with me? I thought you loved me."

Her heart cringed with the memory of that horrible night. "I did love you, but I was scared. Daddy had died. You were coming to Boston, but he wanted me to finish school. I couldn't stand the prospect of slowly losing you over a long-distance relationship, so I pushed you away."

"Why didn't you agree to marry me? You could've stayed in school. I would've agreed to anything to be with you. I love you, Abby."

"If you loved me, why did you get engaged to Lyndsea?"

"Abby, you were my life. I was living in your house. When you kicked me out, I had nowhere to go. Lyndsea offered her couch, and one thing led to another. I felt horrible afterward, and she ended up pregnant. She lost the baby shortly after we left for Boston, and she moved back to Dallas. It's been the worst time of my life."

She dropped her head to her hands. Abby had driven him away out of fear and had broken his heart. How could she have blamed him for trying to find some happiness? He hadn't betrayed her. She had betrayed him.

"I thought there was no chance I would see you again, but then your mother showed up. She said you would come looking for me, and I hoped…Abby, if you still love me…."

She wanted to comfort him, make his hurt go away, but she couldn't make it worse by leading him on. "Chad, I'm so sorry. I'm in love with someone else. It's so complicated—I can't begin to explain—but my heart isn't my own anymore. Any help you can give us I would appreciate, but I understand if you can't."

"Of course I'll help you." He went to his bedroom, came back, and handed her an envelope. "Your mother left this for you. You'll find the way to contact her in there. Abby, she said this might be dangerous. Please be careful." He glanced down at his hands. "Do many people from the other world have this kind of ability?"

"They don't, and I am surprised that you do."

He nodded in understanding. "Raieda said my father was able to do something like this."

"Really? I never knew…I guess I didn't know a lot of things. How does my mother know your family?"

"Raieda brought me here as a child. My real mother, who is from Jastain, was in some trouble and had to protect me."

"Jastain? What?" *Oh my God!* She'd forgotten Chad was adopted. Chad was Sentieve's son! Raieda hadn't chosen Chad because he loved Abby. She'd chosen him because he was a part of this. "Chad, how much do you know about your biological parents?"

"Not much really. I have a couple of pieces of jewelry. Apparently my father was killed before I was born."

Abby tried to keep her breathing even but hysteria knocked at the door of her muddled brain. Chad had the emeralds. And was possibly Avant's son! She couldn't work this through her mind right now. Avant was waiting downstairs, and he would need some time to absorb this. *She* needed some time to absorb this.

"I'll do whatever I can to help you, Abby. Give me your cell phone number, and I'll call you in a day or so."

"Good. We definitely need to talk…later, but now I have to go."

Holy crap. She called the hotel shuttle on her way to the lobby, where she found Avant pacing in the foyer like a caged tiger. Still too furious to talk, he said nothing, although he might've growled.

They caught the shuttle to the hotel, and then rode up the elevator in complete silence. She couldn't speak. Hell, she could barely think. How was she going to tell him?

Avant unlocked the door to the suite and allowed her to enter. She plopped down on the bed. *In love with my ex-boyfriend's father.* In her whole life, she'd had two lovers. Two. And they were a father/son combo! It was all so *wrong.*

Avant walked to the end of the bed and stared at her. She covered her eyes with her hand. Couldn't he see she was having a Jerry Springer moment?

She pulled the envelope from her purse and opened it. Another letter.

Avant continued to stare at her. "What did he say to you, Abigail?"

He wasn't ready to hear the answer to that question, and she wasn't ready to tell him. Taking a deep breath to quell the nausea, she ignored him and tried to read the letter.

Abigail,

If you are reading this, you are close to finding me. I am longing to see you, my darling. Many are looking for you. You must be diligent. Tell no one. Chad will help you. Bring him with you, so you won't be alone. You have been—

"This Chad is still in love with you?" Abby cut her gaze to Avant and then looked back to her letter.

—on your own so much of your life, Abigail. My heart breaks for you, so alone. I don't want you to be by yourself ever again.

"And I suppose you are in love with him, too?" He was trying to engage her in his emotional warfare, but she was determined not to participate.

You must find me, my darling. You will need to come to St. Louis, Missouri. Do not use your Implanting. It can be traced here—

"It seems, Abigail, you can fall in love and into bed with any man who happens to be standing in front of you. I should have expected as much from a woman."

That did it. Avant's words cut more deeply than she could handle and a thorn pierced her heart. What difference did it make to him whom she loved? He would never allow himself to love her, and even if he did, he would never trust her. She was alone now and would always be alone.

Tears spilled from her brimming eyes. Had it only been a few hours ago they had made love?

"Then I guess it's time for us to part ways. I'll take you back to Jastain, and you can be rid of me."

No matter how much she wanted it to be different, it never would. Too many obstacles kept them from ever being together.

Looking up at him with broken honesty, she whispered, "I love you, Avant, but you know that. No secrets, right? I thought I could hold out until you decided to love me too, but that was just a dream." Her voice shook so badly her words were almost lost. "I pray someday you'll find someone you can love and trust. You deserve to be happy."

"Abigail...I didn't...." The sharp lines of his face fell, and his eyes widened in shock at her words.

"You know the saddest part is that we're the same. I wanted so much to be the person who would never leave you, the one you could depend on no matter what. I wanted you to be that for me, but we're too broken for that kind of hope. Some people are meant to be alone."

*****

"Abigail. *No.*" Avant's heart broke with her words. He rushed to her side and took her in his arms, but it was too late. The light amassed and flashed through them. They stood at the falls. She softly kissed his lips and stepped away. He reached out to grab her, but she was gone.

Avant, what have you done? Jealousy had raged within him and, unable to contain it, he had lashed out at the one person he could trust. He trusted her as he trusted his own heart, the heart that now ached with her absence. He squeezed his eyes shut and shook his head.

Abigail was alone on this task with no way for him to get back to her. She was in danger. *Damnable Darkness.* The salt of her tears clung to his lips, and her sob still rang in his ears. If something happened to her.... He pressed a fist to his forehead, the pounding of the falls a mirror of the pounding in his temples.

He hurt her more deeply than Aesdil and his entire army ever could've. The very thing he never wanted to do. He'd been so careful since the cave. Abigail was right: His brokenness precluded him from love. He certainly was alone now. And so was she. *The Light protect her.*

Making love to her had been the purest, most beautiful moment of his life, but now, because of him, it had been tainted.

His Gift had failed him. After all the long years, he'd relied upon and rested in the truth of his Implanting. He had taken solace, and even pride, in knowing he would one day be king. He threw his head back and stared up at the early morning sky. How could he have been so wrong?

Sickened by his circumstances and his own actions, he turned for home. He may not be able to get back to his angel, but he could prepare for when she came back to him. For surely she would.

Chapter Thirty

Abby implanted back to Chad. Although surprised by her sudden appearance, he asked no questions. She returned to the hotel, where she read the remainder of the letter.

She couldn't use her Implanting to get to her mother? Why? She threw on a nightshirt and fell into bed. Something in Raieda's letter didn't add up, but she couldn't put her finger on it. Well, she and Chad would find her mother tomorrow and hopefully get some answers. The more she learned about her Gift, the more secure she felt in using it. Obviously, she could Implant to places she loved as well as to the people she loved. A sob escaped her. She could also use her Gift to leave those she loved. Thoughts of sapphire eyes and warm lips saturated her mind. Her body ached for him and she cried herself to sleep.

The next morning, she met Chad at his apartment. Wanting to make it through the day without having a meltdown, she would not allow herself to think about Avant until the evening, when she was alone.

"My mother wanted you to come, Chad. She said it was important to restoring the Crown."

They took a cab to the airport. She paid for their tickets in cash. During the two-hour layover, she took the opportunity to catch up and clear the air. Chad was a good man. She owed him an explanation, and an apology.

"After Lyndsea lost the baby, I was still willing to go through with the wedding, but she knew I didn't love her. She'd gone into a severe depression within weeks of coming here. I thought it was just hormones. One night I came home from the lab and she was gone. My mother's diamond ring was lying on the bar."

The ring. Sentieve's ring. "Chad, I met your mother when I was in Jastain."

"You did?"

"She told me to tell you that she loved you. Of course, I didn't know at the time you were the son she referred to."

"What's she like?"

Abby sat back in the airport seat and stretched her legs in front of her. "Sentieve is tall and regal with brown hair and your brown eyes. She's a queen. She sent you with Raieda because your life was in danger."

"A queen? Was my father the king?"

Abby took a deep breath and closed her eyes before speaking. "She believes your father was the man she was married to before she married the king. She thought he was dead and only recently found out he was still alive."

Chad sat forward in his seat, his elbows resting on his knees. "Do you know who he is? Have you met him too?"

"Yes, and so have you. It's Avant." Tears pooled in her eyes at the taste of his name on her lips.

"How is that possible? Abby, that man is not old enough to be my father."

"He's forty-eight. Aging in Jastain is a little different than here."

"Is that why he left? Because he found out I was his son?"

She shook her head and dropped her gaze. "Avant left because of me. He doesn't know you're his son."

"What happened, Abs?"

She told Chad the whole story, beginning with Sentieve's infidelity, the king's treachery, and Avant's vendetta. She explained his irrational jealousy and inability to love or trust a woman. "Chad, he already loves you and doesn't care if you're his biological son. He thought you'd died before you were a year old."

"How do you know he'll even want to know me, Abby? The guy wanted to beat the crap out of me yesterday."

"I know his heart. Trust me. He loves you, which is more than I can say for how he feels about me. He has a boy he raised and loves like a son." She'd forgotten Chad's resemblance to Petra. Now that she knew them both, they seemed as different as night and day, and it rarely crossed her mind. If Chad was from Jastain, surely the resemblance to Petra couldn't be coincidence, but what did it mean?

"You're in love with Avant?" Chad asked.

"Yes." Abby felt as if her heart had trekked across the Valley of Umbra in her Dolcini sandals. "Chad, the jewelry from your mother, may I see it?"

"Sure." He opened his backpack and pulled out a small wooden box. "Here's the brooch."

Studying the two green stones, she explained about the Crown and jewels. Raieda had requested, in her letter, that Chad bring them.

She couldn't guess why her mother needed the emeralds or how her own Implanting could be traced. She knew so little about her mother. Her family's mysteries kept unfolding like an accordion. What would Raieda be like? Why hadn't she tried to contact Abby before?

They talked all the way to St. Louis and, in the conversation, many things were healed.

He rented a car, and they drove to her mother's apartment, which was located in a questionable part of the city. A couple of shady-looking guys stood by the building and watched them as they pulled into the parking lot. Abby put her Gift on alert, ready at a moment's notice. She eyed the lean scientist next to her. Chad's presence didn't instill a strong sense of protection, but she'd do her best to take care of them both if needed.

The apartment sat on the ground floor at the end of a dilapidated breezeway. They walked to the door. She knocked but had no way of knowing if anyone was even in there. Her stomach lurched.

She knocked again. A woman in a hooded cloak opened the door. She couldn't see the woman's face, but her first instinct was to run. Speaking into Chad's mind, she asked, *"Is that my mother?"*

"That's Raieda. She wore the cloak when she came to see me."

Abby's concern eased, and she stepped into the apartment. Chad followed and closed the door. The apartment held nothing but a small huddle in the far corner next to a sliding glass door. She couldn't shake the feeling that something was hideously wrong. The room had no light except what seeped in from under the vertical blinds, and the dank smell reminded her too much of the dungeons.

She grasped Chad's hand.

The woman turned to the huddle in the corner and spoke in a melodic singsong voice that snaked a sickening chill down Abby's spine. "Look, my sweet. I told you they would come. They come to take the last of what you have, my poor sweet child, but you won't let them, will you?"

The woman—the *creature*—removed the hood and turned to face her, but she already knew who it was. "Hello, Abby. I'm so glad to see you again. We parted badly last time, but this time will be better, I think."

Abby glanced up at Chad. His eyes were glazed over like he was in a trance.

"Chad, do not listen to this creature or speak to it," she said into his mind. He blinked and some of the fog cleared. *"Chad! Do not speak to this creature!"*

"Seppitent, where is my mother?" Abby demanded.

"Abby, pardon my little deception. Your mother died years ago, just as you've always known."

Shit. Avant had been right. Why couldn't she learn to see the truth of a situation? The pain of the words knotted her gut, but she had to keep her wits. She wouldn't let this creature destroy her. "Why are you here?"

"I told you, Abby, we're alike. We can find treasure in any world. Sadly, your treasure is now the treasure I'll be taking." His hideous face contorted into an expression of pure evil.

Abby focused her energy to get them out of there. But just then, the huddle from the corner stood and gazed out with hollow eyes— and Abby caught sight of Lyndsea. Abby sucked in a breath in shock. Lyndsea's matted hair clung to her face as her filthy clothes clung to her body. With a blank expression, she stepped forward, clearly out of her mind from Seppitent's lies.

"Lyndsea, it's Abby. Don't believe him. He's a liar. *Lyndsea,* tell him to begone. Can you do that, honey?"

Lyndsea looked so pitiful but also full of rage. They had to escape. Abby's light amassed again. She wanted so badly to run, but she couldn't leave her sister, her friend.

The Seppitent spoke. "Poor Lyndsea. She'll surely do harm to herself and others. Hand over your earrings, and I will release her."

"Seppitent, I'm not handing you shit." She gulped and tried to school her face. At least her voice didn't tremble—too much. "Why do you want my earrings?"

The creature laughed. "Don't you even know, Chosen One? You carry the Stone of Light in your ears, or so the prophecy says. Surely your companion told you that before you parted ways so bitterly."

Abby's heart thudded in her chest and, with each beat, a sharp pain pierced her. How did he know about Avant? How did he know about the diamonds? Light filled her. "You orchestrated this so Avant wouldn't be here. You can't stand against us both, can you? Your enchanted letters caused me to distrust all the people who could help me, and you did something to Avant, too!"

"The queen's true love was in quite a state, wasn't he? I may have put a few simple ideas into his mind, but he did the rest." Seppitent sneered with pride. "I'm looking forward to taking over Jastain and making it my own. I've been working on this a long time. It is the last known world that hasn't fallen to me. You, of all people, should appreciate my plan, seeing as the Light has such a brilliant plan laid out for you. Alas, it is a plan that is doomed to fail. Pity. I must insist on those earrings. Lyndsea, it's time to kill her."

The creature's words moved through the room like tentacles into the mind of the girl, whose face contorted to reflect that of its master.

Lyndsea took another pace forward. Abby gasped. The crazed girl held a baby in one hand and a terrifying Michael Myers knife in the other. Abby's heart stalled. What was Lynds doing with a baby?

"Lyndsea, don't listen to him. He's a liar. You don't have to kill anyone," Abby pleaded, but the Lyndsea she once knew was gone. Only Seppitent's lie remained.

For the first time, Lyndsea spoke. "I have to kill my baby. We have nothing left to live for. What difference will death make?"

"Lyndsea, don't say that. You have your future to live for—and me. I love you. We're family, Lynds." A flicker of life shot through Lyndsea's eyes. "I forgive you, and I'm so sorry you thought I abandoned you."

"Lyndsea, you mean nothing to her. She doesn't want you to be happy."

"Abby, I'll kill this baby unless you give my friend what he wants." She raised the knife high over her head and pointed the blade at the tiny baby.

Abby cried out and tried to pry the knife loose with her mind, but Lyndsea held onto it with unnatural strength.

For the first time, Chad's voice pierced the room. "Lyndsea, stop! Please don't harm the baby." He turned his desperate plea on Abby. "For God's sake, Abby, give him the damn earrings!"

She saw no recourse but to hand the Stone over. *"Lord, please help me."* Abby took the earring and laid it in Seppitent's hand. It disappeared.

"Where is the other?

"I only wear the true Stone." She prayed it was a lie.

He laughed and nodded. "Yes, only true treasure is worthy of wear by the likes of us, Chosen One. Sadly, this is only a part of the treasure I am seeking today. Chad, you have the emeralds in your possession, I believe. Hand those over to me now."

Chad reached into his pocket and handed Seppitent a small felt pouch.

To her astonishment, a familiar voice spoke into Abby's mind. *"I have given you all authority to trample on snakes and scorpions and to overcome all the power of the enemy. Nothing shall, by any means, harm you."*

She focused her energy and pulled the emeralds from Seppitent's hand before they disappeared.

"Lyndsea, kill them now!" Seppitent demanded.

Lyndsea lunged at them with the knife in one hand and the baby in the other. Abby shrieked. Chad shrank.

As Lyndsea rushed near, Abby did three things at once: She pulled Chad's arm around her, she stepped into the path of the knife, allowing it to stab deep into her shoulder, and she gathered her energy, thinking of the one person who was the rock in her life.

The light flashed. They fell into the stables.

Petra took one look and ran to them. Spots flickered in front of her eyes. She had to stay conscious. "Petra...take care of Lyndsea and the baby.... This...is Chad...Avant's son...and I need—"

Abby sat at the desk in her father's study. In the total darkness, she shivered from fear. No one else was with her. The light shone behind her. She stood and turned to find its source. Seeking the warmth of the rays that would dissipate her fear, she spun around and around. As she did, she realized she wasn't alone anymore. Avant stood behind her, his arms firmly around her waist. But someone else was there. The familiar voice she couldn't place. "You've never been alone, Abigail, and now you have the Stone. This task is almost complete, and your destiny awaits you. Finish the battle. Claim your victory."

Abby woke, quietly crying in her own bed, but she couldn't open her eyes for the dizziness. The soft linen smelled of lavender and mint and home. Tears streamed into her ears. Her throbbing shoulder was bandaged, and someone held her and stroked her face. She sucked in a ragged breath. The scent of pine, cedar, fresh earth, and a hint of sweet musk wreathed her senses. Avant.

"Lyndsea. The baby—" Even her own ears could barely make out the sound of her words.

"Petra is caring for them, my love." Avant soothed before she could finish.

"Chad…is…your son," she whispered. Pain pierced her shoulder, and she cried out.

He replied softly into her mind, *"I know. I know, brave angel. Rest now. I'm not leaving. Nothing can harm you. You're safe."*

"Avant, you have the Stone." She slept.

Chapter Thirty-One

For the tenth straight day, Abby lay in bed. Avant sat next to her in the armchair he'd brought from his room. She sighed and blew a wisp of hair from her forehead. He glanced up from his book and caught her gaze. Warmth fluttered in her stomach.

Since being back in Jastain, he'd barely left her side, but he remained distant. She kept reminding herself to let him lead. *Driver's seat. Remember, Abs?*

In typical Avant fashion, he never spoke about the day she left him or the evening that precipitated it. Every part of her ached for him, but he plastered on that damned sympathetic face, closing off his emotions, and nothing short of a two-by-four upside his head would remove it. If the memories of him making love to her hadn't been so strong in her mind, she would've wondered if she hadn't just dreamed it. Unfortunately, they were strong in her mind. All the time.

They'd talked at length about the incident with Seppitent. Avant had not been aware the creature had the ability to disguise himself in her world. He had admitted to speaking with a questionable stranger at the bank in Dallas.

Avant said he'd met the shrouded stranger in lobby of the bank while Abby withdrew funds. The gentlemen had asked him if Abby was his wife and commented on her beauty. The question seemed innocent enough but it was the timber of his voice that held a familiarity Avant had not been able to place. And Avant said it was immediately after that meeting that he began to experience doubts about her loyalty and love.

The sun streaked in through the open window. Stretching her good arm, she winced from the jarring movement. She loved Jastain, but their advancements in medicine left a lot to be desired.

Thank God for Chad. Knowing more about medicine and healing than the local medicine man, he'd removed the knife from Abby's shoulder and was able to stitch the wound. He'd prepared a rudimentary antibiotic and a stiff painkiller, which had kept her flat on her back for nearly two weeks.

Avant had welcomed Chad and Lyndsea into the manor. He supplied them with everything they needed and even hired a girl from the village to cook and clean full-time. Helean had taken over caring for Abby, Lyndsea, and the baby, when she could wrestle the little thing away from Chad or Petra.

Petra sat with Abby each day while Avant left to take care of personal business, but an unspoken rift settled between them. She was unsure of what he knew or assumed had taken place between her and Avant. Either way, he hurt because of it. Bands of regret and grief squeezed her heart. She allowed him his space. It seemed like they all needed space.

From what Petra had said, Lyndsea wasn't sure how long Seppitent had kept her in the apartment, but she'd been dangerously close to starvation. She cried a lot and spent most days in her room. The newly born baby was small and underfed, but was otherwise healthy.

Avant took all his meals with Abby and slept next to her each night. But he never reached for her other than to comfort. He generally stayed at her bedside, except for daily meetings with his military captains, which he held downstairs.

After the failed attack on the Freelands, the king had withdrawn his army but kept spies throughout the region. Avant believed Aesdil was gathering additional forces from the Southern Provinces and from the Eastern Islands to strike another blow.

The pretty servant girl just hired from the village, Saundra, padded into the room with a breakfast tray. She smiled as she placed the food in front of Abby.

"Thanks, Saundra. The panas looks as delicious as your mother's."

The girl blushed and nodded as she left the room.

Abby took a bite of the fresh bread and sighed in delight. Avant took a large piece from her plate. Abby frowned at him. "Hey, get your own."

His eyes sparked with desire as he popped the piece in his mouth.

She exhaled shakily. "So how long are we going to skirt the elephant in the room?"

Avant closed his book and laid it on the table near the bed. His dark brows arched as he held her gaze. "To which elephant are you referring, Abigail?"

A giggle escaped her lips. He was right—it was becoming a legitimate herd. A smile played at the corners of his lush lips, though his eyes remained reserved.

She pulled out two pieces of paper and unfolded them. Lifting the Jastainian parchment, she held it out to him. "This elephant."

He stiffened in the chair, his chin lifted and his jaw clenched. After a long moment, he took the paper from her and read it, even though he already knew what it said.

The final prophecy transcribed by Jo-Naphen during the Festival of New Song the year after Avant was born was the definitive word in naming the next ruler of Jastain.

"This has to be wrong. You're the obvious choice for this, not me."

"Abigail, I seriously doubt that I would make a good queen. The voice of Light is truth. There is no argument. I'd trust the vision of the high priest above all others, including my own." He sucked in a cleansing breath. "The Light has chosen you; you'll be the ruler of these lands."

She eyed him skeptically. His answer was too calm, too rehearsed.

"I admit this was not what I expected. Vain desires of the heart lie in expectation." His eyes became remote.

He laid the prophecy on the bed and picked up the letter from her father. He tapped his finger on his lips as he read it and then tossed it on the bed. "Kasten was Sentieve's father. He went into hiding shortly after Sentieve and I were married. I always suspected Aesdil feared him. He was an austere man, but an excellent judge of character. This must be how Sentieve took possession of the emeralds, but where he placed the amethysts is beyond my ken." Avant stood and paced to the window. "If Kasten hid the amethysts while in exile, we may never find them. It is possible Sentieve might know where they are."

This was the most he'd spoken of Sentieve since before Abby had Implanted into him weeks ago. Had he come to terms with her betrayal? She pushed her head back into her pillow. *If he would just talk to me.* "What Seppitent said makes me believe he orchestrated the death of your father, and it's possible Aesdil and Sentieve could've been under his influence as well."

He rounded to her, fire in his eyes, and she shrank back. "That does not absolve them of their actions, Abigail."

She sucked in a breath and pushed the food tray to the side. Avant took it from her and then sat on the bed.

Light within her illuminated the truth, and she spoke softly, "Avant, it's time to move past bitterness. To win this war, we have to fight the right enemy. You have to let go of this grudge."

"I know you're right, Abigail. All these years I've directed my rage toward Aesdil. It has become so much a part of who I am that I'm not certain I can separate from it."

"But it's done nothing except damage your life. You can't allow Seppitent a foothold in your heart anymore. Destroying those who wronged you isn't going to bring your life back, and even if it could, would you want it?" She took his hand. "It's time to turn away from our own plans and take up the destiny that draws us." Dear God, she sounded like her dad. When had that happened?

She sensed the struggle in his heart. He stroked her fingers and studied them. "I know you speak the truth, Abigail, but I fear I'm not as brave as you. I do not think I've the strength to let it go."

She covered their clasped hands with her other one. "Do you remember when you first found me? You told me I had a purpose. There was a destiny I had to fulfill. Avant, your destiny is as important to this plan as mine, maybe more, but you can't reach it until you let this vendetta go. Twenty years is long enough. Let it go, so we can finish this and bring peace to our home."

He squeezed her hand, and his tears fell on the white linens. Hers fell with them.

They sat in silence for a long while. Avant paced back to the window and stared into the distance.

She stared at his straight back with a longing so deep she barely caught her breath. "So, what's next?"

"How should I know, Abigail?"

She frowned. He resented her role, but he neglected to remember she couldn't have done any of it without him. She still couldn't. "My thought is that if the Crown is back at Naphen's home, we can try to Implant there."

"I did not see the Crown in plain sight during our last visit. Have you an idea of where we should look once there?"

"None, but it's not like there are too many places you could put a crown in that house."

He sat down in his chair and picked up his book. "It needn't be decided today. You're still not prepared for activity. For now, rest." He presented her with his most stern look and that lock of hair fell across his forehead.

Her fingers twitched to touch him. *Driver's seat, Abs.*

*****

She lay in bed with Avant next to her. His soft, even breath blew against the back of her neck. It was the only part of him that actually touched her. Chills shivered down her back, and her nipples hardened. Desire heated the space between her legs. Never had she wanted sex so badly.

She rolled to her back, their bodies barely touching, and then broadcast an erotic vision into his mind. He immediately responded, never waking. *Hmm.* She imagined his hands slipping beneath her nightgown and roaming over her bare skin. Again, he responded. Serious *Manchurian Candidate* reaction. *May as well go for broke.*

He descended on her like a summer storm. He licked across the seam of her lips and thrust deep inside when she gladly parted them. His tongue stroked hers, and his body pressed against her. Her breath came hot and heavy. Careful not to disturb her wound, she wrapped her arms around him. Her imagination stalled as reality was so much better.

He pulled from her lips and kissed down her neck. His hands palmed her breasts, and she arched into his heated touch.

But the movement proved too sharp. "Ohh." The involuntary cry escaped her.

He froze.

The length of his erection pulsed against her inner thigh. She opened her eyes to stare into the sleepy sapphires filled with shock. He ripped his hands from her body and crawfished off the bed, falling to the floor. He stood, never looking at her, and ran out the door.

*****

After two weeks, Abby was ready to get back on task, but Chad said she risked reopening the wound. She could walk around the house and the immediate grounds, but shouldn't wander far. The thought that she'd purposely stepped into the blade made her cringe. The irony was the blade hadn't hurt going in—at least, not until it hit her shoulder bone. The healing was the part that hurt and itched and throbbed. And she was pretty vocal about letting anyone who would listen—which was everyone but Avant—know it. He wouldn't allow her to whine or mope. He made her get outside every day but then, on strict orders, she had to return to bed. *The paradox that was Avant.*

He helped her downstairs to the parlor. Chad had taught Lyndsea how to play chess. When Abby walked in, Chad stood to help her into a chair. Lyndsea remained seated and never lifted her gaze to meet Abby's.

"So who's winning?" Abby smiled at Lyndsea.

"Lyndsea's getting the hang of it," Chad said, putting a reassuring arm around Lyndsea's shoulder as he sat back down.

"Hey, Lynds, how are you feeling?" Abby studied the meek face.

"Good. Petra and Helean have really helped me. Everyone's been so nice." She nodded in Avant's direction.

"Chad, I have a question for you." Avant motioned him out of the room. He stood and followed Avant.

When they were alone, Lyndsea glanced up at her. Regret laced her face. "Abby, I don't have the words to tell you how bad I feel. I'm so sorry."

Abby shook her head. "You weren't yourself. I don't blame you. And I'm sorry, too."

"I never meant to act on my feelings for Chad. I had no intentions of being with him when he stayed with me. I just—"

"It's okay, honey. That must have been so hard for you to have feelings for him."

"Oh, Abby, it was hard, but that's no excuse. You would've never done anything like that to me."

"Lyndsea, if there's one thing I've learned in the past year, it's that no one knows what they're capable of until the time comes." Abby struggled to her feet and shuffled to her friend.

Lyndsea stood to meet her. They hugged and cried.

Lyndsea pulled back and blinked away tears. "I named the baby Abigail."

Abby wiped her eyes and her nose with her sleeve. "You did?"

"You know how I always said I loved your name, and Chad agreed it was a good choice."

She and Lyndsea talked for the next several hours about everything that had happened to them in the past year. It was as if they'd never been apart. Sadness lingered in Lyndsea's voice and her shoulders sagged, but light shone in her eyes when she talked about Baby Abby—and when Chad was mentioned. Maybe they could find happiness together.

Lyndsea had fallen victim to Seppitent's lies shortly before she left Boston. She'd lied to Chad about losing the baby and had left with the creature. She'd apparently given birth to the baby in a free clinic in St. Louis, but her mind had been so muddled, she wasn't sure how she'd gotten there.

"So what's up with Avant? Being around him reminds me of the time we waited in that valet line with Russell Crowe. I don't know whether to pretend like I don't see him or ask for his autograph."

Abby giggled, knowing exactly what Lyndsea meant. It had been a long time since she had a girl talk. "He can be a little intense, but he's charming when he wants to be. Watch out, though—he likes to make girls blush."

Lyndsea rolled her eyes. "That's not really that hard. I blush all the time anyway. I'm sure he doesn't make you blush."

"Not as much as he used to, but you'd be surprised." Abby could think of a few things he could do to make her blush.

"So what's going on with you guys? Petra doesn't say much about it. Are you together?" Lyndsea asked.

"I guess so. It's not exactly defined. I need to read that book again, *DTR: Determine The Relationship*, because I don't really know what *we* are. I only know what I am."

*****

Abby spent the next week wandering the house. Avant had resumed some of his normal routine. He spent the mornings away and returned in the afternoon. Ever since the incident in the bed two days ago, he'd moved back into his own room.

She waited for him to make the next move. The anguish of not having him in her bed had brought on a whole new set of insecurities and doubt.

She peered up at him as they walked through the southern field. The rich bloom of full summer had arrived. A renewed sense of urgency raced through her. Her shoulder was almost completely healed, though she would always have an ugly scar and probably some pain. Now, at least, she would have her own ailment to discuss with Susan if she ever got back to the house in Dallas. But no strapless wedding gown. Oh well, it wasn't like she was getting married anytime soon. Was it? In her heart, a wellspring of knowing bubbled. It was time to get that other circle of gold that was to be part of her life.

"Avant, it's time to find the Crown."

"Now, Abigail?" He stopped to study her, the summer breeze blowing that unruly lock across his forehead.

She nodded. "I'm anxious to get on with this. I just want it to be over, so our lives can be settled. As long as it remains to do, my life is up in the air."

He snorted. "You may find that the end of one task is only the beginning of many. Your life may never be completely settled again, and you need to come to terms with that possibility. Perhaps I am jaded, but my life has not been settled in over twenty years." He frowned. "And since you came, it has been nothing but constant change."

Chapter Thirty-Two

After a lengthy conversation in which she and Avant agreed to go immediately to Naphen's, they returned to the house. Abby went to her room to gather a few things and then met Avant in his chamber. He wrapped his arms around her, and for a moment, she just absorbed the feel of him. A soft sigh escaped him, too.

"Abigail—"

Not wanting to hear the reprimand, she concentrated on the little home built into the side of the mountain. A light flashed. They were inside. Neither of them had thought to bring a lamp. They stumbled in the dark for several minutes trying to find a light source. Avant stumped his toe and cursed loudly. Finally finding a candle, she lit the wick, and he started a fire in the hearth.

"Where should we look?" Abby held out her hands in a plea for help.

"This main room seems as likely a place as any."

They searched the small sofa, under a straight-backed chair, and on top of the mantle. They searched under any flat surface they could find, looking around the wall, and even checking the stone for hidden compartments. Hunting for hours in every room, they tore apart anything they thought might hold a crown.

"I don't think it's here." She threw up her hands.

"It is here." His eyes glinted with determination, but then he added, "I'm hungry. We'll eat something and begin looking again."

He pilfered through the kitchen while she felt along the stone wall for a hidden compartment. She shot a worried glance at Avant. What was up with him? He never stopped a task until it was completed, at least not for food. He wasn't himself, and she had a pretty good idea what the problem was.

He found a small amount of oats and some four-hundred-year-old dried beef. She wrinkled her nose when he offered her some.

"You go ahead." If she got hungry, they could go home and eat, but not until they found the Crown.

"I'm going to the stream."

She nodded and kept looking.

*****

Avant walked from the mountain dwelling. In truth, he was not that hungry, but he needed air, space.

His mind whirled like eddies in the brook. How could Abigail be named rightful ruler? This was not the future he'd seen. *He* was the rightful ruler of Jastain. That was the truth that had kept him sane for the last twenty years, the truth that had kept him alive. Countless dreams and visions all pointed to the fact that he would be king.

He fisted his hands. His Gift had never failed him. He'd trusted it implicitly, never doubting. Now, on the precipice of victory, it betrayed him? The *Light* betrayed him? His knees almost crumbled.

Trudging to the stream, he struggled to find an answer. It made no sense. He was supposed to be *king*, but now that could never be. There could be no king while a queen ruled.

The prophecy was authentic, he was certain. He'd seen enough of Jo-Naphen's inscription to recognize it, and the cadence of the foretelling was undoubtedly his father's. Avant exhaled. How could Abigail rule this land? She was just a young woman with no experience. Yes, she had come far and proven herself brave, but the skill it took to rule the kingdom seemed beyond her ken. He scoffed at the idea of her on the throne, but his heart smote him.

Abigail. His chest tightened with the thought of her golden curls and silky soft skin. Of course she could do it. He knew her as well as he knew himself, and loved her better. She was as capable as he. She was the bright and shining triumph in the whole plan of the Light, truly the Chosen One. She had been the one true thing. He wanted her more than he'd ever wanted anything in his life, but he didn't deserve her. He never had, and he never would.

At least with the promise of the kingdom to extend to her, he'd felt worthy of the Seed of Light, but without even that as an offering, he had nothing to give that she didn't already possess. He had offered to make her his queen. What a laugh. Queen of what, when he was never meant to be king? A pain pierced his heart. Taking back the kingdom had been all he lived for.

If his place was not as ruler of this land, where was it? Was he expected to live quietly in the castle and be ruled by a woman? He set his jaw and narrowed his eyes. Far from it! *That will never happen.*

He pulled out his leather pouch and bent to fill it in the stream. The sound of a sword sliding from its scabbard sliced through the air.

His pulse jumped, but he rose slowly and turned to face his assailants.

Four men stood with weapons drawn. The king's captain spoke, "Commander, we have orders to take you into custody. Please do not attempt to fight or we will end you, sir."

Avant sensed several more sentries behind him. Damnable Darkness! He had left his sword at the manor. *Foolishness*. Taking a lesson from Abigail, he used his Implanting and began to hurl large stones in the soldiers' direction. Several boulders struck their mark and left a clear path of escape. He fled back to the mountain home with the soldiers in close pursuit.

*****

Abby stood in her grandfather's bedroom, the place she first met him, the place he'd died. She shoved the straw mattress back on the bed and plopped down. The memory of the frail man rang through her like musical notes to a song she couldn't quite remember, and his love for her warmed the damp room.

Naphen had been her family, living here in the cold mountains alone for so many years. That was what the Darkness had done. It had separated them from each other: her grandfather, her dad, and her mother. They had all given their lives so she could accomplish her task. They'd sacrificed themselves for the Light and for her. The weight of what they'd done lay heavily on her shoulders. Sometimes sacrifices had to be made by a few so the whole would benefit. Her family wasn't the only one that had suffered. When the Darkness covered Jastain, all families suffered, not the least of which were Petra's and Avant's. She could see that now. To restore the Light to this land, her land, she would make any sacrifice to guarantee that happened.

"Where are you, little crown?" She scanned the room. The wooden box perched on the bedside table caught her eye. Deep inlaid wood in an ornate carved design decorated the top and sides. During the last visit, she'd taken Naphen's writings from it and left it there. She picked up the solid frame, turning it over in her hands, studying the structure. A smile spread over her face. Similar to the box in the safe of her father's study, it wasn't big enough to hold a crown, but maybe something else.

Feeling along the inside edge like Avant had done, she pushed the hidden button. "Yes!" A compartment opened to reveal a heavy iron skeleton key and a piece of paper with one word on it: *kitchen*.

Key firmly in hand, Abby sprinted to the kitchen and started pulling shelves off the wall. Canisters clattered, spilled, and rolled across the floor. She searched under the simple, wooden table and behind the pots and pans. Nothing. One tiny cupboard filled with plates and cups hung untouched. She ripped out the contents and peered into the small compartment. It was too dark to see. She grabbed the candle and stuck it in the space. In the back of the cupboard sat a small wood and iron door with a keyhole. That had to be it.

Bang!

Avant stormed in from outside, slamming and bolting the door behind him. "Abigail, we must leave! The king's men were waiting at the stream."

"Avant, I've found the Crown!"

"For the Light's sake, retrieve it and come!"

Unable to hold the candle and the key in the confined space, her hand fumbled in the dark cabinet, but she couldn't fit the key in blindly. What she wouldn't give for a flashlight!

Avant rushed to help her. Pulling her arm out, he bent to look in the cabinet. "What are you trying to do?"

Bang! A heavy force rammed the front door. Dust fell from the ceiling on their heads. The encroaching men's shouts could be heard beyond the wall.

She took a sharp breath and held up the key. "This fits into the keyhole at the back of the cupboard, but I can't open it up without being able to see."

The force pounded again. The front door cracked and began to give way. They only had a few seconds.

"Give me the key."

She tossed it to him. Avant took one look in the cupboard with the candle, stuck the key in, and turned. She probably shouldn't be thinking about how incredibly sexy he was at that moment, especially when their lives were on the line, but God, he was so hot.

"Abigail, get ready."

The front door splintered and gave way. The king's men pushed in.

Avant stuck his hand back into the hole. "I have it. *Go!*"

She grabbed his arm. A light flashed. A soldier reached out to grab her, but caught empty air.

Standing in the parlor, Abby had a vise grip on Avant.

And Avant held the Crown.

Chapter Thirty-Three

Petra and Lyndsea shot up from their seats, and all four of them locked their gazes on the Crown in Avant's hand.

Finally, Petra, who held Baby Abby, said, "So I guess you found it."

Abby started giggling, which turned into laughter, which morphed into downright hysteria, and she couldn't stop. It wasn't really *that* funny, but the near miss made her giddy. Once she started laughing, they all laughed. Even Avant couldn't force the smile from his face.

She fell on the sofa in relief, and Avant sat next to her. He reverently wiped the dust from the shining circlet as he turned it in his hand. The solid gold band was barely an inch wide. In the front, fitted holes where the jewels would sit adorned the ring. Each hole was shaped to fit the unique cut of the different stones.

Avant held the Crown a long while and glanced up to find the other three staring intently at it.

Abby reach out her hand. "May I?"

He nodded, with reluctance etched across his face. Even after it was clear Abby held it in her grasp, he wouldn't let go.

"I've got it, Avant."

He released it like a hot potato and stood abruptly. "I'll get us something to eat."

Lyndsea stood, her straight brown hair falling into her eyes. "Oh, I'll get you something. I helped Saundra put the food up earlier and know where it is."

Avant nodded and sat down. "Thank you."

She blushed and scurried to the kitchen. Abby turned the Crown over in her hand. The cool metal weighed heavier than she'd anticipated, but was smooth to the touch. A ring of intricate scrollwork about half an inch wide above the solid band graduated to a rounded point in the center of the circlet—the space where the Stone of Light sat above the others. She considered trying it on her head to see how it fit, but one sideways glance at Avant confirmed that was not the best idea. The skirmish with Aesdil's men, and presumably his empty stomach, had made him snappish.

Abby fingered the last hole in the Crown. "Where are we going to find the amethysts?"

Petra stared at the circlet. "Those are the last stones you're looking for?"

Abby sighed as she gazed into his chocolate brown eyes. His face showed no hint of previous hurt, but he hid his heartbreak well. She knew he still loved her even though she'd chosen Avant, but she also knew he would do whatever it took to keep the peace and relieve the awkwardness.

Avant focused on the Crown. "Once we find them, the Crown can be completed, but we are at a loss as to where to look."

Abby held up the Crown to Petra and pointed to the pentagon-shaped opening at the end. "The amethysts go here, in these holes."

Petra stared at it with a puzzled expression. "May I take a look, Abby?"

She raised her brow and nodded. "Sure."

Petra stood and walked to Avant. "Here, take the baby." Petra quickly handed him Baby Abby before Avant could protest.

Abby passed Petra the Crown. He held it close to his face and fingered the opening. "Abby, what color are amethysts?"

"Purple usually."

His face clouded, and he stared past her. "I have two purple stones this shape."

"I don't think you can put just any purple stone in there."

"No, Abby. I think I have these stones."

"What? Avant, did you hear—" She turned to him, but Avant hadn't heard a word. Mesmerized by the sweet-faced little angel in his arms, he sat holding her with a gentleness she'd only seen in him once before, in a cave. Her heart melted like marshmallows in hot chocolate. In all these weeks, he'd never once held the baby girl who could be his granddaughter. In fact, she was certain he'd never held any baby.

Abby suspected the little thing had been born premature, but Lyndsea couldn't remember Baby Abby's exact birthday, only that she thought it was early April. Abby glanced over at Petra, and he grinned knowingly. The child had now captured the heart of every man in the house. Abby smiled. Lucky little girl. These men were the best she would find anywhere.

Petra handed the Crown back to Abby and ran upstairs to get the jewels. She scooted next to Avant. "She's beautiful, isn't she?"

His face glowed with wonder. It was as if the baby had been invisible until she was placed in his arms. Her heart hurt for Avant. He would've had the joy of his own children if it weren't for the Darkness. *Maybe one day.*

"She is so small and weightless." Baby Abby gripped her little hand around Avant's pinky, and at that moment, he was wrapped around hers.

Lyndsea and Chad arrived with a tray of food and drinks. Lyndsea took the baby from Avant. He stared at them. "Your daughter is beautiful, and she always has a home here, as do you both." He picked up a piece of bread and looked around the room. "Where is Petra?"

Abby was in the middle of explaining when Petra bolted in with a large wooden inlaid box.

Avant took one wide-eyed look at it and asked, "Petra, where did you get that?"

"This is the wooden box I had when you found me, Avant. It's all I have of my family."

Petra opened the box to reveal several items made of silver, a white-gold, filigree locket, and a rounded cylinder of amber. He removed each item reverently. When the box was empty, he felt along the inside edges for the trigger. A small drawer popped out of the side. Petra pulled it out and handed it to Avant. Inside sat two pentagon-shaped amethysts.

"I found these shortly after you took me in. I've always believed they had a special purpose, but hadn't thought about them in years— until Abby showed me the Crown. The unique shape of the stones triggered my memory."

Avant put his hand on Petra's shoulder. "I am sorry I have never asked you more about your family. I felt you would tell me if you wanted to talk. Do you remember the names of your parents?"

Petra nodded. "My father's name was Fortis and my mother was—"

"—Ferial." Avant looked at Petra as if for the first time.

"Yes."

Abby rubbed down the hair on her arms.

Avant said, "Ferial and Sentieve were sisters. I heard she and her husband went into hiding after Sentieve married the king. You and Chad are first cousins, which explains the striking resemblance. Abigail, I am shocked we didn't see it before. The Light has provided everything we need through those whom we love most."

Chad brought in the emeralds, Abby ran and got the rubies, and Avant got his sword, which he swore never to Implant without again. For the first time in over forty years, all of the pieces were together in the same room.

"How do we get the jewels reset? None of us are jewelers," Abby asked.

Avant smiled. "The Light always provides. There is someone who can set the stones."

"Hossa?" Petra asked.

Avant nodded.

The next morning Abby and Avant made a trip to the home of Hossa and Annova. Riding south through the valley, they stopped in the village for their favorite panas and ate their breakfast on the way to the vineyards.

Avant had been unusually quiet. The fact that he hadn't touched her since they'd made love in Dallas weeks ago gnawed at her heart. Vicious thoughts plagued her mind. Thoughts of him hating her, leaving her, and breaking her heart sliced like sharp glass in her stomach, and she hadn't been able to eat since they had acquired the Crown.

She knew the prophecy weighed on his mind, but it wasn't her fault. She didn't want the damn job, and if it made him happy, he could have it. God knows, he'd be better at it than she would. Besides, when he became king, everyone would assume he made the decisions anyway, including him. Then they could live happily ever after just like in the fairytales—she raked her gaze over his body— only hotter. Way hotter.

He turned his head toward her as if he'd caught the tenor of her thought. "Hossa was a commissioned artisan of the previous king, but when the king killed my father, Hossa and Annova fled to the west and eventually made their way north, where they found me. He forged my sword."

When they arrived at the house, Avant opened the door and entered without knocking. "Annova, are you home?"

The graceful beauty glided down the stairs. "Avant, you bring Light into my house. I perceive you've found the Crown!"

"It is finally time for the restoration. We have all the pieces." He beamed at her.

Annova took both of Abby's hands. "Abigail, we have all longed for this day, waiting patiently for the Light to bring you to us." She pulled her toward the stairs. "Hossa is preparing his tools upstairs. I saw you coming last night. You were in darkness, and Abigail found a key which led to the Crown."

Abby's eyes widened and she nodded. "That is pretty much what happened."

Hossa took the Crown and spent the next few hours setting the jewels into the band. Abby and Avant sat, stood, paced, and watched in silence.

Finally, Hossa looked to Avant. "It is time. I need the Stone of Light."

Avant didn't move but stared at the Crown.

Abby glanced over at him. His face was lined with stress, his eyes remote. "Avant, are you okay?"

She reached to stroke his arm. His muscles tensed, and he flinched. Hossa walked to the hall to find Annova, but she was already there and came speedily to them.

"Avant, my love. It's time to let the Light go." Annova touched his shoulder. He looked up at her and nodded.

Abby held her breath and a knot formed in her throat. With a gesture that clearly caused him pain, he took the diamond from his ear and handed it to Hossa.

Hossa set the Stone of Light in the glittering band. A bright light flashed and a sound like thunder cracked. Abby's heart jumped to her throat, pounding out a beat and reminding her of that scene in *Raiders of the Lost Ark* when people's faces melted off as they turned to dust. She hid her eyes to escape impending death. That is, until a perturbed Avant poked her in the arm, and she realized her face was buried in his chest. She lifted her head to find everyone staring. With her cheeks the temperature of magma, she mumbled an apology and tried to smooth out the wrinkles she'd made in Avant's linen shirt.

Their gazes turned to the finished Crown, and they let out a collective sigh. As a piece of art and adornment, the Crown was splendid, but as a tool and relic of the Light that brought life to the kingdom, it was transcendent. They all stared wide-eyed at its splendor.

Avant was the first to break the spell. He held out his hand, but Hossa shook his head and held the diadem out to Abby. Avant glared at her. She shrank back.

Focusing on Hossa and the Crown, she shook her head. "I can't."

Hossa's quiet voice held an authority she couldn't place. "My dear, it's your destiny. You must or no one will."

Annova spoke quietly to Avant, "Support her. It's your destiny."

Abby could see the weight of Annova's words press on Avant. He squared his shoulders. "Abigail, the Light has spoken. Take the Crown." He nodded solemnly. "It belongs to you."

Avant was a warrior of great pride. She knew what it cost him to utter those words. She smiled appreciatively at him. He truly was the bravest man she'd ever known. At his encouragement, she reached out her hand and curled her fingers around the band.

A bright light shone from the golden circlet, all colors of the stones illuminating the faces in the room. Her hands trembled and vibrated. The power was as real as the pull of the Great River. It poured through her with a mighty, rushing current, flowing deep and wide.

The weight of the Crown became the weight of the world, her world, in her hands. She studied each set of sparkling jewels, unable to tear her gaze from them. The amethysts, provided by Petra, flanked the row of stones on both outer sides and glinted with peace and diplomacy. The emeralds, provided by Chad, were set next. They represented the knowledge and skill to make the world better. Then came the rubies, carried by her own mother, which represented sacrifice and love. Finally, the sapphires that Avant had skillfully pried from his sword represented loyalty and strength. The blue gems surrounded the Stone of Light, protecting all that was holy and pure.

Each stone and setting glinted with a beauty and uniqueness all its own. Each was wholly necessary for the completion of the task. But, together, they represented the greatness of a people for their land and country. The completed Crown represented everything good she'd come to love in Jastain. A stillness settled over the room, a quiet wonder. She'd never felt so honored or humbled by any sight.

Reality and reverence swept her over. Their success or failure meant the literal difference between life and death, and for the first time since the Great Heights, she felt the grace of the Light infusing her with the ability to accomplish the greater task.

Every face dimmed as the Crown burned brighter and took focus from all else.

*****

Avant paced the parlor while he and Petra mapped out the plot to take the castle. He tapped his lip in contemplation. With the additional men from the southern territories, he had six thousand troops at his command, but the king had more than fifteen thousand. Through spies, he'd learned the king had sent nine hundred men to guard the Northern Passage of the Itehris. Aesdil also had the roads and bridges leading to the castle guarded with at least two thousand men and ten thousand more ready to move at a moment's notice.

Avant spread a map over the small table he'd moved in front of the sofa. "In open battle, I am confident my men can best the king's army though outnumbered almost two to one. The difficulty lies in the castle stronghold. Aesdil reserves the best and strongest soldiers for his personal guard. I trained many of them myself. They are far better equipped and number at least three thousand. Within the confines of the castle, I need every available man of my six thousand to breech the keep, which means we cannot sustain heavy casualties in open battle."

He huffed out a breath and steepled his fingers. The king would do whatever it took to keep himself safe and maintain the kingdom—even if that meant sacrificing his general army to Avant's men. They must find a way to lead the troops to the castle without engaging the majority of Aesdil's army.

Another issue was how to actually breach the castle. The wooden gateway was, as always, the weakest point, but the dual ironclad doorway sat twelve inches thick and would not yield easily to anything with which they could batter it.

Chad stared at Abigail. "Abby, didn't you say you Implanted here in your Xterra?"

A twinge of jealousy shot through Avant's heart, but he snuffed out the emotion. As it had been from the beginning, this was now a task that required levelheadedness, free from sentiment.

"Yes! Do you think we could use it against the gates?" Abigail's beautiful face lit with her reply.

His love for Abigail had only intensified since they'd made love, but he'd kept those emotions firmly in check. Once the battle was over and peace was restored, he could attend the emotion. Until then, he must maintain his distance. Or so he told himself.

The others watched in awe as Chad took a quill and did some mathematical equations on a piece of parchment. Pride welled in Avant's chest. *With his mental faculties, this young man is surely my son.*

"Avant, do you have access to a blacksmith?" Chad asked.

"Yes."

Chad explained, "I believe we can reinforce the front end of the vehicle so a velocity of eighty-five miles per hour would be strong enough to penetrate the gates. The challenge will be in exiting the moving vehicle prior to impact. No one could withstand the impact at that speed and live."

Abigail spoke up. "I could do it and Implant out before—"

Fear and horror overcame Avant before the words left her mouth. *"No.* You could not." He thundered. "I will not allow it."

His gaze traveled the room. Everyone had frozen in silence, staring wide-eyed at him. He had not intended to sound so stern. Schooling his face, he spoke softly, "Abigail, you're too important to risk your life. You'll stay here at the manor during the battle."

The others looked at her. Her eyes smoldered like a glowing blade on the forger's anvil. "I'm not staying here. I'm going with you." She crossed her arms over her chest and set her face in determination.

He rubbed his forehead. "This is not up for discussion; you *will* stay here."

"No, I will not, and there is no way, in this world or any world, you can make me," she growled petulantly.

His pulse throbbed in his temples. The desire to throw her over his knee compelled him to press his fist into his side and pace to the window.

The group silently watched the volley.

Petra spoke diplomatically, trying to diffuse the tension that clouded the room. "Abby, I don't like the idea of you being in battle either, but perhaps we can come up with an agreeable compromise."

"Me either, Abs," said Lyndsea.

Avant released the breath he'd been holding and turned to look at Chad, who held up his hands in neutrality. *Coward. Perhaps he's not mine after all.*

Upon hearing he had reinforcements, Avant's voice steadied. "This is not something we will decide right now. We still need to determine battle strategy."

Abigail fumed in his mind. *"You will not allow it, my ass! This is absolutely not decided."* She stood and stomped from the room, just like a spoiled child.

Avant sighed. He would appease her later, but she could not be allowed into battle. And that was that. He turned his attention back to Chad. "Is Abigail's carriage capable of crossing water two feet deep?"

Chad narrowed his eyes and looked to the ceiling. "I'd have to check the owner's manual, but I seem to remember that the under-carriage has a specific depth capacity."

"What are you thinking, Avant?" Petra asked.

"We could travel to the Northern Passage of the River Itehris and subdue the king's troops there, cross into the Valley of Umbra, and come to the castle by way of the southeastern road. Aesdil will have minimal troops to the south, not expecting an attack from that direction. The key will be to make certain we quickly capture all of the troops at the river. We must contain every one of them to keep them from reporting back to him before our arrival from the south," Avant said.

They mapped out their battle plan in detail. Chad could have the Xterra completed in a week's time, and Avant could mobilize the troops by then. After the plans were settled, Avant headed to Abby's room.

*****

Rap. Rap. Rap. Abby glanced at the door, and her pulse jumped. She'd already dressed for bed and was now brushing her hair, because her hands needed something to do. If she won this battle, the one to come would be victorious. If she didn't, something bad was going to happen. She didn't know what, or even how she knew, but that didn't make her any less sure.

"Come in." Abby sat on her bed.

Avant opened the door and strode into the room. With his usual straight-lipped-no-freakin'-emotion face in place, he calmly turned to her. "Abigail, I understand you do not want to be left behind, but you are too important to risk in battle."

The tension in his body charged the room even if she couldn't see it in his features. "You're wrong this time. I'm too important *not* to go. I need to be there. I feel like something bad is going to happen to you if I don't go. *Avant, please*," she entreated, trying to appeal to reason and maybe some of his hidden feelings.

He sat next to her and took her hand. "Abigail, nothing is going to happen to me, and if it does, all the more reason for you to be far from harm. Open battle is no place anyone should have to be, but especially not you."

Abby placed her other hand over his and pleaded her case. "I thought we were partners. We've done everything together. Since when do you get to arbitrarily choose if I go or not? If you would just listen to the Light, you'd know I need to be there."

He pulled from her grasp and stood, tall and straight. "I do not need to listen to the Light to know that a woman does not belong in battle. You will not go, Abigail. I'm sorry, but that is my final word."

His final word? Oh. Hell. No. Her blood bubbled and churned. She fisted her hands at her sides to keep from slapping him. "I'm the one who's sorry, Avant, because I don't see how you have any authority to order me to do anything! You're not my father or my husband, and you certainly are not my king!"

She winced as the hurtful words sliced their intended target with rapier skill. Her chin fell to her chest, and she covered her face with her hands. *Shit.* Sometimes he brought out the worst in her. She could pull her entire body weight up by the tips of her fingers, but that little muscle in her mouth she could not hold. She peeked up at him and bit her lip.

The hurt in Avant's eyes turned to smoldering rage. "*My authority* is that I am still the lord of these lands and commander of these armies, and as such, I decide who goes into battle." He cocked his brow and smirked. "If I have to, Abigail, I will chain you hand and foot to this house and post a guard at your door. Your Implanting will be of no use in this argument."

Her stomach fluttered with need. She couldn't help herself. An overwhelming desire for him flooded her. Her heart pounded in her chest, and her body throbbed at his show of dominance. She caught a twinkle in his eye. The blue-eyed devil was using her desire against her as a battle strategy. *Oh, he's good!* She took a deep breath and tried to settle her thumping heart. He wasn't the only one who knew how to use an advantage. She'd done a little strategizing of her own, and he wasn't playing the right game. This wasn't chess—it was poker, and she held the cards.

Schooling her face, she smiled sweetly. "I'm disappointed in you, Commander, for not thinking this through before making threats. You need me, Avant. In fact, you can't do this without my help."

He met her gaze with intimidating confidence. "Abigail, I can assure you, I do not require your help to fight the king's armies, and I do not wish to argue any longer. You will be safe here until I can send for you."

She stood from the bed, sashayed past him toward the window, and then spun to face her opponent. "Really? Would you care to wager where I'll be during the battle?"

Realization flashed in those blue eyes; he'd walked straight into the ambush.

Abby held out her hand and studied her fingers in mock boredom. "Since you don't require my help, out of curiosity, how do you intend to get *my* Xterra here? And, assuming you can get it here without my Placement Implanting, how will you make it run when I've hidden the keys where, *I can assure you,* they won't be found?"

Chapter Thirty-Four

Abby grabbed Avant's rigid hand and Implanted to the Xterra and then back with it in less than a minute. It took hours to get the SUV started after sitting dormant for almost a year, but with Chad's knowledge of battery power, it finally cranked. It had just under half a tank of gas. Chad immediately took it to the blacksmith's shop and got to work.

Avant and Petra rode to meet with the captains at the military compound, and everyone in the house breathed a sigh of relief. Avant had acted horribly all morning, yelling at Saundra and making her cry, slamming doors and dishes, and not speaking to or looking at anyone except to growl or scowl.

Abby smirked, but a shiver ran down her spine. Eventually, Avant had relented and agreed to allow her into battle, but only after he had wracked his brain trying to think of a way to storm the castle without using the Xterra. He'd paced and sworn. Then he stomped his foot like a child and absolutely refused to let her drive the SUV as a battering ram, saying, *The Darkness could consume all of Jastain before that would happen.* It was his version of a compromise. All she knew was she had to be there.

*****

The following week was filled with preparations and time passed quickly.

Abby rode Imperial into the village. She planned to meet with Chad at the blacksmith's and to stop by the military compound to see Avant before the battle began the next day. He'd slept with the troops for the last five nights, but the doubting voices in her head screamed there was more to it than mere battle strategy.

The villagers called out in greeting as she rode through the main square. She smiled and waved back. This place had captured her heart, and she wished for nothing more than to live here with them for the rest of her life. Maybe the city near the castle would be nice, too. But sadness brewed. More change, more upheaval. And no definitive word from Avant.

She dismounted and walked to her reconfigured Xterra. Tears welled in her eyes. She loved that SUV almost as much as Imperial. Knowing it would be smashed against the castle gates broke her heart. Leaning against his handiwork, she smiled at Chad. Creating and inventing, he was in his element and this world needed so much of what he offered. "Looks like you've pimped my ride, college boy."

"Hey, Abs. What do you think?"

The entire front end of the car supported a large phallic mace that protruded out of the radiator grill. Two and a half feet in diameter and two feet long, the iron-covered tree trunk was built to penetrate and weaken the gates upon impact. Just the visual effect made the little muscle car look formidable—and X-rated. She giggled. "Great job. Very subtle. Let's hope it works."

"I've reinforced the radiator and front tire wells, just in case. If the mace doesn't pierce the wood to the point of splintering, the force of impact will. I'm confident the weapon will obliterate the gates."

Watching him show her the mechanics of his creation reminded her of his love for Q's gadgets in the Bond novels. She shook her head and smiled. Boys and their toys. "Has Avant seen this?"

"Yeah, he came by earlier to see if the car was ready." Chad's face beamed with pride. "He seemed impressed."

"I'm sure he was." Abby was glad they'd forged a relationship even under the strange and difficult circumstances. Now that Chad and Lyndsea had decided to make a go of their relationship, the tension had eased. It still freaked her out to think about the situation, so she just focused on the task at hand. "Did he say where he was going?"

"No, sorry." He continued to put the finishing touches on his erotic monster.

Abby walked across the path to the compound. Built with large logs and surrounded by a sturdy wooden fence, the main structure looked like an Old West outpost. When she entered the fort, the youngest of Avant's captain's greeted her. "Lady Abigail, what brings you here?"

"I'm looking for Avant. Is he here?"

"No, I apologize, my lady. The commander said he had business away this afternoon."

She paused and scanned the large open room with its long rustic tables and wooden benches. Soldiers were scattered around, some polishing weapons, others drinking and playing games of chance. "All right. Thanks, Captain."

He nodded and smiled as she walked out the door. Her shoulders fell. Oh well, it seemed she wouldn't have the opportunity to see him before tomorrow night after all.

She rode to the falls. Summer flowers bloomed around the trees, and sweet fragrance filled the air. She dismounted and walked Imperial into the clearing where the water spilled with roaring force. Spiritus stood patiently by a tree, and Abby's heart leapt with happiness. She dropped her reins and glanced around.

Avant sat on a rock by the pool's edge, one knee propped up. He tossed small stones in the water. It had been just five days, but she missed him like it'd been a month. Longing to run and wrap herself in his arms, she resisted. His strong, proud shoulders strained under the burden he carried.

He put his head in his hands. The agony his body expressed broke her heart, and she could just catch the tenor of his thoughts. His men. Death for the Light. He'd never want her to see this. She quietly left him to his warrior's lament.

*****

Avant called loudly to his captains, ordering them to move the troops. He led half the men to the river while Petra remained with the other half a short distance behind. They had struck out from the compound shortly after dawn in an effort to make it to the Itehris by sunset. To subdue the nine hundred soldiers, Avant was relying heavily on both the element of surprise and the cover of night. Though it would be difficult to conceal three thousand troops, the king's soldiers would not suspect a late-night attack at the Northern Passage. After the king's men were overtaken, Avant's and Petra's forces would reunite and march to the castle.

Abigail would drive the Xterra behind Petra and his half of the troops. Avant closed his eyes and let the thought of her beautiful face engulf him. By the Light, he'd missed her. He'd foregone female companionship for twenty years, but being away from her for five days had been torture. Not to mention the physical need that raged in his body since making love to her more than a month before.

It had been his intention to see her before he left, but time had not permitted it. He made certain she would be as protected as possible during the battle. If something happened to her…. He shook the thought from his mind. It served no purpose to dwell on it.

He still fumed when he thought of how insolent she'd been, but he had to smile at her smugness in besting him. She was a woman like none he'd ever met, and he loved her for it. Of course, she had no idea of the horrors she would see or endure in this fight. Nothing in her experience could prepare her for the brutality of hand-to-hand battle. Avant had wanted to protect her from that, but perhaps she was right about the Light wanting her there. He snorted bitterly. How was he to know what the Light wanted?

The journey to battle covered much ground. If everything went according to plan, the king's spies would assume Avant's troops had taken the northwestern route and wouldn't suspect they went south until they'd already approached the stronghold. Four nights' journey would bring them to the castle, and they would attack from the Forest of Aesdil. The king would have fewer warriors guarding the southern gates.

When Avant and his men reached the Ianus Aquilo, the Northern Passage, an hour after sunset, they formed ranks in sets of one hundred troops. Using his Implanting, he gave the silent order, and they attacked.

For barely an hour, the sound of splashing water and clanking swords rang out in the darkness of the cool summer night. The advancing troops swarmed the king's forces and easily subdued the soldiers before midnight. No casualties were sustained, as the younger, inexperienced soldiers surrendered without a fight and Avant's men quickly bested those who fought. Sending word back to Petra by messenger, Avant mobilized his men on the south side of the mountains in the Valley of Umbra. He offered the king's men their lives in exchange for surrender, which all gladly took.

*****

Having received news of Avant's victory, Abby and Petra crossed the river about one o'clock in the morning and found the southern road by daybreak. On their travels to the Valley of Umbra, the moon hid itself, just like her first night in Jastain, but the sky burst with stars. Just before dawn, they stopped to rest under the cover of trees and dense brush in the southwestern part of the Northern Range of Umbra.

Avant's men trekked forward in small units, defeating smaller bands of the king's soldiers and spies and taking them prisoner to ensure stealth. She'd hoped to see Avant when they stopped to make camp, but he'd gone ahead without her.

For three nights, she, Petra, and the troops traveled by night and slept during the day. Most of the men marched, a few rode warhorses, and she drove the Xterra. The determined and somber mood of the men gave her a sense of confidence. Avant had trained them, just as he'd trained her, and that comforted her. They were ready for battle.

On the last evening of travel, they came to the western edge of the Forest of Aesdil, where they met up with Avant's men to realign the troops for the attack.

Abby got out of the car and searched for him. The plan had Avant attacking the castle with a push of the strongest soldiers first, and Petra following in a second wave with the reinforcements after the outside wall was cleared of the king's men. As strong and smart as Avant was, he was still just a man. A man who could die. Worry etched some scary-assed pictures in her mind, and the thought of never seeing him again was unbearable.

She struggled through the crowds, searching for Avant, but seeking him in the darkest part of night through the outstretched troops proved fruitless. She stopped in the middle of the camp and chewed her nails. She turned in a complete circle. No fires burned and the men huddled next to the ground. Making her way back to the Xterra, she found Petra sending orders to his captains.

He stared at her with stern eyes. The authority in his voice surprised her. "Abby, stay out of the action and behind the fighting line. You can help us more if we aren't constantly worried you're going to storm the gates or try to fight Aesdil yourself."

She nodded and hugged him. For the first time since she'd returned from Dallas, Petra put his arms around her. She soaked in the warmth and comfort as she melted against him. She'd never really had a choice to make. After the Implanting, she would forever love Avant, but a piece of her heart would always be reserved for

Petra, even if it wasn't the piece she knew he wanted. A long sigh blew from his lips, ruffling her hair. He mounted Dalitus and rode to the front.

The first-wave attack launched with a shout and an answering thunder of hooves racing to the castle. Avant led the way. In her mind's eye, she imagined his proud frame charging to the castle wall. He was a valiant knight. The thought of him in danger made her stomach lurch. *Oh Avant, please be careful.*

"I will, fair one. You do the same."

The sound of his voice in her mind stopped Abby in mid-step. She hadn't intended to speak to him. *"Avant, how far are you?"*

"We're two miles from the wall. This first battle will be the hardest fought. My angel, no matter what happens, the kingdom must be restored. Do not quit. Take the Crown and return to the fief with Petra."

"Avant, I swear to Almighty God, if you die, I will come back and blow these punk bastards to hell."

He laughed in her mind. A wave of tenderness flooded her. Not paying attention, she stepped in a hole and fell, dewy grass wetting her behind.

"Angel, we're at the castle gates. Be safe. I'll find you at the end."

"I'll be looking for you, honey."

*****

Avant closed his mind, overwhelmed by his love for her. He allowed himself a brief moment to visualize her beautiful face before he raised the command.

With a shout, the battle for Jastain began.

Charging forward, Spiritus took the lead, running through the first line of troops stationed outside the tree line, one hundred and fifty yards from the wall. The brave animal took the fiercest man head on, jumping across the line of encroaching troops as the soldiers dove out of his way. Aesdil must've been concerned about a southern attack after all, because the forces were double what Avant had anticipated. It would take longer to breech their ranks. Hopefully his men's strength could prevail against the larger numbers with few enough casualties to finish the task.

Spiritus galloped toward the outer walls. The alarm sounded within the gate—the king was now aware of the attack. The south gate opened and a thousand horsemen stampeded onto the battlefield.

Few of them would survive this first battle. Sharp pain pierced Avant at having to give the order. He forced the command from his lips and called to his jousting troops, giving the order, sending them forward.

The Darkness would suffer for the loss of his men. Light would be restored. This is why they had come. His men knew the risks and were willing to take them for the same reason Avant was willing to take them: for the good of the land and the people he loved.

As the first wave of jousters clashed, an echo of clanging vamplates rang out over the field. Horses and riders crashed to the ground. Both sides reassembled to take up the gauntlet and run again. After his well-trained troops cleared the way, he sent in more. The king provided answering forces.

Dawn broke over the eastern horizon and lit the bloody field in a golden glow of morning. This was the only time of day the sun shone on the land around the castle. Haze covered the sky and choked out its rays. Avant looked to the Great Heights. They shimmered. The Light was on their side; they would prevail.

Noise from the battle raged, and the field in front of the wall ran with the blood of men. Carcasses of horses littered the land, and the painful cries of the wounded stabbed the air.

"Avant, are you okay?"

"I'm here."

"Just checking. I can Implant you out of there anytime."

"Abigail."

Her voice in his mind, like a magical elixir, infused him with resolve.

His jousters had broken through the king's ranks and charged the sentries along the outside of the walls.

Avant raised his sword high in the air. The men behind him answered with a shout. He violently swiped the weapon in a command of attack. Spiritus flew through the beleaguered field to engage the advancing sentries.

High over the castle wall, on a landing near the southern tower where Avant had played as a boy, Aesdil stood like a marble carving of a mythic creature. The anger that welled up in Avant's being caused him to wail. He dismounted Spiritus and rushed the ranks of sentries in his rage. Engaging three soldiers, he ended them all with three blows. Two more moved forward. He wielded his sword with the swiftness of an eagle sweeping over its prey. The soldiers fell lifeless to the ground.

"Avant, are you still there?"

"Busy, Abigail."

"Just checking."

His men fought bravely. The hours flew and his arms and legs ached from fatigue, yet he pressed on. Though the troops from the northern gate stood their ground, the guards at the eastern and southern gates fled or were killed. They were making progress.

It was time to bring in the next wave.

Chapter Thirty-Five

Pacing the same patch of ground, Abby had worn a path in the grass next to the beefed up Xterra. She hadn't mindspoken with Avant for a few hours. Their brief conversations were the only thing that had kept her from Implanting to him. Her fingernails were bitten to the quick and she hadn't sat down since the sun rose. When the call came from the front to mobilize, she climbed in the driver's seat and followed behind the last battalion. A shudder ran through her.

Positioned behind the ranks, she jumped out of the Xterra when they reached the edge of the battlefield. With the fighting in front of them, Abby frantically searched the carnage for Avant. He fought on the far side of the battle, near the wall, commanding troops in a successful campaign against the western gate.

She gazed up at the castle. Aesdil stood high, commanding his troops in battle but not joining.

"You cannot prevail, Aesdil. Your reign is broken. Avant and I have the Crown."

"But you do not have the Stone of Light, Chosen One. I do."

So he had the earring from Seppitent.

"You're deceived. Seppitent didn't steal the Stone. The Crown is restored. Aesdil, give up the fight. It's not too late. There doesn't need to be any further bloodshed."

"I'll not be defeated. Avant cannot take my kingdom from me."

Her heart twisted in pain at the thought of more lives being lost. Battle was ugly. Soldiers from both sides already lay dead and injured on the ground. Body parts, strewn like litter in a city park, lay discarded across the meadow. Bright red painted the sweet summer grass and the rusty tinge of blood permeated the air. Abby fought the urge to rush and help them. There was still too much fighting, and if she was caught or hurt, her mission would be thwarted.

Her mission. She didn't even really know what that was, but she did know that when it presented itself, she needed to be ready. Following the Light was not always about seeing what was coming, but trusting that when she did, she would be victorious.

"Avant."

"Still here."

Her gaze searched for Petra, who commanded the troops around him, directing them to advance on the gate and push the king's dwindling forces back as far as they could. She said a quick prayer for him and returned to scanning the field, letting her gaze linger on the formidable wall.

The gate made of heavy wood and metal loomed in the distance. When she'd escaped a few weeks ago, it had been too dark and she'd been in too much of a hurry to get the crap out of Dodge. But now, the massive keep towered over the field like one of the Great High Places. The menacing gray stone blended with the cloud-covered sky. She focused on the figure near the front lines.

Avant's head turned when Petra's new battle cry sounded. Disposing of the sentry he fought, he dashed back to Spiritus and mounted the horse. In one fluid motion, he galloped toward her.

He flew straight for her and dismounted the proud stallion. Then he swept her off the ground and into his arms. Covered in the blood and sweat of battle, he brushed her lips in the most romantic kiss of her life. Just as quickly, he dropped her on her feet and climbed into the Xterra, which sat two football fields from the gate. The path filled with soldiers. She tried to yell at them, but only those closest could hear. Avant could not gain enough speed unless the way was cleared.

"I'll try to force the men out of the way with my Implanting. Can you do the same?"

He nodded at her.

Joining their minds, they pushed the fighting to the sides with an invisible river of force. The pressure of their combined energy parted the troops like the Red Sea, leaving the path open.

Avant released her energy and revved the car's engine. He threw the Xterra in drive.

"Please be careful. You can't be in that car upon impact, Avant."

He smiled and slammed down the accelerator. She shook her head. Even in the midst of a violent battle, the speed thrilled him to the core.

The Xterra sped through the crowd, racing toward the castle gates. Abby gathered her energy to hold Avant off the ground when he jumped from the moving vehicle.

"Abigail, my feet are locked, and my hands frozen to the steering wheel. I cannot stop. I'm pushing against Aesdil but he has more power here."

Shit! Aesdil had bound Avant inside the car using his Implanting. Abby pushed against the king's force also, but her Gift wouldn't loosen Avant from its grip. He would die in the impact. Her heart seized. *Think, Abby.* She searched for a way to save him. He would never swerve into the soldiers.

The gates! With all of her Implanting, she unbarred the gates and pushed them open with the force of her mind. The car sped through the opening and inside the castle grounds. Several surrounding horsemen followed after their commander.

Aesdil, realizing the wall had been breached, released Avant and slammed the gates closed again. He now had Avant trapped on the other side with only six or seven reinforcements.

She had to get inside those gates. *"Avant! Can you hear me? Are you okay?"*

*****

"I'm unharmed for now but surrounded by a garrison of soldiers."

Avant slammed on the brakes. The Xterra screeched to a halt in front of the palace's southern entrance. A group of sentries surrounded the vehicle. Six of his men on horseback had already engaged the king's troops behind him in a vicious battle. They would hold out a while but were severely outnumbered. If he could only reach the palace....

A soldier jumped on the hood of the vehicle. Avant revved the engine and lurched the car forward. The sentry fell to the ground and Avant rolled over him. Aesdil's men surrounded the car. They began to rock and shake the SUV. Soon they would dump it to its side, and it would be useless. Worse, he would be trapped. Realizing he had to exit, he parked the car and jumped out, engaging the two sentries nearest his door.

The clanking of metal on metal rang through the air. These soldiers had been trained by his standards. Their skill made it difficult for him to engage more than one. The blades whipped through the air, their flashing sparks catching the attention of more soldiers. Avant was surrounded. He struck a man across the neck, sending his head over the yard to hit another soldier. When the soldier saw what struck him, he dropped his sword in shock and Avant's horseman ran him through.

Avant held his sword in front of him as he paced in a circle, holding at least a dozen soldiers at bay.

"Avant, distract the king, and I'll open the gates again to let our troops in."

"I'll hasten to do that after I fend off these twelve men, Abigail."

"Just do it, Avant!" The authority in her tone offended and compelled him. He gathered his energy and knocked Aesdil's feet out from under him. That gave him the idea to do the same to his opponents.

*****

"Go, Abigail." Avant's voice thundered in her mind. Abby pushed the gates open with her Implanting and eight men stole into the castle grounds before the gates closed again. She grabbed every soldier she could within arm's reach and put their hands on her as she Implanted to Avant. The light flashed. She and ten soldiers appeared next to Avant in front of a garrison of twenty men.

Aesdil stood on a balcony above them. "That is impressive, Chosen One, but it will not help your lost cause." He gaze cut to the soldiers and he commanded, "Take them and bring me the Crown!"

Avant glared at the king. Avant's rage was fierce, powerful enough to cause a fissure in the foundations of Jastain.

"Remember who the enemy is. Keep your wits," she reminded Avant, and then focused her attention on Aesdil. "Aesdil, you won't win, no matter what you think. You can't stand against the Light."

"Damnable Darkness, Abigail. Get out of here." Avant roared inside her head.

Soldiers surrounded them, but adrenaline must've taken hold, because she felt neither fear nor rage. Instead, confidence surged through her veins. They weren't in this battle alone. They'd been sent, and the Light who had sent them would keep them safe.

She studied Avant as he fought beside his men and now understood the ingeniousness of Aesdil's plan to kill him. Avant would never leave his men in battle, even if they left him. And if he wouldn't, neither would she. *"You know I can't leave any more than you can. What do we need to do to win?"*

He cursed again. She knew this had been his fear about letting her come all along, but he couldn't stop destiny, and he knew it. *"I estimate twenty-five soldiers here and at least that many more right inside that door. We need to capture Aesdil to break their allegiance to him. If one of us can make it to the car and cause a diversion, we could give the other an advantage to take the king. I trained most of these men, Abigail. As long as Aesdil holds power, the soldiers will follow him, but if we can lay hands on him...."*

Abby assessed the distance between her and the Xterra. She could make it to the passenger side if she went quickly.

"I'll make it to the car. How much time do you need to capture him?"

"A few moments only."

Abby gathered her inner strength and, with her Implanting, pushed a group of six soldiers to the ground in front of the SUV. She ran like hell and jumped in, locking the doors and sliding to the driver's side. She drove over the soldiers she'd knocked down. Their bodies crunching under the car tied her stomach in a knot. Their howls of pain ripped at her. *Damn.*

Knocking people in the head was one thing, but running them down in a car was something else. All their lives were at stake. The kingdom, the Light, hung in the balance. Spinning the giant erection around, she accelerated for the largest concentration of soldiers that stood between Avant and Aesdil. She winced and said a silent prayer as she neared the cluster. They scattered like mice before the aroused SUV. She hit two more sentries before wheeling around in the other direction to make another pass.

Along the steps leading to the balcony, Avant had already defeated ten men with only three soldiers at his flanks. He could almost reach Aesdil. The king would not stand to fight face to face. Even from this distance and speed, she could see the fear that filled his eyes.

By his sheer will, Avant stormed the last five soldiers and climbed over the balustrade to put Aesdil at the end of his blade. *OMG!* Her man was a force to be reckoned with. A sexy shiver ran through her. *For God's sakes, not the time or place, Abs.* Apparently, it was true what they said about adrenaline rushes and sexual arousal.

*****

"Finally, *Brother*, I see my enemy face to face. I've wished for this many times," Avant growled.

"You look well, *Lord Ventium*. I'm certain my queen will wish to greet you also," Aesdil taunted.

"You dare mention her to me, Aesdil?" Desire to run his sword through the king pulsed like sweet wine in his fingers. His hands vibrated with bloodlust for his stolen life.

"You need not feel alone, Avant. It seems you're not the only husband Sentieve betrayed." Aesdil trembled but his voice remained even.

"You're not her husband, Aesdil. As you can see, I'm alive, so you are not joined to her."

"But we are joined in other ways you couldn't understand. Were you aware we have a son, an heir to the throne? I believe you've met him. Bring out my son and my queen."

Two sentries stepped onto the balcony, shoving Chad and Sentieve before them. Chains bound their hands in front of them. Chad was badly beaten, and Sentieve looked as if she hadn't eaten or bathed for weeks. Avant turned his head, swallowing back the bile that rose in his throat.

"Surely, Avant, you didn't think this boy could be your son? He doesn't have your strength or boldness; he has my clever mind."

"Let them go, Aesdil, or I'll run you through with my sword!" Avant snarled.

Seppitent appeared. He stepped even with Aesdil and his wicked voice chimed, "Perhaps, Avant, if you'd known your wife better, you would have realized she'd given herself to another long before your unfortunate accident."

*****

When Seppitent appeared, Abby slammed on the breaks and jumped out of the car. Now it was time for her battle. "Men of the kingdom, Aesdil has lied to you. He has betrayed the Light. Abandon the works of Darkness and align with us."

Avant's men had already defeated the bulk of the king's soldiers. Four horsemen opened the gates. Two battalions, led by Petra, flooded into the keep. Many of the king's soldiers dropped their swords and surrendered to the regal-looking Petra as he entered.

Abby's gaze met Petra's brown eyes. He gave her a reassuring nod. With Petra's assistance on the ground, she rushed up the stairs to support Avant. *"Close your ears to that monster. He's trying to ensnare you."*

She bolted up the last steps and stood beside Avant. "Seppitent, you don't belong here. This is not your world, and you are not welcome."

"You're the one who is unwelcome, Chosen One." He laughed a hideous laugh that pierced her ears, but she knew it hypnotized and deceived those under his spell. "I have the Stone of Light. I told you this journey would only mean ruin for you. Now your quest has failed, and all those you love will die."

She gazed around the gathering faces, lost and remote. She was the only one who saw his hideousness and heard the truth of his soul-scraping voice. Even Avant was not immune—his face was clouded with confusion.

"You're mistaken, Seppitent." She reached for her backpack and pulled out the diadem. A bright light shone from her, illuminating the circlet as she held it in front of her.

A collective gasp sounded from those around her. The creature's deception broke in the light of the Crown. Even Aesdil stared, horrified, at the reality of Seppitent's loathsome appearance.

The creature laughed. The shrieking sound sickened her soul. "Abby, you are. As long as the hearts of men choose to listen, I'm welcome. I will eventually rule in Jastain as I do in other worlds."

Abby looked directly at the hideous creature. The light within her built in intensity until it beamed out of her toward the deceiver. He shielded his eyes from the rays. She spoke with a power beyond her ability. "I am the Chosen One of the Light and you, Seppitent, are under my authority. I bind your words from you, and your tongue is tied in a knot. *Begone!*"

Seppitent let out a screech that forced hands to every ear; then he vanished.

All within the castle wall, including Aesdil and Avant, had halted to listen to the exchange between Abby and Seppitent. Upon his departure, a cheer rose from the crowd of soldiers gathered on the grounds. Even the king's men lifted arms in triumph and praise at the defeat of the evil creature.

Abby turned back toward Aesdil, seeing him through the light that now possessed her. She saw, as through a window, into his mind and heart. Though he'd seen the truth of Seppitent's deception, his heart was too hardened to seek repentance and too proud to admit defeat. Looking into his tortured soul, Abby realized how very similar to Avant he was.

Aesdil grabbed Chad and held a knife to his throat. "Would either of you risk this boy's life? Back up or I'll kill him. Chosen One—I'll take my Crown now."

She shook her head and spoke with power. "Think of your life, Aesdil. Do you believe the Light will allow you to reign with this Crown? You're a mockery, and your covetousness will destroy you as it destroyed your father."

His hand trembled. Shaken by the truth and authority of her words, he considered them but would not drop the knife.

Still seeing clearly the intent of his heart, Abby entreated him. "You have the opportunity for repentance, but the window is closing even as I speak. Drop your knife."

"I will kill this boy and then I will dispose of his mother." Aesdil glanced back at Sentieve. Abby looked into the hollow eyes of the queen, a flicker of hate flaming from the woman toward him.

Aesdil's heart iced over and became implacable. His opportunity had past. He was lost. "You are the one for whom opportunity passes, Chosen One. Hand me the Crown."

"Abigail, I will chop off your hand if you hand him that Crown." Avant did not break eye contact with Aesdil.

"I wasn't planning on it, but thanks for the warning, honey."

Avant's rage burned within him, and Abby feared it might consume them all. Aesdil's hand twitched. Sentieve caught Abby's eye, the woman's intent written in the depth of her gaze. Abby opened her mouth to speak, but her voice was lost.

Abby became a spectator outside the action. The events happened as the Light allowed them to unfold. Everything ensued in slow motion, and she was helplessly frozen in place.

Sentieve grabbed the sword of a nearby sentry and stepped in front of Aesdil. Raising the blade above her head, she stabbed him through the heart with her bound hands.

With unbridled rage, Avant lunged at the same moment, piercing through Sentieve's back and into the stomach of Aesdil, both skewered on his blade. The life immediately left Aesdil. He fell to the ground. Dropping his hold on Chad, his body slipped from the weapon that impaled him.

Avant released his sword, frozen, with palms up.

Chapter Thirty-Six

Abby, still unable to move, held her breath. A lump formed in her throat.

Sentieve slowly turned and fell to her knees before Avant. Tears spilled from her. "Avant…I'm sorry, my love…please…forgive me." She labored to speak. She grasped his arms, her eyes begging for absolution. "I always…loved…you."

His face contorted as horror and disbelief drove him to his knees. Tears filled his eyes, and Abby tried to swallow around the painful lump in her throat. He supported Sentieve's frail body and whispered, "I know, my darling, and I always loved you."

"I didn't know…but I see…it now." Into his mind, Sentieve placed a vision. Through her connection to him, Abby also witnessed it.

"My lady, does your husband truly love you?" Seppitent *softly sang to Sentieve.*

"Who are you, beautiful creature? Yes, he loves me." But *doubts had already begun to form with his toxic words.*

"Has he told you that? He is much gone, my lady. How lonely it must be for you."

Seppitent's words had pierced Sentieve's heart with thorny darts, and she wouldn't escape them until she heard of Avant's death in the field several months later.

Sentieve revealed the daily professions of love that had come from Aesdil along with his advances on her. The night she betrayed Avant was after he'd left her crying in the threshold of their home and begging him to stay. Aesdil had found her weeping in the garden, where he seduced her.

"I forgive you, my love. Rest." Avant pulled her body to him and wept in her hair.

Her breaths came in shallow gasps. Blood trickled from her mouth as she whispered, "It is only an explanation. You did not…deserve to be betrayed." Her hand lifted to touch his cheek. "It was not your fault…*please*…explain to my son…tell him I love him."

Sentieve closed her eyes and didn't breathe again.

As Abby returned to self-awareness, the hush of the court contrasted the earlier turmoil. She reached her hand to her face. Tears coursed down her cheeks and dripped from her chin. The Light within her faded and full range of motion returned to her limbs.

Chad lay on the ground, unconscious and bleeding from a short gash on his throat. Abby rushed to him and ripped the sleeve from her shirt to compress the wound. The cut had narrowly missed his pulsing artery. It was Sentieve's blow that had saved his life.

The soldiers began to mill around in a haze, and the din of soft voices echoed across the stone steps of the castle. Petra dismounted and called out orders to the troops on the ground. Abby watched as he climbed the steps, strode to Avant, and pulled the sword from Sentieve's lifeless body. He laid a comforting hand on Avant's back. Then he marched to Abby as she applied pressure to Chad's wound.

He knelt beside her. "Will he be all right?"

"I think so, as long as I can stop the bleeding."

He nodded and squeezed her shoulder. Standing tall, he called to other soldiers, his voice ringing with command, and instructed them to help the wounded.

Avant stayed with Sentieve.

*****

Abby woke just after dawn the next morning. Sitting up from a chaise lounge in the castle's solarium, she stretched and tried to focus her clouded vision. The previous day's events flooded back to her.

Relief that her family was safe poured over her. "Lord, thank you for the lives of all the men who survived. Help us heal this land and restore the kingdom."

Avant's men suffered fewer casualties than expected, taking into account the ferocity of the battle. Only thirty-three of them died, but two hundred were seriously wounded. Unfortunately, the king's army sustained causalities in the hundreds.

Miraculously, none of the men she ran over died, although most of them had at least one broken limb. Chad had regained consciousness in the triage, but suffered deep bruises and abrasions from the beating he had endured. His spirits were solemn but high, and he'd met the adversity with the logic of his scientific mind. He told the caretakers how to make painkillers and antibiotics for the wounded before prescribing a sedative for himself. Only then did he agree to rest.

She giggled at the memory, yawned, and rubbed her eyes. Petra had organized a makeshift hospital in the ballroom of the palace. He had taken command of the king's army and tasked a garrison of soldiers to bury the dead. Then he worked with the local merchants and tradesmen to organize meals and accommodations for Avant's men. At Abby's request, he had men dig two graves in the royal cemetery. Aesdil and Sentieve were buried there.

She'd slept for a few hours in the small solarium. Standing up from her makeshift bed, she glanced around the bright room. One entire wall was made of leaded glass and overlooked an enormous garden. A large fireplace stood angled in the corner, and soft, overstuffed furniture took up most of the intimate space. Everything there screamed luxury and elegance. This was where she would live?

Her stomach growled. She headed to look for food.

The cooks rattled away in the kitchen, already preparing breakfast for the wounded and the other palace occupants. When she entered, all movement ceased. The cooks stopped their work and then turned to bow and curtsy to her. Her jaw fell open. She stood still, her eyes drying out because they wouldn't blink. *What the hell?* "Please continue your work," she finally said.

They rose and carried on with their tasks. Her eyes wandered around the room. Did these people know something she didn't? She grabbed a sweet roll and ran like a scampering rabbit to find Petra. One of Avant's men patrolled the hall, and she nearly knocked him down. "Do you know where Master Petra is?"

"He was organizing men to repair the damage to the castle walls and clean up from the battle. You will most likely find him there."

"Thank you." She headed out the door and found Petra helping men guide the horses to the king's stables.

"Petra." She ran to him.

When the men heard her, they stopped their work and bowed where they stood. She stared at them and then looked to Petra. She grimaced and bit her lip, silently pleading for help.

"You may continue." Petra gestured to the men to rise. "Abby, let's take a walk."

He took her arm and strolled toward a maze of hedgerows filled with sweet-smelling flowers. "Since yesterday, a change has come over this land. Word of the king's death and the restoration of the Crown of Light has traveled to the farthest reaches of the kingdom. In the minds of these people, you're now their ruler."

"What? But Petra—"

He took her hands. "The kingdom hangs in the balance, and you must take the role. The people need a leader. I understand you weren't expecting this right away, but now you have no choice."

"I don't even know these people, much less how to rule them." She pulled her hands from his and pressed her palms against her cheeks. "What am I going to do? I'm not ready."

"Avant and I will help you. You can do this, Your Majesty." He bowed. "Tell me I may rise," he said, looking up at her.

"You may rise." She rolled her eyes and paced to a shrub with little pink flowers. She snatched a flower from the bush. "Seriously, Petra, how can I do this?"

"I am serious. What you're going to do is be a queen. Have you seen Avant this morning?"

She dropped her gazed and shook her head. Tears welled in her eyes. "I have an idea where he might be."

Her stomach knotted with a tangle of emotions. Her heart and mind were not yet ready to sit at the negotiation table over the issue of Avant. After the smoke of battle cleared, she'd paced the floor back and forth, wondering if she should try to find him or if she should leave him to grieve. She had started up the stairs at least five times only to turn around. By default, she'd chosen the latter. Her heart throbbed. She wanted to comfort him, but her own pain and fear kept her at bay.

Petra lightly touched her arm and, with his soothing, confidence-building way, he infused her with strength. "You should find him. He's had enough time to wallow in guilt for something that wasn't his fault."

Treating Petra's words as permission, she sped to the castle. She grabbed the first chambermaid she found. "You may rise." *Oh, for the love of God.* "Please show me to the queen's chambers."

The young girl led her up the stairs and down a long hallway to a large door.

"Thank you. Please have three baths prepared."

The girl nodded and curtsied before hurrying to complete her task, apparently thrilled *the queen* had given her something to do. Abby watched the girl and shook her head. *What a crazy rush.*

She entered a sitting area with rich gold and emerald jacquard fabrics, a large room as elegant as the woman to whom it belonged. A massive portrait of Sentieve, dressed in scarlet and holding a baby, hung over the black marble fireplace. She was still young and she appeared happy to have the baby in her arms, but the artist had captured a sadness in her doe eyes.

Abby quietly moved through the sitting area and into the bedchamber. Her heart thumped against her chest. The oversized bed was elevated on a two-step carpeted platform. The rich cream fabrics of the linens were softly visible through the yards of sheer fabric draped over the canopy that surrounded the perimeter of the dais. Her breath caught in her throat. Avant sat in a cushioned armchair facing the window. He held the queen's dressing gown loosely against his face and looked out over the mountains with empty eyes. Abby swallowed the knot of her own hurt and sat on an ottoman in front of him.

His gaze flickered to her and then away. She climbed into his lap and wrapped her arms around him. His arms enveloped her, and he buried his head in her chest.

She whispered in his ear, "Honey, you're not alone. I know you feel like the Darkness won, but it didn't. The Light has returned. We paid a high price—you paid a high price." She kissed his head and straightened his disheveled hair with her fingers.

"I killed her. I broke her heart and withheld my love. I only ever hurt her."

"That isn't true. Seppitent's words caused her doubts, and the king's dishonor took advantage." She held his face in her hands. "You loved her, and if she had forgotten, seeing you again made her remember. Let it go."

At her words, a peace filled his eyes and color returned to his ashen face. "You were right, Abigail. It was your destiny to be here. Had you not, all would've been lost."

This was so not how the I-told-you-so conversation had played out in her mind. She leaned over and kissed him lightly.

"Your words have healing power, Abigail. You're the Chosen One, and you will be queen." He searched her face in wonder, but then concern lined his face. "Was Chad harmed?"

"Chad'll be fine. Petra has taken over the reconstruction. I swear, he would make a better ruler than either of us. We buried the dead, and the wounded are downstairs being cared for." She looked at Avant's clothes and hands. "I'm having a bath drawn for you, and afterward we can decide what else needs to be done."

She stood, but something compelled her to turn back to him. "You know I love you?"

"I know." He gave her a weary smile.

Her heart sank. She hadn't really expected that he would say that he loved her back, but she had hoped. Shaking it off, she left and found the chambermaid and a bath of her own.

Abby sent Petra to take a bath and rest, too. He'd worked through the night and most of the day. Other than the fresh graves, there was scarcely any evidence that a battle had taken place little more than twenty-four hours before.

She and Avant ate dinner in a small dining room off the kitchen. Abby told the kitchen and serving staff to keep it simple, with no fanfare. She made them put the silver serving trays away and told them to bring in prepared plates only. Avant sat quietly and showed no emotion during the meal, except for a half-smile he gave at her crinkled forehead whenever a server bowed and backed out of the room.

He pushed away from the table and sat back in his seat. "Abigail, we must make arrangements for your coronation. A dress must be made, a celebration planned. A portrait will need to be commissioned. There is much work to do. We will use the flag of the previous Kingdom of Light to fly over the castle until a new one can be designed."

"Those things seem kind of trivial and excessive to me, Avant."

"Those things are not for you, Abigail. They are for the people. A funeral is not for the person who dies; it is for those left behind, to give resolution. A coronation is a declaration to the world of a new ruler. To some extent, the extravagance of the affair denotes the power of the ruler, and as backward as it seems, it instills confidence in the people of the land."

She could see the wisdom of his words, but she still felt like the royal title was two sizes too big for her. There had been a day when she would've been ecstatic to plan a party of this scope, but the last year had given her a love of simple things, the quality of companionship over the quantity of it. In the other world, she had three thousand and sixty-eight Facebook friends; in this world, she had family.

"In addition, we need to decide who will preside over the coronation ceremony. Do you have any ideas?"

Avant's inquiry snapped her out of her thoughts. She leaned toward him. "Can you do it?"

"I do not think that would be appropriate, but may I make a suggestion?"

She frowned, not exactly sure why he couldn't. "Okay, who should do it?"

"I believe Annova is the appropriate selection."

Her eyes widened, and she nodded. She had only met Annova a few times, but knew her to be a woman of character and a prophet of the Light. "That's a good idea. Do you think she would do it?"

He smiled. "I believe she most likely already knows she is going to do it." He took his last bite of roast pork.

"Good point."

"I need to lead my soldiers back to the Freelands tomorrow. I'll stop on my way and speak with her."

"We're going home tomorrow?"

"I am going. You must stay. This is your home now."

Home? No, it was not! "You can't leave me here." She scowled.

"Abigail, I am not leaving you. I need to take my men back to their families and speak to Annova about the coronation. I will only be gone a few days. You should Implant to get Lyndsea after dinner."

Abby hadn't even thought about Lyndsea. The king's men had abducted Chad from the manor. Her friend must've been scared to death. They did need to check on her, but as for the rest of his statement: Abby couldn't stand the thought of Avant leaving. "I'll get her as soon as we're done. Can't you send Petra with the men?"

"No, I cannot. It is not Petra's responsibility to lead the men, and you have already indicated his value to you here."

Feeling hurt and alone, her mouth spewed words her brain never qualified. "I could order you to stay if I wanted."

His face took on a frightening formality. "And you would be wasting your breath. You are not queen yet, even if the people think you are, and we will discuss this no further."

For the remainder of the meal, he planned and she pouted with her head propped on a fist.

As promised, she Implanted to the manor. She found Lyndsea, who pulled her into a bear hug. "Abby, I was so worried."

Abby took hold of her sweet little namesake. "Hello, dear girl." Then she grabbed Lyndsea's hand. "Everything is fine, but you need to care for your man, because he's too busy caring for the wounded. I think he should've gone into medicine."

Relief flooded her friend's face and they Implanted back to the castle.

Avant slept in the barracks with his men and left for the fief the next morning, but not before he commissioned her coronation dress, left instructions with Petra regarding the plans for the celebration, and ordered both royal chambers be completely refurbished. He had time for all that, but not even a moment to spare for a good-bye.

Abby roamed the castle in a funk. They hadn't been together since the night they had found the prophecy. That had been over a month ago and seemed further away than ever.

She wandered upstairs, where designers, tradesmen, and carpenters worked on Sentieve's chambers. She was expected to occupy the much more grandiose master suite.

A tall, finely dressed man sauntered into the sitting room. "Your Majesty, may I introduce myself?" She recognized him from Avant's memories. He'd been Aesdil and Avant's tutor and a member of the Council of Elders, which acted as advisors to the king or, in this case, queen.

"You are Master Galwyn, I believe. You may rise." Though Aesdil had taken very little advice from the council, he maintained their positions in court as a show of solidarity.

"So, Avant told you?"

Avant hadn't spoken to her since dinner last night, and now he was gone. "No, he didn't. I know you from Avant's…stories."

"Ah, I see. Your Majesty, you will need formal training for the coronation ceremony. There are many forms and customs you must learn, and Avant tells me you were not raised in a monarchy."

"That's true. What kinds of things do I need to know? Avant has taught me quite a bit."

"Initially, you'll need to know who you are. By that, I mean what your formal title will be and what it means." Galwyn cleared his throat and smoothed his brocade vest.

Abby furrowed her brow. *Persnickety* was the word that came to mind. "What will my title be?" Clearly, Galwyn was ready to step back into his role of advisor and watchdog of the kingdom.

"Her Royal Majesty, Sovereign Queen and Supreme Ruler of the Lands of Jastain, the New Kingdom of Light."

What? Sovereign Queen Supreme sounded like a combo meal. "That seems kind of...clunky."

"Each word has a meaning, and it is my charge to teach you. I'd like to begin your lessons this afternoon, if it pleases you? By the way, your current appropriate title is Queen Regent of the Eastern Lands of Jastain, the Kingdom of Azdil."

Ha! Avant was wrong. She was queen already, although she had no idea what that meant. "This afternoon is fine. I've got nothing else on the *royal* agenda. Can I ask you something?"

"Of course." The elderly gentlemen's slate eyes scrutinized her.

"If I ordered another ruler to do something, would he have to do it?"

"That would depend on the ruler and the land from which he came. If I were to assume you were referring to Lord Ventium, for instance," he said, his smile wry, "then I would say, most likely. Domentus Ventium is currently a lordship in the independent Freelands of Jastain; however, the Freelands fall within the Kingdom of Light. Therefore, upon your coronation, all of the Freelands will be under your rule."

Her mind spun. She hadn't realized that Avant would be her subject, and she really didn't like the idea. She frowned. He wouldn't either.

"Could I give someone, as a gift, full reign over certain lands? Lord Ventium, for instance, could I give him the Freelands to rule?"

Galwyn looked at her like she had a booger hanging from her nose. "You cannot give the rule of your lands away, and even if you could, you should not. It creates division and unrest and would be seen as weakness by those who may want more than you are willing to give. You could, however, bequeath regency to your consort upon marriage."

Huh? "You mean, if I get married I can give the king authority to rule with me?"

"To an extent, that is what I mean. However, there can be no king while a queen rules. This will all be part of your lessons, but I'll explain briefly. Upon marriage, you may give your prince a ruling claim over some of your lands."

"Why can't there be a king? There was previously a king and queen."

"I can see we are beginning our lessons now. Please sit. We are currently in the consort chambers of the castle."

Galwyn explained the difference between a ruling queen and a queen consort. As Abby understood it, the title of king held more authority than queen, therefore couldn't be used when a sovereign queen ruled. The spouse of a ruling queen was known as prince, which finally made sense because she'd actually seen Queen Elizabeth and Prince Phillip during a vacation to England. Galwyn spent the next three hours explaining all of the different titles, and when she left him, her mind swam with dukes, regents, consorts, and regent queen supremes.

She wandered down the hall into the king's chambers. His lavish sitting room overlooked the kingdom to the east. The ocean was visible from windows that spanned ceiling to floor. The haze had cleared from the sky and only a remnant of fog remained. She walked through a tall threshold into a bedchamber as large as the sitting room. The opulent accommodations dripped with elegance and excess. Rich velvets and brocades decorated gilded furniture. Large intricately woven tapestries and massive oil paintings adorned the walls. From the northern windows, a stunning view of the Great Heights overwhelmed her. The sight of the High Places made her smile with joy. She had stood on those peaks and looked down on this very castle. A chill swept over her, and the room thickened with destiny realized.

She stepped over to the dressing table and fingered Aesdil's personal items, which still lay there. Something sparkled on a silver tray. She picked up the three-carat diamond and twirled the stem between her finger and thumb. Where had her father gotten this stone? It was the perfect mate to the Stone of Light—*the commitment of sacrifice*. There was only one man who would possess this stone, but she'd save it until the time was right. She smiled as she put it in her ear.

The thought of staying in the rooms where Aesdil plotted his evil plan didn't give her a warm, fuzzy feeling. It was most likely the reason for Avant's hurry to have them refurbished. She also didn't like the idea that Avant would occupy Sentieve's old rooms. Once he was the official consort, she would talk him into staying in here, with her, permanently. Petra could have the other chambers; she would rename them just for him.

It still seemed like a mistake that she should be queen. Avant had wanted to be king, expected to be king. But now he could *never* be king. No wonder he'd acted so strangely. He'd understood the implications from the moment he read the prophecy, and still he did what he had to, making sure she could rule, even though it crushed his own dreams. She would just have to make it up to him.

Now that all of their obstacles were removed, they could be finally together. She knew he still had a hurdle to overcome. Except for that brief moment in Dallas, he'd not initiated a relationship with her. Her heart filled with dread. *It has to be his decision.* She'd given him the driver's seat. The answer to that familiar question was the same: She trusted him. What would he do with it?

Chapter Thirty-Seven

Abby paced back and forth in the northern drawing room, which gave her a panoramic view of the west—the direction from which he would come.

The coronation was to take place in two weeks. How everything could possibly get done before then was an effin' mystery. Every available woman in the land worked around the clock in multiple shifts to piece the material for her dress. Petra organized the invitations and sent messengers out to the regent and steward rulers of Jastain.

Huge orders of perishables from the Eastern Islands flooded into the market for local traders to distribute. The whole kingdom labored like an anthill with preparations. Carpenters and tradesmen of all kinds worked diligently in the upstairs chambers, which were close to completion.

Although she'd expected him back the day before, Avant still hadn't returned. He'd been gone five days already. Though he promised he wouldn't be long, she hadn't asked for a specific timeframe. She rolled her eyes. Based on experience, his idea of time and distance didn't correspond to hers.

Staring out the window, she spied a small caravan. Her heart leapt in relief and she rushed down and through the castle to greet it. Annova descended from the carriage, looking as regal as ever. Her red hair glistened in the sun. She wore a simple traveling dress, but that in no way detracted from her stunning beauty.

Abby craned her head to find Spiritus. Maybe he'd gone straight to the city. "Did Avant go to the city?"

"No, my dear. He stayed at the fief on business matters."

"He's not with you?" She felt as if someone had opened a trapdoor under her feet. She fell into a cold, dark well of disappointment. Closing her eyes, she tried to quell the threatening tears.

Annova wrapped a comforting arm around Abby's waist. "Give him time. He still must find his heart."

Another five days passed. She thought about Implanting to him but kept reminding herself: *driver's seat.*

Between dress fittings, menu tastings, and coronation lessons, no time remained to do anything but sleep and eat, and barely that. She never saw anyone she knew and loved anymore, except Lyndsea. Lyndsea and Baby Abby kept her company during some of the preparations, when the new mom wasn't spending time with Chad. It appeared she and Chad truly shared a bond since the ordeal with Seppitent. *At least somebody had found love.* Petra was gone most days and didn't even eat dinner with them, although Abby knew he spent nights in the castle. She understood that he was still trying to sort through his hurt.

Being queen was more of a pain that anything else. The people in the castle accommodated her every need. They quickly provided her with any whim of a request she made. If she complemented a particular flower in the gardens, the vases around the castle were filled with them. If she commented on the pleasant temperature of her bathwater, the chambermaids would argue on how to maintain that temperature. It was all so goofy. She sighed.

The best part about being queen was the chocolate from the Eastern traders, and Abby made a career out of eating it. The bakers and chefs had duels to see whose dessert she liked the best, and usually they all won.

She spent any spare time studying maps of Jastain and learning the names of the different lands and rulers, filling in the gaps from Avant's Implanting. Studying hadn't ever been her strong suit. It still wasn't. Some days, she took long walks in her private garden with Galwyn to make the task more palatable.

The enchantment of the place could charm even the fussiest curmudgeon, but it didn't feel like home. Something was missing. Someone was missing.

Fourteen days and five hours after he'd left, Avant had the nerve to return. She told her staff that she was to be immediately informed of his arrival. One of the lady's maids told her he'd traveled to town to follow up on arrangements for the coronation and would meet with her afterward.

She watched from her windows as he casually bounded up the steps of the palace like he hadn't been gone a day, and like she wasn't mad as hell at him. Determined to be the epitome of reserve and coolness, she sat in her newly refurbished chambers like the regal queen she was—sort of.

The teal blue and silver rooms overflowed in luxury and beauty. The artisans and craftsmen who completed the job in a little over a week could have given the crew of *Extreme Home Makeover* a run for their money. Calm colors provided the soothing tranquility she needed.

When Avant strolled in, she didn't lift her gaze but sat on her cushioned sofa eating chocolates.

"Abigail, I'm sorry I was delayed…. My Light, these are the finest rooms I've ever seen. Do you approve of them?" He rose from a shallow bow to gaze around.

She glanced at him from the corner of her eye. Her heart pounded. God, did he have to look so damned good? He gaped in wonder.

She scowled up at him and continued to eat her chocolate.

"I must say, the carpenters did a magnificent job, and the fabric workers—" He stepped over to peek into her bedroom.

If he thinks he's getting in there anytime soon, he's sadly mistaken!

"I've come from a meeting with Petra, and it seems the arrangements are in order. A week from today you will ascend the throne."

She glared at him again and bit hard into a piece of chocolate.

He took in a long breath. "Abigail, I understand you're angry—"

"Well, aren't you the clever one?"

"—but as I explained, I was delayed. I'm sorry. You have important matters with which to concern yourself. Put away this childishness. Is this really how a queen is to behave?"

He was right, but he'd been gone two weeks and didn't even seem to have missed her.

"You mean important matters like dress fittings and coronation lessons? Oh, how will I ever manage?" She put her wrist to her forehead.

He frowned and furrowed his brow. He wasn't exactly a fan of her sarcasm.

"No. Like what you're going to do for the families of the men who lost their lives in the battle. Are you going to provide for the injured men who can no longer earn a living? Do you have enough excess grain in the storehouses to feed the people through the winter? I could continue, but I believe you understand. This is not a game, my lady. These people are depending on you. They are looking to you for answers. You can no longer afford the luxury of pettiness."

She felt like she was two inches tall. The weight of the kingdom came down on her shoulders. Tears pooled in her eyes. "How am I supposed to do this? I don't want to."

Avant sat beside her. He sighed heavily. "How did you restore the kingdom, Abigail? Are these problems any more difficult than defeating Seppitent or talking down a mountain lion? The Light will guide you and provide everything you need to accomplish your task." He took her hand. "You were not Chosen because you could accomplish this; you can accomplish this because you are Chosen."

She gazed into those blue eyes. The hardness of her heart melted. She didn't understand the philosophy lesson, but holding his hand made everything okay.

*****

The next seven days were a blur. Although Avant was back in the castle, she rarely saw him. He was busy with the final preparations. Foreign dignitaries and the stewards and regents of the lands flooded into town and stayed in the palace. Avant took a small guest room down the hall from her and, occasionally, sat in on her lessons with Galwyn. She offered him the consort chambers, but he refused, saying one of the regents from the southern lands whose daughter had accompanied him should occupy them.

Avant made it a point to never be alone with her, and while he claimed it was for appearance sake, she knew he continued to shut her out. She held out hope.

It was the eve of her coronation. Abby sat in front of her windows, staring out over the Great High Places.

A knock echoed, and she opened the door to find Annova. The woman curtsied gracefully and swept into the room. She took Abby's hands in her own. "My lady, soon to be queen, how you have grown in the Light! I'm honored to be of service to you on this most blessed of occasions. To see the kingdom restored is a desire I have long held, and to be a part of it is singularly special."

"Annova, thank you. I'm honored you agreed to preside over the ceremony." Abby squeezed her hands.

"My dear, the trials of the past have merely prepared you for the future task, and the familiar will guide you on this next journey. You must understand you are not alone, nor have you ever been."

They discussed the details of the coronation and Annova took her leave. Abby quivered with nervous energy. Requesting a small meal in her room, she stayed in her chambers for the remainder of the evening. She would socialize enough tomorrow.

In the morning, she was to ride to the center square in town and walk up the platform. Annova would preside over the crowning. Then Abby would return to the castle to sit on the throne and greet important leaders seeking an audience with her. Finally, after a grand luncheon, there would be a celebration and Coronation Ball where she was expected to…act queenly?

Her body trembled. She wanted to do a good job, and though Avant vowed to remain by her side all day tomorrow, she couldn't help but feel alone. He'd been less and less available, and though she tried to tell herself he was just busy, she knew it was more than that. Eventually, they'd have to have it out.

Sitting on floor in front of her bedroom windows, she leaned her forehead against the glass and gazed out on the Great Heights. The feeling of invincibility she'd had standing up there so many months ago, overlooking the land, came to her mind.

"You are not alone. I am here with you." The familiar voice reverberated in the chamber. Chills raced up and down her spine. She looked around the empty room.

"Look with your heart. You are not alone."

Where had she heard that voice before? It was so familiar.

A revelation, so broad it spanned across worlds, swept her over. She'd heard that voice in answer to every prayer, in the spilling of the waterfall, in the blowing of the wind, in the stillness of the night sky crowded with stars—and in her dreams.

It was the same Voice who answered every time she called. The Light who never left, who always loved, and, even when she was too blind to see, provided. He had always been with her. He never left and with Him, she was never alone.

"Thank you, Lord. Give me the wisdom I need to lead your people to new life."

The answers came as quickly as the words were spoken, as if they had been waiting before the question was asked. She had all she needed to accomplish this task—or any task. Feeling at peace for the first time in days, she climbed into the massive bed and slept.

Her personal maid woke her from a restful sleep the next morning. Accosted by a mob of well-meaning house staff, she was bathed, dried, and dressed in the fine brocade gown, teal green, of course. The chattering maids ushered her in front of the full-length mirror. Looking at the splendid woman in the reflection was like looking at someone Abby could've only hoped but never believed herself to be. The woman staring back was strong, capable, and prepared—everything a queen should be. She smiled at the sight.

A knock sounded. Avant entered at her greeting, and her heart leapt at the sight of him. A small shuddering sigh blew from her lips. If she looked queenly, he looked every bit the part of her king. He wore black pants and a charcoal gray tunic with his royal blue cape. Upon seeing her, he stopped and stared, his face masked in impassivity. Did he approve? She waited.

After a while, he spoke softly. "Abigail...*my Light*, I dare say the halls of this palace have scarcely been graced by such beauty."

She smiled. "Thank you." That was all the encouragement she needed. She took his hand. "We'll be a handsome pair. You look magnificent."

He removed his hand from hers and offered his arm. "Let us go."

A feeling of rejection swept over her at the insignificant gesture. She told herself it was her stupid imagination getting the best of her. Instead, she took the arm he offered and let him lead her downstairs to the waiting carriage. Thousands lined the streets, and the royal coach could barely pass through the crowd. Children threw flowers on the road and greeted her as she passed. She waved fondly out the window.

Bright colors decorated the square with flags flying from every building. At least ten thousand people were crowded into the plaza, every one dressed in their best and brightest.

Avant gracefully stepped from the carriage and held out his hand to help her descend. When she stepped down, the crowd erupted like fans at a football game. She half expected the Aggie fight song to play.

A four-tiered platform sat in the middle of the square. Larger than Ventium Village, the city was surrounded by buildings for long blocks, stretching all the way to the harbor. The streets were crammed with people, but a hush settled over them in anticipation of the coronation. Soldiers dressed in their finest uniforms stood at attention along a red carpet that led from the carriage to the dais. In fact, the military presence was almost as overwhelming as the crowd of onlookers. Petra stood at the end of the line with several of the Elders and above them, on the platform, Annova waited, dressed in a golden gown. A company of musicians sat behind her. As the door of the carriage opened, they began to play.

Avant escorted Abby to the platform, where she ascended to the step next to the top. Annova stepped to the front of the dais and said a few words to the crowd. She then began the Dictum of Coronation spoken by every ruler in the history of the kingdom.

Annova said, "Raise your right hand. Thou shall keep full peace and accord in the Light for the sake of the people and the prophets."

Abby raised her hand and answered, "I shall."

"Thou shall keep in all these domains righteousness and discretion with mercy and truth."

"I shall."

"Grant thou all rightful laws and customs to be upheld and that thou wilt defend and strengthen them to the Light, to the might and powers which it shall choose."

"I shall grant and defend them."

When Annova took the Crown from a nearby pedestal, Abby knelt.

"I crown you Her Royal Majesty Abigail, Sovereign Queen and Supreme Ruler of the Lands of Jastain, the New Kingdom of Light." Annova placed the Crown upon Abigail's head.

Light in every color burst from the golden circlet and shone in every direction. She turned to face the crowd. A bolt of current coursed through her. Individual beams of light shone from each person there. Her eyes opened in revelation: The Light was in each one of these people, and they all had destinies to fulfill. For the first time in over forty years, the sun broke through the haze of the City of Light and glowed down on the crowd. The people bowed in reverence to the Stone of Light, and Abby knelt with them.

After a long moment of silence, Annova rose and signaled to the musicians. The air filled with music. Avant stepped up on the dais and lifted Abby from her knees amidst cheers from the crowd.

*****

Avant took Abigail's hand and led her back to the carriage. The shock of her warm fingers against him shot desire straight up his arm. He smiled when she wiped the perspiration from her brow like she'd just climbed a mountain trail. He handed her a handkerchief as he helped her up into the carriage, the memory of their training sessions firmly seated in his mind. A wave of nostalgia washed over him, causing an ache deep in his chest.

She patted the silk square over her damp face. "Did I do okay? The sun came out, and it got really hot in this dress."

He smiled, tamping down the thought of how quickly he could divest her of the offending garment. "Your Majesty, the ceremony was a sight for the ages, and I have never been more proud or in awe of you."

Her eyes shone with love, and he dropped his gaze, unable to conceal his own emotion in her openness. It wouldn't do to encourage her feelings. Not now.

She reached up to feel the weight of the circle on her head. The golden curls of her hair glittered with the gold of the Crown as if her head was where the royal diadem had always belonged. The streets filled with people cheering and clapping. Abigail looked out the carriage windows. She waved, sending blessings and throwing gold coins as she passed.

It was a custom Galwyn must have shared with her. He, himself, had forgotten it until that moment. Avant tilted his head to her. "How did you know to do that?"

"It seemed appropriate. Was that right?"

Avant stared and nodded slowly.

It seemed she knew exactly which steps to make, hands to take, words to use. Endeared to all who sought audience with her, she found favor in their eyes. Avant stood in the background and watched her emerge like the first flower of spring. The Light had brought forth its Seed and she bloomed in glory. The grace of heaven poured over her in wisdom and love.

They made their way to the pronouncement ceremony, where the royal court and various regents presented their allegiance. Several times she glanced back, searching for him only to find his gaze locked on her in wonder and amazement. He smiled tightly, watching with such a tangle of emotion he wondered how he'd make it through the day.

Where was he to fit in her life now? He didn't even know where he fit in his own life. The dull ache in his chest became a sharp pain in his soul.

By the Light's mercy, the luncheon flew. Avant escorted Abigail to her chamber and bowed to leave so that she could ready herself for the coming ball.

She grabbed his arm, the touch of her hand igniting acute desire for her. "Please stay with me. I've missed you so much."

His arms shook with the effort to resist wrapping her in his embrace. He removed her hand and stepped inside her rooms, trying to regain control of his senses. "As it pleases, Your Majesty, but only for a moment."

"I was so nervous." She narrowed her eyes in disapproval. "You just had to have the train of this dress ten feet behind me, didn't you?"

"But of course. It was the final test." He smiled roguishly. He'd wanted her subjects to see her in all her glory. That's why he'd had that dress designed. Now, all he could think of was her out of the dress. His gaze raked her body, and hot need flooded and thickened in his veins.

She smiled and glanced sideways at him as if she knew his thoughts. He cleared his throat and shifted uncomfortably. They sat and talked about the ceremony. He used his Implanting to show her a picture of it from his perspective, a sight to behold.

Every time she moved closer to him, he rose and paced to the window. Her frustration was evidenced by the clip in her voice. He couldn't fault the Light for choosing her as queen. He himself would've chosen her as his queen, but she needed to rule her kingdom, and in time, find a worthy consort to share in that responsibility. Bile rose in his mouth. Avant knew he didn't deserve her, but he would be damned to the Darkness if he watched her find someone else. He stared unseeing over the Great High Places. There was only one alternative—he must leave.

Lyndsea, Chad, and Petra joined them in the chamber, and for a brief moment, it was like the quiet peacefulness of their days on the fief. Avant held Baby Abigail while Lyndsea helped Abigail change into her ball gown.

Her evening dress of deep crimson sparkled with gold embroidery, the color causing her eyes to turn a deep blue and her hair to shine like spun silk. His heart pounded in his chest as it had the night of the Harvest Festival when they'd danced. He swallowed his passion and took her arm, leading her to the Coronation Ball.

Tall gilded chairs with bright crimson cushions lined the walls of the long, narrow room. The lords and ladies of the court milled in a din of conversing voices. After so long an absence, he marveled at the grandeur of courtly life. A white marble floor and red carpet led up to a dais where the throne sat. Dark oil paintings of former rulers adorned the stone walls and gave a sense of history, majesty, and power to the Great Hall.

Upon the entrance of the queen, all the nobles and the palace guard bowed. Abigail gestured for them to rise. He led her down the aisle, and she took a seat on her throne at the front of the room.

A large stained-glass window resided over her head. Set high on the wall over the throne, it depicted the coronation of the first ruler of Jastain. The brightly hued glass cast rays of color across the floor.

The celebration commenced with a song from the court musicians, and the guests chattered. Abigail danced numerous dances with Petra. Jealousy burned bitterly in his throat. Avant had to continually remind himself she didn't belong to him.

The formalities of the evening ended with entertaining spectacles performed for the queen's benefit. Guests in the palace and all over the kingdom danced and celebrated well into the night. Petra finally left Abigail's side. He kept busy dancing with the regents' and stewards' beautiful daughters.

One particularly lovely young girl caught Abigail's eye. She leaned over to Avant and asked, "Who is that young lady?"

"That, Your Majesty, is the Lady Brislyn of Komissa in the Southern Provinces."

"She is quite beautiful."

"Indeed." Boldly, he caught her gaze. "There is an abundance of beauty here this night."

For the first time that evening, he allowed his emotion to reflect in his face. He smiled when he noticed she couldn't gather her breath.

Later, as the celebration continued, he caught her in a barely concealed yawn. The heaviness of her eyes filled him with compassion. He leaned over and whispered in her ear, "Your obligation is fulfilled for the evening. You may leave when you wish."

A shiver ran visibly through her, but she nodded. Taking a last liberty, he breathed in her strawberry scent before leading her to her room.

He reached his arm around her to open her chamber door, his fingers brushing against her back. A blush covered her cheeks. "Can you come in for a moment?"

His breath caught in his throat. His hands ached to touch her. His senses screamed for her. He knew he should leave immediately, but couldn't bring himself to do so. "Only for a moment." He walked her to the sofa but didn't sit. That would be a mistake. Every nerve in his body sang with need—the need to hold her, kiss her, claim her as his, but that was impossible.

"I had a vision today during the coronation."

His sight cleared and he focused on her words, forcing down the desire that tried to strangle him.

"The Light shined from every person, and I realized we're all created to rule the world around us, to have dominion over it. We can tame all living things and help them grow into something worthy." She stood and paced in front of him, her excitement barely contained. "I believe every person has the Gift of Implanting inside of them, like they have the Light."

He tilted his head, focusing intently on her. Of course the Light would speak to her. The Light had chosen her, and now it was her appointment to guide the people. An appointment he'd expected for himself. A coldness settled over him, and he stiffened his spine and his resolve. His presence in the castle must be short-lived, for her sake as well as his. He must return to the Freelands and his fief, where he belonged. She must settle into her role as queen and later find her prince consort. The thought of Abigail with another man stabbed daggers into his heart.

"If we can teach our people to use their Implanting, Seppitent can never again have power over anyone in this land, and we'll remain safe from the threat of Darkness."

"Your Majesty, these words astonish me, but I perceive truth in them. Though I never before realized the possibility, I see the wisdom of it, and I see they could have only come from the Chosen One."

"I believe this is the purpose of my reign. I've been Chosen to bring this to pass in our world." She took his hand. "And there is no one better than you to help me accomplish this edict of the Light. Will you help me?"

He removed her hand from his and stood to leave. "As it pleases Your Majesty, and as I have always done, I will certainly help you."

She grabbed him and hugged him tightly, refusing to let go. In truth, he didn't want her to.

She whispered, "Can't you stay with me tonight?"

He shook his head. "I'm afraid not, Your Majesty." He fisted his hands into his pants to keep from embracing her, to keep from scooping her up and carrying her to the bed. He couldn't remain here.

The hope on her face fell with his rejection and formality. It took every last shred of will he possessed, but he said good night and left.

New are the eyes that Light's morrow breaks
And hope the companion of love's great mistakes

Keeper of Stone and Wielder of Sword
Grace to the humble whether Lady or Lord

Come forth the lovers, hearken and quick
To rebuild the Kingdom brick by brick

To the King, love awaits at the door
Until such is the time it opens once more

A smile on his face and arms open wide
To welcome the Queen alone as his bride

Rushing then, in will he bound
And on the head of the Chosen set a new Crown

On the last eve of her twentieth year, the Seed of Light will be fully grown and the Crown of Light fully known.

> Annum 1567 — Song of the High Priest
> Festival Keihev Neous (Festival of New Song)

Chapter Thirty-Eight

Abby sat on her throne, trying not to look uncomfortable. She really wanted to fold her legs under her or drape one leg over the arm of the gilded chair, but according to Galwyn and the Elders, that was frowned upon.

During certain hours, she was expected to make herself available to hear petitions from the people. Most often the matters were simple disputes to be settled, but occasionally she had to seek council. Generally, she sought that council from Avant, but he'd been less and less accessible in the two weeks since the coronation.

Although both Avant and Chad had seemed touched that Abby had included Sentieve in the memorial service honoring those who'd fallen in battle, Avant had fled like a refugee afterward, not even speaking to her.

Since being crowned queen, Abby had reestablished the Festival of New Song, celebrating the ability in each person to Implant and have dominion over the world. The people had whole-heartedly embraced her and her ideas.

She'd made plans to educate the population in their Gifts, and she'd tasked Avant with establishing the training program. Seppitent would never have access to her home again without the collective knowledge of her people to defend against him. His power lay in isolation and deception, and together, the people could combat his lies with knowledge and truth. Their connection to the Light would be the backbone of the New Kingdom, keeping it strong for many years to come. She dreamed that one day there would be no one in the land who remembered the Darkness, and that the kingdom would be ruled in perfect peace.

She'd appointed Petra as ambassador to the lands and stewards of Jastain. It was her hope that they would join her in the fight against Seppitent and could be encouraged into the kingdom, but she would by no means force them. She'd also asked Petra to teach and train the people in successful farming and animal husbandry. She prayed for him to find someone who loved him as much as she loved Avant. More than anyone she knew, Petra deserved the happiness the Crown of Light brought. To see him filled with love for someone who loved him was the desire of her heart.

Lyndsea and Chad decided to remain in the Freelands. They were engaged to be married. Chad felt he could do more good in this world with his scientific knowledge than finishing his studies back home. He now worked on providing running water to every dwelling. Although it still wasn't clear who his biological father was, it didn't seem to bother him. Avant thought of Chad as his own.

Abby missed Helean and had offered her a prime position in the palace, but she wouldn't leave the manor. Abby understood. No matter where she lived, the Freelands and Domentus Ventium would always seem like home.

Everyone held his or her proper place. Lives broken by the effects of the Darkness had been restored. She appointed Annova as her personal advisor on matters of prophecy. Annova promised to come to the kingdom twice a year for the festivals. Though the position of high priest was not officially reinstated, Abby considered it the joint task of Avant and Annova. At least, until she and Avant were married. Then the position would be solely his. She counted on him to fulfill the calling of high priest—and husband.

The victory over Seppitent, restoration of the kingdom, and the realization of her own destiny—all of these things added to the richness of her life, but it wasn't complete. And she waited.

Days passed, but her hope didn't wane. Just as she might have anticipated hearing her favorite song, she knew it would eventually play and she would dance again.

Two days before her twenty-first birthday, Avant finally came to her. "Your Majesty, if I may, I seek an audience with you."

Her heart beat wildly against her ribs. Just to see him was a treat, but he had something to ask her? The desire to leap into his arms almost overwhelmed her. "You know you can see me anytime and say anything."

"You're wrong, Your Majesty. Your position requires more from us than that." Avant stood rigid.

Was he nervous? Her stomach knotted in anticipation. "Maybe. But I can't see how those formalities apply to you. You'll have to help me work through it." She smiled and wiggled her eyebrows.

He faintly smiled and nodded.

"Always so serious. What do you want to tell me?"

"It is time for me to care for my own lands. I ask leave to return to Domentus Ventium."

Bands of stress tightened around her chest. "Leave? For how long?"

"Indefinitely." Those blue eyes were as unreadable as they'd ever been.

Her heart caught in her throat. "Avant, no. *Why?* I need you here."

"Everything you've asked of me I can accomplish from my home, and you're more than capable."

"But I-I thought…why are you leaving me?" Her voice cracked. Her eyes prickled and burned as she stared at his rigid form. He had completely closed himself off from her.

"My presence is no longer required, and I need to return to my home. I'm available for you anytime." He spoke with a cordial formality that nauseated her.

Her heart felt as if it were being ripped in two. "I need you now. You're my family. You belong here with me." The words came out as more of a sob than a statement.

"No. I do not belong here. There is no place for me, and I have my own responsibilities."

A cry escaped her. She couldn't speak the words out loud. *"Why are you doing this? I didn't want this job. It's not my fault, but still you're punishing me."*

He stood, a stone statue, and said nothing.

Fighting the tears that wouldn't be pushed back, she held his impenetrable gaze and somehow forced the bitter words from her mouth. "You're free to go."

"Thank you, Your Majesty. I'll be taking my leave immediately."

The sound of his footsteps fading down the hall fell like death.

*****

Avant left at noon and traveled straight through without stopping, arriving in the Freelands by dawn. A quick departure bode better than a lingering good-bye. His gut knotted. It seemed his only destiny was to hurt the women he loved, which made it imperative that he remove himself.

Abigail didn't need him any longer. Great and mighty Light, his chest ripped open to leave her. He had no place in the kingdom when he couldn't even read his own Gift—if he ever had a Gift. She wanted him to establish the Implanting training program. That was comical. What could he possibly teach about the Implanting?

How could he be worthy of her when his own Light failed him? She'd blossomed into a great woman—a noble queen—and the New Kingdom of Light was stronger for her leadership. But she'd outgrown him.

Grief impaled his heart, and he stifled a gasp. He dashed away foolish tears. *You are accustomed to living with heartache, Avant.* He had done it for many long years, but this—this rending was more than his will could bear. Leaving her there had been the single hardest thing he'd ever done. The sound of her words sliced through him. *Why are you leaving me?*

She'd held to her promise to allow him to lead, a fact which made him love her more. He hung his head. Without her, he'd never again be whole.

He found himself walking the path to the house in the vineyard. "Annova, are you here?" He stepped into the gray stone home and found her in the main room.

She rose to greet him as he entered, a question in her eyes and voice. "Avant, what are you doing here?"

"I've come home. There was no need for me to stay at the palace any longer, and I've my own lands to attend to." He stood stiffly in front of her in an effort to justify his presence there.

She searched his face through narrowed eyes. "What do you mean? This is not where you belong. Your own Gift has told you that."

"My Gift has betrayed me, and I am no longer able to discern it." He did not meet her gaze.

She lifted his chin to look into his eyes. "How has your Gift betrayed you?"

He jerked from her scrutiny and paced the room. "You know full well I've dreamt on many occasions that I would be the ruler of the Kingdom of Light, but clearly that was …an error."

"Was it? What exactly do you remember of these dreams?"

"My dreams showed me that I would be king. Many, including you, believed that I would be king, but we were misguided."

"Avant, my love, your pride has deceived you, not your Gift." The wretched woman laughed. "You are determined to destroy your own happiness with your implacable will. I told you long ago, this journey would not be what you thought, but to trust your Gift. Does the Light now require more than you can give?"

He balked at her askance. "Annova, you know I would do anything the Light asked of me."

"Then do you not see what the Light requires?" Her mothering tone filled him with shame. "For you to rule would be like breathing, for that comes naturally to you, but to follow—that is a sacrifice which you are, apparently, unwilling to give. Perhaps it is not on the throne where you are to lead, Avant."

"Then where?"

"From the altar."

The power of her words hit him with the brunt force of a mace. Air whooshed from his lungs, and his body froze. Was it possible? The divine symmetry fit perfectly: a married couple to rule and lead. A high priest and a queen.

Annova continued, "For the Light to truly reign again in Jastain, a high priest must lead the people. Is that not the role you have been born to? Is that not the reason for your existence?"

The full revelation weighed upon his shoulders. He sank on the closest thing he could find: a footstool that forced his legs into his chest. His head dropped into his hands. In his arrogance, he'd assumed he would rule the Kingdom of Light, not that he would stand beside the ruler. But his dreams had shown him he would be king, or at least, he thought they had.

"Do you not love Abigail, Avant? You have forced her to endure more than anyone should for one they love."

He sat, silently absorbing all Annova said. High priest? Like his father?

Guilt swirled with revelation and understanding. His Gift had not deserted him. He'd somehow misread the signs. He'd left Abigail alone, without a spiritual head, without his love and support. Urgency tore through him. Avant jumped from his seat. "I have to go, Annova."

He bolted out the door to find Spiritus. If only he had Placement Implanting, he could right this horrible wrong within minutes, but his heart leapt with joy as he suspected, sensed, she might actually be somewhere close by. If not, he would make his way back to her in the palace.

As fast as Spiritus would fly, Avant headed to the falls. His patience had finally reached an end. There would be no more waiting for his life to begin, no decades of martyrdom. The present and forever after was with Abigail. Now, all he had to do was convince her.

She sat on a rock near the lower pool, crying. He leapt from the stallion and ran to her. Sweeping her up from the ground, he held her close. As long as she was in his arms, in his heart, in his life, he could do anything.

*****

Abby's head rested on Avant's chest. His strong arms encircled her, and his scent filled her nose. Cedar, pine, and sweet musk. As much as she wanted this, his touch only made the heartache worse.

"I've been a fool. Please don't cry," he softly pleaded.

She pulled away and turned her back, wiping the tears from her cheeks. "What do you want, Avant?" The brokenness in her voice reminded her of how she had felt that night in Boston.

"My angel, I am so sorry. Please forgive me."

"You're forgiven. Just go."

"Abigail, please don't shut me out."

She spun around and glared at him. "Why not? Isn't that what you do?"

He winced but redoubled his pursuit. "That doesn't make it right."

"It does when it comes to you, Avant. All you've ever done is rip me apart. The moment I saw your heart I fell in love with you, and every time I tried to love you, you pushed me away. You rage with jealousy and then pretend nothing bothers you. You make love to me and accuse me of being unfaithful. You ask for my trust; then you abandon me! You're cold and heartless." Uncontrollable sobs wracked her chest.

He grabbed her hands. "I'm only heartless without you."

She jerked her hands from his and plopped on a rock. "Don't do this to me." She pointed an accusing finger. "I gave you the driver's seat. Do you know how hard that was? You betrayed my faith." She wiped her nose on her sleeve and tried to turn away, but his blue eyes still held her captive. Even if she wanted to run—and she didn't want to—she couldn't.

He fell on his knees in front of her, his heart open and vulnerable, begging for help just as he had the first time she saw him.

"Please, Abigail," he spoke into her mind, the familiar surge shocking her.

But she wasn't ready to forgive. Not yet. She steeled her reserve and lifted her chin.

Opening his mind like the annuals in the Great Hall, he allowed her access, revealing every thought, word, and deed since his last Implanting. He showed her his love. His torment and anguish over her memories of Chad. She saw his guilt and despair at losing the throne. They coursed through her like the Itehris River.

She stared, mesmerized by his intimate display, and swayed from the dizziness of his Implanting.

"No more secrets. Please don't push me away. Can't you see? I felt unworthy of you. I still do."

"Unworthy of me?" Her heart softened; it always did when it came to Avant. He owned her, lock, stock and barrel, whether she wanted him to or not.

He cupped her face in his hands. "That's how I've always felt about you, from the moment I met you. I thought I would be worthy of you when I became king."

"You're still destined to be king, Avant."

"Abigail, you know that is not possible. But now, I know it is not necessary. I'll be your stable boy if you'll have me."

The honesty in his eyes broke her defenses. She smiled. "Stable boy is not the title the Light destined for you. In fact, your title is already waiting for you to receive it."

"Whatever you title me in public, call me your lover in private, for I will not live without you any longer."

He pulled her from the rock into his arms and ever so gently kissed her lips, sending rippling waves of passion through her neglected body parts. His slow, deep kiss heated her all the way to her curled toes.

Forcing herself to concentrate, Abby pulled from him and whispered in his ear, "Aren't you curious about the title I created for you?"

He kissed down her neck and pushed the fabric of her gown away to press an opened-mouth kiss on the scar of her bare shoulder. "Indeed. I am."

His hot breath tingled against her skin, and she almost forgot her purpose. She let out a little whimper, the smoky sound of her voice surprising. "His Royal Highness, King Consort of the New Kingdom of Light and Imperial Regent of the Freelands of Jastain"

That got his attention. He pulled his head from its descent, his brow furrowed. "Abigail, there is no such title, nor would the Elders agree to ratify one."

She smiled, drowning in the depths of his eyes. "Oh, but there is such a title, and they did agree to it."

"What? How?"

She shrugged. "I told them it was a deal breaker. If they didn't play along I'd take my crown and go home. I can't help it if they understood home to be Dallas." She snickered, remembering Galwyn's scrunched face as he reluctantly signed the formal decree. "At any rate, they agreed, and I sealed it with my signet ring the day of the coronation."

She placed her palms on his cheeks. "Your destiny is with me—as king. I can't do this without you anymore than you can do it without me. We're stuck with each other."

"*Abigail.*" He stared into her eyes in a communication of his heart that was deeper than telepathy.

"So you see, your Gift was right all along." Abby looped her arms around his waist and held on with all her might. "Don't ever push me away again. Or I may have to hurt you."

He laughed. "I couldn't even if I wanted to, angel. I'm yours forevermore." Cupping her head to his chest like a cherished treasure, he whispered, "I love you, Abigail."

Chills ran up and down her spine. She closed her eyes and smiled. Her favorite song finally played. And her heart danced. Home was no longer a faraway place where she'd never belong. It was him.

Avant tilted her head up, leaned in, and tenderly kissed her.

It was a familiar kiss that went on and on, but this time, she sensed his strong arm around her waist and his hand supporting her head. The soft stubble of his whiskers and the woodsy scent of his skin washed over her. When he pulled away and looked into her eyes, she murmured, on cue, "I love you."

He kissed her again.

She broke the kiss and pushed that wavy lock behind his ear. "I have something for you." Reaching to her ear, she removed the three-carat diamond and placed it in his. "It didn't seem fair that you had to relinquish all your jewels."

A smile lit his face, and his eyes shone with love. "Abigail, this is not a gift to be given lightly."

"No, it isn't. And now it really is a kingly gift, and only a small token of all I have to give." She laced her arms around his neck and pulled him to her lips. As desire for him flooded her body, a memory surfaced. "There is still an unfinished matter which needs to be discussed."

Concern and suspicion filled the blue eyes she loved. "What unfinished matter is that?"

"I believe you owe me dinner and dessert in a nearby cave." She bit her lower lip suggestively.

He arrested her gaze with confidence. "As far as dessert goes, I'm sure I can satisfy your craving. And for dinner—there's always squirrel stew."

She wrinkled her nose. "Let's just skip the dinner part."

"If you would care to accompany me to our cave, my queen."

His words sent shivers down her spine, or maybe it was the thought of the icy water, but she didn't hesitate. Immediately, she began to unlace her bodice.

"Abigail, what are you doing?" He gave her that familiar you've-lost-your-scruples look.

"I can't swim to the cave fully clothed, now can I?"

"You do not have to do that—*yet.*" He halted her hands. "We can walk to the other entrance."

"What *other entrance?*" His new memories came rushing into her mind and she playfully slapped at his chest. "You told me the only way to get into that cave was to take my clothes off and swim through the tunnel in the freezing water."

Avant laughed devilishly. "Yes. I did."

With her mouth in a tightlipped smile, she rolled her eyes and shook her head as she took his hand. "I know an even quicker way."

The door of his heart was finally open, and it wouldn't close. His will was settled, and she knew he would never change his mind.

*****

As the prophecies decreed, the king and queen took their rightful places as leader and ruler. The kingdom was restored; Seppitent, cast out. The fruit of love and joy reigned in the hearts of the people. Long life, health, and abundance again blessed the land through the Implanting of the Seed of Light. However, unannounced to the lovers, another seed was planted that day. A seed that would grow to have dark hair and teal green eyes and, one day, would rule the land in perfect peace long after the Darkness had gone.

THE END

OTHER TITLES IN
THE REIGN OF LIGHT SERIES

NOW AVAILABLE AT YOUR LOCAL E-BOOK STORE!

The Pirate Princess

The Prospective Princess

ABOUT THE AUTHOR

Kary Rader is a stay-at-home mother of three, avid reader, and slave to the characters and worlds inside her head.

Always creative, she's drawn to stories with fantastical worlds and creatures. With a little bit of magic and divine guidance, there isn't anything that can't be accomplished. It's the power of words that creates and destroys.

Vanquishing evil and injustice while finding eternal love in the process is all in a day's work. And with the help of her critique partners and master cartographer, imaginary places come to life. Come join her for an adventure and maybe you, too, will be claimed by passion and changed by love. Let the fantasy begin.

You can find her at www.karyrader.com.

Did you enjoy this book? Drop us a line and say so! We love to hear from readers, and so do our authors. To connect, visit www.boroughspublishinggroup.com online, send comments directly to info@boroughspublishinggroup.com, or friend us on Facebook and Twitter. And be sure to check back regularly for contests and new releases in your favorite subgenres of romance!

Are you an aspiring writer? Check out www.boroughspublishinggroup.com/submit and see if we can help you make your dreams come true.